Patriots

Patriots

Kenneth Royce

1

CROWN PUBLISHERS, INC.
NEW YORK

Published in the United States by Crown Publishers, Inc., 225 Park Avenue South,
New York, New York 10003
Originally published in Great Britain under the title
The President Is Dead by Hodder & Stoughton Limited,
47 Bedford Square, London WCIB 30P, England
CROWN is a trademark of Crown Publishers, Inc.
Manufactured in the United States of America
Library of Congress Cataloging-in-Publication Data
Royce, Kenneth.
    Patriots.
I. Title.
PR6068.098P3   1988   823'.914   87-27612
ISBN 0-517-56943-4
10 9 8 7 6 5 4 3 2 1
First American Edition

For all my friends in West Cork

1

The sky parted cautiously to allow the first streak of grey to come through. The difference was so slight as to be almost indiscernible but Colonel Freeman noticed it, as did his co-pilot Lieutenant Colonel Scarpetta: both men had seen that gradually widening band of shifting sludge many times before. The real dawn was yet to come but even to so experienced a crew as that on Air Force One, the result would still manage to astound. Meanwhile, apart from the wavering line hugging the earth's rim, the night was black, pricked by the ethereal flashing glow of the plane's tail and fuselage lights and those on the port and starboard wings. There was an eerily peaceful pre-dawn silence among the flight crew of five.

The strange detached glows stressed the immensity of space and the relative puniness of the giant aircraft. The massive array of instruments glowed on the flight-deck panels. The Lieutenant Colonel serving as navigator was performing his routine checks. His presence highlighted the importance of the flight: the President of the United States of America was on board, at this moment asleep in his room with the First Lady.

There were other distinguished visitors on board; too many for Bill Freeman's comfort. He was used to carrying all kinds of VIPs but the Soviet Ambassador to the United States was an uncomfortable first. The reason was obviously political, and he preferred not to dig any deeper. His job was to get them to London with as little fuss as possible.

The real problems occurred pre-flight: the planning, the enormous security precautions for the aircraft and the passengers who, regardless of status, all had to obey certain safety measures in order to get on board. The Secretary of State was on board with the National Security Advisor, the White House Chief of Staff, five top-ranking Senators, a handful of carefully selected journalists, including two women, Secret Service men, and a bevy of White House aides from advisors to secretaries. And that was excluding the medical team, galley chefs and other service personnel.

The passengers were split up in order of importance. The forward cabin contained five Secret Service men, four Air Force Security Guards and a nurse. The Presidential suite contained the inner sanctum, an office linking up with the outside world. The bedroom had two single beds and was adjacent to a convertible sitting room and bathroom.

The main cabin aft was largely for White House staff and visitors. Electronic typewriters had been removed to make room for two extra seats for the Soviet Ambassador and his wife. For reasons not disclosed, the Ambassador's wife had remained in Washington thus allowing her husband to remove the arm between the seats and to stretch himself.

The least comfortable compartment was at the rear where the engine noise was the loudest and aircraft movement more noticeable. Here sat factions of the various news media. Throughout the aircraft most passengers were still asleep, but here and there, a reading light was on where the restless studied papers or relaxed with a book.

The President woke just before dawn. He switched on a table lamp and gazed at his wife who was still asleep in the next bed, her hair cascading over the pillow. He smiled and moved quietly to the bathroom, closing the door carefully behind him. His wife was still sleeping when he re-entered the bedroom. He dressed quickly, checked his appearance in the mirror between the two easy chairs, glanced once more at his wife then left the room. He took the port-side corridor to the forward passenger compartment and then proceeded up the aisle between the seats. Two Secret Service men and one Air Force Security Guard were wide awake and stirred attentively as the President went past; he smiled reassuringly at them, signalling them to remain seated, not wanting fuss. It made no difference; by the time he reached the crew's rest room, the forward galley just beyond, Colonel Freeman had already been warned of the President's approach by intercom. The flight-deck door was open for him when he arrived.

"Shouldn't you be flying this thing instead of worrying about the boss looking over your shoulder, Colonel?"

It was a standing joke between them, voiced in different ways on different flights but always meaning the same thing. The President had long since accepted that he could not avoid attention but there were times, on minor occasions like this, when he yearned to move just once without his actions being monitored. The Aircraft Commander smiled back. In the pale cabin light he appeared like a younger version of the President himself: tall, debonair, upright and dark, with a good head of hair and deep brown eyes. But he was slimmer and there must have been at least twenty-five years between them. He said, "The usual, Mr President?"

"As sure as hell I haven't gotten up this early to ask about your health, Bill." It was all a routine; the President had always longed to paint some of the remarkable dawns and sunsets he had seen from high altitude. As he lowered himself into the observer's seat, he added, "I'm late. I've missed the deep stuff." He meant the deeper shades of intermingling colour following the first touches of dawn.

The men in the cockpit remained quiet as the President relaxed while the prisms unfolded, spreading and lightening and for ever changing until it was just one more bright morning seen from the top of the world. Bill Freeman stood beside him. "Would you like my seat, Mr President? Up front."

"No. I'd hit something I shouldn't."

"We're on auto, but Colonel Scarpetta would look out for you."

"No, this seat is okay. Do you remember that trip to Scandinavia via Anchorage when we not only got the dawn over the winter ice fields of Alaska but later the aurora borealis? That was something, wasn't it?"

Freeman nodded. "Yes, sir, it was."

The President rose. "Well, I guess that was a short one, but still worth it. How much longer?"

Freeman glanced over to the navigator who had overheard the question. "Touch down at Heathrow in two hours forty-six minutes, sir."

9

"Good. I can get some work done."

The President was at his desk when his wife entered his office. She sat down on the sofa and crossed her slim legs, the pastel pink shade of her dress complementing her complexion. "I should have brought my hairdresser," she said.

He glanced up, smiled wryly. "Seats are too tight on this run. Anyway, you look fine. Besides, you like that guy in London – can never remember his name." He looked down at a pile of notes: remembering them would be no problem.

"Two days in London isn't enough, we've so many friends there."

"That's all the time we can afford. More than enough to discuss with the PM a common line to take in Moscow. This trip is important, honey. The most important of them all. I'd like to finish my term on a high note, but it's not just that. I really believe we can get somewhere this time. Not all the way, that will never happen in my lifetime, but nearer than ever before. That would be something, wouldn't it? And you haven't been to Moscow before."

She wrinkled her nose. "I won't let you down. But I won't be sorry to stop in Paris on the way back." She realised the selfishness of her comments. "I hope you pull it off."

He chuckled. "It'll need more than me. However, I believe there's now a real desire for peace on both sides. *I feel there's a will*. They've come some way towards us. A good way. That's why we've got Anatole Bruslov on board. A goodwill gesture. He was going to Moscow anyway and this is a damned sight better than travelling Aeroflot."

"Is he travelling independently from London?"

"It's up to him. His seat here will be available and I think he wants to use it, but he's left his options open. He might go straight on or he might stay with his ambassadorial colleague in London until we leave. It would be good propaganda if we all came down the steps together in Moscow. Maybe that's what they're trying to figure out: is it our gain or theirs?"

Sam Baites woke up slowly. By the time he looked out of

the window the sky was bright with only wisps of cirrus about ten thousand feet below. The tail of the 707 was twitching and the muffled roar of the four Pratt & Whitney turbo-jets filled his head. He held his nose and blew, clearing his ears for a while. He glanced at the toilet lights: all "occupied". He needed a shave and a wash but would have to wait. He opened a packet of moist, scented fresheners and wiped his face over, feeling better afterwards. The turbulence was tugging at the tail again making him feel slightly queasy.

"Feeling better?"

Baites turned. Suzy Damberg pushed her long dark hair back. She looked far fresher than Baites and had also applied a little perfume, fresh and subtle. An anchorwoman with CBS, she was moderately attractive without her studio make-up and could soften her high cheekbones with well-practised, professional smiles. She was intelligent and probing, unrelenting when necessary, and had devastated more than one interviewee. Baites had not met her before this flight but had seen her often enough on television.

"Why? Was I feeling bad?"

She pulled a face. "You look awful. There's nothing worse than early morning stubble."

"You obviously know." He remembered reading that she was still single.

"That was unnecessary." She was more annoyed with herself than with him; she was used to winning exchanges and Sam Baites' appearance belied his sharp mind.

"You made the play," he said. "Don't beef if you muffed your lines."

Suzy Damberg laid a long-fingered hand on his arm. "I'm sorry. I should have remembered that the *Washington Post* pick their journalists for their brains and not their looks or manners." She smiled sweetly.

He smiled back good naturedly. "You should see me after the sort of repair job you've just done. I drive women crazy."

He watched her lips tighten; she was too used to getting her own way. "Let's start again," he suggested. "You look pretty good and I look my worst. That should make you feel better."

11

Baites suddenly rose and grabbed his toiletry bag. "The john's free. I'll spruce up for you." He climbed past her and she pulled her long legs to one side, her expression carefully guarded. After he had gone she swore softly. But even sitting next to someone she was rapidly beginning to dislike would not prompt her to exchange her seat. It was a privilege to be on this plane at all – so few journalists ever made it.

Suzy sat listening to the steady hum of engines and gradually calmed down. It was too early in the morning to start scoring off other people. And he wasn't as unattractive as she had made out. He was tall and rangy with a seen-everything air about him but his overall manner was not hard bitten – unlike other personalities in the business. She mused for a while. The plane was waking up. Light was now flooding in and voices were mingling with the aircraft noises. The cabin staff had come to life and, when she looked round, breakfast trays were already being distributed.

"Excuse me."

"Oh!" She looked up to see Baites standing beside her. "I didn't realise you were there." She moved her legs again. "I can smell bacon."

"Is that a truce?" he asked as he pushed his bag on to the rack and sat down.

"Truce it is," she agreed. "And you are quite right; you do look better – enough to make women crazy. But you're a bit on the thin side for a tall man."

He allowed her the mild dig; her tone had changed, no longer viperish. "My hair's my own," he pointed out. "And you could fatten out my face with make-up or a silicone job. That should be good enough for a job on your show."

She smiled warmly and patted his arm. "That's a much better start. I hate these early-morning calls."

They ate in silence; the cabin had quietened down again with the advent of food.

"I suppose you're going on to Moscow." Baites wiped his lips.

"Isn't everybody?"

He shrugged. "I guess so. I just wonder if it's all worth the effort."

She turned in surprise. "Just when I'd decided I'd met a

12

newsman who wasn't a cynic; well, not an obvious one. You think it's all a waste of time?"

He gazed out at the bright sky before turning back to her. "It always has been before. I'll admit the President threw out his best speeches so far in the days leading up to departure." Thoughtfully, he added, "Oddly enough it was the Irish dimension that impressed me much more than his latest instalment on sharing star wars. For someone of declared Irish ancestry it took guts."

"Did you ever doubt he had them?"

Baites hesitated. "No. But he resisted some pretty strong opposition from his close advisors. And there *is* the question of the Irish vote."

"Knowing that he won't run again, perhaps he decided that the pro IRA American Irish wouldn't hold it against the next President. I'll admit that his effort to outlaw Noraid was a courageous step. He's determined that the Anglo-Irish agreement is given a fair chance. But it's his continuing insistence that 'conspiracy' must be included in the Anglo-American extradition treaty that has really angered his opponents. He's preventing our courts being used as an escape route for terrorists. Strong stuff."

"It'll be interesting to see how Congress takes it. He's staked a lot on this but he has a strong card in his claim that the FBI have proved how communist bloc money has filtered into Noraid funds in large amounts in the last year or so. I shouldn't think that will improve the ambience when he arrives in Moscow."

Suzy shrugged. "I don't think it will affect the main peace talks. It will help the British and Republican Irish Governments, though. If he gets away with effectively stopping the flow of Noraid funds for IRA arms to Ulster he will have cut them off at the knees, and opened up the way to pour funds into redevelopment over there."

"Underneath that cheese cake you're really a rabid optimist, Suzy."

She tossed her hair back, smoothing it thoughtfully. "He deserves to complete this term on a high note. He's taken a lot of guff and he's nowhere near as dumb as his enemies make out."

Baites slowly clapped his hands. "Bravo. A disciple. You gunning for Ambassador some place?"

13

She smiled wickedly. "For one thing I'm too young and for another I've a short fuse when talking to idiots."

"Ouch! But I hope you're right, I really do, even if I've long since believed him to be an android operated by remote control. For the sake of the country, for all of us, I hope he succeeds." He lifted his coffee cup. "Here's to him. God bless America."

Suzy eyed Baites warily but detected no sign of sarcasm. "I'll drink to that," she said.

Sitting forward of the press corps, Anatole Bruslov felt alienated, but it was something he was well used to. Behind him the twin seats of the main cabin faced each other so there was companionship among the other passengers. It was true that a Senator would call on him, from time to time, sitting in the seat originally reserved for Bruslov's wife, and they would talk for a while. Yet the conversation was always guarded and usually trivial; nobody, himself included, wanted to be drawn into predicting the prospects of what lay ahead in Moscow.

Just the same he was lonely and missed the reassurance of having his own embassy staff around him.

Everybody had been caught up in a new spirit of hope after the President's recent series of speeches and the guardedly warm response from the Kremlin of which his presence here was one manifestation. Put bluntly, Bruslov resented being used as a goodwill pawn. Not that the plane was Spartan; it was fantastic as planes went. Nixon's pilot, Colonel Ralph Albertazzie, had called it the Flying White House, and he had not been far wrong. A man would want for nothing here.

A steward approached him, the Presidential seal on the man's jacket. "Colonel Freeman's compliments, sir, and would you like a spell on the flight deck?"

Why not? It would pass some of the time. Something to tell his wife and children when he finally caught up with them again. Bruslov eased his chunky form from the seat and smoothed back his thinning hair as he followed the steward forward. He spent a pleasant few minutes in the observer's chair while Freeman explained the cockpit controls to him. He suddenly realised the immense

14

compliment he had been paid: for this was no ordinary Boeing 707 – an aircraft, as a type, long out of date.

"What is the range of this aircraft?" Bruslov asked in heavily accented English.

"Officially, just over seven thousand miles, sir." Freeman smiled. "But with the extra fuel we carry we can do quite a bit more."

"So you could turn round and go back without refuelling?"

"That would depend on altitude and head winds and so on. In theory, yes, but I wouldn't be all that happy about it."

"So the consumption is what?"

"About sixteen hundred pounds of fuel an hour."

Bruslov wanted to ask more but was not sure what his questions should be. The Colonel seemed to be hiding nothing from him but Moscow probably knew almost as much about this plane as the pilot. "You are with the 89th Military Airlift Wing at Andrews Air Force Base?"

"That's well documented, sir. No secret."

"Would I ask you to reveal secrets, Colonel?"

Freeman laughed. "I'm sure you wouldn't, sir."

When Bruslov was ready to leave the steward escorted him back but stopped outside the President's suite where a Secret Service man lingered. "The President would like to see you, sir." As he tapped on the office door Bruslov felt lonelier than ever. And for some inexplicable reason, he suddenly felt afraid.

Nearing the end of their journey the passengers felt restless, intermingling and blocking the aisles, making it difficult for the cabin staff to carry out their duties. There was a good deal of laughter and leg pulling. Three Senators visited the rear cabin to exchange words with the press correspondents. Only in the forward cabin was it business as usual for the Secret Service men and the Air Force Security guards.

Sam Baites eased back to his seat having chatted with colleagues seated further forward; he and Suzy Damberg occupied the very rear seats. When Suzy eventually returned to her seat Baites decided that the time was right. "Have dinner with me," he said. "Show you're not

15

prejudiced." He lightly took her hand; she made no objection but left it lying limp in his.

"Where do you know in London?"

"There are plenty of good restaurants. The White Tower in Charlotte Street? They do a very good crispy duck."

"I'll settle for that." She smiled. "You've upgraded me in the last hour or so. Realised my true value. I eat a lot, though; can you afford me?"

"I thought you were a feminist? I wouldn't want to interfere with your right to go Dutch."

Her smile disappeared. "You putting me on?"

"Sure I am. You staying at the Grosvenor? I'll get a table at the Tower as soon as we've finished the arrival rituals."

"It's only the meal I want," she cautioned.

"And it's a meal you're going to get. Right through the menu."

She tried to take her hand away but he was now holding it too firmly. "Don't get ideas," she warned, not sure of his tone.

He laughed. "You don't know when to take me seriously, do you?" He lifted her hand and lightly kissed it. "Nice hand," he remarked. He leaned forward a little to look her straight in the eyes. "And beautiful . . . "

The words died on his lips. He felt an enormous pressure beneath him and the deafening roar that came with it began splitting his head in two. The plane was exploding around him, disappearing in great chunks in every direction. He was suctioned up through a gaping, ragged hole in the fuselage and through the haze of pain, bewilderment and sheer terror, he realised that he was still on his seat but there was a massive battering ram beneath it pile driving him from the plane like a rocket.

In the second or two before he died his last bemused realisation was that he was still holding Suzy's hand. But it was attached only to the bloodied stump of what remained of her arm. It was the last thought Sam Baites ever had.

The impact on the flight deck was initially less dramatic but no less fatal. With its tail section blown off the plane plummeted at sickening speed and began to break up to spew its expensive cargo into the waiting graveyard of the

16

Atlantic. The radio operator had no time to send a message before he was ejected with the rest. Colonel Freeman tried to shout something to his colleagues but the words were forced back into his mouth. His highly professional reflex actions at the controls stood no chance before he and his crew went their separate ways through space.

The Secret Service men had no more hope than the rest. Trained to sacrifice their own lives if necessary in order to protect the President, their terror was no different from anybody else's. They died in a group, unable to say goodbye or express anything except a shout of alarm or fright. They plunged with the rest, involuntarily deserting their President when he needed them most. Their duty was over for all time.

Anatole Bruslov died a lonely man. In his last living moments he craved his friends, his family and familiar soil. Another thought pushed its way into his consciousness – a fleeting suspicion – but there was no time before he died to nurture it.

In the President's suite it took a split second for the President and his colleagues to be hurled forward as the plane was torn apart in huge jagged pieces. He never saw his wife but she occupied his last screaming thought as he joined comrades in an act that provided no differential for Presidents. Terror and death were great equalisers. Air Force One was no more. The President was dead.

2

The air traffic controller at Shannon airport was a highly experienced man – one of the best – but when the blip disappeared from his screen he could not believe his eyes. He swallowed awkwardly and worked the radio with a heightening panic as he raised no answer. Everything had gone dead. The pale glow of the blank screen mocked him. There had to be a malfunction in the communications equipment; the radar was playing up. The alternative was unthinkable.

It was to his credit that he pushed the awesome possibility of what had happened from his mind and set a rescue operation in motion seconds after the screen had shown its negative. Search and rescue units were immediately alerted. Radio stations, lifeboats, Air Corps, surveillance aircraft, and the Royal Air Force in Britain were urgently requested to fly over the position of the last radar contact.

In less than twenty minutes of the first loss of radio contact, Valentia Radio broadcast a warning to shipping. Ships in the general area headed towards the last reported position. In just less than an hour from the first emergency call an RAF Nimrod sighted wreckage in the indicated position which triggered a full-scale search and rescue operation. Everyone's worst fears were realised.

And it was news which stunned the world. Some of the most important people in the United States had been aboard Air Force One, including uniquely, the Soviet Ambassador to that country. This was either the most tragic of accidents or mass murder on an unbelievable scale.

Reaction to the horrific event was staggered through the various time zones. Most parts of the globe were horrified; here and there were pockets of secret satisfaction behind pious and public regrets. But all that was certain so far was that the plane, for reasons unknown, had crashed about ninety miles off the coast of Cork and that wreckage had been sighted over a fifteen-mile radius. In Washington it was still only five thirty in the morning but there would be no more sleep for those on call, nor for an increasing number of others. Like the spread of a massive bushfire the news rolled out of control. In the nation's capital, sleep was shaken off but the nightmare had just begun.

Cork Airport was closed to all but those involved in the rescue operation. Prejudices were broken down in a common cause when Sea King helicopters of the Royal Air Force flew in from Woodbridge in England to land on Irish soil. Just behind them, covering the longer distance from their Air Force base in Yorkshire came the USAF Navajo and HH 530 helicopters. On their way to the crash zone were the Irish vessels *L E Emer* and the *Aisling* and the Royal Navy's *H M S Challenger*. But these were merely the early movements. More ships were en route from points further afield. Meanwhile the RAF Nimrod had marked the zone with white smoke flares and bright green and yellow sea dye. The international co-operation was remarkable.

In Washington British Airways put a Concorde at the disposal of the American Government. National pride was swallowed in the interests of speed. Six experts from the US National Transport Safety Board had been quickly roused from their beds, and, together with other experts, were flown to Shannon where a helicopter would take them on to Cork. The epicentre of operations lay over six thousand feet down on the bed of the Atlantic.

In Europe it took until late-morning for matters to simmer down; the tragedy was never far from anyone's mind. This was no time to voice pro- or anti-American views; all would be affected in one way or another. People's thoughts harked back to Kennedy in '63, but this was a disaster of even greater magnitude. So far some seventy people were missing and the final manifest was being checked in Washington. Not a huge number by air-crash standards, but it was the nature of the passenger list which made the difference. The very heart of an entire government had just been ripped out and yet the calamity, as explosive as it was, might still turn out to be a mere ripple compared with the eruption which could follow. Some

19

people on both sides of the Atlantic had already begun to anticipate the worst.

A haggard-faced Michael Dwyer, United States Ambassador to Eire, flew from Dublin to Cork in a chopper provided by the Irish Dáil. He sat shivering in his seat, holding his ear pads as an extra shield to hide his face from the pilot. He was close to tears, and earlier, with his wife, had unashamedly broken down in their Dublin home. A close friend of the President for many years he still found the catastrophe difficult to accept. He had learned that Air Force One had been cleared to proceed to London by the Shannon flight controller just before it had disappeared from the screen. The search for survivors was on; he must be as close as possible, and a room had been booked for him at Jury's Hotel in Cork City.

Dwyer was a tall man, almost gaunt, but he possessed a renowned sense of humour, appreciated by the Irish, and his readiness to smile had often worked to soften what might otherwise have been a grim image. Behind him sat the Embassy Air Attaché, an ex-pilot, now purporting to do an almost meaningless job in a country with virtually no airforce. It was generally accepted that he belonged to the CIA with a brief, amongst others, to keep an eye on some of the activities from the overlarge Soviet Embassy in Dublin. Britain and Eire had open frontiers for each other's nationals, a useful back door for entry into the UK for those who might not otherwise be allowed in.

Glenn Rees had the sense to be silent in the face of Dwyer's obvious grief. He sat there trying to shut out the thunder of the rotor blades as he mulled over the possible causes of the explosion. He had discussed the issue with the Ambassador before the news had really sunk in. He had shaken his head in disbelief and said, "It can't be a malfunction. The goddamn airplane has more servicing than a commercial fleet in total. It's the most thoroughly serviced airplane in the world – bar none."

Dwyer was still largely numb but had forced himself to respond. "If they took the thing apart and put it together again it could still happen. Human error."

"I don't buy it," Rees had snapped in a tone he would not normally use to his Ambassador; nerves were stretched to the limit. "It's not just the general servicing.

20

The engines, tyres, anything susceptible to wear is changed long before a commercial airline would deem it necessary to do so. You can't imagine the number of checks. Day in, day out. Even the runway is inspected from end to end before Air Force One is allowed to take off. And it is never, ever, overloaded."

The two men had looked at each other, both standing near Dwyer's large desk with the Stars and Stripes draped behind it, neither able to continue the conversation. Apart from his private secretary, Dwyer had avoided speaking to the rest of his staff. The usual embassy business had ground to a halt.

"You realise what you're suggesting?" Dwyer kept his voice low.

"I don't buy that either, sir." Rees had clearly given it thought. "I said it was the best serviced airplane in the world; it was also the best protected. Everyone connected with it is checked repeatedly. The security overlaps. Every visitor, known or not, is signed in and never let out of sight once in the hangar. There's a permanent armed guard at a vital vantage point high above the plane. Catering, baggage, everything is checked."

"And the passengers?"

Rees shrugged wearily. "The passengers are collected from hotels or homes with their baggage, for which they are personally responsible and which is never left out of sight. Once collected everyone remains supervised."

Dwyer turned thoughtfully to his subordinate. "Where do you get all this information, Glenn?"

Rees smiled grimly. "I did a spell with the 89th Airlift Wing out at Andrews. It's on my record. I'm telling you, sir, either way it's impossible."

"Just the same something terrible happened."

"Sure." Rees shook his head. He had been thinking like a pilot. "As sure as hell I don't know what. We'll just have to wait until we get some of the pieces together. And bodies, maybe."

Neither man wanted to dwell on that possibility. Rees said, "If they recover any of the wreckage we're going to need some real crash experts on this one."

Dwyer nodded. "Washington has told me they've already contacted the Royal Aircraft Establishment at

Farnborough and some of our own boys from the National Transport Safety Board are on the way. The Irish are bending over backwards to co-operate; they're doing everything possible and they've taken over Jury's Hotel for us in Cork."

There had been nothing else to discuss and now both men were grateful for the noise of the helicopter as it sped south; it offered an excuse for remaining silent. The Irish pilot, sensing their mood, was uncharacteristically quiet.

Just after the helicopter arrived at Cork airport and before the two passengers were besieged by reporters Dwyer spoke quickly. "Apart from the tragedy itself the White House is worried sick over the loss of the 'football'." He was not talking of the so-called "black box", the flight recorder kept near the rear of the plane, but the box of codes the President took with him everywhere he went and with which he could start a nuclear war.

It was something Glenn Rees had already considered. But he did not reply.

They met at the entrance to Central Park on 59th Street. The mid-morning October sun was weak but the breeze light and it was a pleasantly fresh autumnal day. The carriages were already lined up off Fifth Avenue, the horses content to wait, sensing perhaps that the tourist season was drawing to an end. People were moving slowly, a weird sight in Manhattan. Few were talking. A nation was mourning, openly showing its grief. People appeared drawn and, here and there, wept. It was the most calamitous national disaster that anyone could recall and the echoes were still gathering strength round the world.

Farrell led the way, taking the path towards the Wollman Memorial Skating Rink, the lake to his left. Ross scurried after him, his shorter legs trying to keep pace with the taller man. The grimness both displayed blended well with the general mood; no-one would be able to discern that their motives were quite different.

Farrell stopped at the first empty bench and sat down, crossing his long legs and gazing idly at his polished shoes. He was wearing a light fawn coat over a well-cut suit and did not look up as the untidier Ross joined him. Farrell disliked the whole idea of meeting like this — they

22

appeared such an unlikely couple – but it was better here in the open than anywhere near his home or office or the confined space of a restaurant. When Ross had briefly telephoned him at home he had accepted that he needed too many explanations for a callbox-to-callbox "meet". Anyway, on a day like this most people would be too preoccupied to notice them. He moved his gaze slightly and saw the scuff marks on the shoes stretched out next to his. "Pull your feet in, for God's sake. Someone will trip over them. What the hell do you do with your money, you scruffy devil?" The question was rhetorical, but Ross pulled his feet back and tried a conciliatory smile.

Farrell adjusted his hat, tilting it slightly over his eyes. "What went wrong?"

Ross scratched his chin. He had the appearance of a drunk but a closer look revealed that it was only his way of dressing that gave that impression. His round, pale face looked unshaven and his thinning hair was like a wind-blown thatch. Overall, he appeared to be down and out, but he was far from that: his eyes were clear and sharp. "Nothing. It went according to plan," he said.

In a low, cutting tone, Farrell persisted. "I said what went wrong?"

"And I said it went to plan. The plane crashed. What more do you want?"

"It was supposed to crash in the middle of the goddamned Atlantic not ninety miles off the coast of Ireland."

"It makes no difference. It's done."

"Don't give me that. Don't feed me with that sort of crap. They're getting chunks of wreckage out of the sea. They'll find out what did it. And then our plan is blown sky high. The whole idea was that effective evidence would be impossible to find; it would all be miles down under the ocean, too far out for land-based helicopters, too deep and too complicated to recover in the mountains and valleys of the mid-Atlantic Ridge. A mystery crash. Whatever the suspicion nobody would ever know for sure. We could be in real trouble."

"I was in real trouble when I first agreed to make the bomb. They won't find much. The plane would have been

23

blown to bits, and what they do recover won't tell them a thing."

"No?" Farrell said with obvious suspicion. "And what about the passengers?"

"Same thing. Most of them would have finished up in pieces. There would be no air in what was left to float the remains. And the scavengers will clean up." Then he spoke with sudden irritation, "For Chrissake, you can never tell with fuses. There are too many factors on that sort of job."

"That's not what you said at the beginning. Who're you kidding? You can handle a fuse like a gigolo can handle a woman. For the last time, what went wrong?"

Ross sucked at his lip, distorting his indeterminate features. He half turned his head. "You think I'm talking crap because you don't know about fuses and detonators, how sensitive they can be, how unpredictable; you got it right when you mentioned women. The problem's the same. All you understand is banking and finance. Don't you ever get hiccups in your deals?"

"Okay. But it's lives we're talking about, perhaps our own. This was a one-shot, not an occasional bad move among mostly good ones. There was no room for mistakes. You knew that. Explain so I can understand."

"I couldn't use an out-and-out time fuse. The President has a history of running behind schedule. Where would we have been had the flight been postponed? That's happened before. The plane would have blown up in the hangar, and we'd have been in the shit sure enough." Ross fumbled inside his coat and eventually produced a crumpled packet of cheroots; he took one out before continuing. "I decided on a bi-metal strip fixed to a contact."

"A what?"

"Two metal strips separated until contact is made . . . "

"Keep it simple."

Ross hid his contempt as he took his time in lighting the cheroot. "Temperature. The temperature is constant at around thirty-six thousand feet. It is not quite so simple but I'm trying to be non-technical. There was a refinement, a delaying device otherwise the explosion would have happened as soon as they reached height and that

24

might still have been overland. It was fixed to give a three-hour delay after reaching altitude, so it took a little longer."

Farrell shrugged in exasperation. "You make so damned light of it. We could be in dire trouble for God's sake."

"There are so many factors. Engine heat, the amount of baggage packed in the hold, all these things can affect temperature. There might have been a temporary short circuit due to contraction. Maybe they flew at a lower altitude for a while. Anything."

Farrell said nothing, not sure whether he had been hearing the truth. He sat in silence for a while, bent forward with head down dejectedly.

Beside him Ross added, "If I hadn't used enough explosive you'd have had cause for complaint."

Farrell straightened, his dark good-looking features set grim. He was a man who carefully watched his weight and health. At forty-six he normally looked at least five years younger. But not at the moment. He ran a hand over his face. "There are too many loose ends which didn't matter so much before. But they matter now, by God. And if anything goes wrong you're one of those ends."

"Are you threatening me?" Ross smiled bitterly. "Don't waste your time. Loose ends lead back to me from all over the place. The day I disappear is the day that they all join together and pull the others in. I look after myself, Farrell. And don't you ever forget it. Anyway do you think I'd sing? What do you think they'd do to me? I can't afford to risk going to jail and you can't afford to risk putting out a contract on me. Pull yourself together, man. There's nothing to worry about. We're okay."

Farrell looked thoughtful. "We have to think it through, keep ourselves covered."

"We *are* covered. With maybe one exception."

Farrell nodded slowly and then lifted his head to gaze at his colleague. "If something was done about that it would certainly cut off our trail."

Ross smirked. "If that little problem was left to me I'd have recommended doing it in any case. You'd be wise to see that it's done."

"I won't have time. I've got to think up some excuse to

go to London. From there I can go to Ireland. But it won't be easy. I have colleagues to convince."

"You're the boss, you don't need excuses."

"No, but it would look odd if I gave no explanation. Someone must go over there to keep an eye on developments."

"They'll be doing that anyway."

"Sure. But we need to know. Need to tie this up once and for all. You take care of the other business while I'm away."

"I'll need paying and it won't be cheap. It will need planning."

"When have you not needed paying? Money is no problem. But you'd better not plan for too long."

Ross was suddenly condescending and a certain pride crept into his tone. "I'm a professional and I also believe in what I'm doing. You have the money but you're an amateur. Keep cool, man. I've been in this position too often before."

"Not over the President of the United States, you haven't. The enormity of this just hasn't reached you, has it? You scare me; none of this seems to touch you. You do that job and do it quick."

Farrell rose slowly, his face drawn. "I'll make arrangements to keep in touch. Let's just hope that they never find the flight recorder."

"It'll be too far down," Ross assured him. "Even if they trace the damn thing they won't be able to retrieve it."

Farrell was not convinced. Ross was far too sure of himself. He was an expert, it was true, but perhaps he wasn't giving sufficient credit to other experts. There may yet be many more dangers to straighten out before he felt safe. But even so he sensed a certain satisfaction and, for a moment, a deep fanaticism showed in his dark eyes. He may have been a little too critical of Ross but it was no use pretending that everything was perfect. "See you," he said, turning towards the south entrance and Fifth Avenue.

Ross did not trouble to say goodbye; he continued up towards the Zoo and Transverse 1, walking slowly. For the first time in his life he had blown a job and he didn't understand why. He might have convinced Farrell but he

26

could not satisfy himself. Something *had* gone wrong and the fact worried him a great deal.

The first bodies were sighted later that same day and the rescue helicopters started the grim business of winching them up one at a time while the nearby ships were notified. Chunks of aircraft wreckage were being lifted by the ships in the vicinity. Parts of the plane had been scattered over an area of fifteen miles but the drift was making things worse by the hour. Constant air surveillance was necessary to direct ships; the whole area was littered with them.

The first evidence began to emerge as it became obvious that no life-rafts or life-jackets had been inflated, which meant that there had been no time for anyone to do so. And that virtually excluded engine failure; even if all four turbo-jets had failed simultaneously the plane would have continued to glide until it reached stalling speed. There would have been plenty of time for a Mayday and for crash procedure.

Sabotage had been high on everybody's list as a possibility. This was a stage where the media relayed what they considered people wanted to believe. But for once the very idea was muted as if nobody really wanted to accept the possibility that it could have happened to this particular aircraft.

Meanwhile Cork Regional Hospital was hastily reorganised to cope with the covered corpses as they arrived and seven pathologists and their assistants were on stand-by. Rumours were rife that the President's body had been recovered but, in fact, it had not; nor had his wife's. Two senators and a steward had drifted up and it was quickly established that they had not drowned; there was far too much oxygen in their bodies, which was why they had surfaced so quickly.

Recovered wreckage was placed under armed guard at Cork Airport, anything brought in by sea was taken to the Naval Shipyard at nearby Haubowline. The Taoiseach, the Prime Minister of Ireland, had already flown down from Dublin to cut through any red tape that might hinder the search and the land arrangements, though he need not have worried. The tragic crisis was producing the best in everyone. But it was still too early for any definite opinions

27

on the cause of the crash, on site anyway. Elsewhere it was a different story. Especially in London and Washington.

Paul Sutter flew into London's Heathrow on the special Concorde which had dropped other American experts off at Shannon. He did not go through immigration or customs but was met by a smart young man with a ready smile and non-committal eyes. The polished greeting was formal as Sutter was ushered into the rear seat of a Daimler limousine. The polite young man climbed in beside the uniformed driver.

Sutter felt lonely in the back. Coming over to England had been one mad rush and his brief was scanty. The few hours on the plane had given him more time to think and when it came down to it he was best left alone to try to sort things out coherently.

Sutter was heavily built with the comfortable well-to-do appearance of a banker or a lawyer, though he was in neither profession. In his early fifties, his features were florid and his facial muscles sagged but overall he carried a pleasant image: seasoned, efficient, with an exceedingly sharp mind often hidden behind a slowness of speech. He watched the London scene unfold; nothing spectacular greeted him on the way from the airport to central London – he had seen it so often before. There was a glass screen between the rear passenger seats and the driver's section and he realised that the young man had climbed in front to avoid talking about the one subject on everybody's mind. He closed his eyes and tried to relax until they reached the Thames Embankment, close to Northumberland Avenue. This meeting would be crucial.

"A black day," said Sir Gerald Fowler in his quiet, unassuming voice. "We are all so sorry." He walked across the office to shake Sutter by the hand. "Let me take your coat." He reached for a hanger on an old-fashioned hat stand as he helped the American. A slight figure, Fowler had never been known to raise his voice whatever the provocation. His perpetual coolness was displayed in an almost serene expression; his pale blue eyes were benign behind bifocal glasses.

"The furniture's been changed since you last called; try

that chair there, it's not as hard as the others." Fowler returned to his desk. The office was rather old fashioned, the fittings heavy, and the window drapes dark velvet, but it was the way the Head of Security Service preferred to have it in contrast to the modern starkness of Century House. He noticed that his guest was rubbing his left arm. "London damp playing it up?" He was referring to an old wound Sutter had suffered during a brief spell in the field; mortar shrapnel that had sliced a sizeable piece from his lower arm.

Sutter smiled, masking his slight annoyance. He thought he had kicked the habit of rubbing his arm when worried.

"Would you like some tea after your journey? My own, not the official brew."

"Thanks, Gerald, I would. I feel bushed but it's not due to the travelling."

"Perfectly understandable." Fowler pressed a desk button twice.

"This is the darkest day of my life," said Sutter with feeling. "I keep telling myself that it could not have happened. I still can't come to terms with it. But it has happened and we'd better start thinking about repercussions. We've got to get on top of it before someone gets the idea that knocking off our President is a pushover."

"So you think it was a bomb?"

"I've never considered anything else since the first news. *It was a bomb.*"

The tea arrived and a middle-aged secretary poured it, handing Sutter a cup, and pushing milk, lemon and sugar to the edge of the desk for him. When she had left Fowler cautiously observed, "There seem to have been an awful lot of tail units falling off recently. Particularly on planes that, hitherto, were considered to be extremely safe."

"I know all about them. But this was no metal or any other kind of fatigue. This was sabotage. Pure and simple."

"Paul, have you news that I haven't had? Have they found evidence of an explosion?"

"Not that I know of." Sutter grimaced. He was under great strain and it showed. He stirred his tea slowly. "The sort of checks commercial airlines made after those crashes were going on all the time with Air Force One. It was routine. And you think it was sabotage, too. You don't fool me."

"So who would want to do it?"

"The possibilities can be lined up. Who can tell at this stage? The only certain thing is the careful planning behind it. But you can run through from some of the South American states, to opponents, to star wars. And then there's the IRA having their Red funds cut off and Gaddafi not forgiving us over the bombing of Libya. The President had a lot of enemies but then I suppose that's nothing new."

"What's your guess?"

"There's nothing open and shut about this; nothing's straightforward. At the moment we're trying to find out how the bomb got on board. That has got to be our first priority." Sutter gazed across at Fowler with a mixture of desperation and dejection. "I need your help."

"What can we do?" Fowler was puzzled.

"You must have deep cover agents in the IRA."

Fowler was immediately cautious. "Go on."

"I'm about to ask a big sacrifice, Gerald."

Fowler made no reply but he was watching Sutter closely. He knew what was coming next but made no effort to help.

"Could you activate an agent or two for me?"

"What for? You think the Provos did it? For having their funds cut off? If it was a bomb it was planted your end."

"There's a chance. American funds have risen very considerably over the last eighteen months. The next President, if he's the present Vice-President, is already known to be against bringing in so tough a legislation. It might be that the boyos saw an opportunity of putting things right." Sutter rubbed his arm again. "That's only one of many possibilities, but it is an area where you could help us."

Fowler put his cup down slowly. "You're tired, Paul. Which is not surprising with the news you've just had. You know how long it takes to get them planted, and all the time they are a murmur away from a bullet in the back of the head."

Sutter nodded slowly. "I understand. But we're not only talking about the murder of our President. We don't want

30

the kind of nonsense we had when Kennedy was killed. We want to nail the ones who did it. And fast."

Fowler was silent for a while, gazing at Sutter thoughtfully. Suddenly he felt less friendly. Sutter was nobody's fool whatever strain he might be under. "I'm surprised you take the IRA possibility so seriously. They're *our* terrorists, not yours. Your average American would react to this scenario with utter incredulity."

"Sure. They're no big deal over there. But I'm an intelligence officer like you, not your average American. And if you're going to raise the question of motivation there have been far more obscure reasons for murdering our Presidents than this one. If the IRA can restore their funds in this way they have all the reason they need and it would mean that nobody, but nobody, would be safe from future intimidation. You've got to believe that." He paused wearily. "You're my first call abroad. I must admit that I intend to ask favours elsewhere. Anywhere there might be a possible lead. This is just a start."

"What about the home front?"

"As you know, the FBI handles that. But I have the gut feeling that the roots are not at home."

Fowler inclined his head. "If you're right there will be problems in Ireland if evidence to support you is produced."

"Well, as you know, the stuff being pulled out of the sea is under armed guard but there are extra precautions I would like to see taken. If I can get some help from you I'll fly to Cork. We're on tricky ground. The Irish are being marvellous over this; they could not be more co-operative. But they might be sensitive to any suggestions from us of an IRA connection, big brother."

"Indeed. Any suggestions about extra security would be better to come from you, though. We're outsiders." Fowler suddenly looked amused. "I never thought I'd live to see the day when the British Forces would be welcomed in Eire. But that is what is happening over there now. The RAF rescue teams and the Royal Navy have been greeted with open arms. Two of our frigates have been sailing up the River Lee to Cork. It has taken a mammoth tragedy to make this happen, but I agree that it must be sensitively handled." Fowler was pensive for a while. He quietly finished his tea. "All right. I accept that this is the darkest day the West has known for all the obvious reasons, and for many that are yet to show themselves. I'll do what I can."

As Fowler helped Sutter on with his coat the American said quietly, "When Jack Kennedy was killed it rocked the nation to its foundations. The only thing like it since was when Challenger blew up off Cape Canaveral killing seven astronauts; that rocked everybody, brought it right into the home." He turned as he buttoned his coat. "You can imagine how they feel now."

When Fowler returned to his desk after Sutter had gone he gazed thoughtfully at the door. Something told him that he should not have agreed so readily to the American's request.

3

Laurie Galvin put down the telephone, his features grim. The message had been extremely brief and had merely prepared him to be on stand-by. The general practice was that a more explicit but coded message would follow at home. From past experience that would mean going to England for a briefing. He looked round the makeshift office which was an extension of the garage next door. Apart from crumpled spiked papers the old desk was reasonably clear but the room itself was filled with oil drums and spare exhausts, tyres and dirty rags. The hand still holding the phone was greasy.

Galvin was worried. He knew that the call was something to do with the tragedy ninety miles off Cork. Nothing had been mentioned on the phone, they would not dare, but he was convinced of a connection. With great sadness he wondered how Riley Brown would take his absence.

Galvin was dark haired and well built. He was not over tall, with features that looked as if they had spent some time being battered and had later been roughly restored. His nose was just a little too wide where it had been flattened and was slightly bent. His usually lively grey eyes were at the moment sombre. The garage he ran catered mainly for tractors and the farmers trusted him to do a good and reasonably priced job.

His mind was far from tractors now and the banging from the workshop was an intrusion on his thoughts. He must get back to Dun Laoghaire. It was only five miles away on the Bray Road. By this time, late evening, he was usually home but there was still a little work to do.

He checked that the door was closed. The smell of exhaust fumes was escaping into the office from a wide gap under the door. He dropped to his knees behind the desk and peered up under it. The gun was still taped to the underside with the spare magazine. He'd almost forgotten it was there and he wondered why he was so certain that he might need it now. It was a crazy sensation but one he could not ignore.

Con Tierney watched with the crowd around the perimeter of Cork's small airport. A military cordon kept the public away from the activity and among them was a mass of cameramen and reporters. Flashes pricked the encroaching twilight like star bursts. Occasionally someone would try to get through the barrier but they were quickly turned away. Some onlookers had brought binoculars and would report back to those around them; it was a bizarre running commentary.

Everyone could see the helicopter arrivals. They came droning in, sounding weary and listless like their overworked crews, sometimes with bits of wreckage suspended beneath them. But it was the bodies they carried on board that provoked the interest. Everybody was waiting for news of the President and the First Lady. There had already been several false rumours but a correction had always filtered back.

Tierney made no move to get nearer the actual scene. He could just about see the corpses being off-loaded. He made a point of drifting around the press personnel who had flown in from all over the world and were still arriving. He moved among them and kept his ears and eyes open. He did not look particularly Irish. There were certain types of features, all different but all unmistakably Irish whether dark, fair or ginger haired. He was short and stocky, ill dressed with torn jeans and a well-worn wind-cheater over an open-necked check shirt. His features were pinched but strong and uncompromising with deep, sunken blue eyes. His hair was black and unruly.

Tierney had spent some hours at the airport. He had come down from Dublin after hearing the first radio report, and had driven the one hundred and sixty miles down the N11 to Cork where he knew that if any worthwhile news was coming at all that would be its source. He had not eaten all day but he did not feel hungry until it became increasingly clear that he would not hear anything of use that day. He wondered if he could get a sandwich from the airport lounge but had doubts about getting into the airport building. He would not try too hard; the last thing he wanted was to draw attention to himself.

He moved away from the crowd and trekked along the airport approach road, past the custodial barrier, now permanently down to prevent more traffic getting in. The airport car park had already been full by the time he had arrived in the early afternoon and he had left his car on the main Cork–Bandon Road along with hundreds of others. It was fortunate that the road was wide at this point and could cope with the extra parking. A good sprinkling of garda were around the junction to the airport road but the police paid no particular attention to him; there were people on the move everywhere.

Locating his snub-nosed Morris 1000, an ancient model that seemed to go on for ever in rural Ireland, he pulled out and headed for the nearby Douglas Road, a smart suburb of Cork City. He passed the entrance to Musgraves, the huge cash-and-carry store, and continued on until he found a narrow lane on his right. He turned on to what was no more than a wheel track, the uncut grass brushing the underside of the small car. The farm was on slightly higher ground about a mile further on. When he swung on to the neglected cobbled yard, he spotted the tail end of another car parked just round the corner of the near dilapidated building. Tierney pulled up, climbed out and slammed the car door angrily.

The sound brought another man to the battered door of the stone-built farmhouse. A tall, thin, bearded man, he came towards Tierney with fervent eyes and outstretched arms. "Con, me old darling, I wondered if you'd be here."

They shook hands warmly enough but Tierney still felt disturbed. "What the hell did you come down here for, Eugey? You must be mad."

Eugene Hayes was surprised by Tierney's vehemence. "That's no greeting at all, for God's sake. What did you expect me to do? It's all happening down here. Sure, I had to come."

Tierney pointed to the protruding tail end of the Ford Escort. "Get that bloody thing out of sight. Put it in the barn."

"What's wrong with you? There are plenty of UK number plates in the Republic; they're all over the place."

"Not with Belfast registrations. You should have stayed there until you heard from us."

"Wasn't I trying to ring you this morning? No reply. I knew you'd be here. For Christ's sake I've been motoring all day. I can do without the aggro."

Tierney calmed a little. "Okay, okay. Deal with the car first, then we'll scratch up something to eat. If you're staying here you'd better change your number plates; there are plenty of spares."

Later, sitting at a huge kitchen table, they drank soup and ate heated tinned stew with large chunks of Irish soda bread which Hayes had brought down with him. They talked excitedly. The difference in accents between the two men could not have been more marked. Hayes spoke with the difficult-to-understand grating and harsh Ulster tones while Tierney possessed a softer Dublin accent. Finally, Tierney poured two generous measures of Middleton's whiskey and added white lemonade without asking Hayes. Hayes took his glass. "*Slainte.*"

"*Slainte,*" Tierney toasted back. "I'll fill you in. That Brit-loving Taoiseach of ours has been holding court with a press conference at Cork airport. He's offering the moon and by God he's supplying it. He's handed over the whole county to the Americans and the Brits and anyone else who cares to play. There are more 'experts' floating around than press men." He took a gulp of whiskey and quickly added some more.

"There's no positive news as to the cause of the crash. Yet. They're dredging up all sorts of gadgets. The Brits have some sort of submarine with grapples and the French have something called a Scarab, remote controlled, which can operate at depth and is also fitted with grapples and lights. The general feeling is that the main wreckage is too far down, at a depth not successfully tackled before."

"I don't like the sound of it, just the same." Hayes made no effort to disguise his concern. "I don't like that one little bit."

Tierney shrugged, but the gesture wasn't convincing; he was worried.

"So we just sweat it out and hope for the best? Is that what you're saying?" Hayes was watching Tierney's reaction closely and was not comforted by it.

"We do more than that. We've got to get organised in case

they do come up with something. We must be ready. The Dublin boys are well aware of the need for quick action. It's being organised."

"I can get some experienced men down from the north."

"We don't want Belfast accents running loose in Cork. That's the last thing we need. You'll be a magnet and there are far too many suspicious minds around right now. All we can do is to wait and be ready to move as soon as necessary. We've got to keep cool. You get back. I'll ring in the usual way if we want you."

Hayes bridled, eyes narrowing dangerously. "We're doing all the danger work up there in the six counties while you do the talking down here. You'd better get yourself sorted out. I'm not standing for that kind of stuff."

Tierney backed down. "Look, we all know what you're doing up there; you're doing a terrific job. But you're a give-away in the Republic unless you can hide that accent. They're on the look-out, for God's sake. It's not a question of what you can do but of keeping a low profile. It's our turn now, that's all. It's our patch. And we'll cope. We've all the arms we need and some very good soldiers. We'll keep you in touch all along the line and we'll give you a shout as soon as we need you. Okay?"

Hayes knew he was being brushed off, but he conceded that the difference in territory could create problems for those up north; even a Dublin accent was noticeable around Cork and the Cork people weren't all that keen on Dubliners.

Watching him, Tierney recognised some of the problems. Hayes knew that those north of the border were far better, and far more practised at killing, than their colleagues down south. And Hayes sensed the approaching necessity for the gun; there were none better at using it than he. But to advertise their presence in Cork would invite trouble at a time when they already had more than enough.

In the makeshift morgue at the Cork Regional Hospital covered and strapped corpses lay in three rough lines. In death there was no protocol; Secret Service men lay alongside Senators, White House staff and air crew. And without distinction they took their turn for the over-busy pathologists who worked round the clock, straining to find some evidence of the cause of the crash. Doctors refused to discuss with the media the mutilations found on the bodies already brought in, and would only say that every post-mortem would be thorough – and therefore time-consuming. The gruesome procedure was not one that could be rushed.

The salvage work continued and the helicopter crews were beginning to look haggard. Out at sea there were now too many ships and a danger of collision became real as national rivalry crept into the grim search. So far fourteen bodies had been recovered, and a mass of aircraft parts. But a more important search was also taking place. The British ship *Gardline Locator* had been chartered with special equipment to locate the voice and flight recorders now lying somewhere on the seabed. Each box emitted signals which could be picked up if a rough location could be determined. It was a wide area and the work was painstaking but was deemed a priority.

"Where've you been? I've been worried about you." Riley Brown uncrossed her long legs, switched off the television and hastened towards Galvin as he entered the room. She put her arms round his neck and kissed him quickly, for once feeling little response. She arched her body back from his. "What's the matter? You look awful."

He gazed down at her, his arms round her waist. He raised a hand to pull her head against his chest, stroking her long fair hair. "I should think that on a day like this everyone is feeling pretty jaded. It's also been a long one, though."

"You mean the crash? It's terrible news all right. Dreadful. But it can't affect us, can it?"

Galvin smiled unhappily. "You'd be surprised how many people this will affect outside America. Most of us one way or another. It's bad news, Riley, in all sorts of ways." He suddenly held her from him. "Come on, make some tea."

As she left him to go to the small kitchen he said, "I do have to work, you know. It seems to take me twice as long

38

as anybody else to make half as much money." Why hadn't she told him about a call from England? It must have come through by now.

She called back, "But when I rang you weren't there. You usually give me a call sometime during the day." She had a part-time job as a dentist's receptionist and spent most of the rest of her time painting oils in a small studio that opened off the living room and attracted the best light in the apartment.

He crossed to the living-room window and looked down towards the quay where the ferries departed for Wales. "It's been one of those days. Paddy and I've been out road testing a lot." He looked back towards the kitchen door. "I'm knackered, Riley. Out on my feet. That was a shattering business about the plane crash. It's all people are talking about ."

"I know." She returned with a loaded tea tray and put it down on a glass-topped table; he hated the table but it was a present from an aunt of hers so he kept his counsel. He sipped his tea. "Nice cup. Sorry I didn't ring; it's not often."

She sat across the table from him, a slender, lovely girl who could feel things deeply. She followed more causes than he could recount, becoming genuinely enmeshed in them. At the moment it was Save the Wildlife but she never deserted anything she took up even if she was forced to give it less time. That was one of the reasons he loved her. She put down her cup and her hand flew to her mouth. "I forgot to tell you. Your brother-in-law rang up from England; your sister is ill. He *did* sound worried."

Galvin was relieved that the call had come through but felt alarmed at its nature; the code was top priority. "Which brother-in-law?" He had to go through with it.

"Oh," Riley gazed at the table for an answer. "Joan's husband. Tom. Tommy, he said it was."

Casually he said, "I wouldn't worry. Joan's always ill. It's a neurosis. But I'd better ring."

He finished his tea and crossed to the telephone on the spindle-legged table beside the television. He flicked open the telephone pad, checked the code and dialled a Newbury, Berkshire number. As he waited he noticed Riley taking the tray to the kitchen. He called out to her,

"It's okay, nothing private." And then, "Tommy? Damnit, you should know my dulcet Irish brogue by now. It's Laurie. What's she got now?" He winked at Riley who had come back into the room and was sitting on the arm of the sofa, one leg gently swinging. He listened, his expression changing. "Oh, Christ. Does the doctor know what he's doing?" Now he was slightly alarmed as he returned Riley's soft gaze. "Okay, it's difficult, but I'll come over. The Denbridge Nursing Home in Reading? You want me to call on you first? Okay. The flights will be overloaded with the present crash crisis, but I'll do what I can." He hung up.

Riley rose, her gaze anxious. "She's bad?"

"I won't really know until I get there. Tommy's a bit of a panicker, but I must admit it sounds bad. An internal haemorrhage." Galvin appeared worried. "I'd better see about a flight."

It was far too late to despise himself for deceiving her; he had been doing it for far too long now. But he adored Riley, despite the ultimate hopelessness of their affair. Things would have to run their course, the rest he pushed to the back of his mind.

Galvin's show of concern was genuine but it was not about his sister Joan. This was only the second time he had been recalled in this way. He had taken the call openly because it was by far the least suspicious thing to do. Galvin pulled Riley to him and he had to check his emotion as he buried his face in her hair; her grandfather had been a member of the old IRA and had been killed by the Black-and-Tans.

In the early nineteen-twenties the occupying British troops had been popular with most of the Irish even if the fact of their presence was resented. On the other hand the Black-and-Tans were detested and it was this background and the legends that grew from it that had influenced a warm-hearted and highly impressionable Riley Brown all her young life. Her father, before he died two years ago, had been a staunch Republican, often recounting to his children the anti-British exploits of his own father and the brutal way in which he had been killed; murdered, as he had put it.

In fact Riley's grandfather would not have described

40

himself as anti-British. He liked the British. But he did not want their Government running his homeland; he wanted them out and he had died for that belief. Those who had known Riley's grandfather, and there were still a few around, had said that he was a man who would have kicked the British out and then, with a handshake, would have invited them back for a holiday in *his* country.

Galvin remembered the stories as he drove the seven miles to Dublin airport and parked his battered old Mercedes. Beneath the rust the engine was in fine condition; he would have preferred a Jaguar but that would appear to be trading with the enemy. Small give-aways like that were always a potential trap. When he checked in he found, as he had expected, that flights were overbooked, and all had waiting lists. It did not worry him. He knew that there would be a seat on a British Airways flight in his name, and he was right. He paid for the ticket and went into the crowded departure lounge. When his flight was called he tagged on to the queue. Although it was not officially needed for travel between Ireland and Britain he carried with him a green Irish passport. He arrived at London Heathrow about an hour after take-off.

Sam Squire lived in an old terraced house on Q Street between 29th and 31st in Georgetown with his wife Mandy and their two young daughters. During the early after-noon of the day that the President died, while the children had yet to return from school, Sam and his wife were sitting in the kitchen at the back of the house.

Mandy Squire gazed across the kitchen table at her husband. "Look," she pleaded, "I know it's a terrible day for all of us, okay, for you in particular, but you're taking it too personally. You weren't even on duty."

She had seen the change in him about two hours after the first news flash. At first he had been deeply shocked as they had all been, but then he became morose and withdrawn. He kept both radio and television on all the time, frequently switching stations to devour all the news he possibly could. He had then retired to the main bedroom where he locked himself in and kept the spare television on full blast until she had been forced to pummel the locked door and scream out at him to reduce the volume.

Apart from anything else Mandy was beginning to worry about the neighbours. Eventually he had turned the volume down and she had managed to persuade him to come out. In a matter of hours his face had sunken and his eyes grown wild as if he'd been suffering a fever and was still very ill. The straight-backed man she knew was slumped, round shouldered, and avoided looking at her as he emerged. She hardly recognised her husband of eight years.

"My God," she gasped, "Whatever has happened to you? You're crazy to let it affect you like this. It's not normal."

He had not replied but crossed to the living-room sideboard and poured himself a liberal bourbon. It was his first move towards the bottle; he had always had a contempt of those who could not control their drinking. He had then taken the drink and the bottle into the kitchen, sat down at the table and he had been sitting there ever since.

Mandy could not believe the change in him. It was far too quick for her to absorb. For a time she did not know what to do. She considered calling the doctor until she shrewdly realised that if the doctor saw Sam like this it might put his job in jeopardy. So she had poured herself a drink and sat down opposite him. "What is it, honey? For pity's sake tell me." She checked her tears but could not stop the tremor in her voice. "You're driving me crazy with worry."

He looked at her almost slyly, averting his gaze as soon as their eyes met. His drink remained in front of him, untouched, as if he was still able to exercise self-discipline, but that was the only obvious sign of it. Even as she watched he was receding further inside himself until she believed that he was no longer aware of her. She bit on a knuckle and gazed at him red eyed. Suddenly she felt that she must look almost as big a mess as he. She rose, went into the living room, studied herself in the mirror over the sideboard, and then went into their bedroom and tried to repair her make-up.

While Mandy combed her hair she sat thinking. They had problems enough without this, and she knew that something had been going on. He'd been secretive about phone calls; she had overheard one of them when he had thought she had gone out. And there was the man in the van he had crept out to meet. She had been afraid to mention anything at the time and there was no way she could do so while he was like this. But she had to go back to the kitchen and see what he was doing.

He was sitting as she had left him, his glass now empty. She glanced over to the bottle; it did not seem that he'd had any more. With an effort she spoke matter of factly, "I'll get you something to eat." He made no response.

Mandy fried eggs and sausages, glancing at him from time to time. When she put the food in front of him she noticed that his breathing had become very shallow and he was still glaring at a focal point somewhere across the room. His hand was on the table near the empty glass and his fingers were trembling very slightly.

Mandy gradually realised that her own effort to rouse herself had been in vain and his total lack of response began to play on her nerves all over again. It wasn't long before she began to notice the untidy mess that had first driven her into the bedroom. In despair she said, "I spent time on that meal. *Eat it.*" When he gave no sign that he had heard her she rose angrily. "That's it," she said. "I'm not taking any more. I'm calling the doctor. You're sick, for God's sake."

Mandy crossed to the phone and raised the receiver to punch out the number.

"*NO.*"

The shout was so unexpected that she almost dropped the telephone. She turned to see him move round; he was gaunt as he faced her, cheeks sunken, but a spark of life had entered his eyes. He shook his head in total despair and she felt the old loving concern returning. Mandy put down the phone and went over to him to hold his head against her body. She stroked his hair tenderly. "It's okay, honey. Whatever it is we can lick it together." She looked down at him; he had reached up to hold her round the waist, his grip desperate like a scared child's. "Let me get the doctor. You probably just need a rest."

"No." His head moved under her hands but his voice was much calmer. "It's just nerves. That news has really thrown me." He tried to rise and she helped him to his feet.

"Are you all right, Sam? You're so shaky."

He held on to her. "It's okay." He kissed the top of her head and could feel her relief as she held him more tightly. "I'm sorry." He tried to smile. "I've never felt so shattered but I'll be okay." He steadied himself, still holding on to her. "I must get over to Andrews to find out what's really happening."

Mandy was alarmed. "You're not well enough. And you don't want them to see you like this."

He gently released her grip. "I'll wash up first." He swayed a little then somehow managed to grin. "Stop worrying. They'll have the news straight from the White House there. Anyway I won't be long."

She watched him wash and make himself more presentable but he was still haggard and pale. She was not happy about his leaving and did not think him fit enough to drive as he was but she would rather see him try than have him sitting at the table like a zombie. Yet something he had said disturbed her; he was going to Andrews Air Force Base. Certainly he had friends there, but why do that when he could go straight to the White House Communications Centre at 1600 Pennsylvania Avenue in Washington, where he was known and where the Secret Service had full access. It was a back-handed way of being kept up to date. But she dared not challenge him.

Hank Ross sat in his blue Ford and pondered his next move. The Squire's house was about fifty yards away on the opposite side of the street. Ross had been there no more than twenty minutes and did not want to stay longer in case the neighbours began to take notice. He reached for a flask of coffee and unscrewed the cap. He was weary and wanted to get out and stretch his legs but that would have to wait until he had established whether Squire was at home.

Ross knew that Farrell would in no way approve of what he had in mind. Farrell would want an accident but they weren't always easy to arrange, particularly at short notice. What Ross immediately needed to know was whether Squire's car was in the row lining the sidewalk. There had

44

been no movement from the house since he had arrived and he began to think that he had better return when it was darker. He realised that he was not thinking too rationally but it had been a tiring journey from New York. He had resisted the strong temptation to exceed the speed limit on the interstate and had reluctantly accepted the boredom and fatigue of the long drive; it was better than the possibility of being seen at an airport had he taken the easier course of catching the shuttle to Washington. He scratched his unkempt hair and decided to give it no more than another five minutes. He sipped his coffee and chewed on a stale sandwich. Squire appeared, followed by his wife, while Ross was swilling down the cold dregs; he quickly screwed on the cap and threw the flask on to the passenger seat.

Ross watched him go to a tan Chevrolet, and when Squire pulled out, he saw his wife wave but as far as he could see there was no response from Squire, who looked tired and ill. He waited until the front door was closed then switched on and followed the Chevvy, making a mental note of the registration.

Squire drove carefully at first but as his mind began to fog he became more erratic and the car drifted as if he was drunk. He had only taken the one bourbon but that had been on an empty stomach. Yet that was not the reason for the way the car began to sway dangerously from side to side. Through a clouded mind he realised what was happening and straightened out, much to the relief of his tail, who did not want Squire picked up for drunken driving.

Squire drove steadily now. In a way his mind was clearing. The doubts and the hesitations were over; he now knew exactly what he intended to do and he felt both relieved and sad. Whatever he did could not erase the problems and heartbreak for Mandy and the children; that was inevitable whichever course he followed, but he was now clear cut as to intent. He followed the familiar route into Washington.

He was driving at average speed. There were a good many heavy trucks on the road in both directions, which forced him to concentrate. Then he noticed the blue Ford van on his tail. He adjusted his mirror and awaited an opportunity to pull over sufficiently to pick out the driver. His heart beat faster as he recognised him. At the same time he was satisfied with what he was doing.

It wasn't easy. The tension was building up again and he was holding the steering wheel far too tightly. His mind clouded again until there was little thought left in it. The pressure on his brain was increasingly painful. The blood receded from his face and he was aware that his mouth was open and his breathing heavy. He could hear himself gabbling as tears streamed down to blind his vision. He was now on a straight run on Pennsylvania Avenue and the traffic was thick. He chose that moment to put his foot hard down on the pedal.

The Chevrolet shot forward. Somehow Squire pulled out to avoid three cars in front of him. He was now crying so openly that it was like trying to see through a rainstorm without wipers. The car suddenly went crazy as he pulled as far out as he could. Then he ejected a terrific yell, which at its peak turned to a scream, and he wrenched the wheel to send the car hurtling into the opposite lane to hit a truck head on at a combined impact of one hundred and twenty miles an hour.

The truck skidded to a halt, tyres burning and dragging the mangled wreck of what remained of the Chev and its crushed driver. Sam Squire had at last found peace of mind. The torn remains of the car burst into flame and the resulting explosion of the compressed mess almost lifted the front of the truck. The flames roared up and around and the truck driver and his mate jumped for safety as the on-coming traffic screamed to a halt.

4

When Hank Ross saw what was happening he jammed on
his brakes. It was a wonder there were no further crashes
as cars and trucks shuddered to a halt, hoods to trunks.
When Squire's car blew up he could not believe his luck.
The most god-awful snarl-up was taking place all around
him. Tyres were screaming, horns blaring, and people
were jumping out of cars in an effort to help. But no help
could be given to the crushed and burning body in the
crumpled remains of the Chevrolet. Already a patrol car
was trying to force its way through the mess and an officer
was shouting a warning that the gas in the truck might
blow at any minute.

As the chaos mounted Ross sat there, breathing heavily
with satisfaction. But the increasing sound of sirens
whipped him from his euphoria. The engine was still
running and he realised that he had to get away. The last
thing he wanted was to be questioned as a witness.

Squire was dead; that was obvious. If he hadn't actually
died on impact then he subsequently fried. Ross glanced at
his watch. He wore an expensive chronometer; it was the
one area where his mean nature conceded to financial
outlay. Time was crucial in his business.

He suddenly wanted to get back to New York as fast as
he could. He glanced at the time again and then at his fuel
gauge. He needed some gas. He must reach Farrell before
he caught his flight. It would take about four and half to
five hours to get back. He might just do it. It was going to
be a long, wearying day of driving, but the rewards could
be good. He began to pick his way through the mass of
traffic in front of him, swearing and cursing until he
found sufficient gap to set him free. He started to chuckle,
the dead Squire already out of his scheming mind.

Laurie Galvin's arrival in London was low key compared
with that of Paul Sutter, even though they were both in the

same line of business: no-one waived formalities for the Irishman. Galvin went through immigration and caught an airline coach to the Air Terminal. He bought a bunch of roses before catching a train to Reading, then travelled by taxi to the Denbridge Nursing Home. The Denbridge had been used before and he suspected that it belonged to the firm; it would be easy enough to have calls monitored from Cheltenham. Before he reached the reception desk he was stopped by a young white-coated doctor. "Mr Galvin?"

"Yes." Galvin did not ask how he had been recognised.

"It was good of you to come over so quickly. Your sister's in a bad way, I'm afraid."

"How bad? Terminal?" Galvin fell in step beside the very tall doctor who led the way towards the wards.

The slim, fair-haired doctor became defensive. "I don't believe it to be that bad. But she'll need a good deal of care and perhaps a little luck." He suddenly took another corridor away from the wards and entered an unmarked office. Once they were inside he locked the door.

The office was sparsely furnished: a cheap modern desk, metal filing cabinets and three straight-backed chairs. The desk top had been cleared. Venetian blinds cut out what was left of the late evening light leaving the room shadowy and dull.

"I'm Putton. Do sit down. Incidentally I understand that the switchboard is well versed in giving reports on your sister's condition to any unauthorised callers." The doctor, suddenly appearing less like one, indicated a chair. He made no move to switch on the central light.

Galvin sat on the edge of the desk and put the flowers down. "Where's Jason? With a 'most urgent' I would expect somebody I know."

"Of course. Unfortunately he's sick. Appendicitis. Always boasted that he had everything he started life with; now he hasn't." Noting that Galvin was not satisfied, Putton added, "Sir Gerald briefed me personally. That should convince you of the importance. I mean, you wouldn't expect him to see you himself?"

"No." Galvin studied Putton who now lowered his long body on to one of the chairs and stretched out his legs. Small feet, thought Galvin, and a supercilious attitude.

Putton fancied himself but in what capacity Galvin had yet to learn. Pale blue eyes stared from a narrow, colourless face to challenge Galvin and exert authority.

"You don't hide your feelings," said Putton. "Clearly you are not enamoured of me. But I'm all you're going to get." He smiled. "Perhaps I'll improve in your eyes as time goes on."

"I don't know you. I'd prefer Jason. We have an understanding. We'd better get on with it. I must get back."

"Our cousins think Air Force One was blown up. What's the whisper over there?"

"How the bloody hell would I know what the whisper is? If it *was* a bomb, whispers will be few and far between. And why should there be one in Ireland? The plane started out from Washington." Galvin wasn't quite sure why he was so angry. Perhaps it was the way Putton seemed to talk down to him. He had no idea whether or not the bomb theory held credence.

"Our cousins think it was the IRA. Someone in Belfast or Dublin would have knowledge of it."

"The IRA? Are you serious?" And when Putton didn't reply he added, "God knows why they should think that. But they might be trying to shift the area of obvious blame. It wouldn't be the first time they've killed one of their own Presidents. And this one had ruffled a few feathers. The hand-outs to the wealthy faithful hadn't exactly been forthcoming. And that would annoy some powerful people."

"To the extent of assassinating their elected President? Come now, Galvin."

Galvin shrugged. "What do you really want of me?"

"Assuming it was a bomb, do you think the IRA capable? Do take the question seriously."

"The Official IRA, no. They're no angels but they give the occasional thought to the political consequences of what they do. And they are the least effective in terms of violence. The Provos? They're capable. Factions of them, anyway. They'd have suffered most if their American funds had been cut off. But the INLA are the most spectacular — and most impetuous. They're the smallest group but probably the most ruthless. If I had to choose

49

I'd go for them. Is that taking it seriously enough for you?"

"Thank you. My own feelings exactly."

Galvin looked dubious. The table was uncomfortable but he didn't change position. "You mean that you think it was the INLA, too?"

Putton could not miss the scathing undertone. "You indicated that you do."

Galvin shook his head. He ran his hand through his thick hair. "Oh, no, I didn't. I gave an appraisal in answer to your question. There's no way any of the IRA factions could have done it. On their own. Bombing soft targets in Belfast is one thing, getting a bomb aboard Air Force One quite another. And would they want to do it anyway?"

Galvin stared down at Putton and then proceeded to answer his own question. "Okay, there are a few crazy enough to do it; show how powerful they are, not to be monkeyed with. Don't ever interfere with their fund raising because that can be the beginning of a death blow. If we can knock off US Presidents nobody can be safe anywhere. But would they so soon? The promise to stop the flow of funds was a fairly recent one. It takes time to organise. And the few who are crazy enough would need outside support. Would they get it? And if they did, on what terms? To them and to whoever helped them?"

Putton gesticulated irritably. "I'm not a fool. I under-stand all that but you're going far too fast. It's a matter of where we start. Do you know any of these INLA boys?"

"Of course. You know damn fine that I'm a member of the Provisional Sinn Fein. Most INLA came from the Provos. Some still serve both, wearing whichever hat suits them. You want me to raise my head from the listening post and actively poke around; is that it?"

"Those are the orders I have to give you."

"We're dealing with fanatical, tunnel-visioned terrorists. How long do you think I'd last?"

"We'll pull you out the moment it gets too dangerous."

"You wouldn't have the time." Galvin was suddenly very angry. "Couldn't they find someone who knows more about the Irish problem than you? Do you realise what you're asking? It took me a long time to get where I am and I've already handed over a good deal of information without sticking my neck out too far."

"I'm merely passing on instructions. My personal knowledge of the background is irrelevant. You're a highly experienced undercover man; you'll know when to stop."

"Will they, I wonder? Is this a deal with the Americans?"

"I've no idea." Putton rose and took off the white coat. "I hate this thing. I hate hospitals, too." He hung the coat on a hook behind the door. "Someone will ring you from time to time to give a progress report on your sister. The usual channels will be open to you." He pulled a small slip of paper from his pocket. "An extra emergency number."

Galvin took the slip. The number had been made deliberately simple. "Hope I remember when it matters." He handed the slip back. "*You* destroy it." He turned to the door. "Give my best wishes to Jason. Tell him I hope he'll see me next time." He glanced at the blooms on the desk. "Better give those to a deserving cause."

Hank Ross telephoned Farrell from the Maryland House restaurant near Havre de Grace, just north of Baltimore. He got no further than Farrell's secretary, but extracted from her the information that her boss was catching a Pan Am flight that night, that he would be away for a few days and that the office was about to close. He climbed back into his van, annoyed that he had not been able to raise Farrell.

He kept to the superhighway 1–95, and by-passed Philadelphia in something of a daze, fighting off fatigue as he tried to stay awake. It was important to him that he caught Farrell before he left for Europe and while the issue was still hot. He drove into the October twilight, glad that the rain kept off and that his speed was constant. By the time he passed the New Jersey turnpike exits for Newark he felt all in; apart from the call, he had made no stops and was now driving almost by blind instinct. The build-up around New York forced him to concentrate as he crossed the Verrazano Bridge, the distant lights of Manhattan falling like a fairyland to his left. He was glad to be back in New York; it was the only city he really understood.

He arrived at JF Kennedy and drove straight to the Pan Am terminal and up to the roof-top parking. He took the elevator to the departure level and stationed himself close to the first-class check-in counters. If Farrell was flying that night then Ross believed he had time to catch him but he still felt concerned and edgy.

Twenty minutes later Farrell came through the automatic doors, carrying a medium-sized bag and an attaché case. As Ross saw Farrell make for the nearest first-class check-in counter he scuttled towards him.

Farrell recoiled as Ross approached. The bomber was always scruffy but now, after almost ten hours solid driving on his round trip to Washington, he had reached an all-time low in appearance. Farrell was shocked and livid. "Beat it, you bum. This is a public place. You're mad."

"It'll take no more than a minute. You've got the time." And then slyly, "Better than making a scene."

Farrell veered away from the queue and retreated towards the sliding glass doors, stopping to one side of the end section. "You raving lunatic. What the hell do you want?"

"Money. Lots of it. I fixed Squire. It was a beaut.; one of my best. A dream of an accident outside Georgetown."

Farrell stared in exasperation and disbelief. None of this would be happening at all if Ross had done his job properly in the first place. Things were getting out of control. "Congratulations. You finally got something right. Now get out of my way."

"I want to be paid. This took some planning and a lot of risk. I fixed his car so that it went straight under a truck. It burned out. Nobody will ever know why."

"That's reassuring. I'll arrange for thirty thousand as soon as I'm back. This could have waited till then."

"No it couldn't. I've done my part. I want it now and the price is fifty."

Farrell was looking anxiously around the departure hall. Nobody seemed to be taking any notice but he couldn't be sure. Ross was impervious to everything except getting his grubby hands on money. "You can't be stupid enough to think that I have that much cash on me."

"I'll take a check. Make it out now."

"A check? Traceable to me? You're crazy. You wait until

52

I'm back. There's a lot going on over there that I need to know about. Wait."

"No. I don't know when you'll be back and nor do you. I should have taken it up front. It was a mistake. I'm not making another one."

"There's no way I'll give you a check." Farrell's fury was increasing. "Had you done the first job properly none of us would have ever needed to meet again." He gazed down at Ross with mounting disgust. Everything had changed so much already. "I'll make an arrangement as soon as I reach Ireland. I'll let you know where to collect in New York. Cash. That's all I'm prepared to do. You try making a scene now and you can kiss the money goodbye. Now get out of my way and for God's sake clean yourself up." His anger barely contained, Farrell strode away to the furthest check-in bay he could find; he would have been even more distressed had he known that Ross had openly phoned him at his office.

Heavy lifting gear had to be called in to remove the partially burned-out truck to the side of the road so that what remained of Sam Squire could be scraped up and the gruesome business of identification could start. With the bottleneck relieved, traffic crawled away with little hope of making up for the huge delay. The two truckers had been taken to hospital to be treated for shock, with a separate ambulance assigned for the journey to the morgue.

The identification proved simple enough. Burned and twisted though it might be, the rear number plate was just legible. From then it took only minutes on the police radio to establish car ownership. So far as the police were concerned it was one more crushed wreck to be lifted out and taken away and one more corpse to add to the growing statistics of fatal street accidents. Until the police discovered Squire's occupation.

This information was unearthed by Police Sergeant Ellman whose unfortunate job it was to call on Mandy Squire. When she came to the door of her Georgetown home he at once noticed her distress and sadly recognised that he was about to add to it. He took his cap off and glanced back awkwardly to the patrol car where his partner still sat. This was not the first time Ellman had

53

imparted bad news to someone's wife, but when he saw Mandy's face he somehow knew that this would be different. He could hear the voices of the children in the background. And that made it even worse.

From the moment he asked her if Squire had been out in the car her face froze and the little colour she'd had left her. Ellman wanted to put his hand out to console her, then he realised that he hadn't even told her of the accident. Instead of leading into it he blurted out, "I'm afraid your husband's dead, ma'am. An automobile accident."

He thought she was going to collapse and this time he did offer a supporting hand; it was like holding frozen meat. She was rigid with shock and yet in spite of this he got the impression that she was not really surprised. There was a feel about this particular tragedy which warned him that it was anything but straightforward.

"You'd better come in." She held the door wider, her voice strangely strong and calm. He glanced back to his colleague and finding no support there followed her into the living room. He could now hear the girls in the kitchen, laughing and bantering innocently. Mandy Squire opened the kitchen door and told the girls to stay there. She closed the door again and folded her arms defensively across her chest. "What happened?" She seemed to have found new strength.

"Won't you sit down, ma'am?" Ellman felt like a rookie on his first bad news call.

"You've already told me he's dead. I want to know how it happened."

Her voice was matter of fact, firm, but Ellman thought she was about to fall apart; she was just hanging on. All he could do was to try to play it down. "Instantaneous. Head on. He didn't feel a thing."

"Head on? On the way to Andrews?"

"He could have been going anywhere. If he'd turned at 23rd Street and then on to the Beltway, he could have gone on to Andrews. There would have been several options open to him beyond the crash point." Her hand went out to the table and Ellman stepped forward. She raised an arm to stop him. "I'm okay." She sank slowly on to the edge of a chair, one elbow on the arm, her head

54

supported on her hand, hair hanging forward. What did it matter if he was going to Andrews or Washington? Yet she felt that it did and formed part of the pattern of his evasiveness as if he had found it necessary to confuse every issue.

Ellman felt desperately sorry for her; something had obviously gone wrong before the tragedy. He hitched the belt on the thick waist of his short stocky frame and the butt of his gun stuck out; it had no part in this scene and Ellman hastily pushed it out of sight.

"Head on! Do you know what training he has had? He was a marvellous driver." Without raising her head Mandy spoke in a monotone. "The car had just been serviced. He never broke the speed limit, not even off duty; his position would not permit it."

Ellman was uncomfortable. He said quite gently, "Eye witnesses testify that as sure as hell, he broke it this time. But maybe he *was* on duty. What was his job, ma'am?"

Mandy lifted her head, her features crumbling. She now knew for certain what had happened but there was no way she would tell Ellman. "He was in the Secret Service. On the White House detail." There was no point in trying to hide it.

Ellman's instincts had been right. "I see. In that case I'd better notify the FBI, ma'am."

"Why?" Her head shot up as she whipped out the demand. Her reddened eyes shone with fear.

"Just routine, ma'am. But under the circumstances they would want to be notified. Now is there anyone you can get to stay with you? Anyone you would like me to contact?" Ellman covered his impatience to get to the car radio. He had side-stepped the problem of asking her to identify her husband's remains; he simply could not see how she could face up to it. Let the FBI decide.

George Farrell boarded the first-class section of the Pan Am 747 bound for London. He placed his bag in the locker, slipped his attaché case under his seat and sat back with eyes closed, barely aware of those boarding around him.

His mind was still reeling from the encounter at the airport. Ross had appeared so competent before the crash, and had certainly come with the highest recommendations. But how little of themselves people revealed until something went wrong. He was even finding things out about himself that he did not much care for. This was quite different from a financial crisis, something he could handle without qualm. The present situation, however, was getting out of control.

The plan could still work, but it was not in Farrell's nature to sit back and hope for the best. It was necessary to cover his own tracks at whatever cost. If he didn't others, so far silent, might become as concerned about his capabilities as he was with Ross's. Even at his own investment bank, Farrell and Hammel, some reactions had been surprising and in some ways useful. He recalled the events earlier that day when shortly after leaving Ross in Central Park, he had gone back to his office to confront the gloom that engulfed everybody. Later, Dave Santos, one of his partners, had walked into his office and they had had coffee together.

The conversation was naturally sombre. Then the silver-haired, usually silken-tongued Santos remarked, "I hope you don't take this the wrong way, but a lot of people are going to be relieved that this happened." Hastily he added, "Not with the *way* it happened, but that this particular President has gone."

At first Farrell was alarmed, his conscience flying to his guilt, but as Santos expanded he began to appreciate his colleague's position.

"The country is rollercoasting to disaster. With a national debt of over two trillion dollars and last year's deficit of almost a hundred and fifty billion, we are heading for broke. And still it didn't get through to him." Santos was gazing out of the wide expanse of the fortieth-floor window, his cup in his hand but the coffee untouched. He looked every inch the banker he was.

Farrell watched him, fascinated now. It was by no means the first time this subject had been raised; they constantly discussed the problems that so easily influenced the markets. But Santos was becoming uncharacteristically blunt. "That ass-hole of a Defence Secretary was smiling his dumb head off when it was announced that, in spite of the nation's plight, his budget was to be increased considerably over the next four years. Our beloved Chief Executive must have worked it out in his goddamned sleep." Santos turned to face Farrell who was seated at his desk. "And not one single tax extra to cover the increased outlay. A paltry cut in public benefits that wouldn't cover the cost of one solid-fuel rocket booster. I tell you, George, it's an ill wind."

Santos drained his coffee in a gulp. Suddenly he looked shamefaced. "I guess I'm out of order to say things like that at a time like this."

Farrell replied carefully, "You're only saying what a lot of people are thinking. But will it help? The next one might be just as bad."

Santos smiled wryly. "Maybe we've had sufficient notice to make sure that he's not. He'll be under a lot of pressure to get on with the real issues instead of pussyfooting around with other nations' problems – the Irish question for one. Let them kill each other. Who the hell cares?"

"You're right, Dave. It's not our problem." The lie had tripped easily off his tongue. Ross, for one, was problem enough.

Now he was airborne. The usual safety announcements over, Farrell could not help wondering just how many passengers were uneasy about flying on that particular day. For a brief spell he considered what it must have been like on Air Force One, the sheer terror of those last seconds. Then he reached for his attaché case and riffled through some papers. After a while he reclined back to sleep, thankful for a few hours when no-one could bother him.

About an hour before Farrell took off the Vice-President addressed the nation on the television network in a speech also carried on the radio stations. Many of his advisors had urged him to go on nationwide television much earlier, given the fact that the initial shock was turning into fear and rumour. People were grief stricken, but now many were becoming paranoid and scared and confused. The country was placed on a medium state of alert having gone to condition Yellow but now it had been dropped to a step below that. Everybody wanted to know what was happening so the Vice-President knew that he was walking on

57

eggs, and to make it worse the President's body had not been recovered.

The news bulletins had been flashing out all day and yet there had been no authoritative political output until now. It was perhaps easy to criticise the Vice-President, who was constantly accused of vacillation, but to be fair, no Vice-President had before been faced with so enormous a national calamity. He had not yet been sworn in; but the President had yet to be declared officially dead.

Everybody knew that he had perished together with his wife and the others, but while the search still went on an unrealistic shred of hope remained. Besides, it would be indecent to be sworn in and thereby endorse what everybody else believed to be true; it must at least appear that he held on to his faith and that a miracle might yet happen. The body had yet to be found. By nightfall, however, he had to do something about it for it could not be left to the following day.

So the Vice-President, in a subdued voice and clearly with genuine emotion, spoke to the nation, his speech translated via satellites around the caring world. Aware of his massive audience he kept it low key and at times appeared to leave the prepared script when his own deep anguish came through. He won many friends that night though ironically it had not been his intention to do so. There were times when he obviously spoke with a considerable depth of feeling and had to pause to collect himself. And he raised an issue that most of the media had so far glossed over. On the plane had been Anatole Bruslov, Soviet Ambassador to the United States of America. It was an important political issue. Bruslov had been on board as a symbol of Soviet American friendship; the dawning of a new age. He too had a wife; she was grief stricken and still in Washington. The nation should also give some thought to her, and above all American hearts should go out to the Soviet people at this time of joint tragedy. It was an issue the press were to return to again and again.

Unknown to Farrell, on the same flight but in the higher density seating of economy class, sat a lightly bearded man in his late forties, with mild eyes and a relaxed expression

58

which gave the impression that largely, the world passed him by. He appeared to take little interest in the movement about him, barely glancing at the stewardess when she brought his meal tray. He wore a dark grey suit of not very good quality and a pale blue striped shirt buttoned at the collar but with no tie. The fingers that unravelled the paper napkin from his utensils were long and sensitive like a musician's. In fact he did play the guitar rather well. His laid-back appearance was a cover; there was little going on around him that he missed.

Don Helary had, for instance, noticed George Farrell at Kennedy airport. And he had also witnessed part of the exchange between Farrell and Ross. As he had not wanted Farrell to see him, although as far as he knew Farrell had no knowledge of him, he had quickly faded from the scene. In any event he could make a fairly accurate guess as to their conversation, if not of detail then of substance. He knew all about Hank Ross.

Beside him, on the window side of the starboard row, sat a mousy-haired woman who had used little make-up and whose dress did nothing for her, the purple material obviously cheap. A closer look revealed that she had good bone structure, clear eyes and a pleasant mouth, features that could be very attractive had they been better presented. Her hands, too, were good and cared for. Her slight figure was lost in the folds of the seat, her head turned towards the black void outside the aircraft. She was Don Helary's wife and like her husband showed no sign of interest in what went on around her. When she turned to speak to him it was almost with a polite indifference. Once she smiled but it was an automatic gesture which displayed little feeling. The woman sitting on the outside seat of the row was barely aware of them and after the first nod and cursory greeting, was encouraged to ignore her companions. Don Helary and his wife, Una, had booked their seats soon after the Air Force One crash had been reported.

Milton Purcell had been even more cautious than the Helarys. He had booked an earlier flight and had done so before Air Force One had crashed. Always perceptive, his sharpness had not let him down this time. There were people he wanted to avoid and the best way of doing that was to leave the country. But it was important to him to go

59

where he might best get help if he needed it. His destination was Eire. He was one hour ahead of the Helarys and Farrell and some two hours away from the crash zone. He thought about that quite a lot. Not the best of air travellers, he nevertheless flew when it was necessary to do so.

An average-sized man, hard, narrow features with an almost aggressive expression, his dark eyes restless like a terrier looking for someone to fight. His black hair was thick like his eye-brows and his short-fingered hands were constantly moving and gripping each other. He was travelling on a false passport.

Laurie Galvin flew back to Dublin a worried man. He could see his cover, carefully nurtured over two and half years, being destroyed. It was not just a matter of taking risks – he was doing that all the time – but of the changed nature of those risks. In order to help the Americans he was being forced to increase the danger to himself in a reckless way: if he was to get results he must step out of character and it could not pass unnoticed. In the fanatical political field in which he moved justice was arbitrary and particularly brutal. He could not help but feel that he was being sacrificed for someone else's cause. He would have been even less happy had he known that he was not the only one to be placed in extra danger. He still found it difficult to believe that the IRA had placed the bomb.

Galvin arrived in Dublin on the late flight and to the news that *HMS Challenger*, using special sonic gear, had picked up the radio transmissions of one of the "black boxes" and could pinpoint its position. It was too dark to operate now but the French, with long experience of aquatic exploration, intended to use their remote-controlled Scarabs in an effort to recover the box at first light the next day. American recovery vessels, with updated Scarabs, were on the way over but it was hoped that the box would be recovered before their arrival.

He had turned on the car radio and normal programmes were intermittently interrupted to give out any further developments on the task of recovery. Sharks were hampering the helicopter rescue crews, something which

60

brought home to him the fact that there were all kinds of dangers apart from his own.

When Riley Brown greeted him as he entered her apartment, he was more than ready for the love and comfort she gave him. But with her too, he would now have to be more than usually cautious. If he could have thought of some way to get her away for a few days he would have been happier but he knew that would raise suspicion; a difficult position had now become impossible for he knew that he would betray her in a way she would never understand. He held her very tightly and mouthed silent apologies she could not see as his hand at the back of her silk-haired head drew her face gently to his.

After he had satisfied her about the condition of his sister and when they finally sat down to a late meal, a news bulletin broke into the last TV show of the day to make the sombre claim that the President's body had been recovered. Delay of announcement had been due to the difficulty of identification but there was now no doubt. The Vice-President would be sworn in early the next day. Somehow, although everybody had known he was dead, the brutal confirmation of it made it worse.

Galvin knew that if the assumption was right about how the President had died, then the wolves would already be gathering. And he had better get among them. When Riley suggested they turned in he followed her into the bedroom with a kind of shame. Whatever his previous commitments, everything had now changed for the worse and would never be the same again. It was almost impossible to hide his feelings from her and his sense of betrayal was already becoming unbearable.

5

The ship hove to, rolling against the increasing swell, lights ablaze to mirror fragmented shafts over the dark restless sea. There were really too many vessels for safety even though some of the smaller ones had left for Cobh harbour. The helicopters had long since returned to Cork airport where tired crews unloaded their gruesome catch, corpses or wreckage, and where they could snatch a few hours' rest before starting again at first light.

This pocket of the Atlantic was festooned with lights but the brightness they cast worked as a warning to other shipping in spite of the almost festive effect. A searchlight suddenly creamed the ocean, bouncing off a rising swell to cast strange reflections into the night as the phosphorus glowed weirdly. A pasty moon face crested the spume to create a chilling spectral view as a body turned slowly as if on a spit. There were only shreds of cloth hanging to it, streaming out like strips of flesh. The beam shadowed the features and exaggerated the water-wrinkled skin.

Someone shouted to alert rescue teams and the body obligingly turned as if it had heard the call. More light was called to bear and a boat was lowered as that particular patch of ocean suddenly became floodlit. And then a second body floated into view like a pummelled doll, dress in shreds, shoes off, arms outstretched as if trying to keep afloat, hair sprayed out like a luminous halo.

"It's her." Someone yelled. "My God, it's her."

But as the boat detached from its davits the figure disappeared in a trough and when the boat rose on another swell the corpse had gone. The man's body was not too far away and was caught unceremoniously with a grappling hook. The long dead Bruslov, stripped of all dignity, was roughly hauled into the boat. Nearby, as if to mark the spot, the bottom section of the tail fin of Air Force One with its famous number 27000 came into view and moved quite gracefully on the unsettled sea.

The boat crew searched on, with loud hailer instructions from observers on the parent ship, but the First Lady had been swallowed up by the waves. She had made a brief appearance as if taking a last curtain call before reluctantly returning to her grave. A buoy was thrown over to mark the last position she was seen. A report was radioed to land and a helicopter would retrieve Bruslov's corpse the next morning; by then it would look the same as the others in its plastic zip-up.

Galvin woke early and turned to gaze at Riley in repose. She had one bare arm outside the sheets and he put a hand out to touch it, stopping just before he did. He quelled the urge and swung his legs out of bed.

"Where are you going?"

He smiled, his back to her. "I thought you were asleep. I'm getting up."

Riley struggled to sit as he turned round; he was always surprised at the way she looked first thing in the morning. She was young, of course, but there was a freshness about her not solely attributable to her youth. Her skin was fair and good and soft and he never tired of touching it. She glanced at the luminous clock. "It's only six o'clock. It's still dark now."

"There's a job I've got to sort out. I might be doing a deal with someone in Cork. It could make some money for us. I'll probably have to go down there."

She became fully awake at that. "Cork? Sure they're heathens down there. What sort of deal could you do with them?"

He laughed as he pulled his socks on. It was an old story; Dubliners believed that the Cork people came up to Dublin to steal their Civil Service jobs. The Cork people's answer to the charge of job stealing was that they were simply brainier than the Dubliners and therefore in greater demand.

"There's a car-hire company down there who want to expand their fleet. They're thinking of branching out up here. If they do they will want maintenance. And they don't want to pay out too much for it. If I can get it I can soak them later."

"It's typical of them. Something for nothing. Anyway, don't forget the meeting this afternoon."

He had forgotten. Damn it. He went to the bathroom annoyed with himself for the lapse. He would have to attend and drive down to Cork afterwards. The meeting was to sort out a more permanent hide-out for two escapees from Belfast who were at the moment hidden near Dublin.

Galvin made no secret of having lived in England and of having useful contacts there. These contacts had sometimes been used by the Provos for all sorts of reasons. Some were genuine hardline Provos and some were MI5 agents. It was all a very delicate operation and at times he felt deeply anxious about placing his safety into the hands of others "across the water", largely unknown to him and mainly unseen. So far it had worked well. No arrests were ever made in England that might be traced back to him.

Riley rarely attended these kinds of meetings, content to leave it to the men. As he shaved he realised that perhaps the meeting might be a useful start in tapping the grapevine of information about the crash, if there was any to tap at all.

They turned on the radio while having breakfast and the news of the recovery of Bruslov came through and the possible sighting of America's First Lady. But most of the bodies were still missing. The back-up to Air Force One was flying to Shannon to collect the President's body which had been examined by Irish and American pathologists. The examination would continue in Washington but it was already recognised that if there had been an explosion it had not taken place forward or amidships, so the President's body would be unlikely to reveal the cause of the crash.

Galvin had no alternative but to postpone the visit to Cork until after the meeting that afternoon, so meanwhile he set out to cover the few miles on the Bray Road. His garage was on the outskirts of a village, not immediately visible from the road but easy to find to those who used it. The repair shop was an old barn, roomy and solid. He unlocked the office door and turned on an electric fire before sitting at the battered desk.

He sat at the desk wondering how to convince Riley that

he would need to go away for a while. This was where the risks began, where people he knew would begin to wonder, where it would be more difficult by the day to justify his movements.

He went through the job orders and decided that he might have to get an extra mechanic in while he was away. He unlocked the door of the workshop and the smell of engine and diesel oil escaped beyond the big double doors. Inside were two old tractors and a near-vintage Austin. Patrick O'Brien, his full-time mechanic, arrived at half past nine; nothing started too early around here but work could sometimes continue late. Galvin told O'Brien the same story he'd used with Riley and gave him the authority to take on new labour if he was away too long. He would make arrangements with Riley to come out to settle the wages should it be necessary. He handed over the keys to the petty cash, fully aware that his cover story was dangerously inadequate.

Galvin was not worried about O'Brien – he trusted him and they got on well – but others would notice his absence and O'Brien had no reason not to tell them where he'd gone. There was no natural way he could confine O'Brien to secrecy; besides, Paddy was too open and could easily be pumped. Just before lunch he left the garage not at all happy about the arrangements. But at least he had kept it fairly simple.

The meeting later that day was held in an old farmhouse ten miles north of Dublin. The isolated venue enabled each man who attended to check out whether the Irish Special Branch were following anyone. But Dublin was not a war zone like Belfast. Action in the Republic was mainly confined to bank raids and kidnapping of wealthy industrialists, whether foreign or Irish, to raise money for the active units in the North. It also provided, as now, boltholes for those on the run, and rest camps for the occasional battle-weary soldiers.

There were seven at the meeting and the business did not take long. When they had finished Galvin was asked how his sister was. This did not surprise him. Riley had probably mentioned it to someone and the bush telegraph was rapid and effective among these men. They had earlier tried to get him to use his sister in England but he had easily skated round it by pronouncing her unreliable; she had no idea he was in Sinn Fein, which happened to be true. Talk drifted to who was doing what and where and someone remarked on the absence of Con Tierney – an active member of the Provos – who was usually at these meetings.

When it was suggested that Tierney had gone down to Cork it produced uneasiness among the seven men. Yet nobody passed any kind of comment until Galvin said, "I've got to go down about a deal. If I see him I'll let you know, if anyone's all that interested."

Nobody said they were but it gave Galvin an opportunity briefly to state why he was going. It was much better than them finding out by gossip. He left for Cork during the early evening after a touching farewell with Riley.

In Washington, Lydia Bruslov was in her private apartment at the Embassy, desolate at the news she had received about her husband. They had been married for thirty years and, on the whole, the marriage had been successful. She had enjoyed being in America and the diplomatic bag had always been a useful way of getting things back to her son and daughter in Moscow.

Now things had changed irreparably. Not only because she had lost her husband – she was strong and resolute and in time would overcome the tragedy – but because the life she had got to know had now come to an end.

The whole embassy staff had paid their respects and the higher ranks had gone out of their way to offer condolences. The atmosphere in the building was subdued and her housekeeper had kept a discreet distance so that her mistress could bear her grief in private. When Mikale Nikov, the Second Secretary, called on her for the second time that day she imagined it would be to ask if she was bearing up under the strain. Instead she received her second shock of that day, which, in its way, was as traumatic.

Nikov entered the large, superbly furnished drawing room and from the way he stood Lydia knew that this was no solicitous visit; his stance had duty etched all over it. "Comrade, I've had word from Moscow. They would like you to return at once."

Lydia was stunned and bemused. She knew that she could not stay indefinitely but she believed she would be given time to collect herself and to have a decent interval to do some final shopping and pack at leisure. A few days at least. The request was indecent. "It is too soon. I don't want to show my grief in public. The airport will be crowded with reporters; I am not ready for that." A plump, but still attractive woman, her dark eyes sparkled with defiance.

"Comrade, it is not a request but an order. There is a plane on its way. You will fly out in four hours' time." Nikov was coldly correct.

Lydia knew, as they all did, that Nikov was the KGB Resident in Washington. She normally had little to do with the man but it would be naive of her to pretend that she did not know his true position. "That gives me no time to pack."

"I will detail help for you." Nikov looked at his watch. "Will you be ready in ninety minutes?" It was not really a question. "There will be no restriction on the amount you take back." He smiled politely. "Provided you don't include the furniture." He offered a short bow. "I must not detain you." For a moment he hesitated uncertainly then added, "I am merely passing on the order, Comrade. I am sorry it is so soon, we shall all miss you." He left the room closing the door very quietly.

Lydia suddenly burst into tears. She sat on the edge of a brocaded Empire chair and sobbed for a few minutes. Why the haste? Why couldn't she stay for a few days longer? What possible harm could it do? There had to be a reason but she could not see one. She rose when there was a tap on the door: her helpers. *There was always a reason.* So what had happened? What had gone wrong?

Sir Gerald Fowler sat back thoughtfully. He reached out to touch a button on the intercom then stopped, hand poised. He remained still for some time. Eventually he rose, left his office and walked down two flights of stairs, along a corridor passing several offices but stopping at a door with a brass number seven on it. He went in without knocking.

Reg Palmer was slouched in his chair, talking on a green

scrambler as his chief walked in. His office fittings were strict government issue but he had somehow scrounged a Victorian seascape from the property office, a gloomy oil painting which adorned the wall opposite his desk. He glanced up and straightened as his exchange became more precise, but he continued talking as Fowler signalled him to carry on.

Fowler wasn't influenced by Palmer's air of near indolence. It was part of an act to cover a very specialised expertise; he was a red-hot operator. He had occupied his present position for over four years and was only in his early forties. Fowler rated him highly but rarely indicated so; he sat down and waited, aware that Palmer was frantically wondering what had brought Mohammed to the mountain.

When Palmer finished he put down the phone, gave an apologetic smile and started to rise until Fowler waved him down and came straight to the point. "How do you rate Laurence Galvin?"

As Palmer was exclusively attached to Irish affairs the question was easily answered. He was responsible, through his link man, Norman Jason, of placing Galvin where he was. He did not need to reach for a file; he carried most of the detail of his specialised agents in his head. "First-class man. Stands up to stress particularly well."

"Is that all?"

"What exactly do you need to know, sir?"

"Tell me all about him. I'm trying to make a decision."

Palmer decided not to trust his memory. He said into the intercom, "File IR38, Mary." When his secretary brought it in she discreetly hid her surprise at seeing Fowler.

Palmer slipped the disc into his desk computer and brought the file up on the screen. Yellow text on a brown background sprang up. "He went in under his own Irish name because his background stood up to examination." He glanced down at the detail. "Father was born in Kilkenny and served a short term with the Irish Army. Came to England with one daughter and two sons aged six, nine and ten. Mother died in nineteen sixty-five and father did not re-marry." Palmer glanced across the desk. "Galvin senior was killed by an IRA pub bomb while visiting friends in Ulster in nineteen seventy-five. He did not die immediately. As far as we can see the old man had no strong political views and was not short of money.

"Galvin was twenty-three when his father was killed. The sight of him dying in hospital remains with him and left a strong desire for revenge. He is the youngest son and was educated here at Repton then Birmingham University. At that time, had he flown a flag outside his home, it would have been St George's. It was as though he wanted to sever all ties with his own country, an understandable reaction just then. Even so he kept in touch with relatives in Ireland, who were then mainly in the Dublin area. He has no problem slipping in and out of the brogue."

"Did we recruit him?"

"Not at first. These kinds of circumstances are always suspicious, and particularly so in his case. But he was so cut up about his father that he wanted to get back at the IRA and approached us in a round-about way. We listened to him but he was too full of hate to be of any use at that time. Subsequently he realised that his bitter attitude to Ireland as a whole was totally unreasonable and he got things into perspective. We'd kept a distant eye on him and when circumstances provided a need, we approached him to sound him out again. By then he had matured and was much more in control of his feelings. He was still an anglophile but he had developed a deep sense of purpose towards his own country. After a great deal of vetting we had him trained with the SAS at Hereford, and eventually set him up in his present business." Palmer smiled. "He actually makes a modest profit."

"You preferred him down south rather than Ulster?"

"He is a natural there. In Ulster he would stand out. Anyway, as you know, a great deal of information finds its way from Belfast to Dublin and he is adept at picking it up." Palmer scanned the screen, scrolling up new data. "In his teens he joined a boxing club and later had a few semi-professional fights. Didn't need the money; simply enjoyed it. Likes animals and can ride a horse rather well. That goes back to his Irish boyhood."

"Any complicated associations in Ireland?"

Palmer grinned openly, aware that Fowler knew more about Galvin that he was indicating. "You mean Riley

Brown? A raver by all accounts. A keen artist. Sells a few paintings but not enough to live on. Galvin lives with her. An excellent cover – *her* background is IRA of the old school. She's really out of context with the present bunch of terrorists. But I doubt that she realises it and Galvin can't risk swaying her. In answer to your unvoiced question, yes, I'm satisfied that he can handle the emotional side of it. He's been through it all before, remember."

"What of his family now?"

"His eldest brother went to Australia, married out there and has two sons. The brothers keep in touch but only around birthday and Christmas time. His sister lives here; also married with children and he sees her from time to time. We use her quite genuine medical history to get him over here quickly if he's needed urgently. Anyone who rings up the Denbridge Nursing Home in Reading will get confirmation if needs be although it would never happen unless someone was suspicious, in which case we'd have to bring him back."

"How have you handled the father's death?"

Palmer wondered why Fowler was so suddenly concerned. Galvin had now been working for them for some five years, more than half of that time in Ireland. His results were good although information gathering was a slow business. "We built a background of the father going to Australia not long after his wife died, which is borne out by the later departure of the eldest son. After all he was killed over eleven years ago, and the IRA have a history of killing innocent people. They're not likely to keep a record of those they shouldn't have killed, even if they knew."

"Is it a weak link, though?"

"No. It would take too much ferreting. Anyway, they wouldn't take the trouble; if there's a hint of guilt, retribution is rapid. They're not the sort to bother with digging up the evidence first. What's the problem, sir?"

"We've made it much more dangerous for him. I wondered if he can cope."

Palmer didn't believe Fowler. Using Galvin in a far more dangerous context had been Fowler's idea in the first place. Why the sudden doubts? "He has instructions to abort if there's any real trouble."

70

"Quite. But have you a replacement in mind should he not have time?"

Palmer did not care for the turn this conversation was taking. There was always a risk to field agents and those risks were accepted and usually put on the line so that the agent knew what he was up against. But this sounded as if Fowler had kept something to himself. With deliberate suspicion he said, "Men with Galvin's background do not come easily. He would be difficult to replace which was why I was not keen on using him the way you suggested in the first place. You don't seem to rate his chances too highly, Sir Gerald."

"My dear Reggie, you know far more about the risks than I. It's just that I feel it might be prudent to groom a replacement. Merely as a precaution."

Palmer said, "If there's something I should know that you're not telling me I think Galvin should be warned."

Fowler shook his head. "I'm not being deliberately obtuse. Really. I don't like risking his cover any more than you do, but there are so many ramifications. I still think we must help our cousins on so important an issue but having given it considerable thought, I'm beginning to believe that Galvin is placing himself in an extremely vulnerable position – like one of the smaller pieces of wreckage being tossed around the ocean out there; he may not get anywhere and if he's the man you seem to think he is, it might be difficult for him to back down. I think he might cope with the 'boyos', given luck, but I'm not at all sure that the answer lies with them. I can't add more; I don't have the answers."

"Then let's take him out."

"We can't." Fowler rose and wandered over to the painting. After a while he turned to face the desk. "I'll go this far. It's not Ireland I'm particularly worried about just now. We might be looking the wrong way." He eyed Palmer quizzically. "There have been one or two interesting arrivals at Heathrow today. I'll gamble that they're in transit. All we can do is hope for the best, give whatever support we can, and keep our eyes wide open."

George Farrell checked in at the Grosvenor Hotel; his secretary had booked him a room from New York. The temptation to continue on to Cork was almost irresistible but he had to be circumspect. The British media had more than adequate coverage of the day-to-day progress of the action off the Cork coast, although there was still no indication of the cause of the crash. The newspapers were full of speculation and had interviewed so-called experts not directly involved in the operation; those on site were saying nothing, mainly at the request of the increasing band of American officials. The actual clearing-up job of recovery and identification went steadily on.

The day after Farrell arrived in London he went to the City and called on friends in British merchant banks to do business that could have been done from the end of a telephone in New York. Meanwhile he booked a flight to Dublin through the hotel. He did not want to make too obvious an entry into Cork City.

In Cork, Galvin too, was arranging his cover. He had arrived very late on the day he left Dun Laoghaire and could not find a room. Apart from stepping too far out of character he did not have the funds to stay at the better hotels, which in any case were fully booked, so he had to go out on the Bandon Road, well clear of the City on the west side, and find a farmhouse with a "rooms-to-let" sign hanging lopsidedly from a tree. It was further from Cork City than he wanted to be but the place was comfortable and he had a large double bed to himself. He left at nine the next morning and arrived in Cork about half an hour later.

Cork City, Corcaig in Irish, meaning a marshy place. Settled at the head of the tidal waters of the River Lee it possesses great charm, different somehow from the other Irish cities. There is a soft, friendly gentleness about it and it is often called the Queen of Cities. To show that there are two sides to its character, it is also known as the "Rebel City", to reflect the unbreakable spirit of independence which has followed it down the centuries during national uprisings. There are good wide streets and bridges and quays of great character. The river is split, forcing Lapp's and Penrose Quays to opposite banks and joining into a main flow beyond them on the way to the sea.

Galvin came in on the Bandon Road from just south of

Ballinhassig and passed the airport far out of sight to his right. He came through Bishopstown and into the city proper south of the river. As he drove he was rapidly recalling the layout of the old city; it was some time since he had been in Cork. He drove up the wide avenue of South Mall noticing that the on-street parking slots were already over-spilling, and he looped round, left and left again into Merchant's Quay, and finally turned into the wide banana curve of St Patrick's Street, where the big stores were. He did a quick turn into the approach to Roche's car park and joined the end of the long queue. It was another fifteen minutes before he passed the barrier and searched for a space in the warren of parking lots belonging to the store.

As he locked his car he sensed the atmosphere of palpable shock all around him. Down here they were much nearer the tragedy, and it showed. He turned into St Patrick's Street and cut through to the much narrower, squashed but delightful characteristics of Oliver Plunket Street to search for O'Malley's Car Hire. He had no appointment but obtained an interview with the Manager to discuss the matter of maintenance representation to cover the Dun Laoghaire area. He did not expect to achieve anything nor did he want to. He left a tattered card and received one from the man who reluctantly interviewed him. In business terms the call was abortive but he picked up a rumour that a body and some wreckage pointed to bomb damage. It was rumour, of course, but it was also an indication of the way people's minds were working. Down here in Cork they knew; they didn't need experts. And as Galvin left O'Malley's offices he reflected that they were probably right.

Having established a checkable alibi it was time to get down to the real work. He collected his old Mercedes and cut through to Evergreen Road and turned off at Turner's Cross on to the airport road. It was almost midday by the time he arrived and he had to park some distance from the airport and walk back, such was the congestion on a normally open road. The onlookers were fewer than the previous day but the press and television coverage had increased and cameramen from all over the world were

73

clustered with reporters, quite often grouped and chatting until the next rumour broke.

The news was, in fact, becoming more sparse as security tightened. But the rumour he had picked up in Cork of bomb evidence was much stronger here. If it was real evidence then this was where the real problems began; and the real dangers. He had to know more. Galvin jostled his way through the press and television crews looking for someone he could isolate and talk to. He stopped suddenly. Just ahead of him was Con Tierney with another taller and darker man. Galvin started to ease back not wanting to be seen by either man but Tierney turned too soon. Galvin and Tierney stared at each other in cold, controlled silence. Beyond them, well on the fringe of the media groups, another man who had already located Tierney, watched them both.

6

Tierney, in his usual torn faded jeans and windcheater, detached himself from his colleague without a word and a slow grin spread across his face as he jostled his way towards Galvin. "Laurie! What brings you to the Rebel City?"

Galvin smiled back. "I came down to see O'Malley's about a maintenance franchise. What's your excuse?"

"Is that why you're dolled up, now?"

Galvin was wearing the neat grey suit he had worn to call on O'Malley's. It was out of character but helped strengthen his story. "That's right. Take a good look; it's likely to be the last time you'll see me like this. So what are you doing down here?" he pressed again.

Tierney's sunken blue eyes gave nothing away; they were chill as they carefully watched Galvin. He was still grinning slightly. "This is where it's all happening, for God's sake. I was kicking my heels in Dublin, for sure. Terrible business."

Nobody quite knew exactly what Tierney did for a living. He was known to do odd deals with tinkers, or "the travelling people", involving second-hand furniture and junk, but whether or not it was enough to sustain a living was questionable. Among the "fraternity" he was linked to two Bank of Ireland raids: in spite of his way of dressing he never seemed to be short of money and always had time on his hands. Behind the smile his pinched face was hard and uncompromising, his stocky frame restless as he barely kept still. Only his eyes remained steady and they were without any trace of feeling.

"Yes, it's a terrible business," Galvin replied, taking his time. "There's a strong rumour that they've found evidence of a bomb."

"Where did you hear that for Christ's sake?"

"At O'Malley's first. But I've heard it since I arrived here as well."

"That's more than I have. Jesus, who'd want to blow up the President of the United States? Except, maybe the communists."

Typically, Tierney did not see the irony of what he had said; his own politics were extreme left. He was a destroyer but never a builder.

"Ask anyone here. With your sharp ears I'm surprised it hasn't reached you."

Tierney waved his arm. "Ah, sure this bunch of pirates would say anything. They're looking for a story, the grimmer, the better. When you going back?"

"I'm not sure. O'Malley's are thinking it over. I'll stay on until I've heard one way or the other."

"You won't get anything from them from where you operate. You're too small, for sure."

"That is a problem," Galvin agreed. "But I'm good and I'm cheaper than anyone else."

"Ah, you're good all right. I'll say that for you."

"You want a lift when I go?"

"I've got my own wheels. When I get bored here I'll go back."

"What about your friend?"

"My friend? The feller I was talking to? He's no friend, just one more bum hanging around waiting for something to happen."

That was not the impression Galvin had gained when he had first seen them together. "Any news from the hospital? How many have they found?"

"The last I heard was twenty-three. They won't find many more. Had a talk to the helicopter boys, not the British, sure it's an insult that they are on Republican soil; the Americans told me. It's rough out there. Sharks and all. They can't keep it up much longer."

As they were talking both men were keeping an eye on media movement. A buzz was going round and two men were running from the direction of the airport building, parts of which were still being used for transit of bodies and sections of the plane. When they reached their colleagues it was as if they had generated an electric shock. A huge wave of excitement swept the crowd. And the word went round. The French had recovered one of the

76

"black boxes". The mystery of the crash might be on the verge of being unravelled.

Galvin kept his eyes on Tierney as the news spread. The normally agitated frame of the stocky Irishman went rigid, the only movement was the slow balling of his hands into fists. The pinched features went completely blank. His stance stood out more because the reaction of all the others was animated; general excitement at what might come out of it.

Galvin chose the moment to slip away. He tapped Tierney on the arm and said, "I'm off. See you." Tierney barely nodded, his tight features grim. As Galvin moved away he noticed the taller man Tierney had been speaking to quickly shift his gaze from them.

Mandy Squire felt that her head was bursting. Her two daughters were with a neighbour and she now had two men in the house asking her questions she did not understand. They had somehow taken over her house and had even made coffee for her. They were from the FBI, polite but insistent to a point where she thought she would go mad, listening to the same questions over and over, sometimes differently phrased but always meaning the same. In some ways they were like her Sam; the way they moved and acted constantly reminded her of him. She had never felt so bad.

After trying to explain to her two children what had happened to their father, she had gone to bed the previous evening after finding some old sleeping pills; she hadn't felt up to seeing her own doctor. Even the girls crying in the night had failed to rouse her. But they had given her some strength and a little purpose. They had brought her a late breakfast and by the time she was dressed friends who had heard the news of the accident were already dropping by or telephoning. In the end she had taken the phone off the hook. The girls had refused to go to school recognising the poor state their mother was in.

In the afternoon, wondering what she should do next, the two smart-looking men had arrived and introduced themselves as Bob Rook and Peter Carraz. They had expressed their deepest sympathies and had almost

77

immediately suggested that her young daughters might be better with a friend or neighbour while they interviewed her.

"We are sorry about this, Mandy. I hope you don't mind us calling you that." Carraz looked apologetic as he now pulled up a chair to sit opposite her. "Sam was in the same professional family as us, so to speak. It's the nature of his job that has brought us here." Carraz glanced up at Rook who had brought in the coffee. "You absolutely sure that it was Sam, your husband, who was driving the car?"

Were they mad? Why didn't they know? "Of course it was Sam. How many more times?" Then a thought struck her. "Shouldn't I be identifying him? Isn't that the routine? Then you could stop asking these dumb questions."

Rook pushed the coffee across the table. "We think we can spare you that indignity."

"Indignity? To identify my own husband?" Her hands started to shake. She glanced at each man in turn, lips trembling. "Was he so badly cut up that you don't want me to see him? Is that it? My God."

Rook, who was standing to one side of her laid a hand on her shoulder but she shook him off. "Answer me, damn you!"

"It's pretty bad," Carraz admitted. "We just think you're going through enough without having to do that." He didn't add that identification was impossible: medical and dentistry records would have to be used.

"If you think I'm suffering too much, why don't you both butt out?" Mandy sat, glaring from one to the other.

"Do you imagine we don't want to? Come on, you know the rules. Sam was one of the President's bodyguards. Now they're both dead, killed on the same day. We find that a little curious."

Mandy flared, sitting bolt upright. She looked from one to the other in total dismay. Her heart was pounding and she felt faint; perhaps she had avoided thinking about it. "No. *NO.*" She tried to struggle from her chair. "*Just what the hell are you saying?*"

Carraz backed off, realising that he had almost pushed her over the edge. "It's okay. We're not suggesting a connection but merely pointing out the tragic coincidence.

Drink your coffee, or have you anything stronger around?" He gave Rook a signal to find some liquor.

Her heart muscles were being squeezed with panic, making her breathing difficult. She gazed at Carraz, red eyed. "What has coincidence to do with anything? Sam wasn't on the plane. He was off duty." She dreaded voicing the next question, feeling as though she already knew the answer. "How did the plane crash?"

Carraz shrugged. "Nobody knows. Was Sam out sick?"

Mandy felt the lifeline of anger. Their questions weren't even subtle. "Didn't you trouble to check before you called? No, he wasn't out sick but if he was what the hell has it got to do with you? Go on, say it, you bastard."

Rook appeared with a bottle of bourbon and some glasses. He placed them on the table and helped Carraz off the hook. "We're only trying to establish his state of mind; whether he was fit to drive or not, that sort of thing."

"Like hell you are. Put that bottle down. I don't want a drink, and I'm damned if I'll offer you one." Mandy rose shakily but both men had the sense not to try to help her. She pointed to the bottle and glasses. "Take those back where you found them."

After Rook had left the room Carraz said, "We have to ask these questions, as objectionable as they seem. If we don't someone else will. Had he been sick at all? Had he been acting normally?"

Mandy was now dreading every question. The danger she felt stimulated her mind. She had to be so careful. He'd been up to something, she was sure of that. And friends might have noticed a recent change in him. "Look, he'd just gotten off a long spell of travel with the President; a swing through the western states where he had a lot of advance arrangements and crowd-control problems. He'd gotten very little sleep and was exhausted, that's all."

"Had he been to the doctor?"

"There was nothing to see the doctor about. He had regular check-ups."

Carraz fiddled with his tie. "Have *you* seen the doctor?"

Mandy was suspicious. "Why should I?"

Carraz spread his hands. "Well, you've had one hell of a shock. I would have thought it a sensible thing to do."

"I'll get by."

"I can arrange for a doctor to see you. No expense. It's the least we can do for a colleague's wife." Carraz looked round for the phone.

Her heart was being squeezed again. She knew why they wanted her to see a doctor, particularly one working for them. They'd detected that she'd been under stress for some time. The right doctor searching for those symptoms would quickly diagnose a long-term deep-rooted depression, and would then try to find its cause. "No thanks. If I can't sleep at night I have some pills." She realised her mistake at once.

"You obviously found the need for them before Sam died."

"A lot of women do use them, you know."

"Sure. Did he have any money problems at all?"

"What's that got to do with it?"

Carraz shrugged. "State of mind again. That's what we're after; was there anything that made him lose concentration while driving, anything that worried him? It's pretty routine stuff."

"There were no money worries so far as I'm concerned but you'll be able to find out from our bank so I've no doubt you'll check for yourselves."

"Right." Carraz stood up and tapped on the table. "That just leaves searching the place. We'll be as neat as we can."

Mandy flared. "Search? What the hell for?"

"Anything that might throw some light on why a perfectly healthy man, regularly checked and a highly trained driver as you pointed out, should suddenly slip up and crash. Anything that will give us some small clue."

"I won't allow it. You have no right." Mandy was deathly white.

"We have, I'm afraid." Rook, who had returned, produced a warrant. "But don't take it the wrong way, Mandy. We're also having the car checked out for defects. We won't take long."

Mandy sank into a chair, dreading what they might find.

Dave Santos rang the apartment bell and waited, aware that he would be viewed through the spy hole set in the polished, solid oak door. He smiled as he heard the chain and the security locks being undone and he brushed back his thick silver hair. He was a tall, imposing figure, with soft speculative brown eyes, a relaxed yet upright stance. His creased features were lightly tanned. The door opened and Judy Farrell smiled brightly as she stood aside for him to enter.

Once in the spacious hall he brought his hands from behind his back and held out a single orchid cased in Cellophane. "Easier to dispose of should the need arise."

Judy took it from him. "It's beautiful, Dave." She closed the door and locked it then gazed again at the bloom. "There was never anything wrong with your taste." She smiled impishly. "I'll keep it as long as I dare." She reached up and pecked his cheek then led the way into the huge living room.

Following, he watched her slim legs and the figure that always roused him. He checked a strong urge to embrace her. This time he was not absolutely sure how she would react.

Different suites of settees and easy chairs stood at each end of the huge living room; soft, dove grey leather one end and pastel rose velvet the other. An electrically operated folding partition could separate the two halves. The drapes were rarely drawn because the fairyland of lights beyond the sealed unit double glazing was among the best views in Manhattan with the East River a fragmented and partially shadowed glittering stream far below.

"I've always envied you this apartment," Santos said as he moved towards the windows while Judy branched off to a curved corner bar.

"I know. Scotch on the rocks? I think it's malt."

He took the glass from her. "Cheers, Judy. It's so good to see you." Then after sipping and with a twinkle in his eye, he added, "And to have you alone for a spell."

She raised her dry Martini, long red nails delicately hiding the stem of the glass. "Cheers, Dave. I don't know which way to take that but I guess I'll find out."

They took their drinks to the settee facing the middle window and sat at opposite ends, Judy appearing faintly amused. "Things still the same between you and Mollie?"

Santos winced. "We're like strangers."

Judy was turning the stem of the glass slowly between her fingers and he watched, aware how so small a movement from her could hold his interest. She crossed her legs slowly and put her glass down on a side table. There was a strange intensity in the way she looked at him. "Did George *have* to go to London?"

He was surprised by the bitterness behind the question. "I guess not. We do things differently. I use the phone when I can; George has to have personal contact. Are you upset that he didn't take you?"

Judy leaned back and placed an arm along the settee. "He rarely takes me. We've been married for eleven years and I still don't know him. Lately he's walled himself in even more. He's involved in something that's eating him, and he's made sure that I don't know what it is. At first I thought it was another woman but I gave up that idea. Whatever it is it's not sexual. I'm surprised you haven't noticed the change in him."

Santos wasn't sure what to say. He had not heard Judy talk like this before. "I guess we're all so busy at the office that I haven't had the chance. What do you think it is?"

"I've really no idea. There was a spell recently when he waxed on about Ireland as if he'd suddenly found some long-lost passion about the country and its politics." Judy waved a hand dismissively. "He didn't convince me, though. It was all too sudden. In spite of his Irish background I've never heard him speak about the place before. It was all stage-managed, as if he was trying to distract me. As if I cared after years of virtually being ignored."

Santos drained his Scotch, holding on to the empty glass. "Why are you telling me this?"

"I hoped you'd have some answers. I thought it might be connected with the business, although financial problems don't seem to trouble him; he's quite cold blooded about them. This is something different; something's preying on his mind. I'm surprised you haven't noticed."

"Maybe he took pains to hide it. And you invited me here this evening to find out what I knew? I'm sorry to be so disappointing."

Judy put out a hand. "Don't be silly, Dave. That was only part of it. But there's something going on and I intend to

82

find out. While he's away I'm going to go through his things and see if I can discover anything illuminating. If I do I'll let you know."

Santos was shocked, not so much about the ethics but the depth of feeling. It seemed that the pent-up emotions of years had reached a culminating point, that Judy Farrell had suddenly had enough.

She turned to face him fully. "Your glass is empty. You want a refill?"

"I'll do it." He crossed to the bar feeling her gaze on his back. He turned. "I'll help you as much as I can. In view of what you say I'd like to find out, too." Then he returned to sit beside her, their eyes met and they both knew that he would not be leaving the apartment that night.

By the time George Farrell reached Dublin speculation in the media was rife. As he climbed from his taxi outside the Gresham Hotel in O'Connell Street, headlines proclaiming the bomb theory glared at him from news-stands. He refrained from buying the newspapers. Once in his room he could follow the more reliable television news in safe anonymity. His mind was so fully occupied with events that at no time did he notice his tail; he had been followed from London by Don Helary and his wife Una, seated separately on the plane. Even if he had seen them he would not have known them.

Helary wore a more expensive suit than the one he'd chosen for the Atlantic flight and a dark green tie against the pale green of his silk shirt. His wispy beard was somehow tidier and he seemed to be taking more interest in everything around him. But the biggest change was in his mousy-haired wife who now wore a brunette wig. The make-up she had applied transformed her to a strikingly attractive woman and she had changed the scuffed patent pumps for elegant high heels.

Husband and wife had separated in London and their reservations to Dublin had been made by a London source who had exerted some influence to obtain them; seats were still solidly booked and extra flights had been put on to cope. Rooms in Dublin had been somewhat easier to obtain as the exodus continued towards Cork City. Don

Helary and Una checked in separately, twenty minutes apart.

It was Don who kept reasonably close to Farrell and hung back in the foyer until the banker had signed the register and was taken up to his room. When Helary took the lift to his room his wife arrived at the hotel shortly after. She sat in the foyer, on the off-chance that Farrell might reappear. Sometime later when her husband stepped from the lift she checked in.

Helary went to the nearest booth and called a number. When he was connected he spoke with deep mid-western accent. "I'll need help. I guess he'll be heading for Cork but he's almost certain to make some sort of contact here. I think it's important to let him do that. I'm calling from the Gresham." He hung up and sat close to where Una had been sitting. Neither had given any indication that they knew each other and they had their own rooms. Helary picked up a copy of the *Independent* and began to read the copy beneath the headlines. It was waiting time; a meal could come later.

Laurie Galvin checked at the Cork Regional Hospital. The staff were working under considerable pressure but matters were slightly less chaotic than when the world had first awakened to the news of the crash. He managed to talk to a couple of nurses going off duty and offered to take them for a meal. They immediately took him for a newspaper man and refused to comment; they had all been warned against talking and official news bulletins were being issued at intervals by the hospital's chief administrator. It was clear that the pathologists were keeping matters very low key and Galvin learned very little.

It was an open secret, however, that the recovered wreckage had now been taken to a warehouse in McMahon's Boatyard on the outskirts of Carrigaline by the Owenboy River. South-west of Cork Harbour, Carrigaline lies about three miles from the bridge at Ringaskiddy which links the Irish Naval Base at Haulbowline Island with the mainland. It was about four miles from the southern edge of Cork City.

Galvin drove out there and it was soon evident that others had preceded him. The traffic was quite heavy and he passed one truck, tarpaulined at the rear, with police outriders and soldiers on the back. More wreckage. It was impossible to keep the fact from public view. When he reached the gates of the boatyard he was stopped. No-one who did not have official business there was being allowed within three hundred yards of the building housing the wreckage, and even they had to prove identity. He identified the actual warehouse by parking awkwardly and waiting for the truck he had passed to arrive. He watched it being cleared at the gates and visually followed its path. The building was more modern than the others, and set slightly apart. It was ringed by police but the outer perimeter of the yard itself was guarded by both naval personnel and infantry men.

Galvin wondered what to do. Real news was short. He was not alone by the gates, but the press coverage was less here than at the airport, dead bodies being more news-worthy. And then he saw Tierney for the second time that day. The short figure was walking away from him along the edge of the yard as if viewing its defences. To a man like Tierney, gaining entry would be no problem, but Galvin decided it was too soon for another encounter and went back to his car. It was already obvious, though, that while he was investigating down here, he would have to watch out for Tierney. He would also have to discover his interest. Galvin drove off.

Tierney turned as if by a signal. He saw Galvin leave and then continued with his inspection. Later, he picked up his own car and drove into Cork from where he rang a Dublin number from one of the saffron call boxes. "How're you doing? Good. I don't know whether the rumour is true or not. We've got to find out. If it is true we'll have to do something, okay? I'll need some of the boys down here fast. They can stay at the farm. Tell 'em to bring bed rolls and some grub. Another thing. Laurie Galvin is poking around down here as much as I am. Now as he's one of us and I haven't been told about it I find that strange. I don't trust him. Have a word with Riley Brown and find out why he's here. Bring the information with you, so move fast.

85

You'd better bring some extra shooters. I'm not sure what we've got at the farm but I reckon we're going to need all we can get. There'll be trouble ahead for sure. And we'd better be ready for it."

7

Glenn Rees, United States Air Attaché to the Republic of Ireland, had ceaselessly sought information. Nothing was yet positive but there were many pointers. And the issue was being made more difficult by the fact that the experts were beginning to disagree over their conclusions. Rees had his own opinion of experts, but he held his counsel on what they were.

He met Paul Sutter in the lounge of Jury's Hotel on Lancaster Quay off the Western Road. The two men shook hands, Rees noting Sutter's fatigue. The heavily built shoulders were slightly stooped as if the weight they carried was becoming too much. Sutter still wore his topcoat and he spoke slowly, his voice echoing his physical exhaustion. "We'd better go up to my room; we're surrounded by the press in here."

The taller Rees followed his chief to the elevator. Rees was a few years younger than Sutter, and leaner; not so ostensibly relaxed. Rees worried about everything except that which really mattered.

Once in the room Sutter took his coat off and produced a bottle of Irish and two glasses. "When in Rome," he said, "although they might frown on this down here. Bushmills Black Label. Made north of the border. And don't ask for it on the rocks. Drink it straight."

Rees didn't argue as he took the glass and followed suit while Sutter sat in one of the easy chairs. Sutter said, "I'm spending most of my life in the air which many think isn't the safest place to be right now. When I've finished with you I'm off to the Hill again. So fill me in."

"There's not much you don't already know. It's a slow game. The First Lady made a brief appearance and then went for ever. Women carry more body fat so are more liable to float. Some victims were drowned which means that they were alive on impact. Whether they were conscious at the time is debatable. All have severe impact injuries: multiple fractures, soft-tissue injuries, haemor-rhages and so on. Nobody would have lived for long after the plane dived and broke up. Seconds, if that: most deaths would have been instantaneous."

Rees glanced across at Sutter before continuing. "The experts are beginning to disagree on the way some of them died. Most had their clothes torn off but there is evidence that many were bombarded by small fragments of the plane and some argue that this could be caused by a bomb explosion. Others say that with any decompression as a plane plunges from over thirty thousand feet there are chunks that explode outwards like rockets."

Sutter opened his eyes. "So nobody knows for sure?"

"That's about it. There's no firm evidence, just arguable pointers. The wreckage looks like a lot down there at the boatyard but in fact it represents less than two per cent of the bodyweight of the plane. One positive development is that the French have now recovered the voice and flight recorders. Quite a feat at that depth. They got them up while our recovery ship was still at sea. This effort is international if nothing else." Rees was aware that he was telling his chief the technical detail, and that was not what was wanted. But there was as yet nothing else. He added pointedly, "You want this explosion rumour battened down? We can kill it with an announcement."

Sutter came to life. "No I don't. It was a bomb. I know you don't agree. I know there's a lack of evidence. But that's what it was. If anything I want that rumour strengthened. I want to bring the perpetrators out of the woodwork. MI5 are helping us here. And the Irish are unofficially helping them – though they'd never publicly admit it; that would be an admission that they're tolerating British agents on their soil."

"I still don't buy it."

"That's because you won't face up to it. My guess is that the idea was spawned here or in Belfast. The FBI are sharing what they've got. Reluctantly. But the issue is far too big to complicate with departmental rivalry, although I sometimes wonder." Sutter was breathing heavily, his eyes hard as he looked at Rees. "I think the IRA are up to their necks in it and I'm sure that events will prove me right." He suddenly realised that he hadn't touched his drink and he stared at the deep amber spirit, giving it a little nod of respect before he drank. "What was the passenger load?"

"Fifty. Maximum. Plus eighteen crew including cabin staff, chef and so on. Sixty-eight dead, twenty-six so far recovered."

Suddenly Sutter said, "What's bugging you, Glenn?"

Rees smiled at being caught out. "Our NTSB boys want to take some of the wreckage back to the States. The Irish and the British crash experts aren't too eager. It would leave them with an incomplete junkyard. Anyway it would mean that once it's back home we lose sight of it. The FBI would muscle us aside."

"Does it need to go back?"

"No. The Farnborough boys easily match ours and they have our full respect. The Irish are willing to give us all we need. I think the real problem is security. McMahon's Yard is fine – and again they're leaning over backwards to help – but the press are a nuisance and if you're right then we need stronger safety measures than we've got."

"Isn't there any place else the bits can be taken? Somewhere out of the way?"

"You want me to raise it with the National Transport Safety Board? I'm sure the Irish will agree."

"They won't take notice of you or me. They're specialists, they'll tell us to butt out. They might listen to our Ambassador. Have a word with Michael Dwyer. Tell him it's my idea. He's a good guy and I know him slightly."

"Okay. That it?" Rees rose after finishing his drink.

Sutter nodded. "I'll keep in touch and you can contact me in the usual way. Just one thing. The goddamned stuff had better be moved at night; loaded trucks won't go unnoticed."

After Galvin left McMahon's Yard he was driving back to Cork on the link road with his mind on Con Tierney, when he decided to branch off on to a rough intersection that looked like a farm road. He tight-turned and faced the main road he'd just left. Traffic was not dense on the link road and he had a clear view. He sank down in the car and waited, his gaze just above the dashboard.

Galvin did not have too long a wait. Just twenty minutes later Tierney, driving his battered Morris 1000 and keeping within the speed limits, went past and was easily identifiable. Galvin took his time in pulling out and waited for another car to separate him from Tierney. They were on the Cork road, so little was likely to happen until they reached the city. Galvin did not get too close; a man like Tierney would instinctively watch his rear.

Tierney found parking space in Grand Parade but Galvin found it difficult to do the same. He had no alternative but to continue and turn into South Mall, left from there into St Patrick's Street, then left again into the Grand Parade. Knowing where Tierney was parked he pulled in and double-parked hoping that he would not be moved on.

Through a line of cars Galvin saw Tierney hasten along from the direction of St Patrick's Street and climb into his car. The Morris moved off and Galvin eased into the traffic stream behind it. The rush-hour traffic was heavy and progress slow. At times he had difficulty in seeing the Morris and almost missed it when Tierney turned on to the Douglas Road. Puzzled, he hung on knowing that he was safe in the congestion but wondering where they were heading.

On the southern outskirts of Cork, as they drew further from the City, the density thinned noticeably and later as Tierney headed towards Donneybrook on the L66 Galvin decided to drop back. He caught sight of Tierney's right indicator and anticipated that he was going back to the airport. With this in mind he hung back still further. Once off the link road the traffic was thinned to a trickle and the danger of Tierney spotting him became real; it was second nature to any Provo to look out for a tail. He allowed Tierney to get out of sight, just accelerating on odd occasions to get a glimpse of the Morris.

A few minutes later Tierney turned right again, his route still consistent with going to the airport. Galvin took a calculated risk and hung back still further. When later he decided to accelerate there was no sign of the Morris. Galvin put his foot down. There were good long stretches along this minor road and little to stop him building up speed. He went on until he was nearing the L42, the airport road and decided to turn back.

He pulled in, wondering just where Tierney had turned

90

off. He guessed that it was some way back on the more open stretch but there was little in the way of reasonable roads before the T-junction about two miles back. In fact, there were two minor roads, one to the right and one to the left, and three tracks which were obviously farm roads. Turning round, Galvin stopped at each of the farm tracks. Two were well worn, giving an impression of regular use. The other, leading off to the right, had long rough grass growing quite high between the barely discernible tracks. He crouched down and found what appeared to be fresh oil drips where a vehicle had slowed down. They were still wet.

It was too risky to approach openly up the tracks. Anyway, Tierney might have turned off on any of them. It was a hunch, no more, but the back of his neck was prickling. He decided to return in darkness. He checked his trip meter from the track to the T-junction and then turned once more to head for the airport from where he could pick up the Bandon Road leading to the farmhouse where he was staying. He had to hope that he hadn't been seen.

Riley Brown stood away from her easel and swept back her hair with a paint-stained hand. It was not a good day. In the absence of real flowers she was using very good artificial ones for a still-life commission but they were not the same; too perfect for one thing. But she had applied her imagination and taken a liberal amount of artist's licence. The water colour was not going well and, unlike an oil, there was not a lot she could do about it.

When the door bell rang she was in a grouchy mood and decided to ignore it, knowing that Laurie Galvin had his own key. She was determined not to show how much she had missed him.

The bell rang again and she swore loudly but still ignored it. She viewed the painting in disgust and almost threw her paints at it. The bell rang again, this time continuously. "Who the hell can that be?" She banged down her palette on the nearby bench and went angrily to the front door, a brush still in her hand.

She opened the door ready to close it immediately. "Oh, it's you."

Gerrard Connolly smiled. He was a tall, rangy man, wearing the usual jeans and jacket. Once-white sneakers covered large feet. His mass of dark hair looked as if it had been permed but the tight curls were quite natural. There was a cockiness about him which Riley had never liked, and his smile was somehow always suggestive, even when Laurie Galvin was there, as if he wanted to see just how far he could go. "Well, my lovely, aren't you going to ask me in?" He was leaning easily against the door jamb.

"I'm busy, can't you see? The last thing I want right now is interruption." She could smell liquor on his breath.

He studied her, smile broadening to a point just short of lechery. "Isn't Laurie interrupting then? It's him I really came to see."

"He's away. Goodbye."

As Riley made to close the door Connolly put his foot in the gap and his weight against the door. Riley pushed it harder but Connolly thrust it right back almost sending her flying. "You thick pig, you nearly had me over. Get out," Riley flared.

Connolly entered the tiny hall, now smiling lasciviously. "Where can I find him?" He went past her into the living room, looking around with a touch of envy.

She followed him in, eyes blazing. "I'll tell him about this, my God I will."

Connolly burst out laughing. "You have me quivering in me shoes so you do. Just tell me where he is, Riley, and be done with it. Or is it that you want me to stay? Are you playing hard to get, now? I'll go along with that."

Riley knew Connolly to be a friend of Con Tierney, and in spite of her background some of the Provos disconcerted her, this one included. She would not admit to being afraid but there were times when she came close to it. She could handle it with Laurie present, or in groups, but this was an open challenge and Connolly was enjoying himself. "He's in Cork. Now get out." It was no secret but she hated herself for telling this man.

"Now what would he be doing there?" Hands in pockets Connolly wandered over to the windows to look down at the harbour.

"Why don't you go down and ask him? Look, push off, I've got work to do. You've already ruined my concentration."

92

Connolly turned. His smile had gone but the arrogance remained on his brutal features. His eyes were suddenly opaque, the killer in him on open view. "What's he doing down there?" He moved towards her.

Riley stood her ground but now acknowledged her fear. "If I knew I wouldn't tell you. Go and ask Paddy O'Brien at the garage. He might know."

"It's business then?"

"No. He's got some floozy down there." She quickly realised that her temper had masked her fear but had created another problem. With dismay she saw Connolly's expression change.

"So you're free now. That's cosy."

As he advanced she reversed the paint brush in her hand so that the shaft was forward; it appeared so puny in her hand. "You touch me and you'll get this in your eye."

Connolly grinned. With a fast movement he tore the brush from her fingers then quite deliberately broke it, holding it up for her to see.

"That's a double 0 pure sable, you pig." Riley went for him but he grabbed her wrists tightly, laughing while she struggled. He gradually pulled her towards him and she caught his breath again. "God, you've been drinking. You disgust me. *Let me go or I'll scream my head off.*"

The threat only stimulated him and he managed to get his arms round her while pinioning her own. His grin changed to a grimace of agony when she kneed him in the groin. As he fell back and doubled up she realised that she had to get out quick. She sped to the door but he managed to grab one of her arms. He pulled her back and whipped her round the face with his free hand. As she fell he doubled to his knees through the sheer agony of movement.

He could hear his own rasping, but when he managed to gaze across the room there was no sound from Riley at all. She had crashed into a chair as she'd fallen and she lay arched back over its legs, skirt ruckled, arms hanging loose. Gradually she slipped down until she slowly fell forward on her face. And then she was quite still.

Connolly began to panic; Tierney wouldn't be too pleased with him for this. A messy assault and no hard news to show for it. He left the room, not happy with the way Riley was lying. "The bloody bitch," he muttered as he walked away.

In Washington, Bob Rook and Peter Carraz had begun to sense the strange atmosphere in the Squire household. *Something* was wrong there — both men felt it — though there was no clear reason to connect two tragic incidents. But the gap was so immense that both men at times felt they had gone overboard. Mandy Squire was holding something back but whatever it might be could be a million miles from their tenuous suspicions. Yet they could not dismiss them.

Carraz went down the corridor and returned with two coffees. The two men sat on opposite corners of the well-worn desk. "Where's the motive?" Carraz probed once more. "We've been through his banking. No problems beyond the usual mortgage. No accounts in any other bank in his name. He doesn't seem to have needed extra money. His colleagues thought he was maybe a little off recently, but nothing serious, and anyway, not all of them agreed. Those who might have are seven thousand feet down in the Atlantic."

"This coffee's lousy." Rook screwed up the paper cup and tossed it in the trash can.

Carraz swivelled to gaze at his partner at the other end of the desk. "What we need to know won't be in any computer. Mandy Squire's state of mind is not in a computer. And anything that was bugging Sam Squire before he took on the front end of a truck won't be there either."

Rook nodded in agreement. "We've got to get to Mandy Squire. She's definitely holding back. Maybe we should speak to her kids. They might have noticed something about their father which didn't seem right."

Carraz gave a low warning whistle. "Thin ice. Bob. And we'd be the ones to fall through it."

Carraz sighed unhappily. "Okay. But think about this. If Squire was involved then there had to be someone behind *him*: unless he'd gone bananas he wouldn't have done it alone. We *must* tackle those kids. We'll be in the shit if we succeed and in the shit if we don't."

*　　*　　*

94

Mandy Squire continued in a state of increasing depression. She tried to cope with her children as she had always done but her own dark mood had an effect on them, too. She realised this but more than anything she knew that she must struggle through for the sake of Sam. She was not going to allow his name to be besmirched in any way if she could prevent it. And the first priority had to be putting a brave front on things: give no-one a reason to force a visit from the doctor on to her.

It had started a few weeks before Sam's death. He'd used to go out in the evenings with scanty excuse, sometimes offering none at all. She also had the impression that he went out to make telephone calls. Sometimes the calls were made to the house, obvious instructions for him to meet someone. And he was so tied up in whatever was bugging him that he probably hadn't noticed the effect on her. At least, not at first. He had become secretive and obsessed.

Mandy knew that what she was holding back could be crucial to the FBI. She had closed her mind to what he might have done. She was hanging on for her own sanity and for love of the kids. Yet she knew that she could not keep quiet for ever. Sooner or later she would have to tell someone about his strange behaviour, and the part of a telephone conversation she had overheard. If she cracked up they would get it out of her anyway. It had made little sense then, but one name had been mentioned and she struggled to remember it. When she couldn't recall it she thought about the blue van that Sam had climbed into one night: anything might help to put the pieces into place. She had even felt guilty about switching the hall light off and opening the door ajar to see what he was doing across the street.

She needed someone to confide in; someone she could trust. There was no way she would tell the FBI about these incidents until she knew more about what they could mean. Yet she couldn't keep it to herself much longer. She suddenly stiffened; she was on the point of recalling the name she had heard but then when she thought she had it, it eluded her. The truth was that she had barely overheard it, Sam had been speaking so softly, and it had left more of a phonetic impression than anything. At the time she had made no effort to remember, being too concerned about not letting him know that she was there. It was lucky that he had gone out afterwards. She believed the elusive name had now become important. But it would come to her, she was sure of it, when she least expected it to. And then she would have to decide what to do.

George Farrell rang a Dublin number from his hotel room. "Teller," he announced once he was through.

There was a silence the other end then a deep Dublin voice answered in some surprise, "Punt." The answering code was simply the Irish name for a pound note. "Where are you calling from?"

"Here, in Dublin. The Gresham."

"Say no more. Be outside the hotel in half an hour's time. If I'm late go back into the foyer and check outside every five minutes. Look casual. And keep an eye out for a white Ford Granada with a black strip along the body. When I see you I'll pull in and cruise just past the hotel. Climb into the back seat." The phone went dead but the tone of disapproval still rang in Farrell's ear.

Farrell checked the time, then went down to the bar for a drink. He did not mix and sat in a lone corner, conscious that he was checking his watch too often. What he found disturbing was the fact that in spite of his background he did not feel Irish here. He felt what he was, a stranger in a strange land, and he was puzzled by his reactions. He should feel at home here of all places. His own parents had been pro-IRA but as he'd made his money his own opinions had changed and he'd taken on a mild contempt for feckless religious lunatics. The Irish connection, however, had proved useful over the last months, and particularly so now.

With five minutes to go Farrell went up to his room to collect his coat and then went outside the hotel, declining the porter's offer to call a cab. There was a drizzle now, what the Irish call a soft day, and he hung back by the entrance watching the hotel lights creep across the wet sheen of the street. The noise of passing cars subtly changed as moisture clung to the tyres. Dimmed headlights approached like low flying owls. O'Connell Street was subdued. Taxis came and went and Farrell was about to go inside again when a white Granada cruised in, slowing down as it passed him.

Seeing the black strip, Farrell hurried after the car, forgetting the instructions to be casual, and finally broke into a jog as it pulled in further along. The windows were tinted and in this light effectively opaque. As the car finally stopped he opened the door and climbed into the back. It pulled away almost before he was seated.

The big dark head of Sean Hogan arched above the driver's seat but the Irishman did not turn or utter a word. He drove towards the back of town, through the darker, murkier areas where the Dublin charm disappeared and the streets looked the same as any other city backstreets. Farrell, finding the need to speak, was aware of the same resentment he had felt over the phone. He did not know how far Hogan wanted to go out of town but it was obvious that he needed to get well away from the city centre. Then, judging by a sudden series of erratic and sharp turns, Farrell wondered if they were being followed.

It was a long time before Hogan was satisfied enough to pull up. When he did Farrell had the greatest difficulty in seeing where they were. The tinted windows were streaming from a now heavy rain. After the engine was turned off the only sound was the swish of the screen wipers and when they stopped he could hear only his own breathing: the small prison was complete.

"Where are we?" asked Farrell at last.

"It doesn't matter. Out of town for sure. I have to make sure Special Branch aren't tailing me. Now, what brings you to Dublin, Mr Farrell?" Hogan turned round in his seat, a thick arm along the back, and a full beard projecting in silhouette. What little light there was reflected in the eyes like pinheads.

"I should have thought that was obvious. You don't seem all that pleased to see me."

"I'm not. Questions might be asked about you. Anyway, there's no need. You've panicked for sure."

Farrell bridled. Had he panicked? He thought of Hank Ross and Sam Squire. "There has been a certain amount of tidying up to do our end. But the main mess is here. I wanted to see what is going on for myself."

"There's no mess. There was bound to be worldwide

reaction to the crash but it's all under control. Go back home to your wife before someone wonders what you're doing here."

Farrell wasn't used to being talked to like this. "I don't like your attitude. You people have had a lot of money out of me and I've collected huge sums for you. It's you who's showing panic. I want to know where I stand and to cover my tracks if needs be. That's why I'm here and this is where it's happening."

Hogan gestured impatiently, with his big, clumsy hands. "Sure, I'm sorry. We've appreciated what you've done. The Belfast lads couldn't have managed without you and that's a fact. But that's your speciality. Money. Apart from knocking off the odd bank and doing the odd kidnap and a bit of industrial extortion, we're no good at it. It's not big league stuff. But what's happening now *is* our speciality. Trouble is like food to us; we have it daily. Leave these things to us. If anything goes sour we'll deal with it. Don't worry. Were you going down to Cork?"

"Yes. If anything goes wrong I must know as soon as possible."

"We'll let you know if there's any need to duck. I'll personally phone you in New York. Anyway, you won't find accommodation in Cork. It's booked solid and if you take the kind of doss house that might have vacancies you'll stick out. Leave everything to us. I'm sorry if I was short but it was a shock to know you're here. I've sent men down there to look after things. And I'm in daily touch."

Farrell, slightly mollified, thought about it. It wasn't easy for a man like Hogan to apologise for anything and he accepted the peace offering. "I'll continue to stay in Dublin," he said at last. "I can justify that."

Hogan sighed. "It would help us not to have to worry about you. And that's best done if you're safely across the pond."

"I won't contact you unless it's absolutely imperative. I must give it a few days to see which way the wind is blowing." And then as a sop, "Anyway, if the clamp comes down on your US funds I'll have time and opportunity to think of some way around it while I'm here."

But Hogan was still unhappy. Farrell was a damned nuisance. His usefulness was not here in Ireland. "If that's the way you want it. Okay. I'll take you back." And then with more interest, "Did your tidying up over there work?"

"Sure. I moved fast."

"Good. That's the way we work, too."

Don Helary was already in the bar when Farrell had entered to wait for the car. He noticed the agitation of the man and ordered another Guinness. The bar was not yet crowded and he was careful in his observation. When Farrell glanced at his watch once again and then left for the elevator it was not difficult for Helary to anticipate what would happen next. When Farrell reappeared in his top coat Helary waited a few seconds before going to the front doors to peer out. Giving the impression that he was weighing up the weather from the safety of the foyer, he saw the Granada slip by and Farrell hasten after it.

Helary left the hotel, walked along after Farrell and did not change pace when the car stopped. He continued on as the car pulled away and memorised the registration number. As soon as the car was out of sight he made a note of the number, sheltering against the wall to keep the paper dry. It had almost been too easy.

8

Galvin cursed the rain. The rubbers on the wipers needed changing, the windscreen was covered in smears, but at least there was no other traffic on the road at this time of night – one advantage of the Irish country roads. It was only about eight in the evening.

Measuring the mileage, he drove past the track he had earlier located and continued on for another half mile. He turned on to one of the farm roads on the opposite side and managed to swing round in an awkward sequence of short movements. Pulling over as far as he could, Galvin switched off the engine and pocketed the keys after locking the car doors. He started the walk back with the soft rain driving into his face.

There was not a headlight in sight but to his left he saw the glow of Cork City rising on an ethereal blanket to hang below the low cloud. The road itself was completely dark and he had difficulty in detecting the edges. Loath to use a flashlight he finally had no choice in order to find the barely discernible turn-off. The small oil patches were no longer visible but he found a sodden, screwed-up piece of paper which he unravelled. There was just enough print left to identify it as a receipt from a Dublin store. About to discard it he suddenly pocketed the paper; someone might be trying to be helpful rather than careless. He started off slowly up the track, increasingly aware of how exposed he was.

Galvin moved carefully. On farms there was always a danger of dogs and he was alert to the first suspicion of a growl. As he continued, finding it increasingly difficult to keep to tracks which were virtually invisible, he was conscious of his vulnerability. Men like Con Tierney reacted murderously to intrusion. He reached a point where he believed that he had completely lost the tracks, no longer able to feel the shallow wheel ruts beneath his feet. In the end he reluctantly dropped to his knees, shielded his flashlight and kept as low as he could. The little pool of light scurried around until he found he had strayed some few feet. He adjusted his bearings and went on.

The ground became rougher and began to rise. Galvin reckoned that he'd covered about half a mile. In spite of its lightness the rain was penetrating and his clothes were now sodden. He trudged on, occasionally stopping to listen and to check on the track which was now dangerously rutted.

He saw lights. Very faint and as far as he could judge, through one window only. He continued more cautiously but still there was no sound of dogs. When the grass and the track petered out he could just discern the rough, undefined shape of buildings. He guessed that the deep clear patch leading up to the farmhouse was partly rough earth and beyond that, where he could see a reflection, cobbles. From behind the building came the "put-put" of a generator.

Galvin lay flat, feeling the rain trickling down his neck. In the gloom the building appeared run down but he kept his gaze on the one lighted room. There was no farm smell to the place and he guessed that it hadn't been used as a farm for a very long time.

It was a long stretch across the open ground to the building and as if to confirm the dangers a door opened at the side of the house and out of Galvin's sight. Light flooded at an angle past the far corner of the house and someone moved over the cobbles. A voice called out but Galvin could not distinguish the words. A faint sound of coarse laughter came from within the house. The light disappeared as the door was slammed. Galvin lay prone.

He wiped the rain from his face and shivered as it streamed inside his collar. He got up slowly and veered well away to his right. He pushed through the rough growth as quietly as he could, flanking the farmhouse with the intention of checking the rear. It was easier to get nearer at the side where the grass grew close to the walls. There was only one small window at the side and the glass was opaque, suggesting a toilet or bathroom. He crept round the back and found another lighted window. Running water gurgled in a nearby drain and he guessed that he was near the kitchen. The sound of the generator was much louder.

Galvin crouched low and gazed around, picking out the ill-defined shapes of out-houses, some big enough to be old barns. The rain pattered on corrugated roofs and cascaded noisily where the gutters were broken. There was a smell of decay about the place and when he came close to the wall he rested behind a rain barrel which carried a strong stagnant odour and probably hadn't been used in years.

He crept round the barrel and below the sill of the lighted window. He rose very slowly and peered through the lower corner. An unlighted pressure lamp hung from an onion hook screwed into a ceiling beam and another was on top of a rough wooden counter. The light was good but he guessed that the power came from the nearby generator and the presence of the gas lamps suggested that it was apt to break down. A huge kitchen table dominated the centre of the room with six battered but sturdy chairs round it. There were gaps round the walls where units had been torn out and the plaster had been chipped off.

Ducking, Galvin scuttled to the other side of the window and repeated his act. He was satisfied that the kitchen was empty. He decided that it was time to survey the front and to risk the more open ground. He had to find out if Tierney was here – and why. The kitchen door was a few feet behind him, an old dustbin beyond that.

Galvin had just started to move when there was an almighty crash from one of the barns. It sounded as if someone had knocked over a pile of empty drums. There were shouts from inside the house and as Galvin dived across under the window he knew his only chance was the water barrel. He swung behind it as the door crashed open and two men stood in a patch of light. Both were armed with shotguns. Flashlights beamed out towards the barn. There was a continuing sound as if a metal drum of some kind was rocking to and fro. "Stay there."

Galvin recognised the voice. Tierney. His cover was too flimsy for him to risk peering round the barrel. He sensed that the other man was standing close by and he could hear Tierney running across towards the out-houses. The

102

other man, barely three feet away, was shining his flashlight and now Galvin could actually see Tierney, gun waist high, reaching the biggest of the barns. He disappeared inside.

Nothing happened for a while and then came a hollow, clanging sound as if Tierney was kicking at an empty container. Repeated swearing followed and Tierney reappeared, his gun now pointing down. "One of the bloody rabbits has gone." He came back slowly still bawling out, "I'd strung them up from the rafter. I don't know how he did it but the bastard got it down."

"Who?" The voice was too near and from the one word Galvin recognised the Belfast accent.

"A bloody fox, for Chrissake. He got on top of the drums and must have dislodged them as he leapt down. Crafty bastard." Tierney raised his gun, and dangling from it Galvin saw a rabbit. "I'm bringing this one in to hang." His flashlight was ranging from side to side in the vain hope of picking up the fox. "I'll blast his bloody head off." But it was an empty boast.

Tierney flashed his beam at the rain barrel and Galvin pressed himself against the wall behind it. As Tierney came closer the other man began to laugh. "I thought the bloody Garda had heard the generator and thought we had a still going or something."

Tierney laughed back. "Well, I hope the boys bring some grub with them; one rabbit won't go far. And with that accent of yours, Eugie, you can't help them with the shopping."

Eugie? Eugene. As the door closed Galvin wondered if he was right in thinking the man with Tierney might be Eugene Hayes, a top Provo in Belfast. He hadn't had sight of him. But at least he'd found out where Tierney was; there was now little he could do without special equipment and he would have to go back to Dublin for that.

Galvin was as careful heading away from the farm as he had been on the approach but once out of sight of the farmhouse he started to hurry. Then, half way to the main road, headlamps came beaming towards him and he threw himself flat, cursing silently because he'd broken cover too soon.

*   *   *

103

James Powell, the Attorney General, walked unhurriedly through the Rose Garden, heading for the East Wing of the White House. He had no idea why the newly sworn-in President wanted to see him in the family quarters rather than the President's office. A big, upright man in his late fifties, with a full head of iron grey hair, he exuded power in a quiet, unobtrusive way that seemed somehow incongruous with the high status of his office.

Powell had known the new President for a very long time. In many ways they were opposites but there had always been mutual respect and even though Powell was such an assertive man he appreciated the more subtle and sometimes seemingly weak character of his friend. Powell saw the President's caring attitude as a refinement he himself did not perhaps possess, and in his own quiet, self-effacing way the President bore his critics more adroitly than most of them realised.

As he neared the East Wing Powell reflected on the tragedy that had engulfed Capitol Hill over the last three days. He couldn't get his mind off the matters and he'd had little sleep. His main concern was whether the new President could get it together fast. The Government had almost ground to a halt. Meanwhile the rest of the world watched and waited. Taking the elevator to the Presidential quarters he went straight to the Lincoln Sitting Room.

The tall, somewhat boyish figure of the President came towards Powell with hand outstretched as if they hadn't seen each other for some time. "Glad you could come so soon, Jimmy. These are sad, sad days."

Powell stopped and said, "Mr President, I came as soon as I received the message." The two men shook hands but Powell had adjusted more quickly to the formalities involved in addressing the nation's new Chief Executive, who still seemed ill-at-ease.

The President waved Powell to a chair. "I suppose you're wondering why I wanted to see you here and not at the office. It's difficult to explain. I see that place as a venue for the affairs of state. What I feel in this suite is personal, the memory of a friendship I don't ever want to forget. These were his rooms, his possessions are still here, his aura is still here. It'll take some getting used to when we move in."

Powell eyed his new President and old friend without expression; he always dressed well but today he looked ten years older. Powell waited to be guided into the right dialogue but it was not difficult to guess what would come next.

"I want these sons-of-bitches, Jimmy. I want every goddamn one of them, and alive if possible. But I'm not willing to split hairs over it if it means . . . Well, I'm sure you get the drift. Just make sure you're right. Now, what's the position?"

Powell was surprised. "You're assuming the worst? I mean, there's been no sort of information on how the plane crashed."

The President looked pained. "Don't play around. It's not like you. We all know the plane was safe. Now, what's happening?"

Powell was suddenly suspicious. "Has Paul Sutter been talking to you?"

"Sure he has. He has no doubts."

"That's more than he told me. If he knows anything he should come across. We've been in touch."

The President brushed the criticism away. "He doesn't know anything. It's a gut feeling a lot of people share. Are you saying the FBI has doubts?"

"No." Powell shook his head. He was quietly seething over Sutter. "But where does this gut feeling of his point to?"

The President hesitated, unsure of Powell's attitude. "I believe he thinks the IRA are in there somewhere."

"How does he arrive at that conclusion? We're not yet absolutely certain that it was a bomb."

"He's on the spot. He'll have his reasons. What's the news your end?"

Powell controlled his exasperation. "We have every possible man on the job. Every informer we've got. We've placed first-class undercover men in the extremist groups. There has to be big cash involved in it somewhere. Ostensibly we're laying back a little. I don't want any impression of panic around the place. And it would be better if we played it cool on the bomb scare. Sutter and his globe trotters don't have to worry about the internal image. They can play away and lose a few times without the home crowd knowing. If we do the same we're in trouble."

"What's your guess?"

Powell shrugged. "We have no pet theories like Sutter's. We're looking into every possibility. What's happening in Ireland? Can't we get the stuff back here?"

The President wearily rubbed reddened eyes. "Our best men are already over there and they have the backing of some of the finest experts around. Sure it's far from base but in many ways that's better. It's isolated over there."

"Too isolated for us. I'd like to get over there myself but I guess that Sutter and his bunch are crawling all over the place." Powell made no attempt to hide his frustration.

"As much as the Irish allow; they know their own back yard best. I've instructed Sutter to keep you informed and I'm telling you to do the same for him. Full liaison. So you have nothing to tell me?"

"One strange coincidence on our own doorstep." Powell related the circumstances of the death of Secret Service agent Sam Squire. "It looks like too thin a connection, but you never know. We're still working on it."

The President slowly rose and Powell stood up at once. "Whatever it takes, Jimmy, bust your ass for if we fall down on this we'll become target practice." He mused for a while before adding, "It was as well they went together; neither would have survived for long without the other." Then suddenly, as if to relieve the nightmare he'd been living, he said, "I shall miss my offices in the Executive Office Building, but one of the first things I intend to do is get rid of that gold-striped chair by the President's desk. Keep me in touch, Jimmy. Daily. Let's see how good you are."

The lights swept up towards him. There was no cover of any kind, just rough pasture land. Galvin rolled from the track, rose and ran as fast as he could before he was caught on the fringe of the beams. As the turn of the track brought the lights his way he dived again and hoped for the best. He flattened on his stomach to face

106

the track and watched the approaching beams bounce as the car covered the uneven surface. It creaked past him about fifty feet away and as there was no braking he assumed that he hadn't been seen.

The crazy thought to go back to find out who was arriving at the farm was discarded almost as soon as it arrived. He rose and jogged towards the main road veering to his right in the hope of finding the track again and direction from there. He was wet, muddy, but reasonably satisfied. He wanted to get back to Dun Laoghaire as soon as possible but it would mean arriving very late and he needed to clean up and dry out first. When he reached his car he drove back to the Bandon Road hoping he could slip into his room without being seen.

Galvin left early next morning and arrived at Riley's apartment by ten thirty. He let himself in and called out but there was no response. The living room was untypically untidy and, still calling he went into the studio. There was a painting on the easel and a palette on the cheap table with the rest of Riley's paints and brushes. The painting was a still life of some artificial flowers still in a pot; not one of her best. Without knowing why he began to feel uneasy. He went into the bedroom and Riley was still in bed with the sheets pulled up over her head.

This was so unlike her that Galvin hesitated at the door. Riley was active; she hated staying in bed. So she must be ill. Galvin approached quietly. "Riley! You all right?"

The hump moved slightly and there was a muffled response. "I'm trying to sleep. Leave me alone."

Her tone wasn't right. He came forward and gently pulled at the sheets but she was holding them tightly. He reached into the bed and prised loose her fingers, slowly pulling back the sheets. "What's the matter, love? What's happened?"

She was curled up on one side in a pair of his old pyjamas as if she needed the extra warmth of them. When he tried gently to turn her over she held tight keeping her face to the pillows. He went round the other side of the bed but she now covered her face with her hands.

"Riley. For God's sake. What's happened?" He sat on the edge of the bed and grasped her wrists, trying not to hurt her. She fought to keep her hands where they were but inevitably he pulled them away and in so doing rolled her slowly on her back. She tried to keep her face in the pillows but once he had her wrists secure he gradually pulled her to a sitting position. "Don't fight it any more," he said softly, "I can see it." He had difficulty in keeping his voice steady. He cradled her against his chest and she clung to him fiercely and began to sob quietly. He just held her and let her cry it out of her system.

When she was steadier he said, "Okay, let me see."

"No." She kept her head against him.

"Come on, love. I just want to see the damage." He eased her back and she tried to avert her head but he held her chin, fighting back his anger at what he saw. The right side of her face was swollen, bruised and torn, and the eye itself was virtually closed, the lid horribly discoloured. Beneath the eye, as if caught by a ring, a deep gash formed a long, jagged, half moon. "Who did it?" he asked quietly.

Riley shook her head. "It doesn't matter. It's done. It will heal. I just didn't want you to see me like this."

It was no time to press her but he had to know. "Come on." He kissed her gently on the forehead. "Who did it?"

"Leave it alone, Laurie. Just let it be."

"You know I won't do that. So make it easier on yourself and tell me now."

"Will you promise to do nothing about it if I do?"

"No. But you're still going to tell me because you know damn fine I won't give up. Whoever it was should be put down."

Riley turned her head away and he did not try to stop her. "I don't want the police here. Nobody."

"All right. When and why was it done?"

"Yesterday. To find out where you were and what you were doing."

That narrowed it right down. "Come on, love. A name to go with it. If you don't you could be leaving us both

108

wide open. Who would want to know something like that? It was no secret. Don't worry, I won't do anything stupid."

He let her think it out. She still wouldn't look him in the eye, as if she was shamed by her wounds and the fault was hers. Her body was gradually relaxing under his hands but it was still some time before she said, "Gerrard Connolly."

Galvin didn't move; his actions were already having a disastrous effect. He held her and murmured words of comfort but his mind was racing and he could barely contain his fury. Connolly had served effectively on both sides of the border and was known to have killed an Ulster policeman, although the constabulary had attached the blame elsewhere. He had been tried and convicted in the Republic as a member of the outlawed IRA and had served his time but had always managed to avoid conviction for the major crimes he had committed. He was a cold-blooded executioner. Connolly. "Why didn't you tell him where I was?"

"I did. He didn't believe me." She dare not tell him that Connolly had set out to rape her. "Have you finished in Cork now?"

If ever there was a time for truth it was now. "No," he replied. "I've got to go back today. I've returned for some more figures. I'll be as quick as I can down there. Connolly won't try it again."

She stiffened and for the first time looked him fully in the eye. "You'll not be seeing him?"

He smiled. "Now, would I do a daft thing like that?"

Riley wasn't convinced. "He'd had a few jars. He didn't know what he was doing."

"Get yourself dressed while I phone the doc." Galvin made her a cup of tea, knowing he had to get back to Cork, yet unhappy to leave her like this.

"Why would they want to know what you were doing down there?" Riley was beginning to suspect.

"I haven't a clue. I ran into Con Tierney in Cork and he knew why I was there. As he's close to Connolly it's all a mystery."

When the doctor came Galvin let him in and left the apartment telling Riley he would return later. Whatever the urgency to get back to Cork there was one job he must do first. He drove into Dublin and parked a little way from Connolly's favourite pub. Nestling unobtrusively in the back streets it was used a lot by the various IRA sections.

The long bar was quite crowded when Galvin walked in. He received nods and greetings from a good many of those drinking inside but he did not stop to speak to anyone. This was not strictly his pub but Pat the barman had worked elsewhere and Galvin had got to know him quite well. Pat started to draw a pint of Guinness as Galvin approached; he pushed the glass aside to let the drink settle before filling it. "Long time no see."

"I've been down in Cork. Trying to do a deal." The more who knew the better. "Have you seen Gerrard Connolly around?"

"Sure. I saw him yesterday."

"Not been in today then?"

"He's pushed off for a few days." It was a man close to Galvin who answered.

Galvin turned as he recognised the soft voice. He had not seen Sean Hogan for some time and could not understand why he had missed his distinctive beard on the way in. There was something about Hogan which separated him from the rest. An intelligent man, he always gave the impression that he was operating well within himself. Galvin had a high respect for him without trusting him at any level. Tierney and Connolly were always men to watch and when the chips were down, totally cold blooded, but Hogan controlled both men and others like them. Yet he had charm and usually a very quiet manner.

"Pity. I wanted a quick word with him." Galvin quelled his disappointment. It would be a mistake to ask where Connolly had gone; this was not the right pub for that sort of question. He reached for the now completely drawn stout and drank deeply. He would have to wait but he could not help reflect on the possibility of Connolly being one of the passengers in the car heading for Tierney's farm only last night.

"What do you want him for?"

110

Galvin smiled. "You know better than that, Sean. It's personal."

Hogan was amused. "Just thought I might pass a message on if I run into him. I always got the impression that you didn't like him."

"I don't. He'll land you in trouble one of these days. Cheers." Galvin raised his glass. He stayed long enough to have the odd word here and there and then motored to the other side of Dublin to search for a phone booth.

When he was through he gave the code and said, "I need some equipment fast. A galium arsenide laser with opto-electrical linkage." He used the full name to make sure there were no mistakes. "And I want as light a battery as you can get. None of the old-fashioned stuff. Miniaturised earphones. Night glasses. Properly packed. I'll be parked on the wide stretch as you enter Bandon, just before it narrows to the Clonakilty – Bantry T-junction. Left-hand side, Bantry direction, and I'll have the bonnet up. Nine p.m. latest."

Galvin listened for a while then spoke tersely. "Then get some from up north. There's time if someone pulls their finger out. And don't raise the problem of customs at the border, there are plenty of unmanned roads. If you can't make that deadline then forget about the whole thing."

Satisfied that his instructions would be obeyed, Galvin drove to his garage about five miles from Dun Laoghaire. Paddy O'Brien had his head inside a tractor hood as Galvin climbed out.

"Ah, you're back. How'd it go?"

"Not bad. They need some more figures so I've got to get back there. Can you cope? I might be a few days. Depends on how long they take to make up their bloody minds."

"It's okay, sure." Paddy wiped his hands on a heavily oiled rag. "Young Niall is helping me. He's a good lad. I let him leave early."

"Fine, Paddy. I'll sort out the arithmetic." Galvin hurried into his makeshift office, made sure that Paddy was still occupied then dropped to his knees to grope under his desk. He produced the Browning automatic and the spare magazine. He stayed a short while in the

111

office for the sake of appearances, grabbed some old papers and went back to O'Brien. "Has Noreen still got that puppy she wanted to get rid of? The Norfolk terrier?"

Paddy pulled his head clear again. "So far as I know. She wants fifty quid for it."

"She's a crafty devil. It'll be the litter runt if I know her. I'll call in on the way back to Riley's. See you, now."

Paddy waved without turning.

When Galvin arrived back at Riley's place he had a squirming bundle of floppy-eared Norfolk terrier puppy in his hands.

In New York Hank Ross checked on the banker's draft that had been arranged by George Farrell in payment for the presumed execution of Sam Squire. As usual, Farrell had been ultra careful. Ross wasn't sure how it had been done but the fact remained that the money paid in to Ross's account was from an unknown source.

Ross returned to his Lower East Side apartment a contented man. He let himself in and entered rooms as unkempt as himself. He would not employ anyone to tidy up for him.

He went into the sitting room and opened a small, second-hand bureau, then unlocked one of its drawers with a key he kept strung round his neck. He went through some statements from various banks, the credits telling him that he was a millionaire. The state of his apartment made this difficult to believe. Yet the fact remained that the competence of Ross in using explosive had earned him a fortune.

He quietly gloated over his success, and was still in a happy frame of mind when the door bell rang. He had few callers and survived with even fewer friends. He did not need people. The ring of the bell surprised him. He squinted through the spy hole and a tall, sallow man the other side of the door held up a police ID as if he knew that Ross was watching.

Police! Ross was startled. He called through the door, "What do you want?"

The sallow face through the fish eye grinned to show large teeth. "I want to talk to you, Mr Ross. You prefer I call up reinforcements? Or will you settle for a cosy chat with me?"

"Have you a warrant?"

"What kind of a warrant? I only want to talk to you."

Ross thought quickly. He was always careful and never kept the tools of his trade in his rooms. He turned the two security locks and pulled the door open a few inches. The cop made no attempt to push his way in. He stood there with an amused grin on his face and spoke easily. "You look guilty enough to have knocked off the President. May I come in?"

Ross withered. He opened the door and as the stranger went past him he said, "What made you say that?" Then he cursed himself for saying it.

The tall man turned to gaze round the room in disbelief. "I was kidding. What are you so uptight about?"

As Ross reluctantly closed the door and then stood with his back to it, he forced himself to appear cool. "I'm not used to having cops knock on my door."

"I'm not a cop," said the tall stranger. He took out his ID and threw it to Ross who caught it awkwardly. "Look at the mug shot. Do I look like that?"

Ross stared at the ID. There was no resemblance. He edged away from the door. His gun was in the bureau but that now seemed a long way away and the stranger was in his path, standing roughly in the centre of the room. "Then why did you say you were?"

"To get in. Call me John Smith. I mean you no harm." Smith removed his hat but held on to it. "I didn't have the time to go through all the usual mallarky of making contact. I understand you know your job pretty well."

Ross had never felt at such a disadvantage. Something was not quite right. Business meetings were always arranged on his terms, safeguards thought out by himself. Now suddenly he was snared in his own apartment with someone he knew nothing about. He tossed the ID back. "You'd better get out."

"I've only just arrived. And if I went wouldn't it worry you that I know where you are? And what you do?"

"You don't know what I do. I don't know what you're playing at, Mr Smith and I don't want to know."

113

"You were recommended. A long time ago. They tell me you do the job well."

"What sort of job are you talking about, and who are 'they'?"

Smith was almost openly laughing at Ross's acute discomfort. "Why, blowing people up. Killing people. And one of those who recommended you is George Farrell."

Ross went white. Farrell wouldn't talk to this man, he was convinced of it. Farrell wouldn't say a word to anyone because he would only incriminate himself.

"You don't believe me? Well, you don't know how well George and I know each other."

"Just what is it you want?" Ross was in a trap and as yet could see no way out.

"I want you to do what you're best at. I want you to kill someone for me."

9

In response to pressure from the US Air Attaché, a suitable site had been found to investigate those parts of the plane that were believed to offer some positive idea of how the crash had occurred. It meant moving equipment from McMahon's Shipyard at Carrigaline to some thirty-five miles away on the Bantry Road. But there would be many advantages. Press harassment could be avoided, and the experts could escape the fishbowl pressure they were at present enduring, and which too often impeded their work.

It was left until the Boatyard had officially closed for the night before the transhipment began. Several sections of Air Force One were loaded on to a truck together with the cockpit voice and flight recorders. Equipment necessary for the painstaking work of investigation was also loaded on to the closed-back truck which was then bolted and padlocked at the rear. Top experts from the investigating team drove off as they would normally do but instead of returning to their hotels they followed carefully mapped-out instructions which took them north for a short distance on the L67 and then west on the L68 to Ballinhassig and then on to Inishannon and the Bandon – Bantry Road. The truck did not leave until eleven o'clock.

Half an hour later, Con Tierney received a telephone call at the farm. "A truck's left with some of the gear," said the caller.

"Where's it gone?"

"Sure, I don't know that. It headed towards Cork."

"Can you find out for sure?"

"How much is your paper willing to pay?"

"Another fifty. It's not worth more."

"When will I get it?"

Tierney checked his temper. "Tomorrow. Outside the yard like before. Half twelve. Now, where's it gone?"

"It's only a whisper, now. They're keeping it dark at the

Yard. I hear it's taking the Bantry Road. Beyond Bandon anyway but I don't know where it will finally pitch up."

"How long ago?"

"About thirty minutes."

Tierney glanced at his watch and swore. Whether he could catch up would depend on how far and how fast the truck was going. He asked for a quick description of the truck and was mollified when he was given its registration number. He hung up and bawled to the other five men in the house, "I'll be back. No time to explain." He raced to his Morris 1000, for once wishing he had something like a Ferrari.

Galvin was at his meeting place at five minutes to nine. The road was very wide at this point, well lit and quite busy. He pulled in, switched off, climbed out and opened the bonnet. He had gone just past the intersection that led into the bustling, once British military garrison town of Bandon. Ahead of him the road narrowed considerably and led to an awkwardly angled T-junction with the Bantry Road peeling off to the right. There was a nearby garage in view.

Galvin kept his head down and took a look at the engine while keeping an eye on the road behind him. Two minutes past nine a Land Rover pulled in behind him and the driver called out, "Anything I can do to help, old chap?" The voice was so public-school English that Galvin almost laughed. He did not know why; English accents were plentiful enough in the tourist season, but that was really over now. He called back, "That's kind of you. Have you any tools to fix this lot?"

"Let me see." The driver climbed out and the coding was complete. As the man approached Galvin thought he looked like a young army officer in civvies. And if he looked like one, as sure as hell he wasn't SAS. He had hoped that authority would have had more sense.

The two men quickly got down to work and the gear was loaded into the boot of Galvin's car. "As small as can be found," said the man. "Bang up to date. Good luck. I'd better get out of Indian territory before I get an arrow up my arse."

*　　　*　　　*

116

In Dublin an increasingly agitated George Farrell made a person-to-person call to Dave Santos in New York. As he sat waiting he could think of one clear advantage of staying on in Ireland: if anything was going to break it would happen here and he would be right on the spot to cope with it.

When Santos came on the line Farrell noted that the time was nine p.m., four p.m. in New York. "Hi Dave; George. How're things?" After the routine exchange he continued, "You'll have figured out from the hotel operator that I'm in Dublin." It was better to say so rather than the fact being found out. "There are a couple of issues I can sort out with the Bank of Ireland while I'm here, so I thought I'd stay two, maybe three days. The place is crammed out with foreign journalists but I managed to get a room. You'd think it was *their* President who'd crashed. Now, can you cope okay?"

Farrell knew that his absence put more pressure on his business partner and that he should really return. He also knew that Dave Santos fundamentally disagreed with some of his trips, that their styles were quite different. He was ready to argue and did not realise just how knotted up he was until Santos agreed easily. "Take all the time you want. There's nothing here I can't cope with." And then, "You said, crash. The word here is that it was a bomb."

"That's just talk. Nobody knows what happened."

"So you haven't learned anything?"

Was there a touch of disbelief in Santos's voice? Farrell looked at the phone and wondered if he wasn't being bugged by his own conscience. "About the crash? No. I don't think anything much will come to light. Anyway, I wanted to call you first before letting Judy know."

He went down to the bar. He was drinking more – not excessively – but apart from keeping in touch with the news bulletins it was difficult to know what else to do. He had considered going back but the urge to stay was too strong. He needed to be on the spot should anything disastrous occur so that he could take immediate action to protect his own skin. This would be where bad news would first break and it would be easier to disappear from here than from home.

Farrell had struck up an acquaintance with a fellow

American who said he had come over on a news assignment about the present Taoiseach, the Irish Prime Minister. The man was staying at the same hotel and was lightly bearded with mild eyes and a relaxed disposition, probably in his late forties. He gave his name as Don Helary.

Helary did not impose himself on Farrell. They always met casually, but he began to take far more notice when Farrell, not long after his two telephone calls, made the announcement that he might go down to Cork. For quite different reasons than Hogan's, Helary didn't want Farrell to go either. The mild-mannered American considered how best to stop him.

Milton Purcell had kept a low profile ever since his arrival in Ireland. He had learnt to blend into almost any situation but he had had to work hard to do it: his thick black hair and eyebrows, his short-fingered, powerful hands and his dark, restless eyes were not characteristics easily disguised. The trick he had come to rely on lay in his attitude: he could always become the most neutral, self effacing person in a crowd.

Purcell carried in his head an enormous store of information and figures on funds raised in America for the IRA: where they came from, and, very importantly, where exactly they were going. Competitiveness for the funds could encourage rivalries and demonstrations of each faction's effectiveness so that the bombs grew bigger and the deeds more daring. And Purcell was adroit at dangling the carrot. He was probably the only man who knew for sure where the money really did go and yet his name appeared on no letterhead, nor was he known to more than three people in the IRA.

Scrupulously honest in relation to the use of these funds, his morality was less clear when it came down to the question of financial sources. Anybody would do, of any political persuasion. It didn't matter that the Russians and the Libyans were considered enemies of his own country, and that he himself was staunchly American; if they supplied funds he would launder them so that the source was beyond discovery. He had slipped up only once – and that had set up a disastrous chain reaction, leading to his

118

presence here. For once in his life he felt that he had been manipulated. And that his life was now in danger. That had to be put right. But it was a question of waiting to see how things worked out before he moved.

Purcell did not see himself as the fanatic which he undoubtedly was, but as a clear-thinking man of honourable conviction. He was a natural, brilliant organiser, and in this way, as shrewd at using vast sums of money as Farrell. He did not want any form of glory but was ideal at providing for those who did, even for those for whom he had little respect. In his way, Purcell was as cold blooded an expert as Ross the bomb expert. He recognised the forces that were building up and the enormous explosion that could follow if matters were not properly handled. And he was convinced that there could be far more than one explosion. He hoped that the air crash would remain a mystery, but suspected the worst: in his field of work he had to.

Purcell returned to the lodgings he had managed to obtain on the outskirts of Cork. Before leaving Dublin he had spotted Farrell and realised that the fool must have panicked and that it was best to keep away from him. Although he knew Sean Hogan well he had made no effort to contact him. In Cork he had noticed Tierney several times although Tierney did not know him. But he was sure that the Irishman would have been sent down by Hogan in preparation for trouble. He wondered just how they would react when the news broke about the bomb and how many of his Irish colleagues had been involved this end in the original decision. That momentous step would never have solely been taken Stateside.

Purcell deplored the present chaotic state of affairs, but as long as he could be sure of his financial back-up when the time came then he would be satisfied. When the dust settled, no matter how long it took, he would be ready.

Linda Rossi was not at all happy to see Bob Rook and Peter Carraz. She was going away to her parents' retreat in California and was in the middle of packing when the bell rang. She guessed who they were the moment she opened the door. She almost closed it again but realised that it would only delay matters. With resignation she invited them inside.

"We're real sorry to bother you at this time." Carraz had so far said the same thing to three other wives who had lost their husbands in the air crash.

"Oh, sure. It's written all over your faces." Linda led the way into the airy sitting room; chintzy curtains and light walls made it seem bigger. She motioned them to chairs and flopped down in one herself, pushing her bobbed dark hair back wearily. It was clear that she was still in a state of acute distress and was trying to put on a brave face. She was pale and her slight figure sagged in the chair as if nothing mattered any more. "I'm going to visit my mother for a few days; please make it brief."

"Sensible," said Rook. "And we are really sorry." Warily he added, "I believe your husband is one of those not yet found?"

"You want coffee or something?"

They declined politely.

"If he'd been found I wouldn't be packing; I'd hang around. Are they flying the bodies back?"

"Yes. But the doctors have to examine them first and there will be a public inquest into each . . . one they find. That's after the post mortem, the autopsy," explained Carraz.

Linda nodded, her deep brown eyes dulled.

"Are you coping okay?" Rook asked. He was noting the difference between the grief etched on the composed face opposite him and the more drastic effect tragedy had had on Mandy Squire.

"Will you guys stop asking the obvious and get on with it? I've just lost my husband; I don't want to talk about it, okay? Now what is it you want?"

"Do you know Mandy Squire?"

"Of course I know Mandy. We're friends. So were Tony and Sam. We were *all* good friends. What happened to Sam the same day was . . . " Linda's lip trembled and she waved her hand to dismiss the question.

"Did they ever change duties around, Mrs Rossi?" Rook elaborated, "You know how some guys do to help each other out."

"No. They were proud of their work, they wouldn't monkey around."

"Of course not. But sometimes there are domestic problems. Wife ill or something like that."

"I guess they could ask, but the reason would have to be good."

"So Sam Squire wouldn't have asked your husband to do his duty for him on a particular mission?" Carraz took over as he watched Rook do his usual apparently aimless wandering around the room.

"Just what the hell are you talking about? What are you getting at?"

"It's a straight question, Mrs Rossi." Carraz's tone was bland.

"And you've already had an answer. What's Sam got to do with anything? They're both dead. Can't you leave it at that?"

Carraz seemed to be embarrassed but pressed on: "Well, we know how they both died but we don't know how the plane crashed or what was wrong with Sam's car. We're just trying to make sense out of a difficult situation."

"Like hell you are. You're asking some pretty strange questions."

"I guess so. Did you all exchange presents at Christmas? That sort of thing?"

"Naturally." Linda stared at Carraz in despair, suddenly unsure of herself. "I do remember that Tony wasn't designated for duty on that trip. Someone else was but he got sick. Both Sam and Tony were off at that time. But Tony was instructed officially. There was no casual exchange of duties: the Service wouldn't take that from anybody."

"Who got sick?"

"Al Bramwich. He's still in hospital. A hernia. We weren't all that close to the Bramwiches although he did boast that the case Sam gave him was better quality than the one Tony was given."

Rook stopped dead and snapped, "Case? What sort of case?"

Linda was startled as the question came from Rook who was now behind her. She half turned. "Attaché case. One of those with a coded safety catch. Sam had bought up half

121

a dozen while he was at San Diego when the President flew down there. He got them cheap – bankrupt stock or something." She turned back to Carraz. "This is all so much garbage. What's going on?"

The two men exchanged glances. Carraz asked, "I don't suppose you have Tony's case here?"

"He took it with him. They were ideal for travelling." Linda stood up. "I don't like your line of questioning. I don't understand what's going on. What are you trying to find out, for God's sake? Why don't you leave me in peace and go fill out your reports?"

"I'm sorry." Carraz rose after a quick nod from Rook. "You're right. We're just groping in the dark. I hope you get some rest with your mother, Mrs Rossi. And our sincere condolences."

As they climbed into their car Rook said, "I'm tired of walking round rooms while you sit down. Next time you stand."

"Sure. If you're tired of standing as sure as hell I'm tired of looking into the desperate eyes of young widows."

Rook gunned the car. "Okay, okay. Now we've got to run down those other cases and that means covering some old ground. They won't be pleased to see us again."

"I go along with that but I would guess that the case we really want is in fragments at the bottom of the Atlantic."

The two men glanced at each other aware of just how far their thoughts had advanced.

Galvin drove back towards Cork and branched right on to the airport road. He reached the turn off to Tierney's farm well within an hour. He stopped short of the tracks to take stock. The equipment was too heavy to carry far and he knew that he would have to take the car at least part way up the tracks. He climbed out after switching off engine and lights and waited.

The quietness of a rural Irish night gave way to the occasional rustling of small animal life. The clouds had lifted and the night was dry. He climbed back in, switched the engine on and put the lights on full beam. Insects winged in to dance in the twin glowing tunnels and a bat flitted towards the car only to soar above it at the last moment. Galvin ducked involuntarily. He headed towards the tracks.

As he drove up towards the farm he dimmed his lights and as he drew closer cut back to parking lights and finally to no lights at all. He veered from the track and the car heaved and bucked over rough ground until he thought the springs might give out. He made a large careful circle and pulled up, facing the road. He climbed out and paced back to the track. He was forced to use his flashlight now and again. He had to be satisfied that he would be out of sight of any vehicle coming on the tracks in either direction. The curves dictated which way the beams would sweep and, by the time he got back to the car, he believed he had got his position right.

He knew that the living room was at the front of the building and he was relying on his laser microphone to pick up the vibrations of conversation from the window panes. Keeping the car between himself and the track he erected the boom, put on the ear phones, directed the "mike", made sure the batteries were working then settled down to a long wait. His main worry was that he'd cut off external sound and would have to rely on sight alone to detect anything or anyone approaching.

The first thing he picked up was the sound of a television, which was a nuisance. They were tuned in to Channel One of Radio Television Eireann and it drowned practically everything else. It was a question of settling down and trying to focus on any voices apart from the overriding amplified speaker. Gradually he began to pick out several voices. By concentrating hard he picked out three, all male, one a harsh, northern accent, and an argument started about the programme that was on. Two of the men wanted the set turned off so that they could concentrate on playing cards. And then Galvin thought he identified a fourth voice.

Four men, at least, for there could be others outside the room. He aligned the track of the "mike" in a slow sweep along the house and then on the upper windows. There was snoring from one of them. Five men. He did not recognise any of the voices as Tierney's. He picked out Gerrard Connolly and felt cold anger.

He still only had the probable number of men at the

123

farm. And then suddenly, there was a reference to Tierney. Somebody remarked that Con was a long time gone and where the hell had he pushed off to anyway? It seemed that he hadn't told anybody where he was going.

Gradually, Galvin built up a picture of men summoned for a purpose for which they were now awaiting instructions. It became clearer, when the television was turned off, that Tierney was the key; he was in charge of this group and would remain so unless Sean Hogan came down. As the men continued to talk Galvin, for the first time, began to believe that the IRA were in some way involved in the Air Force One disaster. It was difficult for him to accept this because he did not think they could cope on their own with so immense and monstrous a crime. But they were mixed up in it somehow. So who was behind them? Meanwhile, where the hell was Tierney?

Tierney coaxed the Morris 1000 to go at speeds it should not have tackled. Its stubby frame coped well with the twists and curves and narrowness of some of the stretches and sped across the bridge to follow the path of the Bandon River beyond Inishannon. Shortly afterwards Tierney cruised past the spot where Galvin had collected his galium arsenide laser. The road was quieter now but it was wise to slow down when going through the town; he wanted no brush with the Garda.

Certain that he had made good progress, Tierney could only keep moving in the hope that the truck carrying the aircraft parts had not turned off somewhere. He had to rely on luck and instinct. The fact that parts of the aircraft were being moved at all was a strong indication that some sort of discovery had been made and whatever it was could not be favourable to him. He just kept driving, accelerating again after leaving Bandon. He stuck to the main T65 and passed through the small twin towns of Enniskean and Ballineen, separated by only a short section of road.

He was beginning to worry now. He had seen no sign of the truck, unless the number plates had been changed, but he doubted that. A little later he ran under the two rows of arched trees which formed a canopy of leaves that cast back the reflection of his own headlamps. It was like travelling in a golden bowl of light, the autumn leaves still

124

falling. Not far beyond them was the town of Dunmanway. He was now well into the district of West Cork. He did not know the area but he did know that if he went through Dunmanway he would be heading for Bantry Bay from where, it was said, the next stop west was Boston, USA. To the north of Bantry lay the Kerry Mountains.

Common sense warned Tierney that the convoy would not go as far as Kerry. It would be important to keep in touch with colleagues in Cork. Thirty or forty miles away would be no problem because the roads were good and largely empty. In these parts it was possible to motor for miles without seeing another car. Nor did he think the truck would be taken further south towards the coast, where the population was denser and where there would still be visitors around the resorts. This part of Ireland enjoyed the warm air coming off the Gulf Stream.

He slowed down, convinced that the truck had pulled off somewhere. He kept a steady look out as he approached Dunmanway, where the wide road narrowed as he neared Main Street. He was no longer sure what to do. He did not want to go beyond the town, thinking it a waste of time. The chase had been hit or miss and he was furious that his contact hadn't given him more notice. It was well past midnight and, although this was not particularly late for the Irish, the town was largely quiet and the shop lights out.

As he approached the town square with the flower beds so neatly planted at its centre, he noticed a group of men talking outside Atkins Stores, the largest in town. The shop faced the square but was on the other side of it so Tierney drove round the square, really a triangle, and pulled up by the group of men. As he leaned across the passenger seat, they all stared at him, listened to his Dublin accent with extreme politeness, then collectively agreed that none of them had seen a truck such as he described.

Tierney drove back the same way he had come. Used to dodgy situations, he sensed that he was not too far away from the truck. The area *seemed* right for it: only thirty-seven miles from Cork but far enough for Cork people to consider it to be in the sticks. Ireland had a lot of space and only around three and a half million people to spread themselves around in it. Once he was the Cork side of the town again he pulled up and tried to think it through. He was tingling; the answer was, tantalizingly, almost there.

He reversed and went back into Dunmanway but took the first turning left instead of continuing on to the square. His beams picked out the sign: Sackville Street. It was too English for him. He continued past a short row of houses, all in darkness, and went round a wide curve at the end of which he saw two double gateways almost opposite each other. Avenues leading to large houses. Ireland was full of big Georgian properties, a legacy of the Ascendancy days and again a reminder of the British. It was easy for his violent anger to rise quickly at the thought. But the two houses, both lying well back and out of sight, gave him an idea.

When he reached a T-junction he was unaware that he was in Railway Street. If he turned right he would head back for the square and he didn't want to be seen up there again. There was room to do a U-turn at the junction and he cleared Dunmanway once again. After about two miles he passed an avenue leading to another, well-enclosed large house. He went past slowly and thought he saw a movement behind the gates. He continued until he reckoned that the sound of his engine would have faded.

Tierney pulled in, switched off and walked back. It was a long walk but the road was empty. He approached the well-recessed twin pillars of the entrance to the avenue, what the British called a drive, and slowed right down. He reached the first pillar and carefully reconnoitred.

There was a very wide forecourt which curved back to another set of pillars supporting the big double iron gates. To get a clear view he had to edge round the first pillar. This end of the avenue was banked by trees which cast it into darkness; a rooks' haven. Even so it was against this darkness that he saw a lighter shadow. He waited until it moved. There was no sound, just the shifting of position.

It was impossible to say how many men were there but the house was obviously guarded. Whether the guards were police or troops did not matter. The Republic took pride in having an unarmed police force, but Tierney was left in no doubt that whoever was there would not only be armed but would have communication with the house itself. He edged his way back to the street. There was no

126

way that an ordinary house, no matter how big or important, would have guards at the gates. And they would be around the grounds too. High walls ran either side of the street pillars.

He silently crossed to the centre of the street and, out of sight of the gates, looked for signs. There were none, not even a house name. Tierney was satisfied and went back to his car. He had found his spot. And the evidence could now be destroyed.

He was deep in thought all the way back to the farm off the Cork airport road. He hadn't many men but although he could always obtain reinforcements the last thing he wanted was an obvious army. Nor did he want the Ulster men to come down.

If the organising had been done in the States the strong support had come from where it mattered and, as it had turned out, Stateside had not done too well. The mistake had to be covered up or confused beyond recognition. Suspicion didn't matter. Solid evidence did. The prospect of action pleased Tierney and it would be easy to justify it under a political banner. He convinced himself that if the Brits weren't up north it would never have happened, overlooking the fact that he was also an enemy of the elected Republican Government.

He turned on to the farm tracks and about half way up his headlamps caught a change in the pattern of the rough grass to his left. He stopped, reversed back, went forward again turning slightly left. He braked hard. Not everybody would have noticed but Tierney was quick to see the crushed grass off the edge of the main tracks. Wheel marks. He followed them until they faded out. He kept going and found some crushed bracken. It was hopeless beyond that point. He drove fruitlessly over the rough ground and then drove back to the main track. He continued towards the house and a little further up discerned another set of wheel marks leading off.

Tierney pulled up. He reasoned that the faint tracks which branched off in front of him were those of the original turn-off, and that those further back formed the exit point, taking the more direct route to the main road. His judgement was based on the direction the grass was flattened. He climbed out and used a powerful flashlight

127

but nothing came to view. For a moment he considered that he might be over-reacting because the tracks were still some distance from the house, but the thought was replaced by strong suspicion.

Tierney realised that he probably wouldn't have noticed in daylight. His lights had simply caught the direction of the crushed grass. He climbed back in, groping under the dashboard for his Smith and Wesson. Listening gear. The distance from the house at which the tracks stopped was all too obvious. They had been used a lot up north by the SAS. Bastards. But how had they found out so soon? Traitor. Tierney's blood went cold. Christ. He'd organise a search around the farm in the morning. But his main concern was the identity of his watcher. Whoever it was had gone, it was now well after one in the morning, but he would be back the following night for sure. Tierney decided to arrange a reception.

10

The news could now be confirmed. Air Force One had been destroyed by a bomb. But the headlines were mere speculation; no official announcement had yet been made. In New York Dave Santos read the accounts. And so did Judy Farrell. They felt uneasy enough to arrange a meeting.

The temptation was to have lunch in mid-Manhattan but they did not want to be seen together in public. Their consciences had driven them underground. So Santos took a cab from the stark, sun-starved canyon of Wall Street to Judy's apartment block and then an elevator to her penthouse.

There was a despondency underlying their happiness but neither had yet mentioned it: it came between them unvoiced yet deadly. When they had finished their drinks Judy said, "I've fixed a cold buffet. Nothing special. It's on the table when you're ready." And then quickly, as she sat down close to him, "Have you found out what George is really doing in Dublin?"

"I can only do that by going over there and the business can't take both of us being away. I'm uneasy about it, though. He's certainly covering something up. The Bank of Ireland excuse was shit."

Judy tilted her head and smiled cryptically. "You don't really want to face it, do you, honey?"

Santos looked puzzled. "Face what? What's on your mind?"

"All right, I'll come straight out with it. Can the crash off Ireland have anything to do with his being there? Right now I would think that it would be a good place to keep away from. Whatever George is, I've never known him to be ghoulish."

"Are you trying to say that he's somehow involved?"

There was a dreadful and prolonged silence between them. They stared at each other, the shock of what had been said clear on their faces. Santos said, "This is crazy. What are we saying, for Chrissake? There's one hell of a gap between the crash and his being over there."

"More to you than to me." Judy stopped fingering her necklace and reached for her glass. "I've been thinking a lot since his phone call. The call itself was strange; normally he wouldn't have bothered, but he's been acting oddly for some time."

"I haven't noticed anything, but then we're pretty busy. Are you saying he had something to do with blowing up the President?"

"*Someone* did it." Judy drained her drink. She put down the glass, rose, and disappeared into the study. When she returned she was holding bank statements.

Judy sat down again. "He keeps all his desk drawers locked which never worried me too much, although I must admit it hurt when I first saw him do it. This time he left in such a hurry that he forgot to lock two of the drawers. That in itself is indicative of his state of mind; he's usually such an orderly person, as you know." Judy handed over the statements. "Take a look at some of the withdrawals. And if you're figuring it was sneaky of me to look through his drawers while he is away, then you're right. But I'm desperately worried about the way he's been acting and his suddenly shooting off to Ireland."

Santos took the statements. "Are you sure you want me to look at these?"

"I thought we wanted to find out what he is up to. I'm worried, Dave. Really sick at heart. I'm not asking this lightly nor simply to get at him. You might even put my mind at rest."

Santos riffled through the sheets. His concentration suddenly sharpened when he realised that he was holding statements from two separate banks in the names of Burns and Driscoll. It seemed that whatever Farrell's deception, by using Irish names it was impossible for him to discard an Irish link.

Santos gazed at the statements thoughtfully, now absorbed in his own professionalism. The different names immediately smacked of a tax fraud. Yet the amounts in the pseudonymous accounts were comparatively trivial. One address was in Long Island and the other in Boston.

130

Santos looked up and flinched as he met her questioning gaze. "You mean these cash withdrawals?"

"Yes. George is a credit-card man. He doesn't carry a lot of cash."

"They're not excessive amounts, honey. Well, I suppose they do mount up." He hesitated before adding, "If I didn't know George better I would have said these could be blackmail payments."

"If George *has* been having affairs he certainly wouldn't be blackmailed over them. I doubt that he'd give a damn whether I knew or not."

"Even if it turned out to be a . . . "

"A man?" Judy smiled wryly and shook her head sadly. "Even that. No, he wouldn't give in to blackmail over those sorts of issues. It's more likely that he gave the money away."

"Are you suggesting an Irish cause?"

"Although he has Irish ancestry he's never shown an interest; not to me anyway. This is like so many things he has done before: sneaky and unaccountable, but there must be a reason."

Santos tidied the statements and laid them down. "It's one hell of a long jump. I just can't grasp it."

"Nor can mothers whose sons turn out to be murderers and rapists. If something else happens to prove a connection what would you do about it?"

"Me?" Santos was startled.

"Okay. We. You and me."

"I wouldn't want to have you by finding a way to get rid of him."

"Nor would I, Dave. He'd always be between us. But just supposing my hunch is right, just supposing he is connected even in a small way, we would have to consider what *he* would do to us if he found out that we knew. Think about it."

"Okay, let's have it. You may as well sit down." Aspel waved generously to the two chairs in his office.

The neatly dressed Rook and Carraz lowered themselves awkwardly. Neither liked sitting down in this office; it lulled them into a false sense of security and they both knew how dangerous that could be with Aspel, no matter

131

how affable his mood. What's more, they both found the chairs too small for comfort.

Aspel added, "I don't want a Tweedledum and Tweedledee act." He signalled to Carraz. "You do the talking. And stick to the point, I've a lot to do."

Carraz related their findings to date and then added, "These attaché cases are a problem. Even Squire's wife remembers his buying *six* of them in San Diego. We can now account for all six right here at home, yet Linda Rossi swears her husband took one with him on the flight. It's certainly not in the house. We had to call her mother's place — that's where she's staying — to get permission to go in. With her out of the way we took our time in going over the place. No case. Nothing that suggests anything at all."

"What about Squire's own case?"

"His wife still has it. It's there in the bedroom."

"Okay, so you've taken a bum steer. There's no significance in the cases. They were cheap, he bought them. Period."

"He bought six. How do we account for seven?"

"Rossi's wife is wrong."

"She's a determined, intelligent woman. She saw him take it with him." Carraz looked across to Rook for support. "We're both satisfied that there were originally six but somehow another one appeared on the scene."

Aspel eyed them both in turn. "Six, seven, what the hell does it matter? Maybe one of them already had one." When they returned his gaze without comment he added in exasperation, "What's the big deal? Are you saying that because there appears to be an extra case you've provided some sort of answer to the problem? You think it was filled with explosive? Then how the hell did it get on board? You think security broke down and allowed Rossi to take it on board to blow himself up?"

To take the weight off his colleague, Rook said, "We'd like to follow it up. Okay, it makes no sense but it itches and we've got very little else. And we'd like another check on Squire. A computer can only have what's been fed into it. We're not satisfied that the clearance is right."

Aspel smiled grimly. "Okay, I'll tell them upstairs that

you think the computers stink and that the whole goddamn vetting system was made up by fairies."

This time there were two men. Hank Ross was deeply troubled as he peered through the spy hole in his door. The tall and large-toothed John Smith was not one of them. What the hell was going on? The bell rang again. He called out, "Who is it?"

"FBI, Mr Ross. Open up please."

That was how Smith had got in. Stall. Standing back a little Ross called out, "How do I know?"

Just as Smith had done the two men held up their warrant cards and this time Ross took time to see if there was a resemblance. It was difficult to be sure through the small hole. The two men looked like the real thing but then so had Smith.

"If you don't open up we'll stake you out until we see you. What would the neighbours say?"

Grumbling, Ross unlatched the chain and opened the door.

"That wasn't so painful, was it?" said one of them, grinning as he went past. "My name is Samson and this is Officer Hartz." Samson looked round the room in open distaste. His nostrils twitched and he didn't bother to remove his hat. "This won't take a moment, Mr Ross. All we want to know is whether you've been approached over the last couple of months to make a bomb big enough to blow up an airliner?"

Ross recoiled. His pasty face went suddenly moist. He slowly sank into a dilapidated chair. "What the hell are you saying? You're crazies, both of you." He glanced over towards the phone and Hartz, reading his mind, reached across and handed it to him.

"You want to check on us, Mr Ross? Here's my card and there's the number."

Ross put his hand on the receiver. Not to take up the challenge could be a mistake. He cunningly dialled enquiries and checked the number of the FBI office on the card. Having done that he then rang the office and said two men had called giving their names as Samson and Hartz. Whoever took the call asked him to describe them which he did with fair accuracy. He had been left in little

133

doubt but he had gained time and Samson's shock tactics had failed. But it had been far too close.

"Satisfied?" asked Samson with a smile.

"No, I'm not satisfied. You deliberately tried to blow my mind. I'll report you for that."

"That's your prerogative. Now will you answer the question?"

"You can't expect me to take it seriously." Ross scratched his filthy hair. "You've got the wrong man and the wrong address. What would I know about bombs and planes?"

"Does that mean no?"

Both men stood over him smiling cynically, deliberately goading.

Ross realised that he had to suppress his panic. He had kept his address as secret as possible and yet within the space of two days he had received callers all claiming to be FBI. It was unnerving but now he began to muster some of the cockiness he had shown to Farrell. "It means that you both leave now or I register an official complaint of harassment. My sheet is clean."

"Sure it is. But we still know you're a bomb maker. A clever one. Maybe the best. We didn't say you had made a bomb, we merely asked if you had been approached to make one. You only have to say yes or no."

Ross replied with a sneer. "You dumb bastards. You're asking me to say I'm a bomber. I wouldn't know a bomb from a cookie."

"Then what do you do for a living, Mr Ross?" Hartz at last removed his hat.

"As little as possible. Get out of here." Ross crossed to the door and opened it wide. "Out."

Samson pointed to the card he had left on the table. "If you remember anything give us a call. We might come back with a search warrant."

"You can search as much as you like. How did you two get the job? No wonder we're crawling with Reds."

"We'll be watching you."

Samson and Hartz took their time in leaving and waited outside as the door crashed shut behind them. They went slowly back to their car, aware of the twitching curtains. "Wadd'ya think?" asked Hartz as he slipped behind the wheel.

"We shook him and I would guess he's hiding something. But he came back strong. Let's shortlist him."

Half an hour after Samson and Hartz had driven off Ross left his apartment and crossed the street to where his car was wedged amongst others. He was so preoccupied that he was actually opening the door before he realised that there was someone already sitting in the front passenger seat. He stiffened; things were getting too much.

"Get in."

It was Smith. In a way Ross was relieved; Smith did not pose the same kind of risk that Samson and Hartz presented. He climbed in. "How the hell did you get in? The car was locked."

"Grow up," said Smith amiably. "When I saw the FBI I thought this was the best place to wait for you."

Ross just sat there, making no attempt to switch on the ignition. "Yeah, well, if you saw them you'll know I can't do anything for you. Things are too hot."

"You promised, Hank. Don't let those guys rattle you. I've got the mug shot, the layout and part of the money. Right here." Smith looked awkward in the car. His long legs were drawn up and a large paper parcel was on his lap. He had thrown his hat on the rear seat and his dark hair touched the top of the car roof.

Ross glanced greedily at the parcel, then shook his head. "No. It's too dangerous." He thumbed in the direction of his apartment. "If those monkeys hadn't called it would be different. Maybe I'm being watched even now."

"You're not being watched. If I thought that I wouldn't be here. What did they want?"

"It doesn't matter. I'm not taking any chances with those guys. They *know* what I do."

"You'd be dumb to think that they didn't. You're not thinking, Hank. They're just shaking the tree to see what falls down. They've nothing on you."

"And I don't intend to let them get anything."

"Okay." Smith gripped the parcel in both big hands. "You're shaken up. I can understand that." He tore open the outer layer of paper and poked a finger through a thin cardboard lid then tore it back a little. He tilted the parcel towards Ross. "A first payment of fifteen grand. It's in

135

here. The rest after the job. The mug shot and the details are under the notes. All I ask is that you take a look, then decide. It's easy but it needs your knowledge of explosives. If you then decline I want the fifteen grand back."

Ross examined the box without touching it. "Ones and fifties?"

"All used and unmarked. Well?"

"I'll have a look and decide. If it's as easy as you say I'll probably do it. Where can I contact you?"

Smith laughed. "I'll give you a call tomorrow. Around this time. Count the money by all means but just remember it's not yours until you okay the deal. Don't try running out on me, Hank. Just a friendly warning." He slapped Ross on the knee. "I'll leave the money on the seat. Tomorrow, then." He reached back for his hat, climbed out and walked away without a second glance.

Tierney's hair had grown so thick the wig wouldn't fit. He got Connolly to give him a haircut with a blunt pair of scissors, the only ones he could find. They were in one of the upstairs bedrooms of the farmhouse, the low, sashcord windows facing towards the coast some few miles away. Cracks in the old plaster had split the covering wallpaper. A worn, moth-eaten carpet, its fringes almost gone, lay between two beds, one of which was still unmade although it was almost noon.

Tierney sat in front of a battered dressing table, its mirror pock marked with age. He swore frequently at Connolly who was no hairdresser. Connolly just laughed. The two men were equally vicious, equally and violently anti-British. They had grown up on backstreet fighting. Both had been involved in bank raids. They lived on trouble and could justify its political motive from their upbringing in violent times: the troubles had spawned their ideas and both men were now proud of their deeds in the name of holy Ireland.

Various disguises had been used many times as occasion demanded. Both Dubliners, they had done limited active service "up north" because the Ulster terrorists preferred to do their own killing. Just the same they had been extremely useful in fund raising and, from time to time, had been able to let their violent tendencies flow in that

136

direction. Banks and wealthy industrialists were considered soft targets. Bank security was nowhere near as tight as it should be because the banks had worked out that it was less expensive to accept the occasional raid than spend millions on additional safeguards.

When Connolly had finished Tierney applied stage make-up to darken his skin; not too much, but enough to give him a Middle Eastern appearance. With the lank black wig over his own cropped hair he looked reasonably more like an Arab than an Irishman. He then inserted dark brown contact lenses, a ploy he had used before.

Tierney went downstairs and grinned at the men idling in the sitting room; they were all bored, but it was nothing new. Waiting was the biggest part of the game. He changed the number plates of the Morris to an old UK number and drove off. He had about thirty-five miles to go but there was no hurry and he had flask coffee and some potato-bread sandwiches with him. Rain clouds were building up but the winds were strong enough to keep them moving in southern Irish skies.

About three miles from Dunmanway he started to search for the avenue leading to the large Georgian house lying well back and out of sight of the road. When he located it he realised just how well placed the house must be. It was a quiet road, sufficiently away from the small town hassle of Dunmanway where, only two miles ahead, the whole scene changed. The site was protected by a tall, thick wall either side of the gates and continued for some way. This time as he drove past Tierney saw nothing of sentries and guessed that they had been warned to keep out of sight. That would make it more difficult.

Tierney drove on for about half a mile and then pulled in and tucked his car into a rough hedge behind which the ground rose noticeably. The area was covered in trees, some dead; two which the gales had uprooted were propped up by others still sturdy. There was no way that he could judge whether the ground belonged to the house or not, but it was certainly neglected.

A tractor carrying a loaded trailer trundled past and Tierney made no effort to conceal himself. When the road was clear again he climbed out and immediately crashed through a weak section of the hedge, tearing his clothes on the stiff bramble. There was plenty of cover as he climbed the wooded slope. He reached the summit and continued down the other side without looking back. Once sure he was out of sight of the road he slowed down to get his bearings. He reasoned that the house would be to his left and began to make his way in that direction, very wary now, frequently stopping behind the cover of trees.

Along the slope there had been some trees felled and great trunks covered the rough ground. It was unsettling but there was no sound of chain saws, nothing but the odd swish of birds as they flighted near him. He kept on, remaining just below the crest of the high ground. He reached the head of a scarp, the ground falling steeply below. He crouched, realising that he could not have chosen a better position.

The scarp fell to a small wood through which he could clearly see a path. Beyond that was an orchard with some two dozen apple trees, to the left of which was the main avenue leading to the house. He judged the avenue to be about a quarter of a mile long and it snaked through palm trees and Rhododendrons and between the odd oak and beech tree; at its head it was flanked by two enormous monkey-puzzle trees which must have taken well over a hundred years to reach their present height. The house itself lay in the very centre of a huge area of shingle, as effective an alarm as anything; as he expected, it was big and square – a typically Georgian structure – with the shallow indented roof at its centre to take the flow of rainwater through interior ducts.

But it was the buildings leading off from the house that really attracted Tierney. A long block of stables that seemed to go on for ever, yet with no horses in sight. A police car was parked near the house with two army jeeps. Soldiers and police were not immediately evident but as Tierney scanned the whole area he began to pick them out, particularly around the stables. He guessed that there would be guards placed strategically along the avenue.

He crept as near to the ridge as he dared. It wasn't a sheer drop down and was as wooded as the slope behind him. There were rock outcrops here and there which might account for the fall of some of the trees. The winds could often be storm force around here and some of the

138

soil was shallow. He could see no guards immediately below him but they might easily be hidden in the small patch of woods this side of the orchard. Two men in white coats left the house and walked towards the stables.

Tierney stayed long enough to memorise the layout and produced pad and pen and made notes. He realised that the possibility of hi-jacking the incriminating debris was virtually nil unless he was ready to start a full-scale battle and he would need far more men than he had for that. As he lay there thinking it out he reasoned that there was only one possible way to destroy the evidence.

Laurie Galvin drove out to the farm again. He had waited for darkness but was much earlier than the previous night. The weather thankfully remained dry. The position he had chosen before had turned out to be quite effective but in spite of this he decided to change it as a safety precaution so he branched right instead of left when he reached the farm track. He set up his gear, directed the boom, and put on his earphones. The television was louder than the previous night and he could pick up no voices at all.

He took off the earphones and stared towards the house. He could just make out the slight fuzz of the front lighted window. Why was the television so loud? He put the earphones back on to pick up a religious discussion and the voices thundered in his ears. He tore the phones off again. Tierney and religion somehow did not equate. He dropped flat and put an ear to the ground. It might be caused by the breeze but there was rustling from the direction he had staked out before.

Without further hesitation Galvin packed his gear and loaded it into the car. He climbed in. His window was already lowered and he peered out across the dark fields. The car was pointing towards the main road and it was slightly downhill but when he took off the brake it refused to move, held by the suction of the rough grass. He rocked her as hard as he dared but the springs creaked loudly.

He climbed out, kept the door open and pushed. The car must have stuck in a rut for it rocked without moving. Movement from the other side of the track was more distinct; someone was being careless. There was a period of stalemate; if Tierney's men were out there they would not want to use flashlights to show position any more than Galvin wanted to start up the engine for the same reason. As he strained to free the car he realised that Tierney must have picked up his tracks of the previous night.

Galvin was a good distance from his original position but he must have made some noise and once Tierney knew he was this side of the track he would hurry this way. And that was what happened. There was a sudden shout followed by the steady tread of running feet. They had given up caution. Flashlights began to probe.

Galvin jumped in and gunned the engine frantically. He kept the lights off and sped down the incline towards the road straining to pick up what was happening across the field. Something pinged above his head and he guessed that someone had fired a lucky shot and it had scraped the metal roof. That meant only one thing. If they got him he was going to disappear for ever. Tierney must have a lot to hide.

Galvin drove as fast as he dare over ground he could not see and which was knocking hell out of the springs. He was thrown about the seat but held on to the wheel wondering if they had yet actually seen him. They must certainly have heard him. He caught a flash of light in his rear-view mirror and saw that someone was running towards the house, carelessly beaming his flashlight; he must be rushing to collect the car.

Flashlights were now openly on view and considerably nearer. One appeared out of nowhere just to the right of him and in the reflected beam Galvin saw a gun being raised. He veered straight for the gunman, keeping low, his gaze just above the dash. The man fired but lost his nerve at the last moment and threw himself to one side as Galvin headed straight for him.

It was time to use his lights. It would pinpoint him but after a very nasty jolt which shook up the whole car he realised that he could easily land in a ditch – for good. He switched on full beam and in a way it was more frightening with lights than without. Every shadow and hollow before him was cast out of proportion so that minor obstacles appeared immense. Unless there was clear danger ahead he had to ignore the frightening distortions his headlamps

140

threw up. He put his foot flat down and aimed straight for the road.

There was no nonsense now. He could hear the impact of shots on the bodywork and then the rear window splintered and spiderwebbed. He zig-zagged. There was another flash behind him but the light diffused on the rear window. He guessed that he had passed remarkably close to someone but no shot followed so far as he knew, then it occurred to him that somebody had shone their flashlight on his registration number. It was standard practice to muddy it up on a jaunt like this but a beam might pick out the detail.

He reached the road and shot across it, braking suddenly into a sliding skid and finding direction just before he hit the opposite bank. He was now flank on to Tierney's mob and far to his left he could see a car jolting down from the house. He could cope with that but the volley of shots now coming his way was another matter. He kept going as fast as he could. The nearer he got to the airport the safer he would be but even as he consoled himself with that thought a hole appeared through the windscreen just to the left of him and as he tried to get more out of the car twin beams glared off his wing mirror as the car engine began to cough. They had got him.

11

Galvin lost speed and watched his fuel gauge plunge. At the rate he was losing fuel his tank must have been hit more than once. At the next turn-off he switched off his lights, veered across the road and entered a farm access. He kept going until the engine cut out

He ran back towards the road, keeping well clear of the farm track. He crouched down in a culvert to wait for Tierney's car to go past, surprised that it was taking so long. When he looked back the twin headlamps had gone. Tierney could be waiting for him, playing him at his own game with his headlights off. He squatted and waited for half an hour. Nothing happened.

His own car was about fifty yards along the farm road and eventually he went back to it. There was not enough fuel to blow it up which is what he would have preferred to do. Instead, he took out the tool box and removed the number plates. The engine and chassis number had been taken off a long time ago. With the plates under his arm he climbed up the track until he heard the distant growling of a dog. He turned back immediately, went as far as the main road, then walked in the direction of the airport.

Galvin kept to the edge of the road expecting at any time to hear Tierney's car speed forward. Its absence was puzzling unless Tierney simply wasn't willing to fight on open ground at the risk of putting his operation on view. And that was just it; what *was* his operation? Galvin had endured two nights trying to find out and already had blown that part of his mission. In the boot of his car was some sophisticated audio-surveillance gear which would raise some stormy political questions when found, particularly as this sort of equipment was known to be used by the SAS in Ulster. The current détente between London and Dublin would be blown sky high. Yet there was nothing he could do; it was too heavy to carry.

He was at most three miles from the airport. He needed

transport to get back to his farm lodgings and the airport might be the best place to find it. He walked on still thinking he was in some kind of trap and unable to fully understand why Tierney's men had dropped out.

He found a Volkswagen Beetle before he reached the huge Musgrave cash-and-carry complex. It was in the drive of a small bungalow tucked behind white-painted gates which he opened. There were house lights on and he could hear music.

The car was locked but he had no trouble inserting a probe to open the driver's door. He slid on to the seat, released the brake and let her freewheel down the slope to the road. He covered some little distance before the ground levelled out and the Volkswagen came to a stop. Galvin went back and closed the gates then returned to the car to fiddle with the leads under the dash. He drove back to where he had left his own car.

When he reached the spot he fixed his own plates over the Volkswagen's; it would take the heat off if there was a quick search. He swiftly transferred his gear to the boot of the stolen car and prepared to drive back to the Bandon Road and his digs. He'd make up his mind what to do with the car once he had safely hidden the heavy gear. He eased the VW down towards the road when he saw two sets of beams coming from his left, the direction of Tierney's place. He snapped out his lights at once.

He coasted down the track, braking well short of the road so that fringe headlights wouldn't brush him. A bull-nosed Morris 1000 went past and behind it a jeep. The Morris was on full beam and the jeep on dipped headlights but it was sufficient to illuminate the Morris for Galvin to recognise Tierney behind the wheel.

Now he guessed part of the reason why Tierney had called off the car chase. He had another engagement and hadn't wanted to get involved in what might have become a protracted pursuit. Galvin had to make up his mind quickly. He drew out some way behind the jeep and started to follow without lights.

After a while it became hopeless. He could see the red blobs of the jeep's tail lights well enough but he could not make out the edge of the road in the darkness. He found he was veering off the road too often and this could be dangerous with drainage ditches alongside. He kept it going for a while but was losing ground and having too much difficulty in steering. Only a maniac would drive on side lights on these roads and would immediately arouse suspicion, and if he put on full beams they would see him anyway and the emptiness of Irish roads would go against him. Apart from being unable to drive safely without lights there was always the risk of being picked up by the police; he was driving a stolen car.

Galvin pulled up, fuming quietly. He thumped the wheel, angry at what he saw as his own monumental cock-up. Two nights of failure. He searched for crumbs of comfort. He had no idea where the two vehicles were going but it smacked of a raid of some sort. The only thing that Galvin knew for certain was that Tierney's men were down here in connection with the air crash. He was about to drive off again when he had a consoling thought. If Tierney's mob were away the farmhouse might be empty. Perhaps he could pick up something there.

He U-turned and headed back to the farm. Now familiar with the general layout he went past the tracks and parked on the road some way from them. He headed for the house. In his hip pocket he carried his gun; they may have left someone behind.

The familiar sight of the sitting-room light broke through the darkness, indicating that someone was still there. Galvin made a straight approach. He wasn't careless but at least he knew that the odds against him had shortened. He crept up to the window and looked through one corner. As far as he could see the room was empty. He went round the back, aware now of the pitfalls of the rain barrel. The kitchen lights were out. He slowly tried the back door to find it locked. He had to get in somehow.

But first he wanted to check the barn. He could make out the dim shape of the main barn and ran towards it in a crouch. One door was broken off and the other hanging from rusted hinges. Galvin glanced back towards the house; there were no lights this side. He stepped inside the barn and used his flashlight. It was a junkheap of straw and discarded farm tools. There were parts of an old tractor at one end. He noticed the beam from which the rabbits had hung on the now empty hooks originally put there for stringing onions.

It took Galvin ten minutes to find where the arms and explosives were hidden. They were right behind the hanging door, the least obvious place. A hole had been dug against the slatted wooden wall then covered by a solid framed lid which was indented enough into the earth for soil to form a layer over it. It had then been hidden with straw; the whole barn floor was covered in this way.

In the cavity were two Ingram sub-machine guns, an Armalite rifle, plastic explosive and detonators, fuse wire, remote control apparatus, and two Browning automatics. He lowered the lid, repacked the soil and threw the straw around. He had no doubt at all that there were other caches but he had at least confirmed the presence of arms.

Galvin went back to the front of the house. He favoured the room he could see into and reached up to slide back the catch of the sash window with a pocket knife. He lifted the frame very carefully, detecting an imbalance in the old weights. He belly-rolled through and closed the window again; sudden draughts could be a warning. As he gazed across the room he noticed that the door to the hall was wide open. A log fire had been burning in the huge grate, its embers still red.

Galvin went past the old settee and the three dilapidated armchairs. The television set was on a rough wooden table against the far wall. He crossed the room and entered the hall. He had to use his torch now. He went quickly round the ground floor, kitchen, a second reception room with a camp bed and some chairs, a toilet with an old-fashioned high level cistern, and a huge utility-cum-storeroom in which was an oil-fired boiler for the ancient radiators and some fishing rods and baskets. Satisfied that the ground floor was empty he started to climb the stairs, aware that in a house this old they were bound to creak.

He took a good deal of his weight on the solid banisters, the ancient boards groaning as he climbed. There was a light on somewhere upstairs and yet he had not seen it outside. He heard a toilet flush and he froze with one foot raised. The sound gushed right through the house. Footsteps scuffed across the landing and Galvin pulled out his gun. He released the safety catch and pulled the

145

hammer back very slowly; there was already a round in the breech.

A door was pushed back and a bed creaked heavily. There was a belch and then the bed creaked again. Galvin waited then continued up, pausing at the head of the landing. The light had disappeared. He decided against exploring the whole of the top floor. He knew that there was at least one man and that he had gone to bed, by the sound of him, full of liquor. Galvin backed down the stairs keeping his gaze on the darkened landing. Already there was heavy snoring. He applied the safety catch and pocketed the gun.

Back in the sitting room he began to poke around. There were a few tattered paperbacks, copies of the *Cork Examiner*, some tidied, others just thrown down. Full ashtrays and a half empty packet of Players cigarettes were on the table. Someone was something of an artist, for rough sketches of animals lay loose on top of a drawing pad, a pencil beside them. He searched around them, inside the books, newspapers. There was a copper log bucket by the fire with some screwed up paper. He bent down and unravelled the sheets.

At once he knew they were important. They were the crude sketches Tierney had drawn of the layout of the house and grounds near Dunmanway. Had someone been careless again or was he meant to find them? Galvin reached for the sketch pad. He drew a more distinctive copy from the originals.

He went over them once more, keeping an ear for movement from upstairs. He then screwed the old sketches up again and threw them back in the bucket. As he turned to the window there was a heavy thump from upstairs followed by someone swearing loudly and he guessed that Tierney's man had fallen out of bed. Galvin opened the window quickly, climbed through, pulled it down but could do nothing about the catch. A man entered the room just as he drew back.

Galvin moved away quickly. Once clear he ran lightly back towards the car. There was no sign of Tierney returning, indicating a protracted mission or a long journey to it. He was convinced that the plans he had in his

146

pocket were important. He started the car to begin a search for the nearest public phone.

On the way to Bandon Tierney was quiet and reluctant to talk to Connolly by his side. But Connolly could sense that it wasn't the caper that was on Tierney's mind so much as who was watching the house. At last Connolly said, "Who do you reckon it was, then?"

"I don't know," Tierney replied grimly. "I don't like it. Eugie reckons he has the car number." He turned briefly. "Michael says he's got a mate in the Garda; he can run it through the police computer. We might come up with an interesting answer."

"Supposing it's the Garda that's watching us? He wouldn't be so keen then."

Tierney shook his head. "It's not the Garda. The guy was too far away from the house. If he was spying he would need the right gear. It might be Special Branch, or maybe the Americans have been put on to us. Or the bloody Brits." He suddenly smiled a little. "Whoever it is won't have found anything out. His tracks had been made before I found out the location, so there was nothing for him to pick up. And tonight we stopped the bastard before he got going."

"We should have finished him. Gone after him."

Tierney dimmed his lights as a car went past. "No. We missed our chance. The last thing we want is an open street battle. The bastard was cagey and one of us made too much noise in the first place which warned him. After tonight it won't matter, as long as we do the job right. We'll hang around for a few days more to make it look okay and then we'll go back to Dublin." After a while he said, "I'll check with Eugie when we stop but I'm sure we haven't been followed." He laughed. "We'd better find out if it's the fishing season and get the rods out to make it look good. Do you know anything about fishing?"

"Sure. You toss a grenade in a river and they come up cooked."

Tierney drove a mile beyond the house. It was still a rural area and would be for another half mile. The actual approaches to Dunmanway were short, just a few dwellings on the way before reaching the small town. He squeezed the Morris in as far as he could, doused his lights and saw the jeep's headlights creep up behind him. He climbed out and went back to Eugene Hayes who was driving the jeep.

"See anything?"

"Not a thing. I thought we had company when we first started but it must have been in my head. I've been watching all the time."

"Good. It's about a mile back. I'll lead the way with Gerry. Give it a good five minutes and then send Michael and Johnnie. Same wait and then you follow with Pat. Make sure you've got everything. I'll be on the look-out, ready to give the signal. Just keep going until you hear me."

Tierney went back to the Morris and lifted two back packs from the rear seat. He passed one to Connolly and slipped into the harness of the other. He locked the car, glanced at his watch, and led the way back. One man would remain with the jeep to cover an emergency; they could all fit in if they had to.

"Hey!"

Michael Daley stopped and gave Johnnie a quick nudge. The sound had come from the other side of the hedge.

"Through the gap. A bit further on. Gerry will guide you."

It was Tierney calling but Daley still thought it uncanny the way the voice had come from nowhere. The gap was slightly easier to get through than when Tierney had first blazed the way. Once the other side the four men joined up.

"Anyone see you?"

Daley knew that Tierney could not have missed the car that had gone past while they were on the road. "We faced the hedge and did a pee as the car reached us. No problem."

By the time Eugene Hayes and Pat Sullivan were signalled in the others had drawn their Ingrams from their packs. When they were all assembled Tierney gave the word to follow him and he took the route he had taken earlier. It was much more difficult now. It was pitch dark; the six men had to maintain contact in very difficult conditions and it was essential to move quietly. But they were well trained and Tierney was a natural leader in this sort of situation and possessed good directional sense.

They climbed up to the ridge and Tierney went forward alone to peer over the edge. The long stables were in darkness – the scientists had at last been forced to take time off to rest – but there was sufficient light from the house to illuminate part of the courtyard to provide a focus.

Tierney took his time. It was almost one in the morning; he would have preferred it to be later. The approach down the wooded scarp was slow, a stage at a time. It was hard, tedious work even over the easier sections. The mass of bramble impeded and tore at them all the way, and stinging nettles had to be borne without murmur. Blistered hands clutched at any support they could find, and booted feet groped for every root or ledge.

They were a long time getting down and at each stage two men always remained stationary to give immediate covering fire should it be necessary. As they drew nearer to house level there was a faint sound of laughter. A bat winged over them, swooping and flapping but eventually tired of their company. The last stage to the bottom was the slowest of all because they knew that guards, police or army or perhaps a combination of both, would be somewhere around the stables.

There was movement below. A patrol. Tierney's men froze immediately. Two men. And they were talking. When the voices and footsteps had gone Tierney led the way on the final descent to reach level ground. One by one they joined him. The rear wall of the stables was only fifty feet from them. To their left, unseen in the bad light, was the small orchard and behind that the woodland which formed part of the gardens.

Motioning the others to stay where they were Tierney went off on a recce. The ground between the foot of the scarp and the converted stables was open but rugged and full of ankle-breaking potholes with too much give on the surface, probably a warren of fox holes. He reached the rough plastered wall and felt his way along, searching for an entry. There were no doors at the back and only upper windows, but the stables were low ceilinged.

As he was about to return to the others a vague shape came towards Tierney; the man was humming. Tierney reached into his belt for his silenced Browning, tensing for the confrontation. The humming ceased as the figure stopped some yards from Tierney who remained absolutely still.

"Is that you, Eamonn?"

The Garda sergeant never found out. Tierney did not prolong the agony; he fired two shots and the sergeant fell on top of his rifle. He went forward to make sure he was dead and on discovering that he wasn't fired another shot through the man's head as wide eyes peered up in silent agony. Tierney pulled the sergeant by the arms some distance away from the wall and went back for the rifle. He hurried now, increasing his risks, not knowing how long it would be before the sergeant was found missing.

He reported back. In a whisper he said, "We've got to move. I had to croak one. There are three rear windows out of reach. You form anchor, Eugie, then Pat and Michael can go on top. And don't make any bloody noise."

They moved off, separating then regrouping at the wall. Choosing the middle window Hayes bent down and Daley climbed on to his back and then to his shoulders as Hayes straightened. With the help of the others Sullivan climbed up Hayes and Daley and stood shakily on Daley's shoulders until he had a grip on the rotting window ledge. The window was so old and uncared for that he had no trouble in opening it by shaking free the loose latch. He pushed the small window open and climbed through, stepping carefully on the boards. He poked his head out and caught the grappling hook now thrown up to him. He secured it on a sturdy part of the window frame and stood by as each man climbed up in turn. When they were all up he pulled in the rope.

"Some of these boards are rotten," Connolly complained. "We'll have to watch our step."

They got down on all fours and felt their way to the open stairs which turned out to be more supportive than the floorboards. Once in the main stable they stood still and examined the double doors and the shuttered front windows. It was pitch black inside – a good sign: but flashlights had to be used carefully. The horse stalls had long since been ripped out to form one very large room.

They posted two men either side of the doors, sub-machines cocked and ready. Restricted torchlight slowed them down but revealed what they had been hoping to see. On the rough concrete floor, laid out in the position they would have formed as part of the aircraft, were three white segments of fuselage. Relative to the whole plane they must have appeared small but in the stables they looked immense. For a while, as they glistened under the guarded torchlight, the three jagged and buckled sections brought the whole disaster much nearer. Even Tierney stood for some moments staring in awe at the damage that had been done. A smile of satisfaction spread slowly over his lips. The lives lost meant nothing to him; the effect of that loss, everything.

The open wooden stairs came down straight from the upper floor and to the left of them was a long wooden bench with various instruments spread along it. One section had plastic dust covers and Tierney moved quickly round the fuselage parts to lift the covers. It was almost too good to be true. The orange "black boxes" were there. The flight-deck voice recorder and the flight recorder stood almost side by side. He didn't understand the sophisticated equipment nearby to assess these recoveries but he intended to make sure that they, too, would be of no further use.

They worked fast. Uncoupling their back packs, Tierney, Hayes, who left his post at one of the doors to help, and Connolly set about fixing charges to everything. They used a mixture of explosive and incendiary devices, attaching a detonator each time to make sure that if one failed the others would do the job, but each was also fixed to two central timers, again to cover against a single failure.

They were sweating and those on sentry at the doors became edgy as time passed. But the job could not be hurried. The men were experts at what they were doing and for once Tierney was glad to have Hayes in the front, northern accent and all.

So far there had been no indication of anyone finding the dead police sergeant. But at intervals they had heard a patrol go past at the rear and had stopped operations with

151

flashlights out each time. When they had finished there were charges fixed to several points of the fuselage sections and separate ones to the "boxes". They had used more plastic than necessary but they knew there would be no second chance.

When finally they were ready Tierney checked the connections and the timer and Hayes, who had more experience than any of them in this field, checked again. He gave a thumbs up. A last look round, a signal to the men at the doors to head for the stairs. They reached the window and waited for the next patrol to pass, gave it a little extra time then lowered themselves on the rope.

Tierney was the last down. There was no point in trying to shake the grapple free as it might make too much noise. They crossed the open ground. Climbing up the scarp came as a relief and they found it easier than the descent. Their elation was barely controllable but when they reached the hedge Tierney enforced discipline and made them go back in pairs as they had come. It was essential that they were not seen as a group. This time he and Connolly were the last to leave.

It wasn't until they were on their way back and after they had passed the gates to the house that they released all the pent up fears they had harboured. They shouted and screamed and thumped each other and gave no thought to the safety of those who were to take the brunt of the explosions to come.

There might have been more loss of life if the dead sergeant had not been found lying in the rough grass. Sergeant Flanagan had been something of a disciplinarian. When he had left the makeshift guard room in the house none of his men were brash enough to query his movements. From time to time he had radioed in but often there had been long gaps and nobody was particularly worried; if Flanagan had expected others to operate by the book he had always been a law unto himself.

The last gap in transmission had been too long, however. Whatever the reluctance of his men to check on him someone at some stage had to do something. So they had found him, rifle by his side but without his two way walkie-talkie, which Tierney had failed to spot when he had dragged the body away. The alarm went up, men came racing forward from all directions except those on stationary sentry duty. The stables blew up while they were still grouped round the body.

To a man they were blown flat; the two men on guard outside the stable doors were killed instantly. With the massive blast came the terrifying sheets of flame that roared out as if a petrol tanker had been inside the building. The heat was intense and the men near the dead sergeant were pinned down while debris hurtled through the air above them.

The stables, some hundred and fifty years old, had been scattered in every direction and with the chunks of the old walls had gone lethal splinters of aircraft screaming through the air like shrapnel. The main fireball stayed within the perimeter of the stable block, huge flames roaring from the gaping interior of four blackened stubs of walls.

Everybody came running from the house, some lifted from their beds and all horribly shaken. Someone had already phoned the fire brigade but the nearest was in Dunmanway and that was a part-time service with only one engine. Calls were put out elsewhere but it would take time for engines to arrive from Bandon, and, in the other direction, Drimoleague and Bantry. The fire might be put out but the damage was already done, as the whole township of Dunmanway was to witness when they jumped from their beds wondering who had attacked them in the middle of the night. Cars and people jammed the roads within minutes and general chaos ensued.

Tierney could not have wished for better. If ever fragments of the aircraft were salvaged they would be of no value with so much damage and so many blast marks on them. The black boxes had gone up like grenades. He'd done his murderous job well.

Galvin didn't hear the news until the next morning and when he did he drove straight out to Dunmanway. He was seething all the way. Reports of the time of the explosion convinced him that he had put in his warning call to London for them to relay to Dublin in time to prevent the disaster. In fact he took the view that the men could have been caught in the act if the guards had been warned directly.

The radio reports had been explicit enough for him to locate the house but, even if they hadn't, the swelling congestion of traffic and people would have drawn him to the area. He had to leave the stolen Volkswagen well away from the scene knowing he was taking a chance even with the false plates up; police had been drafted in from all locations. Nobody was allowed along the avenue to the house unless on official business and Galvin felt the frustration of being able to play no part. He joined the group of press men at the gates and picked up some detail of what had actually happened. The current rumour concerned a tractor driver seeing an Arab in an old Morris near the house the previous day.

He drove back to Cork City, parked the car, and checked with the Bank of Ireland in South Mall on a draft he had been promised to replace his abandoned car. At least that had been actioned. He withdrew the money in cash and returned to the Volkswagen parked not far from the bank. Making sure no police were about, he replaced his old number plates with the genuine ones and then walked to the nearest used car dealer.

He bought a second-hand Ford and drove off with the log book and a tank full of fuel. He was relieved at having discarded the Volkswagen after putting the surveillance gear in the Ford. He found the nearest call box and telephoned his London contact. After the official exchange he blazed, "What the bloody hell went wrong? You could have stopped them."

"Not over an open phone, dear boy. You should know better."

"Sod the open phone. Three are dead, blown up with the evidence. You had time, you bastard."

"There must have been delay that end. You know how it is. Dublin doesn't like interference from London. We have no direct jurisdiction, you know that only too well. We can only pass on what we know. We must terminate this call now."

"If you do I'll make it difficult for you. I don't believe that crap. You could have *caught* them in the act. What's

154

going on? This is something more than a cock–up. Even you don't make that sort of mistake."

The line went dead and Galvin glared at the receiver in his hand. He put it back slowly on the cradle, fighting the impulse to smash it. In spite of his threat he knew he wouldn't do anything; there would be sudden technical difficulties on the line. But something was going on which stank like rotten fish.

He went back to the Ford. He knew there was a pub on the north side of the city frequented by the local Sinn Fein and Galvin drove out there; it was important to keep up his image. He parked in the crowded forecourt and noticed Tierney's Morris. He opened the doors to the public bar and went in. The place was quite crowded and sure enough, Tierney with a satisfied smile on his face, was standing drinks at the bar. He had his group with him but Galvin was surprised to see Sean Hogan there. What was the supremo doing down from Dublin? But the person who really made Galvin's blood run cold was Connolly; and suddenly he decided to hang the consequences and pay him back for what he'd done to Riley Brown.

12

"Well, if it isn't Laurie himself. The black velvet is it?" Tierney couldn't have been more affable.

"I don't like some of the company you're keeping." Galvin made no attempt to hide his feelings not to avert his gaze from Connolly. The area round the bar was suddenly quiet.

"I don't want any trouble," said the barman quickly. Then seeing that he was not going to avoid it as Galvin advanced, added, "You start something and I'll call the Garda."

"Call them," snapped Galvin, knowing that the barman wouldn't with so many Sinn Fein and Provos as his customers.

Tierney looked on, fascinated. He had no knowledge of what had happened between Connolly and Riley Brown but it was clear from Galvin's expression that this was a personal issue. He had no fears about Connolly's fate; the tall red-headed Dubliner was among the most vicious men he knew. And it might be interesting to see Galvin beaten up.

Connolly wore a look of disbelief as Galvin drew nearer. He reached for a bottle on the bar and smashed off the neck, the beer swilling over the floor. The others began to draw back and the building tension spread rapidly among the customers. During the mounting silence the powerful, bearded figure of Sean Hogan detached himself from the bar. He had earlier warned Connolly that Galvin had come looking for him in Dublin, but unlike Tierney he wanted no trouble. "Come on boys, cool it. This isn't the place to settle your differences." He placed a hand on Galvin's arm but Galvin shook him off.

"Keep out of it, Sean," Galvin snapped. "There will never be a better time to fix this piece of slimy woman basher. Is that how you get your kicks, Gerry? Beating up helpless women?"

Connolly felt all eyes on him. The blood rushed to his face in anger. He swung the bottle and Galvin, with apparent ease, caught his wrist, turned and threw Connolly over his shoulder. Connolly crashed near the doors; everyone else stood rooted to the spot.

Connolly rose slowly, the remains of the jagged bottle still in his hand. His face was white with fury and his lips drawn back in a vicious snarl. As he reached a half crouch he dropped the remnants of the bottle and advanced on Galvin like a maddened bear. Galvin's stance seemed casual but his reflexes responded as Connolly came in with a kick which Galvin countered with his instep, scraping his foot down Connolly's shin as the leg rose.

From then on it was the most complete and clinical beating any of those watching had ever seen. Each time Connolly came forward Galvin was ready to oblige. Not only was he beating him to a pulp but he was shaming him in front of his friends, reducing him to a babbling and battered form who could no longer sneer or make threats.

At no time did Galvin ask if Connolly had had enough and none of those watching had the nerve to suggest it. Connolly was defeating himself until finally, barely able to move, unable to open his swollen lips to get his words out, he eventually recognised that he was finished. He glared up malevolently through puffed slits of eyes.

Connolly tried to say something, then collapsed on his face, his breath rasping into the floor. Nobody said a word. The sympathy had been with Connolly from the start. He was among friends, one of the team, and it was Galvin who was the intruder. All they could do was to stare at Galvin in awe.

At last Galvin spoke in triumph. "And that's what happens to anyone who molests any friend of mine. And while you're feeling sorry for this piece of slime let me tell you that you didn't see Riley before the doctor got to her." He gazed down at the inert Connolly; "This his drink?" asked Galvin reaching for an almost full glass of Guinness. He then walked over to Connolly and poured the drink over his head. "Have this one on me. You'd better get a doctor to him." He walked out of the pub without looking back.

It seemed a long time before anyone said or did

anything. Tierney had been shaken to his roots with the rest of his men. He had seen a side to Galvin he had not suspected was there. There were thoughtful and uneasy glances. Then as necessity overcame shock there was a move towards Connolly and someone said he was bringing his car round and knew a doctor who would handle it.

Meanwhile Sean Hogan was gazing thoughtfully at the door. "Now, doesn't it make you think where he learned all that stuff?" he said softly. Tierney caught his glance and with it the strong intimation of danger.

The press were caught flat-footed. They had all been ready to denounce the IRA as having blown up incriminating parts of Air Force One but reports about the sighted Arab grew stronger by the hour. The farmer who had seen Tierney with his darkened face found himself in great demand.

No counterclaims were made and the Arab sighting gathered strength; coloured people in that part of West Cork were as frequent as astronauts on the moon; it would be impossible for them not to be noticed. So the easy hate of all those who were anti-IRA was now tempered by doubt.

In London Sir Gerald Fowler had some lunch brought in for himself and his guest, Paul Sutter. Fowler had his desk cleared and the two men sat on opposite sides of it, flatware laid out and a wine cooler on the floor at the side of the desk.

"I'm sorry about this," said Fowler. "Not for the food – I know the restaurant it comes from – but for not taking you to my club where it's infinitely more comfortable."

"But infinitely less private," smiled Sutter, rubbing his arm.

"Exactly. Tuck in. You realise, of course, that the Arab theory is bunkum. The IRA blew up the plane parts. That solves your problem, doesn't it?"

Sutter tucked a napkin in his collar; he found the chair too low for the desk. "You seem to be very sure that the IRA did it."

"Aren't you? Isn't that what you wanted to hear? You thought them responsible in the first place."

158

"I thought they were one of many possibilities. Have you any proof?"

"Not to satisfy a law court but proof enough for us. Our man in Ireland rang through. He had the names of most of those involved." Fowler cut into his Dover sole. "Unfortunately he was far too late with the information. We needed it much earlier. I don't blame him; he was in a particularly bad situation but the fact is he didn't make contact until the damned evidence had already been destroyed."

Sutter chewed thoughtfully. "So if we know who did it why haven't they been arrested?"

"Paul, really. The Republic has a population of under four million and they don't like being overshadowed, particularly by us. We can only pass on information. It's not always appreciated and sometimes resented. Don't misunderstand me; we have lots of friends there, even in high places, but they can be touchy when we interfere. The fact that we know tells them that we have men working on their patch. Even though they already know that, it won't go down too well to be so pointedly reminded."

"So you think they dragged their heels? Evidence of how the plane was destroyed was blown up in their own back yard and they fouled up the follow through?" Sutter kept his eye on Fowler as he lifted his glass.

"That sounds a bit harsh. These things happen."

"You don't seem too upset."

"We can't do a thing. But, if we pass over the names to you, maybe you can arrange some sort of justice; not necessarily through the courts." Fowler shrugged and dabbed his lips with his napkin. "We're used to what goes on in Ireland. Each time we try to extradite terrorists from there we either cock up the paper work ourselves or some Irish judge with suspect sympathies lets the culprit go."

"Having the names would help a good deal."

"These IRA boys are extremely adept at going to ground. But I'm sure that you'll find a way to cope."

"You seem to be taking this pretty casually."

"Not at all. I just don't think the IRA, on their own, are capable of pulling off such an enormous crime. It suits us to blame them; it will do them immense harm and they will lose very considerable support. But does it suit *you*?"

"Like you, I never imagined that if they had a hand in it they would have done it alone."

"Ah! You've been holding out on me. You thought they might lead somewhere?"

Sutter smiled. "I obviously haven't fooled you. I'm sorry. Of course there's somebody else involved but we first had to establish that *they* were. You're not holding anything back are you, Gerald?"

"Why on earth should I hold anything back? We're discussing who killed your President, for God's sake. It could be our Queen next." He folded his napkin reflectively. "You did ask for our help; we've done rather well in a short time."

Sutter laid down his fork. "Okay. So you think that people will believe that the IRA blew up the plane and then incriminated themselves by blowing up the evidence?"

"What else could they do? Let the findings be published? Their enemies will take the view that they've condemned themselves by their double act and will rightly be reviled by it. But that won't worry the IRA one bit. They were reviled already. They've done the job. Even if the Irish police find them what can they do? There are no eye witnesses. The only actual witness was shot dead."

"There's always your man."

"He didn't see it happen. And he would face a lot of hostility in an Irish court. I don't think it a good idea to put him on open show; he'd be lucky to get out alive once his cover was exposed, and it would destroy a good agent. I repeat, we've passed on what we know. If neither of us are satisfied then I think the answer lies elsewhere. There's nothing more we can do."

Sutter appeared uncertain. "Are you willing to use your man once more? Is it possible that he can obtain actual proof of who blew up the plane parts? If he can it will enable us to put the screws on certain people across the pond."

"Do *you* want it or do you want me to pass it on to Jimmy Powell?"

"I'll pass it on to Jimmy. That way the FBI can't

160

complain they never received it." Sutter, realising that he was rubbing his arm again, suddenly checked himself.

Fowler looked thoughtful and in some ways pleased. "I'll see if I can get our man to produce a little more for you." He was content with the way things had gone. But he wasn't so sure of Sutter's attitude.

Since hearing of the news of yesterday's bomb outrage everything had changed for George Farrell. But he could not accept that he was out of danger. He was confused and bewildered; he was not sure of anything any more. When he had shaved that morning he had almost seen a stranger in the mirror, certainly someone much older than the man who had first arrived. More and more he felt rejected, at times believing that he had been used and that his job was over.

The news of the incident had brought new hope. They had got rid of the evidence. Without that there was nothing. All the police forces in the world could harbour an equal number of suspicions but there was nothing left with which to prove them. The evidence had been destroyed. Even if they caught the men who had bombed the house he knew that there was no direct connection with those in the United States, or with himself. It had been supportive action. One cell helping another.

What was there to stay for any longer? He didn't know but he'd be a lot happier if he could get down to Cork to check out what had been going on for himself. He did not trust newspaper stories nor the many rumours that were circulating, but there was no accommodation and that was that. He went down to the bar and ran into Don Helary, who was with an attractive woman he had seen from time to time in the hotel.

"George. I don't think you've met Mary Poulter. She's staying here." Helary smiled. "Mary's in television. Over here to do some deal with RTE."

Mary Poulter smiled back. "I'm not sure that Irish television are all that interested, but you never know, and it will probably sell in the UK. Nice to meet an expatriate. The place seems full of them right now."

"Most of them are media people of some sort," observed

161

Helary. "The news doesn't improve, does it? One dreadful step after another. Join us, George. On the rocks?"

Farrell sat down. He was having difficulty in concentrating. The woman was quite attractive. He took the drink when it arrived and swallowed half of it in a gulp. "Cheers," he said after he had put down the glass.

The place was filling up around them as it always did at midday. He didn't know what to say to Mary Poulter; he tried to avoid talk of the death of the President and now the latest bomb.

Helary made the first move. "George has been considering going down to Cork but I told him that he'd never find a place to stay. From what I hear it's bursting at the seams."

"It's very pretty down there. Quite different from Dublin. If you really want to go I might be able to help." Mary Poulter had a soft, persuasive voice.

"I've tried every hotel myself. The porter also tried. Don's right; there's not a bed to be had. Unless you own a hotel I'm afraid nobody can help."

"I've rented a villa down there." Mary delved into her handbag and dangled a bunch of keys. "It's not in Cork though. It's in Kinsale, a yacht harbour not far from Cork. Beautiful place."

"I don't understand."

"I've rented it from today on but I'm touring for the next three days. I'm driving down to Bantry this evening. I can't get away until after eight but Kinsale isn't that far off course. If it's important enough to you I could drop you there. I don't mind and I much prefer night driving." She looked slightly embarrassed. "If you don't mind paying three days' rent it would help me."

Farrell couldn't believe his luck. "If I remember right Kinsale's about ten miles from Cork." He produced his chequebook but Mary waved it away.

"We can settle that when we get there. I must stress the time limit, though, because I'll be staying there myself when I return from Bantry. You'd have to find your own way back here."

"That's no problem. I'll hire a car. You've made my day." Farrell called the waiter.

"Can you be ready by eight or just after?"

162

"Sure I can. I don't know how to thank you."

Helary raised his glass. "If you intend to come back to this hotel I wouldn't check out if I were you. They're overcrowded and you'd never get your room back. They won't even take a deposit because they can fill any room that's empty right now. Just a warning. I know a guy who lost his room that way."

"That's okay. I intended to hang on to it anyway. But thanks." Farrell managed a smile for the first time in days.

When Mary excused herself Helary escorted her to the door. "Good work," he whispered. "You sold it to him."

They held each other as if they would never separate and the Norfolk terrier pup, now called Hercules, was already showing his jealousy as he jumped and pranced round their ankles. "I thought you'd never come back. Oh, Laurie, it's so good to see you."

Neither wanted to move or lose contact as they swayed together in the middle of the living room. Hercules started jumping up over the furniture, frustrated by not being able to reach higher than their knees. Finally Galvin scooped the dog up and handed him to Riley.

"You want a whiskey?" she asked at last, trying to cope with the squirming Hercules.

"Too early. Tea will do fine." Behind his smile he took stock of her cuts and bruises. If he had suffered any remorse over Connolly's humiliation he certainly suffered none now: looking at her he knew that he'd happily have done the same all over again.

She suddenly saw his hands. "Holy Mother of Jesus, what happened to you? And don't think I haven't seen under your eye. You've been fighting?"

"I don't know how." He chuckled. "I was looking in the engine of a car and some fool closed the bonnet on my hands before I could remove them."

"Was your face still under the bonnet too?"

He saw where she was looking and his hand went up to his eye. "Oh that. I fell off a stool after drinking too much trying to relieve the pain in my hands."

She started to laugh. "I hope to God it wasn't Gerry Connolly you fought. He's not worth it and he has too many friends. They're a wild bunch for sure. You don't want me to ask questions about it, do you?"

"No."

"Don't you think you should contact your sister? It's days now."

"I rang the nursing home while I was in Cork. But I'd better give her another ring." The lies were beginning to be more difficult. He and Riley had been very close before, in love even, but something much deeper had bonded them during these last few days and it was difficult to know why feelings had intensified so much. He tried to avoid thinking about it but when he did face it he knew that there was a limit to living a lie and he was no longer sure he could handle it. The prospect of hurting her was suddenly much more difficult to face.

After tea he went through the motions of ringing the nursing home and Reg Palmer, head of Irish affairs at MI5, answered guardedly as he quickly picked up the fact that Galvin was ringing in someone else's presence. He told him that his sister had suffered a relapse and it was advisable that he come over.

Riley picked up the gist of what was being said, as she was intended to. She cuddled Hercules as Galvin spoke, noticing the annoyance on his face.

When he had finished she said, "She can't help being sick, Laurie. She is your sister after all."

He glanced at the old wooden clock on the mantelpiece. "I won't get back tonight. First thing in the morning, though. It's a bloody nuisance."

"She wouldn't say that if you were ill."

The growing deception made it worse for him, and he wished at times like this that Riley was less understanding. "If I can get a seat," he said. "I believe the flights are still crammed. Maybe I'll be lucky on stand-by." He gave her a long, tender kiss. "I'll miss you. I seem to be travelling a lot and getting nowhere. Even that Cork franchise didn't work out though there's still an outside chance." He grinned, eager to make the right impression. "I'll be back before you know it."

Farrell packed enough for three days. But while he was folding his clothes he had moments of doubt; what would

164

he do when he visited Cork? What *could* he do? But that was where the truth was. He had to go.

He took his grip downstairs and left it in the lobby, intending to wait in the bar. He wasn't sure why but he'd expected to see Don Helary there. When he'd eaten earlier Helary had not been in the dining room. Just after eight Mary Poulter arrived a little breathless and dressed in smart slacks and an open jacket with a blue roll-neck underneath. He rose to greet her as she approached.

"You look very chic."

"My driving gear." Her hair was tied back in a pony tail. "My luggage is in the car and that's across the street." She led the way out and he was surprised that he hadn't given her more attention before. He picked up his grip and she led the way across a busy O'Connell Street. She opened the boot for him and he placed his grip next to her two cases. The car was a roomy Ford Granada and he climbed in beside her.

She pulled out into the traffic stream, watching her mirror, one small foot hitting the central brake pedal of the automatic drive. Right from the start he knew that he was in the hands of a very competent driver. She spoke little while they were in the hustle of Dublin but began to ease up when they reached the outskirts.

The motoring became pleasant on the open road. "It will take about four hours. You want to stop for a snack or a drink on the way? I've got to get some gas. I think there's a filling station in a couple of miles. The price here is out of sight."

"No, I'm quite happy." Farrell found her easy to be with. "You want me to share the driving?"

She turned to smile. "No thanks. I like driving and almost always travel distances at night. Here it is."

The glow of the filling station approached like a battery of television lights, high and suspended and almost blinding as Mary slipped the car into a bay. She filled up and went into the office to pay in welcomed dollars and they eased out on to the road again. They did not go far. On the darkened road, the filling station now out of sight behind them, Mary came to a halt, complaining about the position of her seat. She asked him to ease it forward for her while she released the catch. He heard the nearside

165

rear door open but by the time he turned round to see what had happened, Don Helary had slipped on to the rear seat and was holding a gun against Farrell's head.

"One dumb move and I'll blow your head off," he said without expression. "Okay, drive on."

Farrell was petrified, the more so because he had not the slightest idea of what was going on.

13

Galvin reported to the Denbridge Nursing Home in Reading and was met by a white-coated Reg Palmer, complete with stethoscope sticking out of a side pocket. They went for a walk in the grounds.

"At least, thank God, it's you; I couldn't stand the other supercilious so-and-so," Galvin said with feeling. "I've got a bloody bone to pick with you."

Palmer knew what Galvin was going to say.

"You ballsed up my phone call." Galvin felt his blood rising as he considered his position. "You had plenty of time to contact the Irish Special Branch or the Garda and get Tierney's bunch of bombers. You could have got the lot. It was a cock-up and three poor bastards died because of it."

"I understand how you feel. It was unfortunate. But as I said before, we can only relay information. And we did that promptly. After that it was completely out of our hands."

"Are you saying the Irish deliberately did nothing?"

"It's not something we're likely to ask them, is it? And if we did we'd get a short answer. I don't know what happened there."

"I just won't accept that the Irish sat on it."

Palmer thrust his hands in his pockets. "It's getting chilly. Perhaps," he continued thoughtfully, "Dublin finds it more expedient to deal with completely discredited bombers than cope with dead or captured martyrs."

Galvin saw some truth in it but he was far from convinced. "There's too much involved for the Irish to take that line. There are too many Irish Americans. No, I don't buy it. I think it was a cock-up your end."

"Don't be absurd. We want proof of who did it and we want you to get that proof. The circumstantial stuff is all right for us but not for juries."

"Ask the Garda or the Irish Special Branch to do it. I can't do it alone. Besides I'm pretty well blown."

"The Irish will be working on it, but you're the one who's already near to the answer. We're trying to help our American cousins."

"Then let the bloody Americans help themselves."

"Come on, Laurie. What happened over there? Is it anything to do with your gashed hands and your black eye?"

"That's personal."

"The girl? Riley Brown?"

"I said it's personal."

"Oh dear. I'm just through telling our beloved leader that you can handle that particular problem. It's obviously worse than I thought. So they suspect you?"

"They've seen me once or twice in Cork. A cover can stand up only so long."

"Can't you look around the farm again?"

"They'll have gone to earth. I'll have a look, sure. But there won't be anything there. You're hoping for bomb material that might match anything Forensic have found in West Cork. Tierney isn't that stupid."

"But you'll have a look just the same? You might get another lead. Who knows?"

Galvin began to stamp his feet. "I miss that chunk of Gulf Stream. It's bloody cold here. Okay, I'll look." He hesitated for quite some time and Palmer could see that he was struggling. Galvin added, "I think I'll have to leave the girl."

"As bad as that? Won't it raise more questions? I don't think you're telling me everything."

"That makes two of us, doesn't it? I told you it's personal. Look, if you don't like the way I do things then bring me back."

"You're no quitter. Besides there's someone over there who might need you." Palmer spoke carefully. "How do you think one of Tierney's men was so careless as to leave screwed up plans in a coal bucket?"

The way Palmer said it made Galvin's blood run cold. He turned to stare at Palmer. "You having me on?"

"I told you there was someone else."

"The poor bastard."

"He can leave pointers in only the flimsiest way. It's up to you to interpret them. Which, so far, you've done."

"Jesus." Suddenly Galvin flared. "That makes the cock-up even worse, doesn't it? The poor bugger's got his head in a bucket waiting for it to be hammered."

"Can you help him?"

"You shit. You know bloody well I have to." He stopped walking. Coldly he said, "But even that's not the real reason, is it? You think there's somebody behind the IRA." Palmer's silence confirmed Galvin's own suspicions. "So why don't you check with the FBI on who funds them, if you don't already know."

John Smith called on Hank Ross well after dark.

"You said you'd call," complained Ross who had just washed his hair and managed to make it look as if he hadn't. His cotton shirt was clean but not ironed, his pants washed but crumpled.

"Your phone might be bugged," Smith wandered over to the window and peered down into the street.

Ross was looking for a bottle of bourbon amongst the clutter on an old sideboard. "You want a drink?"

"I don't touch the stuff. I want it done within the next two days."

Ross poured a shot of whiskey into a glass, then went into the kitchen. Smith heard him open the ice box and drop some cubes into his glass. "That's rushing it," he called out. "All I have from you is a mug shot and an address." He walked back into the room, sipping his drink. "It will be too risky to get into his place unless you've got keys. Better done through his car. A good, old-fashioned job. Sometimes they're the best."

"That's a bit old hat for what I'm paying you, isn't it?"

Ross shrugged and spilled some of his bourbon. "Do you want the guy dead or an art display? I'm taking the risks; I'm not likely to cut corners. I never do that on a job. At the same time you won't get a two-foot crater in the road. I know my job."

Smith suddenly leaned forward on the chair. "The

169

sooner the better and the sooner you get your balance. Now you want details of the car . . . "

James Powell sent for Joe Aspel; there had been some interesting developments. "Okay," said Powell, "let's have it."

"Carraz and Rook have been pushing their pet theory: that Mandy Squire knows more about her husband's death than she is willing to say. So they concentrated on her two kids. It took time to gain their confidence – they had to use one of our more attractive women agents to help them out, Harriet Grossly, and she also got friendly with the girl next door who's a friend of the Squires." Aspel correctly read the impassive impatience of Powell and hurried on.

"The upshot is that Mandy Squire was worried sick about a meeting between a man and her husband some time before the crash. He didn't come to the house but it was clear that they had arranged to meet and he had waited in his small van across the street from the house. It so happens that all three girls were leaving the car next door and saw both men and the truck. The two wives took turns in picking up the kids from school. They didn't have a close-up view and weren't interested except when the Squire kids heard about the second visit on the day that Squire died. It seems that the van followed Squire as he drove off that morning. Mandy Squire talked to the kids about it to unburden herself. She would sometimes think aloud in their presence.

"They described the man in the van as messy and dirty. Hair not combed, scruffy. They didn't like the sight of him. The van was a blue Ford with New York plates."

"No number?"

"It was too much to expect."

"You've been in touch with New York, of course?"

"We've been checking all known and suspected bombers nationwide. The computers throw up a few possibilities. Old blue vans aren't unique but the general description of the man fits only three. One of those is in New York." Aspel glanced at a slip in his hand. "Harry Ross. No convictions but a suspect for some time. It is believed that he does quite a few jobs abroad, even going as far afield as

Europe if our information is right. Someone like that could have made the bomb."

"And used Squire to get it on board?"

"That's much more difficult to answer. After all, Squire was never on the duty roster for that flight."

"Have we got enough to pull Ross in?"

"We've got nothing yet. If we assume he's the bomber, then who ordered it? From what is happening over in Ireland right now it seems that the IRA did it."

"Is that what you think?"

"I don't know what I think yet. The rest of the world seems to think it. I've set a surveillance on Ross but I would guess that he's long since stopped communication with anyone who paid him, assuming he's our man. But if he is he's only the technician. We want who's behind him."

"What about Milton Purcell?"

Aspel smiled wryly. "I've been waiting for that. The son-of-a-bitch has disappeared. We've got a nationwide APB out on him. Nothing."

"Maybe he's gone to Ireland?"

"What could he do there?"

Powell offered a twisted grin. "Keep away from us? Or is he running from someone else? Keep at it. I'll get in touch with the Irish Special Branch."

Galvin rang Riley Brown from London airport and told her he would have to stay over a day or two. Riley's concern for his sister made Galvin uneasy. He was chipping away at their relationship each time he lied to her. With a heavy heart he dashed for the departure gate. Reg Palmer had smoothed the way for him to avoid the usual check-in procedures in order to catch the flight. His boarding pass was waiting for him at the boarding point.

Just over an hour later he was in Dublin. Cork would have been nearer to where he had to go but his car was at Dublin airport.

A long drive offered time to think, but he didn't much care for what came to mind. His personal life was going to fall apart but it was the effect it would have on Riley that really hurt him. It might leave her twisted, even more hatred building up against the Brits. But he had been activated with a specific job to do and that was that.

171

He had put a retainer on his room at the farmhouse near Bandon but he took a detour towards the airport when he finally reached the south. He drove along the road where Tierney had stayed in the farmhouse and turned up the tracks without lights. He became careless in the amount of noise he made, but operated efficiently enough and rigged the laser gear that he still had in the boot of his car.

As he listened he got soaked in the heavy rain, but he stuck at it. So far as he could judge there was no life in the house. With great difficulty he lugged the batteries and the boom to a new position and listened again. The longer the silence the more he tried to penetrate it. He took the extreme risk of loading the gear in the car and driving round the rear of the house stopping just short of the large barn.

He rigged his gear again and listened carefully. There was no response on either side of the house. It was an indication that Tierney thought the place had served its purpose and that could be because Galvin himself had given too much away during his fight with Connolly. The whole place was dead. It was no use searching now. The police would almost certainly have already done that and they wouldn't expect anyone back; the farm was blown.

Galvin dismantled the gear and loaded it in the car. He would come back in daylight and do a thorough search. For the Americans. Sod the Americans. Let them do their own dirty work; there was a colleague with Tierney's mob who had already risked his life for them because the Americans demanded information. It was their bloody mess, not anybody else's.

As Galvin eased the car over the ruts he knew that his attitude was unreasonable. The Americans would be taking their own risks elsewhere. The British and the Irish authorities knew more about the whole IRA structure than anyone and he had no doubt that the Irish were following their own leads. Providing the various national authorities weren't pulling against one another, matters might, in the end, come together. But Galvin wasn't at all convinced that co-operation was really happening; he was still not satisfied with what Reg Palmer had told him.

He decided to risk returning to the farmhouse in daylight.

Farrell was terrified. He had been shocked when Helary had first jumped into the car and had pointed the gun at his head. It was difficult looking over his shoulder at the gunman so he had turned to appeal to the woman, but Mary Poulter was staring ahead through the windscreen, concentrating on her driving as if nothing had happened.

"Is this a joke?" asked Farrell, disgusted with himself as his voice shook.

"No joke," replied Helary. "Don't ask any more questions because you won't get answers. Just sit there like a good banker and give us no trouble."

"For God's sake tell me why."

"No questions," repeated Helary. "It's just not your day, George. Be philosophical about it." As Farrell was about to ask another question Helary jammed the gun viciously into the top of his spine and Farrell yelled out in pain.

Farrell sat there rubbing the back of his neck. He said nothing more as the miles rolled past and all he could do was to try to get a sense of direction. The fact that they didn't mind his doing this alarmed him. They didn't care one way or the other. The bile of fear suddenly rose to burn the back of his throat. Dear God. He wanted to be sick and retched. Nobody took any notice of him. He retched again but nothing came. Tears began to prick the back of his eyes; how had it happened? How could he possibly be in this situation?

His mind slipped into limbo. Nothing was real any more. He felt sick and his stomach kept heaving. He could not come to terms with his position; the gun behind his head, the woman driving on as if nothing had happened at all; the occasional traffic they passed, the road signs here and there and as they reached more open country the odd sign of nocturnal wildlife scurrying across the road. Where had he gone wrong? Why was it happening at all? It was this most of all that really frightened him. He was unable to isolate the error that could have got him into such a situation.

173

He averted his head so that they should not see, but he sensed the woman's glance and he had the feeling that Helary could see the reflection of his tears trickling down his face. The dreadful thing was that they did not seem to care what he did. They were completely unmoved.

They passed Wicklow but shortly after turned inland towards Kilkenny. They were in rural Ireland again, with the roads almost completely empty. They turned off and followed farm tracks on to rising ground. Ireland was covered with farm tracks and these were no different from the others. The headlamps bounced over rugged ground and eventually, intermittently, picked out a single-storey stone cottage partially hidden behind a dump of old cars piled high on one another like a metal graveyard.

They pulled up in a muddy yard and a strong, sweet, sickly smell pervaded the car; somewhere near there must be manure. Mary Poulter climbed out and Helary warned Farrell to stay where he was. It was so dark everywhere. No flicker of a friendly light in any direction and the threat of rain kept the skies closed up. A light flashed as Mary picked her way towards the door and fiddled with a key as she opened it. The hinges hadn't been oiled for a very long time.

Lights eventually appeared in the house and Farrell guessed that propane gas cylinders were being used. So there was no electric power laid on. On a signal from Mary, Helary climbed out and told Farrell to precede him. The smell was almost overwhelming and this time Farrell managed some relief as he retched once more. When he straightened he noticed a small car parked at one end of the cottage. He was pushed inside and the whole place smelled stale as if it hadn't been lived in for years.

The small sitting room was identified by three easy chairs, quite new, and a cheap, modern table. Farrell was prodded through to a room furnished with hard country chairs round a solid kitchen table, a crowded dresser one end with pottery mugs hanging from hooks.

"Sit in that chair. There," ordered Helary.

Farrell sat down and then to his dismay Mary Poulter bound his arms and legs to the chair while Helary covered him with the gun. "I'll get cramps," Farrell said tremulously. "I suffer from them."

"Then you'll have to hope they won't reach your guts because if they creep up there they might kill you."

"Look, if it's money we can figure something out. That's no problem."

"It's not money, George." Helary looked at Mary. "You finished? He's secure? Okay, I'll be away for awhile. If he causes trouble, kill him. Don't make it hard on yourself."

Farrell's fear tightened as Mary came round to face him, reached for her handbag on the table, and produced her own gun. Helary left the room without another word and Farrell heard the car start up and squelch away. Mary sat across the table from him and started to read.

The terror wouldn't leave him now. When his mind drifted it would suddenly sharpen to make his heart race and his guts churn. Helary and the woman were not wearing any form of disguise, which meant that they didn't care if he could identify them again. And that meant he was not going to leave this grubby and evil-smelling cottage alive.

Helary drove back to Wicklow in the small car he had left at the cottage that afternoon. Now alone, some of his tension showed. Sweat beads brightened his skin. It was all right keeping calm for a job, and certainly he was well used to crisis, but it took its toll on his nervous system no matter how experienced he might be.

He saw the isolated glow of the phone booth on the edge of town and pulled in. Once in the booth he pulled out a slip of paper to check a Dublin number and then dialled. A woman answered his call. He took a deep breath and concentrated hard. He spoke in a carefully measured Irish accent. "I want to report a kidnapping. Put me in touch with a senior officer."

"May I have your name please, sir?"

"Don't mess me about or the black tulips will stop growing, so they will." Helary was sweating freely now, the effort of concentration immense.

After a while a man answered. "Chief Inspector O'Riordon. What's this about a kidnap and black tulips?"

"Have you ever seen one? Squeeze them and they run red."

"What do you want me to take down?"

175

"We've kidnapped an American banker. George Farrell. He was staying in Dublin and lives in New York. We want a million dollars. No arguments. Do your homework and contact his family. We'll give you three days. I'll be in touch." Helary hung up. He leaned against the side of the booth and felt utterly drained.

Chief Inspector O'Riordon picked up the slip from his desk and decided to report it to Detective Chief Superintendent Keane. "Strange one," he said when the overworked Keane reluctantly signalled O'Riordon to sit down. "Otherwise I wouldn't trouble you with it." He glanced at the slip and then at the heavy grey-haired man across the desk. "The IRA just phoned to say they've kidnapped a George Farrell, an American banker. They want one million dollars. Contact in three days."

Keane sighed. "Why contact us? We're not an intermediary for kidnap demands and he must know we'll resist it. Why didn't he contact Farrell's family? Hand it over to the Garda."

"There's something odd about the call. Can't really place it but some parts don't measure up. For instance it was not one of the usual voices. I'll run the tape through but I'll bet my pension the voice is new. Now the arrangement is . . ."

"I know what the arrangement is. It would be better if we had a proper code instead of this business of using certain callers and Mickey Mouse language. What's worrying you?"

"The voice. The accent was Dublin most of the time but now and again there was something else there. I can't put my finger on it."

"The tape should throw that up. Did he ring the Special Branch direct? Not the local radio station first?"

"Straight through. He knew the routine all right. Said Farrell was staying in Dublin but not where. That won't take long to check out."

"Inform the Garda and we'll sort out the discrepancies as we go." Keane gave O'Riordon a shrewd look. "What's really worrying you?"

"It's difficult to pinpoint, but the more I think about it

the more I believe there was no real menace in the demand, as though the caller was concentrating too much on the actual message and not enough on its import."

"Jesus, are you saying it's a hoax?"

O'Riordon shrugged. "No. I don't think so. I'll find out if he's missing." He hesitated. "As you say, why call us about a kidnap?"

Keane stared. "If Farrell's missing see that it gets full media coverage stressing the call, the demand, and who made it. It might stir something up."

But as O'Riordon left the office he could not rid himself of the feeling that that was precisely what the caller wanted.

14

Galvin slept badly and woke up late. He was at a low ebb. After a breakfast he hardly touched, he almost gave in to the mad urge to ring Riley Brown. He resisted because there was little he could tell her except more lies. It wasn't difficult to imagine how she would feel if she knew he was back in Ireland. He drank black coffee and went out to the car.

He drove back to Tierney's farm, about half an hour's journey, and drew up where the tracks began. The rain had stopped but the ground was wet and he decided to motor up to the house; at least he could make a faster get-away if he had to. His heart was no longer in what he was doing.

When the farmhouse was in sight he stopped, unsure of himself. The place still seemed as dead as the previous night but what surprised him was the fact that there were no police on duty. The Garda would surely have searched the place. He supposed a really thorough search could be done in a day but he would expect them to leave someone to watch the house. He drove up to the front door, turned the car so that it was facing downhill and left the engine running.

He raised the old-fashioned knocker and hammered the door, ready to run for it if any of Tierney's men appeared. Nobody answered. He hammered again. The sound rumbled round the house. He pulled out his gun and went round the back feeling uneasy at being too far away from the car. There was no sign of life and while this confirmed his audio surveillance of the night before he was less satisfied now than then. The location of the farm was in his report to London for them to pass on. So why at least weren't the police here? He asked himself the question again and again.

It was easier to get in at the front and he slipped through the same window as before and stood with his back to it. The room had been tidied up. There were no papers in the fire bucket, no books, and, as he slowly gazed round the room, no evidence at all of finger prints being taken.

It might be that Tierney and his gang had wiped the place clean but it would have been a full-time job with so many of them in the house, and anyway, the police would still have dusted around the door handles and other obvious places. None of what he saw looked right.

He went round the house, upstairs and into the rooms he hadn't seen before. Beds had been stripped of blankets and sheets which were not to be found anywhere. There was no sign that anyone had recently stayed here. Tierney had done a first-class clearing-up job. Even the kitchen had been stripped of foodstuffs which had mainly been in cans, Galvin recalled. The bin was empty. He appreciated the sheer professionalism of it. That left the barns.

He knew where one cache had been and was not surprised to find the cavity empty. As he searched he became more convinced that the police had never been here. There had been no search. He gazed over at the rusted remains of the ancient tractor and was filled with increasing uneasiness. If London had passed on his information why hadn't the Irish acted on it? *If* London had passed it on.

Galvin rose and went outside. Someone was playing a very strange game. There were two other smaller, ramshackle barns adjoining a large paddock where horses had once roamed, uphill from the house. He went through them and found two more empty arms hideouts. In one was an unloaded automatic pistol magazine, the spring rusted and stiff. At the base of the spring, within the lower body of the magazine, he noticed a piece of paper crammed in; he had to force the spring before he could get it out.

No bigger than a cigarette paper, it was screwed up so tightly that he had to unravel it very carefully to avoid tearing it. The writing on it was so minuscule that he took it out into the light and even then had difficulty in reading it. It contained an address, just two faint lines.

So the infiltrator was still working; he was taking

179

desperate risks and for what? He must feel totally cut off, the kind of dangerous loneliness that can break the strongest nerve. Galvin suffered a wave of humility. If there was one thing he must do it was to take some pressure off his unknown colleague.

He went back to the car unaware that much further up the incline, behind a distant hedgerow, he was being watched through powerful binoculars.

Farrell's kidnapping did not take up the column inches it might have done had the other terrorist news not been so spectacular. But it did reach the front pages if not the major headlines. It took the police a little time to be convinced that he had actually been kidnapped. The bar staff at the hotel remembered seeing him with Helary and the woman called Mary Poulter the previous evening. But he had told nobody he was going away.

A trace was put out for Helary and Mary Poulter but Helary, who had by now returned to Dublin and had read the report went straight to the police anyway. He told them that Mary Poulter had gone somewhere into Kerry, he didn't know exactly where, she was simply touring, and that she had offered Farrell a hitch as far as Wicklow. Helary told the police that he had been there when the offer had been made and that he hadn't the slightest idea why Farrell wanted to go to Wicklow. It didn't occur to him to ask. He believed the two of them had set off some time after dinner and this was confirmed by the hall porter. He considered it inconceivable that she could know anything of Farrell's disappearance, although he admittedly had not known her long.

Smart police work produced the garage Mary Poulter had used on the way to Wicklow and the pump man remembered the two well, as the woman had paid in dollars. The garage man had seen Farrell in the car, not a good view but enough, and there was no way that he was being forcibly detained. The two were simply motoring through. Meanwhile Mary Poulter had not yet been found.

Special Branch made the decision to release the IRA claim that Farrell had been kidnapped on the premise that at least it might produce him if he hadn't been. And if he had then they had wasted no time. The recovery rate of kidnapped victims was very high in the Republic. The concentration of the search was in the Wicklow area. There were at present no photographs of Farrell. He must have taken his passport with him as it wasn't in his room, so telexes were sent to the FBI to contact Mrs Farrell at the address given on the hotel register.

Judy Farrell couldn't believe it. She stared at the FBI agent as if he had gone mad. She was numbed by the news. "A million?" Judy was still dazed. "Then we must pay it." The words came uncomfortably.

"I must tell you, ma'am that the Garda Siochana, the Irish police, are strongly against any form of ransom payment. They will block you as much as they can. I have to say that we agree with them. It's a mistake to give in to ransom demands."

Judy stood there not knowing what to do. She still could not grasp what had happened. She wanted to get rid of this man as quickly as possible but realised that she must hear him out. She was well aware that he was assessing her reactions and she tried to be more composed. "I'll *have* to pay," she said flatly.

"Can you give us a photograph of your husband, Mrs Farrell? We need one to wire over to Dublin. At the moment they've got nothing to print."

As she crossed to a side table to remove a framed portrait she echoed, "Print?"

"It helps if there are mug shots in the newspapers. People might have seen him, that sort of thing." He took the photograph from her without looking at it. "Thank you, Mrs Farrell. I'm very sorry about this. I'm afraid it's a hazard for wealthy businessmen these days. They're soft targets. But we'll keep you informed. We're putting a tap on your phone just in case direct contact is made. It's unlikely, but as there are IRA supporters at this end they might just possibly use one to relay messages to you."

"I don't want a phone tap." Judy realised that the sudden outburst could be a give-away. "I don't like the idea of it, the intrusion."

Rolf Kerr stared at her, mildly surprised. "It's the only way we can get a trace on a voice. I take it you want the men caught if possible?"

"Yes, of course. I'm sorry. I do understand, but I just don't like the idea."

Kerr was reluctant to go. It wasn't often that he had the opportunity to talk to such a beautiful woman. Shrewdly he said, "We don't want to spy on you, Mrs Farrell. But your husband is being held and we need all the help you can give us. Meanwhile don't agree to paying a thing. At this moment don't say no and don't say yes."

When Kerr had gone Judy immediately reached for the phone. She drew her hand away as if it had burned her. Was there already a tap on it? She put on a coat and took the elevator down. She caught a cab to Wall Street and alighted outside Farrell and Hammel, hesitating only fractionally before entering the huge bronze portals. Reception seemed a mile away and she only vaguely knew the girl behind the long curved desk.

"I must see Mr Santos at once. My husband's been kidnapped in Ireland." It was the best excuse to be there.

"Oh, my God." The receptionist got through straight away and within seconds said, "He'll be waiting by the elevator."

And he was. Santos took her by the arm to lead her down the carpeted corridor to his office. He could see she was distraught but said nothing until they were inside the office and the door was closed behind them.

"George has been kidnapped in Ireland. The FBI have just seen me."

"*What?*"

"The IRA have claimed responsibility. They want a million dollars ransom."

"Then I'd better organise it. Good God. I can't believe it." Santos held her at arm's length. "This thing is going from bad to worse. Just what the hell is going on?"

"I don't know. I can't take it in."

"You want coffee?" And when she shook her head, "Sit down. We must think."

182

"I can't sit down." Judy clasped her coat and began to pace the room. Finally she went over to the window to stare at the hazy New York skyline, its square-edged jagged peaks looking like a sales graph in the poor light. She shivered and he put his arm round her. He suddenly swung her round. "There's an organisation in London who specialise in handling kidnap demands. They're first class and know how to negotiate, how to see the whole thing through; they're all ex-cops, mostly from the anti-terrorist squad at Scotland Yard. Leave it to me."

"Don't you think we should tell the FBI what we suspect about his being over there?"

"Not yet. We don't actually know a thing but an organisation like the one I'm talking about might come up with some answers. It's worth a try."

Milton Purcell read the newspaper accounts and saw the news bulletins on television. And his terror grew. So far he had felt that he had everything under control. Even though he had sensed a growing pattern he now had the worst possible kind of confirmation of his fears. They would be looking for him.

When he had left New York he had done so before receiving news of Sam Squire's death. By the time it filtered down to him in Ireland he took the worst view: that Squire had been murdered. He had no doubts as to who had kidnapped George Farrell and he wasn't misled by the announcements. He wondered if there had been any other killings, in the USA. But the disappearance of Farrell was crucial because he could be linked to him.

He sat on the edge of his bed wondering what to do. So far he had played it very close to the chest. He had kept clear but as an American visiting Ireland out of season, he'd soon be noticed. Being on the run wasn't the answer either; it could be effective for only so long.

He was staying near Kenmare, approached on a road built through solid mountain rock, a day-tripper's dream. It was time to make contact. The telephone in his lodgings was too public and Purcell set off with ample change and a small diary which would have to be disposed of. He found a booth, checked the number, and dialled. The calling tone rang out for so long that he was about to hang up when the breathless voice of Sean Hogan came through sharply. "Yes?"

"It's Milton. We've got to talk."

"Milton? *Milton*, Holy Mother of God, where are you?"

"Here. In Ireland. Is it safe to talk?"

"That depends. Are you anywhere near Dublin?"

"Not near enough to drop by if that's what you have in mind. We'd better arrange to meet. It's important."

"Sure, if you think we must. Where and when?"

Purcell had been looking up a map. "On the Tipperary – Cashel Road."

"Jesus, it would take me hours to get there." Hogan made it clear that he wasn't keen on the idea at all; this was the second American who had come unwanted at a critical time, but this one was important.

"Three. That makes it half way. Okay?"

Hogan worked it out and covered his annoyance. Purcell was not a man to panic; this had to be vital. He glanced at his watch resignedly. "Can do." Then hung up.

Purcell returned to his lodgings and sat in his room planning the route. He was a man who never carried arms, and up to now had not had reason to, but now he desperately felt in need of a gun. He had a long way to travel but what he had to say could not be risked over an open line. He had a late dinner, snatched an hour's sleep lying fully clothed on top of the bed and woke up ready to move instantly.

The route was circuitous; he knew how easy it was to get lost on the minor roads so he first cut up to Killarney and then turned east on to the Mallow Road. The rugged beauty of the country he was passing through was lost in the surrounding darkness and the lakes were no more than huge distant patches in the poor light.

He considered the man he was about to meet. So far as he was concerned, Sean Hogan was the brains of the Dublin crowd and some of his thinking should have been better heeded over the border. Ostensibly Hogan was Sinn Fein, a political animal rather than an actively violent one, but Hogan knew how to cross that narrow

184

divide only too well and was an enormous asset to those in the field when he did.

Purcell drove on through the night, his only company the suicidal insects sucked into his headlights. He was glad of the straighter roads as he got nearer to Mallow but there was still a long way to go.

Meanwhile a tired Hogan was travelling south-west down from Dublin. He had only just returned to the city, in fact, had barely opened his own front door when Purcell had rung. Hogan held a tremendous respect for Purcell. He recognised the financial genius of the man, the deceptive coolness in someone who could, on occasion, be fiercely aggressive. But Hogan had never known Purcell to be aggressive about anything except positive administration. He was a tremendous fund raiser and had been particularly good to the Provos. Hogan would do well to remember that.

His route was more straightforward than Purcell's. He followed the National Primary through Naas and then the long stretch down to Cashel. The whole journey was scattered with old IRA war grounds but they had been of a different breed. It was not something that touched him as he motored on. He lived for the present; the past was only the tenuous excuse for what he did now.

The secondary route linking Tipperary and Cashel was twelve miles long. On leaving Tipperary Purcell stopped just outside and set his trip meter to zero. He drove on slowly, well within the time limit he'd set himself. Driving on the left-hand side of the road – even with virtually no traffic at this time in the morning – wearied him and the hedgerows had thrown up dark barriers like a prison. But he was nearly there. After travelling precisely six miles he pulled in and switched off his lights.

Some twenty minutes later when he saw the distant glow of approaching headlights he switched them back on. The headlamps bounced into the night like low-slung searchlights and then he could actually see the twin orbs which flashed at him; he flashed back. The approaching car slowed perceptibly and slid past him by some twenty feet before stopping and the main beams were switched off.

A tired Hogan climbed out and walked back to Purcell. He climbed in the front passenger seat and shook hands warmly with his American colleague. "As pleased as I am to see you, what the hell brings you to Ireland, Milton?"

"The same thing that brought Farrell."

"But he's a panicker, you're not. And look what's happened to him. So what are you doing here?"

"Keeping my head down. Did you do the Farrell job?"

"Now, why would we do that? I was trying to get him to go home, for God's sake." Hogan tried to turn his bulky figure in the seat. It was strange sitting in a car in the middle of the night talking in this way. "You didn't bring me half way across the old country to discuss Farrell?"

"The implications of the kidnap. If you didn't do it who do you think did?" It was important to know which way Hogan's mind was working.

Hogan waved an arm. "Pumped-up gangs are always taking our name in vain. It sounds like some amateurs who are trying to make a fast buck. Don't worry about it." He grinned in the darkness. "It keeps Farrell out of our hair for sure."

Purcell spoke quietly, "You've got to repudiate the claim then."

"You can't be serious. It's not worth it. And anyway nobody would believe us."

"Don't you see? Whoever they are, they're trying to blame you, the Provos."

"So what's new? Jesus, you couldn't have dragged me out for this." And then with sudden suspicion, "You know who did do it?"

"I have an idea. The whole object is to draw focus to the Provos, to discredit you in any way possible. First Air Force One, then the plane parts and now an American businessman in order to raise funds that have been cut off Stateside. You're going to be landed with the whole thing."

"Jesus, but didn't we have a hand in it all but for Farrell?"

"The force of the accumulated points against you will make it all hang together. You will lose support in places where it matters most. You'll be wound down, Sean, for a long time to come. Suddenly there'll be a lot of informers."

"The Official IRA have always informed on us. They know nothing of any of this."

"They don't need to, do they? The whole goddamn world knows. It's gonna stick, Sean. That's the object, to discredit you in such a way that nobody is left in doubt. You'll lose important friends. Repudiate the claim about Farrell. Do it convincingly and you'll create confusion. If you're being set up for one thing then why not for another? You'll create doubt and you can capitalise on that."

Hogan tugged at his thick beard. "Are you saying that whoever took Farrell did it simply to pass the blame on to us?"

"That was one reason."

"How do you know?" Hogan's tone hardened.

Purcell suddenly wanted a drink and sensing it Hogan passed him a flask. Purcell drank sparingly and returned the flask which Hogan screwed up at once. "There's nothing I can prove. You must trust me. That shouldn't be so difficult. I'm trying to protect all of us. They've got Farrell; they'd also like to get me."

Hogan swore. "Are you going to tell me who and why?"

Purcell had gone over this repeatedly during his drive here; he knew the question was inevitable. "I can't tell you without losing credibility and I need to retain that to preserve the money sources I tap. I'm trusted. I cover up contributions to everybody's satisfaction. It took a very long time for me to dispel uncertainty in potential sponsors before I reached that position. I've built up our finance from an almost derisory figure, but over the last year I've really broken through with some staggering contributions that will rival what you raise from intimidation. That's what's at risk. And I can't let that be endangered."

Hogan sat thinking; he was beginning to have qualms.

187

Suddenly he said, "Look, we did do the bloody job, didn't we? You were over here while we planned it."

"The planning took place in New York."

"Don't bugger around, Milton. You know what I mean. We sanctioned it because we were going to be on the back end of nothing for a very long time. The detail *had* to be done your end. You were being squeezed out. Answer my question."

Purcell took a firmer line. "Get one thing clear, it would have happened with or without you. There were outside supportive motives. Plenty. It was done with our funds. All the planning was done there, all the risks taken there."

"Until now. This is when you need us."

"We've always needed each other. Don't let's fall out now that the going's tough. I'm trying to explain that all the help that can be gotten for a job like that has to be examined carefully. Nothing is straightforward. Our purse strings are far flung, the money comes from all over, and for many reasons. I have to protect those sources. Even from you."

"Even if they're out to kill you?"

"Given a little time I can take care of that."

Hogan sat gazing out into the darkness feeling very uneasy. "You seem to be saying that our supporters in the States stage-managed the operation but someone else pulled the strings and they are now nervous because things didn't go quite to plan."

"It's not even that simple. We had to have channels to the right people in order to stand any chance at all. Sure, the original brain work was ours but of necessity we had to co-opt others: the bomber, the inside man, extra finance. It was no small operation, was it? I'm surprised to find you so naive."

"I'll let that pass, Milton. I knew you would have to use or buy people. But I've always understood that George Farrell supplied some of the contacts."

Purcell smiled in the darkness. "He did his bit. But there's another aspect. If we didn't achieve the result we wanted, if the new laws went through in spite of the assassination as unlikely as that might be, I had to be

sure we could get the loss underwritten. It was important that we didn't lose money in any way whatever
happened. I achieved that."

"Jesus, you're implying that someone wanted to kill
him even more that we did and was willing to see that we
weren't out of pocket over it." Hogan balled his powerful hands and his tone changed. "No, by Jesus, you're
going further; you're suggesting that we've been used."

"Calm down. How the hell can we have been used
when, as you yourself say, the idea originated here and
now it's been done? What I'm saying is, that because it
didn't go quite according to plan some important people
are worried, people who would not have been worried if
the goddamned plane had blown up and scattered in
mid-Atlantic. It's made all the difference. It will suit
some people if the blame rests firmly on the Provos to
show that there were no other interested parties. The
inside man is already dead. I dunno about the bomber
but I wouldn't like to be in his shoes right now. Farrell is
as good as dead. Then there's me floating loose."

"Damnit, they can't kill everybody. What about me?
The boys? You think we'll sit around waiting to be
killed?"

"It's the link-men they want. Those who were positively
involved. Those who carry evidence of one kind or
another that might point the FBI in another direction.
People like myself. You must remember that we've had a
lot of money from the Russians, the Libyans, the Syrians
and various organisations in the States. Okay, I've
laundered the money, but people like that won't be too
eager to contribute again, or at best not for a very long
time the way things are going. They'll wash their hands
of us."

Hogan shook his craggy head. "Shit."

"Meanwhile someone's measuring the Provos for the
coffin; they want to be sure the blame sticks to you like
glue."

Hogan sat thinking and when he didn't reply Purcell
added, "It's not just the job, Sean. Most people are
already satisfied the Provos pulled it. It's the insidious
building-up of lies on a basis of truth. It will come as no

189

surprise to me if eventually odd clues come out of the blue linking our organisation and the Provos with the inside man's death. You're already linked to Farrell. What'll be the public reaction when they find him with a bullet in the back of the head? It's a build-up of public revulsion. Link after link until it won't matter what you say for you'll take all the heat. Then the arrests will start and the false evidence be produced. You're being trussed for the kill, Sean, and you don't seem to grasp it. They don't want to hurry this: they want it to fester first in the influential mind of world opinion before they make their last move."

Hogan thought it through. "So you reckon that if I can unscramble the Farrell business it will cast some doubt on the rest – that Farrell isn't the only set-up? That we're being used as patsies all along the line?"

"It's the one genuine area to work on. Done properly the rest could go our way."

"It won't be easy."

"You're the one man who could do it. They won't expect an approach from you. Can you find Farrell? He might still be alive. They won't blast him until they're absolutely sure he's of no further use."

"If whoever's doing this is as good as we are at it then it won't be easy. But we've got a lot of ears to the ground. And you refuse to tell me who we're up against?"

"If we're to have any future at all this is the time when I must show that I'm totally, unquestionably, reliable. Knowing won't help you in any way but it could implicate you. Better not to know. Can you find a place for me?"

"You'd better hole up with Tierney. He's at a villa in Kinsale. A yachting place. Plenty of foreigners even at this time of year. There's a boat available, too, in case you suddenly need one." Hogan groped for the interior light and wrote quickly on a small pad. He tore off the sheet. "That's the address. It's better if you can remember it. Go straight there." He switched off the light again.

"I remember seeing Tierney; he's a hot-head."

"Some of us have to be. But I'll sort him out for you."

*　　*　　*

190

They broke up shortly after and Hogan was very pensive on the way back to Dublin. He reluctantly accepted Purcell's need to protect his money sources and indeed it was best that he didn't know the full story. And there were others he'd rather *not* know about; that way he had no need of a conscience. Anyway, it was exclusively Purcell's domain and an extremely complex one. He thought over everything they had discussed and the dawning was slow to come. When it did he slammed on the brakes and the car skidded dangerously. He pulled up slewed across the road. He started to swear violently, hammering the steering wheel. Hands still on the wheel, he lowered his head and cried out as if in pain. He believed he knew who had taken Farrell. And he now knew what he must do.

15

Galvin approached the long, low-slung concrete bridge
that crossed the estuary and realised how difficult it would
be to observe from this position. Cars moving along the
coast road could be seen from any villa on the opposite
bank. To get behind the villas was difficult as the ground
rose sharply, while the buildings themselves were scattered
along the incline with drives shooting off from the curving
roads.

The ancient town of Kinsale with its old harbour and
winding streets was behind him. He had left it on the L42,
a route he was still on and which formed part of Western
Bridge, a modern construction which somehow failed to
distract from the mixture of wild and cultivated scenery
around it. As he reduced speed he accepted that all the
advantages lay with those overlooking him from across the
estuary. Old, ribbed hulks reclined on the mud flats and
near the inlet were the shallow oyster beds. Yachts of
differing sizes were buoyed on the water, turning this way
and that as fickle winds played with them. It was a tranquil
scene and somewhere in it nestled a bunch of killers.

Galvin didn't cross the bridge although he was tempted.
He took the minor road beyond it and wound past
Ballywilliam. It was narrow here and difficult to find
somewhere to pull in without hindering other traffic. He
finally found a place leaving just enough space for others
to squeeze past. He climbed out and mounted the bank.

He grabbed at the bushes to pull himself up to a vantage
point. He had plenty of cover from the opposite banks and
knew that for the moment he was out of sight of anyone
over there. The sun filtered through scattering clouds and
sparkled off the water, at times blinding him. Galvin
levelled off and worked his way along. He had selected a
spot that was thick with cover. He wedged himself behind
a bush on the slope and unhooked his binoculars.

There was a cluster of three villas on the lower slopes
across the water. They seemed to be very close together

but there was a good deal of dead ground between them and Galvin knew that they were very well separated. He raised the glasses to the higher points and the villas became more separated still; some of the approaches to more isolated dwellings were more difficult to negotiate and he could pick out the stone-lined drives sprinkled with cascading border plants and flowers, some still in bloom.

It was a painstaking vigil for he wasn't exactly sure which of the villas housed Tierney and his mob. His reason told him that it was likely to be one of the more inaccessible, and the more isolated. Some of the villas were second homes or weekend cottages and weren't always occupied. Some were rented out on occasion, others empty for most of the year. Strangers wouldn't be particularly noticed because strangers were drawn to the place. And nearby Kinsale, because of its attraction to the international yachting fraternity, boasted some fine restaurants. It was a good place not to be noticed; Kinsale survived on visitors.

Galvin picked out a car on the forecourt of one of the upper villas, huddled below the rugged skyline of bush and trees. He stiffened. Round the corner of the villa, almost out of sight, he could just see part of the bullnose of a Morris 1000. There were so many of them around in Ireland that at first it wasn't significant until he considered that the type of person who owned villas like these might run to a more expensive model. It was too far away and the angle too difficult for him to read the registration number. He concentrated on the windows. There was no immediate sign of occupation.

It was difficult to know what to do. He wasn't in the best position and he was becoming too aware of how awkwardly his car was parked. The last thing he wanted was the police to become interested, and he wasn't even sure that he had located Tierney's villa. It had a name according to the slip he had picked up at the farm but there was no name outside so far as he could see. He hung on, reluctant to give up.

Someone came outside and went to the car on the forecourt. An average-sized, dark-haired man, with a positive, restless movement. He opened the car door sharply and although Galvin couldn't see him poking around inside he had little difficulty in recognising the quick, almost impatient, movements. When he had finished and emerged with a coat over his arm he moved swiftly round the car and it was obvious that he was quickly assessing the tyre pressures. Satisfied, he went back inside.

Galvin sat back. He had seen that man before somewhere. He raised the glasses once more but either by accident or design, whoever was in the villa was keeping away from the windows. He was sure that he knew the man. Galvin was suddenly very alert. It wasn't one of Tierney's mob, at least not one of those he had previously seen, and yet *if* Tierney was there he had to be.

Galvin was suddenly alerted; he scrambled down the bank to blasting horns from below and when he reached ground level a truck was trying to get through the narrow gap he had left. The truck driver was cursing and Galvin squeezed his car out and continued up the rise heading for a connection with the Inishannon road. When he reached the junction he turned right and headed back towards Kinsale; it was his best chance of getting accommodation, providing he was willing to go out of town to a farm or boarding house. While he drove his mind was working furiously. The man he had seen was out of context; he was sure he wasn't anyone from Dublin or up north.

It took time, flicking over the pages of memory. During his training he had gone through all the photographic files of known and suspected Irish terrorists but he was sure it wasn't one of them. And yet he had seen this man in Ireland; it was the one thing he was convinced of. The answer came suddenly and with it surprise. Milton Purcell. The American fund raiser. He had once come to Dublin a long time ago, not under his own name, for the meeting had been clandestine.

Milton Purcell. What the hell was he doing in Ireland? Galvin was now completely satisfied that it was Tierney and his crowd who were in the villa. Although he saw Tierney and Purcell as incompatible, for some reason they had found a need to be together. Galvin slowed as he reached the fringe of Kinsale. He would have to find

194

out what was happening. And for that he would need to get a damned sight closer to the villa than he had just done. He would have to wait for nightfall.

George Farrell was close to collapse. He was trussed in an airless cellar at the derelict farm. After he had been tied to the chair, and Helary had left, Mary Poulter had sat reading a magazine as if he wasn't there at all. When he had tried to talk to her she had gagged him with freezer tape and had gone on reading.

Cramps had started early in his lower calves and he had struggled in the chair trying to draw Mary's attention but if she heard him it made no difference; so far as she was concerned, Farrell did not exist. The pain had become so excruciating that he had finally toppled over, the sweat pouring off him and in the end had fainted from the pain.

The faint must have relaxed his muscles for when he came to, head on the floor, the pain had gone. He was conscious of being wet all over, a mixture of sweat and urine. He had never in his life felt so helpless or so degraded. Between the table legs he could see the carefully creased slacks and the neat ankles and shoes of Mary Poulter. He heard a page turn.

A long time later she said, "I'm tired of your fidgeting. I'm going to put you in the cellar." What remained of Farrell's spirit left him.

She released him from the chair by untying one limb at a time, after warning him that she'd shoot him if he struggled. In fact he could barely move at all. She told him to lie face downwards, holding the gun at his head as a reminder of what would happen if he didn't, and retied his wrists together behind his back and then bound his ankles. He was now free of the chair and she dragged him clear of the table. The cellar was under the kitchen and was reached through a tattered carpet-covered trapdoor.

Pushing the big table aside to gain access she pulled back the shabby carpet and raised the trap. There were wooden steps leading down into the gloom. Farrell could smell the foul dankness mingled with other, nauseating odours; the trap probably hadn't been opened for years and it was best not to think about what the cellar might have been used for.

Mary Poulter showed no expression as she dragged him to the edge, her gun in her waistband. Farrell silently pleaded, eyes full of fear. But his plea left her untouched and she pushed until he fell down the stairs.

He was a quivering, bruised mess when his body stopped rolling and by that time the trap had already been closed. Oh, God, why hadn't she removed the gag? He wept unashamedly then, for there was nobody to see him and he could feel his tears moistening the crust of dust covering the stone floor. He was going to die slowly and painfully, trussed like a bird, alone and in the darkness and filth.

Where the hell had it all gone wrong? What of all the effort and money and the danger? Where was the reward, or at least the recognition, for the sacrifices he had made? He was even being denied a priest. He needed a priest as never before. But if he had one what would be his confession? Where now was his defence for what he had done?

Something moved a few feet from him. Not rats. Please not rats. A lifestyle of wealth and comfort had been reduced to this; he was being denied a decent death and had become a grovelling derelict, but even they died better than this.

As time wore on, he had no idea whether it was night or day for the darkness was constant. He began to hallucinate. He started to see images of the last minutes aboard Air Force One. Of the President. And his wife. Of the VIPs. The Soviet Ambassador. They had all gone. And he had played a large part in their going so violently. Perhaps it was right that he should die so slowly and in such uncomfortable degredation.

Farrell tried to sit up. If he wriggled backwards he might find a wall to lean against. It took some time to cover the ground, but when he found the support he needed he enjoyed temporary relief. But he knew he couldn't endure these conditions for long; no-one could. Okay, if he was guilty what of the people who had brought him here? What of them? Weren't they as bad? Weren't they killers

196

too? And just who the hell were they? The obvious never occurred to him.

"I want Detective Chief Superintendent Keane. This is Sean Hogan."

The switchboard operator kept him waiting, then Keane came on. "Hogan is it? What happened to the procedure?"

"Balls to the procedure. I've got to see you."

"Well now, are you coming to give yourself up?"

Hogan controlled himself, knowing that he had already gone too far at a time when he had to be diplomatic. But he was not forgetting that Keane, of Special Branch, was one of those hard-headed coppers who believed that the Sinn Fein should be outlawed just as the IRA had been so many years ago. However, it was the wrong time to argue. "Can we meet outside somewhere?"

"What's it about?"

"Someone has claimed the Provos have kidnapped an American called Farrell. It's in all the papers. It's nothing to do with us."

"Us, Hogan? I'm glad you're admitting membership at last."

"I meant them; I'm speaking on their behalf." Hogan was annoyed that he was so shaken as to make such an elementary mistake.

"Okay, Hogan, I'll make a note of the protest. Is that it?"

"It's not as simple as that. I need to see you. Christ, do you think I'd be ringing you if it wasn't urgent?"

"You mean urgent to you. There's a little matter like the murder of the President of the United States that takes a little of my time just now. Unless you can help us on that you'll be wasting my time right now."

"We're being fitted up for that, too."

Keane laughed. "Well now, you poor bugger. Hogan it's not you who should be making this call. You're supposed to be the innocent, political animal; get Tierney or one of your other gorillas to get in touch. Or are they otherwise engaged just now?"

Hogan was having difficulty in keeping himself in check, although he well knew that Keane was trying to goad him. "So you won't see me?"

197

"I'll send a squad car round to your place to pick you up."

Another provocation. "I can save you the journey. I'm not too far from Brown Thomas. I'll wait there for the car."

Keane delayed his reply. Then quickly, "Make sure you're there in half an hour." He put the phone down, looking thoughtful and not a little smug.

Brown Thomas – the Dublin equivalent of London's Fortnum & Mason – was owned by the same Canadian multi-millionaire, Galen Weston. The original Georgian property was in fashionable Grafton Street, an unlikely place for Hogan to be.

When the car arrived Hogan was standing outside the central window of the store between the two doors. He did not realise that it was a police car until it pulled in and to his surprise the rear window wound down and Keane shoved his lined face out and shouted. Hogan crossed the pavement and Keane spoke brusquely. "Get in."

Hogan opened the door not too pleased about sitting so close to one of his sworn enemies. But there was nothing he could do about that. Both big men, there was no room between them as the car pulled out.

"Okay," Keane said briskly, "Out with it."

Hogan could feel the heat of Keane's leg and tried to pull his own away. "Someone's trying to drop the Provos in it."

"My heart bleeds for you. You told me that much over the phone."

Hogan felt a fool; he should have thought through more carefully how he should tackle this and Keane had no intention of making it easy for him. "Look, there's something funny going on. Just how professional was the Farrell kidnap?"

Keane smiled. "You seriously expect me to tell you? It's not just the kidnap that's troubling you, is it? There's something else on your mind. Well, you'd better be quick. I've got an appointment."

"There's a whole pattern of things. That bombing the other day; everyone's come down on us, yet an Arab was seen around the place according to the papers."

Keane smoothed back his thick hair. "You really take the

198

biscuit," he said, openly voicing his contempt. "Everyone knows the Provos did it. You know, I know, the Yanks know, and even the Brits are convinced. Your bunch were getting your Yankie colleagues off the hook. It wouldn't surprise me if they planned it."

Hogan kept his temper. "If you're so bloody sure why haven't you pulled them in?"

"Don't keep insulting my intelligence, Hogan. I could go through the motions and pull a lot of your crowd in, make waves, please the public and a few politicians. But this job is too big to bugger about, we're too stretched to ask a lot of questions when we already have most of the answers." He glanced out of the window to see that they were now crossing the Liffey by O'Connell Bridge. "Certain of your mob have gone to earth. We're a comparatively small force covering a huge area. You know this and trade on it."

Half way down O'Connell Street Keane called out to his driver, "Turn into Talbot Street and head for the Station." He then turned to Hogan. "You're a pain in the neck, Hogan, and you're wasting my time. Tierney and his boys have got to surface some time. We'll squeeze them out. And you'd better remember that this time they have nowhere to run. No country will have them, unless they want to spend the rest of their days rotting somewhere like Libya. But they have to get out first. And all we have to do is to wait."

"I keep telling you we didn't do the Farrell job and we didn't do the West Cork job; we're being fitted up."

"I know you do and I keep asking myself why you're suddenly denying something your mob would normally brag about. I tell you something else, too; when Tierney comes from his bolt hole it won't be any use his chasing off to America. Even the American Irish Senators who have so often helped you by fighting the extradition laws wouldn't be so stupid this time. They must get their beliefs from fairy stories, the little people. They know as much about modern Irish affairs as you do about speaking Mandarin. They won't protect you. Nobody in the western world will. You're in the proverbial shit, Hogan."

"Okay. I've wasted my time. I thought I'd be helping us both."

"Balls. You're trying to help yourself."

"Supposing we find Farrell for you?"

"That wouldn't be difficult as you already have him."

Hogan felt his gorge rise. He cursed Purcell. Not only had he achieved nothing but this meeting had probably made matters worse. "I wouldn't be sitting next to you in a police car if that were true. I thought we might swop a little information and find him before it's too late."

"Okay, let's do that. You produce Farrell and we'll take it from there. And I'll give you any pointers I get. Quid pro quo. At the moment I've nothing to give you because I think your lot did it."

"Thanks for nothing." Hogan replied heavily.

Keane called out to his driver, "Stop here." He turned to Hogan. "This good enough for you?"

Hogan hadn't been following the route. He looked out and realised he had to get back across the river. But he climbed out without another word and slammed the car door behind him.

A little later, when Keane was discussing the unusual meeting with his friend, Chief Inspector Matt O'Riordon, he took a different view from the one shown to Hogan. "I think your hunch was right, Matt," he said. "Hogan's worried and I believe him; I don't think the Provos did do the Farrell job but why has it driven him to contact us openly? Keep an eye on him. It might be worth it."

Ross left his house in a benevolent frame of mind and went down the steps to the well-worn pavement with its filled-in pot holes and crossed the street to his car. His professionalism was not affected by his buoyant mood. He was adept at taking stock without seeming to. Even in the car he skilfully used his mirrors, almost like a cockpit drill, and he didn't drive off until he was quite satisfied.

The moment he crossed the street FBI agents, who had rented an apartment slightly up the street from him, locked up and ran down the stairs. They had their car facing the same way as Ross's and pulled out behind another car which passed them. They had done this for the last two days and guessed that Ross was heading for one of two destinations. After a short while they knew which of the two and they relaxed a little; he was going to get his gear. With just a minimum of luck, before the end of the day they should have prevented a murder and would have arrested Ross in the course of committing a felony. And that would create a firm platform for launching an attack against him on the much bigger issue. They too were feeling good that day.

They followed the familiar route through Brooklyn around Jamaica Bay heading south towards Floyd Bennett Field and the Marine Park Bridge. They could afford to drop back even though they changed their car daily, a condition their chief had imposed, because they already knew the route. There could be no negligence over this job and they took care to keep him in distant sight.

Once they were on the Marine Park Bridge they dropped back even further; ahead was the Nassau County peninsula which fingered out into the sea forming the bay on one side with the Atlantic brooding off the other. As they reached the end of the bridge Fort Tilden occupied a site to their right on the other side of the peninsula, and to its left was Jacob Riis Park.

Now was the time for extra caution as they were more easily on view. They had Ross well in sight and eased off still more as he headed towards the tip of the peninsula beyond Fort Tilden. They pulled in behind an old building which had once been part of a boatyard but which was now mainly used as children's unofficial club house. At this particular time the place was deserted and one man climbed out with binoculars to watch Ross's movements.

He stopped outside a rough wooden building which in its time had served as a small warehouse, lockups and even a marine supply store. It had been in a bad way when he had bought it. He unlocked two heavy padlocks and pulled back one of the doors. There was nothing visible inside but junk. Empty paint and oil cans littered the place and to his right a workbench with an old-fashioned vice was bolted to the concrete floor. There were tool boxes, broken crates and planks of wood and another workbench over by the far wall. It wasn't until he had locked himself in that Ross began to reveal the workshop's true purpose.

It was a tedious procedure but had nevertheless stood him well. The sound legs that held the huge benches were wood, encased in solid steel and he had to unbolt these to get at the contents they held. He could only unbolt one leg

201

at a time otherwise the hefty bench top would have toppled.

So that the explosive did not sweat Ross never over-loaded the cavities and there were air holes bored through the wood and the steel on the inside of the bench legs. As he went through the routine of moving one of the legs he noticed that one of the bolts was loose; he was always careful about tightening the bolts before leaving; it was an imperative safety precaution. For a moment he thought someone had been tampering. He hastened to make sure everything was there, the inventory kept in his head.

The watching FBI agents were blown off their feet even though they were still some distance away. The massive blast seemed as if it would rupture the whole peninsula, it went on and on as each hidden cache of explosive was caught by the enormous detonation. The earth trembled and a huge fireball belched smoke and flame which cut off the sea and formed a searing barrier that continued to explode intermittently. As the badly shaken FBI agents clambered to their feet they could only stare at the continuing devastation enacted before them. Ash and debris cascaded down and with it tiny, unrecognisable pieces of flesh and bone that had once been Hank Ross. One short pull on the bench leg had triggered the sophisticated booby-trap and cost Hank Ross his life.

16

John Smith saw Hank Ross leave his house and remained seated in his car. Although some distance away, he had a sufficiently clear view as Ross crossed the street and drove off. Not long afterwards the FBI agents came hurrying into view; Smith watched them follow Ross. He climbed out and walked slowly towards Ross's apartment house. He went up the steps and let himself into the hall.

He had no problem in springing the lock on Ross's front door and he slipped inside the overcrowded and untidy living room. So much was strewn about the place that it was ready made for what he wanted. He slipped a clip of old British newspaper articles about the IRA in Northern Ireland into some magazines, some going back as far as the death of Bobby Sands. And he placed a few stained beer mats, each with a printed shamrock and a Republican Irish slogan, into a drawer of the shoddy sideboard.

He pondered the danger of over-kill and resisted the temptation to leave the official Sinn Fein news-sheet; it might be better not to plant anything so blatantly obvious. He decided to leave it at that. Satisfied that he had done enough, he left, locking up carefully after him.

The Liffey closed in, lights stringing along the shoreline reflecting gently on water now so smooth that the wind seemed never to touch it. The dark line of the bridge humped over the river leaving murky smudges under its arches. And beyond Inns Quay and the far side of the bridge, the Law Courts lifted into a rotund silhouette, the main building beneath the dome partly lost in the darkness except for the huge, almost luminous pillars.

The sea-going launch barely moved, the swing of its bows almost imperceptible. It was movement enough for Sean Hogan. He had never liked being on or in water.

He couldn't swim and had long given up trying to learn. He was a landsman and Tyson's suggestion that they should put out to sea had been one more upset on a whole day of them. They were overshadowed by the bank, beautifully private, and he had seen no need to move at all.

"For a strong man you're acting like a rabbit," Tyson observed acidly. On a personal basis he had nothing in common with Hogan at all and detested the rough character of the man, even though he acknowledged Hogan's astuteness.

"It's all right for the likes of you," Hogan retorted. "You were born with money, had your first yacht shoved in your Christmas stocking as a kid, so you did. And all at our bloody expense."

It was an old argument. Tyson was Anglo-Irish, his Irish ancestry going back four hundred years. But to Hogan, Tyson's loyalties were clearly on the other side of the water, in England, where he had been educated: Harrow and then Oxford like his father before him and his children since. He could not accept the obvious contradiction.

Yet Tyson's background had perhaps been as influential to his later actions as had Hogan's. Somewhere, somehow, Tyson had followed a course as unlikely as the circumstances which had led to his present meeting with Hogan. They had nothing in common except perhaps the most binding thing of all. In just one respect they followed the same path. Cynical of almost everything about Tyson, Hogan was satisfied that whatever Tyson did was for money, even though there was no evidence that he had ever been short of it.

Tyson had only to open his mouth to make Hogan squirm as the English public school accent flowed out. The other thing that annoyed Hogan was that Tyson was undoubtedly highly intelligent and that he sometimes made Hogan feel inferior. As Hogan saw it, a man like Tyson, born with a silver spoon in his mouth, Irish silver at that, should be a high-class buffoon and it riled him that he was anything but. Hogan saw Tyson as a champagne communist.

The two men rarely met and even that was too often

for Hogan. When they did meet it was always important. They now sat in the large cabin, Hogan with a pint of Guinness on the polished table and Tyson opposite him with a glass of white wine; they never sat side by side.

Tyson wore a blazer with a yachting emblem on the brass buttons, and grey slacks. He was a tall, elegant man with thin aristocratic features and a slight look of disdain as he stared at the rough-and-ready Hogan sitting opposite with his pint.

"Right, old chap. What's the problem?"

"Lay off Milton Purcell. Get the message back to your Russian friends."

"Purcell? Good God, is he here?"

"Wherever he is."

Tyson gazed across the table, incredulous. "That's why you've come here? To say that?"

"It's important to us. There'll never be another like him. It could take years to replace him. He's a one-off; the one man *everybody* can trust. The one man who can cope. He's done a terrific job for us."

"I'm not arguing. He's a very sound man. Why are you concerned?"

"Don't try bullshitting me, Tyson." Hogan was in his element when he had reason to be coarse to Tyson.

"I'm sorry. I don't understand. Is he being threatened?"

"Sure, he's being threatened. Like Farrell's being threatened and God knows who else."

"Who the devil is Farrell?"

"You don't read the papers? Who're you kidding? I told you to cut the bull."

"*That* Farrell? Good grief what are you saying? Someone claimed that the Provos did it."

"And as you well know someone wants it believed that we did. It can work both ways, you know, Tyson. We're bloody livid about this. Tell them to lay off or Farrell won't be the only bugger to disappear. You sort it out or you'd better go over your bloody boat every time you come aboard; she'd make a nice firecracker. I'll say it one more time, tell them to *lay off Milton Purcell.*"

Riley Brown gave Hercules his meal, topped up his

water, and wondered why Galvin hadn't telephoned. It was unlike him. It was not knowing what was happening that niggled her. Why was she so worried about him?

She made some tea and drank it absentmindedly while she stood in the kitchen. On impulse she put down the cup and rang the garage. Yet when she spoke to Paddy O'Brien he knew less about Galvin's whereabouts than she did; for some reason he thought he was still in Cork; Galvin hadn't told him he was flying to England to see how his sister was progressing.

The next thing to do then was to telephone the Nursing Home or Galvin's brother-in-law. She remembered the name of the home, the Denbridge at Reading, but did not know its number. She turned to the table where Galvin kept his little book of telephone numbers. It wasn't there. She searched around and still could not find it. He must have taken it with him. Her heart began to thump.

Riley realised that she could get the number through directory enquiries, but she did not know his sister's married name. Joan was it? But Joan who? The same thing happened when she thought of his brother-in-law who lived in Newbury. It was a silly thing but she simply did not know the surname and didn't think it had ever been mentioned. She had no way of contacting him. She had been cut off. But why would Galvin do this to her?

After his unwelcome guest had left the boat Tyson took his time. As he replenished his wine, the ice bucket now openly on the table, he knew that the advice he must give would have to be accurate, for none knew the Irish political scene better than he and that included the outlawed organisations in particular. Tyson was respected on both sides of the law, which would have amazed many people. Equally, he himself would have been surprised that others well knew of his adroit political juggling.

He finished a second glass of wine and made his decision: a priority had been established.

He made a telephone call from the nearest public phone booth, and asked for an extension number. Once through, on recognising the voice, he spoke the sentence:

"It would seem that the elusive Purcell is here somewhere." Then he hung up.

Paul Sutter met Glenn Rees in Cork. They walked up St
Patrick's Street and turned into Merchant's Quay, crossed
the busy street and leaned on the parapet overlooking
the River Lee. To their left people hurried across the
bridge and behind them could be heard the constant
noise of traffic. The river was low and sluggish and the
sky overcast but it was quite warm for a late October
morning and neither man wore a raincoat.

"A helluva lot's happening and I'd like to know what
it's all about," Sutter said with feeling. "I've got precious
little out of Gerry Fowler and I think he's playing some
crafty game of his own. He's a cunning son-of-a-bitch
but I can't complain at this stage because he's put at least
one of his deep cover boys on the line. It's just that I find
he's too ready to take the easy option. What have you
found out, Glenn?"

"No more than you. If you think the Brits are up to
monkey business then so are the Irish. Maybe they're
doing it together. We've lost a President but, as shocked
as they undoubtedly are, I've a hunch that it's not their
first priority. It was *our* President. Our issue is simple:
we want the bastards who did it. I think the Brits and the
Irish do too but they see some political mileage in it, and
are trying to turn the situation to their advantage."

Both men were leaning with their arms folded along
the top of the stonework, a smell of oil and petrol fumes
creeping up behind them. The Air Attaché turned his
head. "You can almost feel the undercurrents. This
business about George Farrell is one of them. Now why
would the Provos do that at this time?"

"It's typical of them. Money meets fanatacism. A
dangerous mixture. Had you heard of Farrell before?"

"No. We did an open check through the Embassy. He's
an investment banker. Can well afford the ransom
they're asking but the Irish are dead against paying
anything, as we are."

"But how did they know he was here?" asked Sutter
gazing at a wheeling seagull. "The usual snatches in this
country are of locally established, wealthy businessmen

207

or foreigners who have factories over here and have been living here for some time. They usually take time to formulate a plan. This is a quickie but it still smells like pros. You think there's any connection?"

Rees peered down into the water rippling past the bridge. "With Air Force One? How do you arrive at that?"

"Farrell's an Irish name. Maybe he's tied in with the boyos on our side and they've fallen out. Think about it: when was an American businessman last snatched in Ireland? The FBI are doing an in-depth check on him; maybe they'll come up with a connection."

Farrell was bubbling through his mouth tape. Half deranged, his thoughts became wilder and more confused as time passed. His nostrils were blocked with dust and his breathing was increasingly difficult. At moments his mind cleared and he would conquer the terror that was gradually pushing him towards insanity. When lucid he would think logically, go over everything that had happened and try to produce some answers.

After these spells of futile analysis he would again lapse into despair; his discomfort, the cramps, the terrible darkness, the smells would all get to him and the fears develop again. He was in an abyss and it was far too late to appreciate the comforts he had previously enjoyed: money, friends, home, Judy. He couldn't even bring her to mind, her image hazy. Yet he could somehow smell her perfume. In this stinking, filthy cellar he could still smell her heady scent. And it was driving him mad.

He had found the sitting position, propped against the wall, the best during his waking hours. He never really slept but dozed a lot and the pain of bound wrists and ankles always penetrated to wake him again. Sometimes he was so exhausted that he lost sight of what was happening but those moments of relief were all too brief.

He was sitting in this position when he heard the guitar; it caught him in a moment of relative clarity. The sound came from above and reached him quite clearly. Somebody was up there. Farrell tried to shout but the

208

effort barely penetrated his gag. He forced a scream from the back of his throat and almost choked himself. He pushed himself upright against the wall and his legs somehow supported him.

In a desperate effort he managed to reach the stairs, although he couldn't actually see them. He hooked himself on to the planks and started to climb in a sitting position. He knew that he couldn't get out – for the trap was firmly fixed – but if he could bang his head against it he might be heard. As he worked his way up he was assailed by the stench of his own body. At one time he almost fell off the side of the stairs but managed to hold his position. He reached the trap, the strains of a Spanish lament quite clear and beautiful. He balled himself up and was about to thump his head against the wood when, incredibly, someone opened it.

The light blinded him as the trap was lifted and revealed the form of a woman fuzzed and haloed, a brilliant aura right round her. It was the greatest moment of Farrell's life until Mary Poulter said, "He likes your playing, honey." Farrell nearly fell down the stairs in shock. His spirits sank lower than they had ever been. He gradually eased himself down before they could kick him off the stairs.

Farrell couldn't watch her come down. The light, now dull though it was, was painful to his eyes. He had found hope and it had abandoned him as quickly. Just then he was so numbed that he was incapable of any thought. But he could hear the woman he knew as Mary Poulter and her tread was light on the stairs. The guitar was still strumming above and then suddenly it stopped.

"Stand back." It was Helary calling before he let a chair drop down the angle of the stairs. Mary caught it as it landed. Helary came down swiftly. He had left the trap open so that some light came through but Farrell was in a protective coital position and was babbling softly to himself.

Helary stepped over Farrell and placed the chair in the patch of light escaping into the cellar. He said to his wife, "We've got to get him on the chair, it's too awkward to work on him like that."

Farrell wasn't listening; he had begun to hum to himself.

209

They struggled to lift his dead weight and managed to get him on the chair where they bound him, leaving his present binding as it was, but making it impossible for him to fall or throw himself off the chair. Helary pulled Farrell's head back by the hair; Farrell had his eyes closed and was still humming, at last finding a defensive device.

"Can you hear me, you ass-hole?" Helary shouted.

Farrell didn't answer.

"Hold the chair tight," Helary instructed his wife. When she was ready he gave Farrell a hefty smack round the face sending his head sideways. Blood showed on Farrell's cheek and he opened his eyes in surprise. The blow had been savagely painful but had also cleared his mind.

"Nod if you can hear me?"

Farrell nodded, not sure of this latest development. Without warning Helary reached forward and tore the strips of tape from Farrell's mouth. The relief was so great that Farrell didn't feel the pain.

"Good. Now collect your wits and we'll be kind to you. Where's Purcell?"

Farrell expressed surprise but found he couldn't speak. He was desperately thirsty. He licked his swollen lips and gazed uncomprehendingly at Helary.

"You'd better get him some water. By the stench of him he's lost all his fluid."

Mary went up the stairs and came back with a jug. She tipped some over Farrell's head to freshen him and then held the jug to his lips. He drank greedily and had a fit of coughing. No wine had ever tasted better.

When satisfied with Farrell's condition Helary asked again, "Where's Milton Purcell?"

It took time for the name to register. He shook his head and droplets of water ran down his face. He was finding bliss in unbelievably simple things. "I don't know," he replied.

Helary didn't waste time. "Take his shoes and socks off."

When Mary bent down in front of Farrell she found that one shoe was already off. Keeping her head well back she removed the shoe and socks.

"What are you doing?" croaked Farrell.

"I'm going to burn your feet off until you tell me where Purcell is. It's no coincidence that you're over here at the same time."

"I don't know." screamed Farrell. "I didn't even know he was here." He was barely coherent.

There was a strong ring of truth in Farrell's denial, however garbled. Helary glanced at his wife. "We'd better make sure."

She nodded and taped Farrell's mouth up again as Helary produced a cigarette lighter and some matches. Mary held Farrell's shoulders while Helary went to work. Half an hour later she released the quivering, jibbering Farrell who almost took the chair with him as he fell sideways. Helary quickly caught him and pushed him upright. Mary reached round from the back, apparently unmoved by the torture her husband had inflicted and the immense suffering Farrell had endured, and tore off the tapes once more.

"Where's Purcell?" demanded Helary quietly.

Farrell was almost beyond answering but Helary was an expert on the extent of human limits. Helary leaned close to Farrell and just picked up a garbled "don't know". He sighed with disappointment. Again he looked at his wife. "Maybe we shouldn't be surprised. I can't see Purcell risking himself with this garbage. Okay, we can do no more. See to it."

Farrell was beyond knowing what was happening which was merciful. The excruciating pain in his feet suddenly stopped as Mary Poulter put a ·38 slug through the back of his head with the indifference of the cold-blooded. Farrell did not see the mess it made. His war was over.

Galvin lowered the binoculars. For two days he had been watching the rear of one of the villas from high ground above it. It had not been easy for him to find a convenient parking place where the car wouldn't be noticeable. And the distance had made it impossible to use his galium arsenide laser. It was too heavy and awkward to carry to his present position and from anywhere more accessible he would probably be seen. So

211

he had chosen the hard way.

The view below was of a few well-scattered villas among the shrubs and trees. The sea was blue and empty here, but to his right, where the estuary widened and curved, yachts and boats of all kinds were moored in profusion. But he was not there to admire the beauty of the scenery. He was perched behind a thick clump of bushes in a sitting position, resting his elbows on his knees to take some of the weight of the heavy-duty binoculars. It was wearying work and as yet he'd had little to show for it. Tierney and his mob were keeping a low profile but gradually Galvin had built up a list of those staying in the villa.

The most interesting occupant was Milton Purcell. He was completely out of context with the rest. There had been no sign at all of Eugene Hayes and Galvin wondered whether he had gone back across the border to Ulster. There would have been little point in his staying now that the job was done. But the others had to stay out of sight and must know that the police would be painstakingly searching for them, or waiting patiently for them to show themselves.

Galvin knew that Tierney, and people like him, were used to the waiting game. They could hole up in discomfort for as long as was necessary. They knew how to keep their heads down and when to move on. But here, in this particular villa, they had all the facilities they needed and could take it in turn to go out and to buy food and necessities.

Galvin reached for a sandwich. He needed to get to Purcell. He was a man who would know more about what was actually going on than Tierney. Connolly was also there. It was too distant to see how he appeared after his beating but he was moving around all right. Galvin had to be satisfied with odd sightings. He had established that apart from Purcell, Tierney and Connolly, there were three other men, two of whom he knew slightly and another he thought he recognised. Michael Daley, who idolised Tierney; Johnnie Mooney, a hot-head who would last no time at all without the others to keep him in some sort of order. In a group of hot-heads, Mooney was the most impulsive. Galvin thought the last man was

212

called Sullivan. He couldn't recall actually meeting him but the name and the image had stuck in his memory. Apart from that Galvin knew little about him.

As Galvin picked up his binoculars again he reflected that one of those men was carrying his own life in his own hands and had been consistently laying a trail. Galvin also suspected that the carelessness with the torch at the farm had been a deliberate warning of the trap set for him; he owed this man his life. As Purcell, Tierney and Connolly could be excluded it had to be Daley, Mooney or Sullivan. But there was absolutely no way of knowing which one.

There was no pattern to the movements of the men in the villa and Galvin would have been surprised if there had been. They spent more time in than out and so far they had not all gone out together. The largest number to leave the villa had been three. Purcell had not left the villa at any time except to go to his car or sometimes sit on a garden chair on the rear terrace, but he had never gone for a trip like the others. There had to be a reason and Galvin felt strongly that if he could isolate Purcell he would come up with some answers.

The strong prevailing westerly had broken the clouds up into fascinating formations and a weak sun was misting through. At the villa there had been no outside movement all morning and one of the rear-room curtains was still drawn across as if somebody was still in bed. Galvin changed position to ease his legs. He was wearing a shoulder holster and found it uncomfortable and the Browning heavy. He took a drink from his flask then gazed around the low hills and along his side of the bank to make sure nobody could see him.

It was early afternoon before anything happened and Galvin was finding it difficult to keep awake. He was at an angle to the villa, not directly behind it so that he had a limited view of what happened on the forecourt. It was a compromise position and not ideal. Although he could see movement at the front, initially it was by seeing a shadow and he could not see who it was or how many. A car started up, the engine being excessively revved. Then the Morris 1000 came into view.

Galvin had to be quick for once the car reached the

end of the forecourt it would turn sharp right down the hill and away from him. He was left with a very short time to assess how many were in the car. Four. He couldn't believe it. He visually followed the car down the hill trying to confirm through the small rear window that he had actually seen four heads. But it was impossible to do and he had to be satisfied with his first sighting.

That meant two men were left in the villa and one of those was probably Purcell. They were odds he was willing to take. He waited. The car was now out of sight below him and he wouldn't see it again until it crossed the bridge provided it followed that route. He refocused on the bridge.

Then it came, like a slowly moving beetle crawling over the narrow stretch of concrete supported by its dozen cylindrical pillars with their pancake bases. At the end of the bridge the car turned right and was now side on to Galvin. He tried to pick out the number of passengers again but the angle was wrong and he could only see two men his side. Yet he was sure there were four. He waited until the car disappeared round a curve of the coast road and then focused again on the villa.

All the curtains were now drawn back. There was nobody on view. He could not wait too long. He had to take a chance. He made sure the Browning moved freely in the holster, removed the binoculars and hid them in the bushes. He crawled down the slope trying to keep under cover. From time to time he glanced across the road on the other side of the estuary to make sure the car wasn't returning.

The nearer he came to the villa the less he saw of it as he crawled over dead ground until at times he could barely see the top of its roof. He slowed down and listened. Nothing. He continued on and then the roof began to take more form and the undergrowth thickened.

When a dustbin lid clattered he stopped. He could see nothing but not far from him someone swore and the lid clanged once again. He waited before crawling on. There was a straight line of shrubs some twenty feet

214

from him and he realised that they must form part of the garden.

Galvin approached the shrub line and lay prone to peer through. The villa was less than twenty-five feet from him. Immediately below was a long, wide, multi-coloured slabbed terrace that continued up to the building. The problem was that there was a straight drop of some eight feet almost immediately below him. At the boundary end of the terrace the ground had been excavated sheer instead of being stepped.

He could see quite clearly into a drawing room; one man was reading and another was fiddling with a radio. He edged along so that he was out of sight of the lounge, found he was now facing small opaque windows which had to be bathrooms and toilets, took one last look towards the lounge and then slithered down the bank. The nearest door to him was locked and probably led to the kitchen because two dustbins were at one side of it. He crept round the side of the villa and found bedroom windows. He could see into them quite clearly. All the windows were modern and double glazed; that created a problem.

Edging round the front of the house he knew that the lounge was at the far end and he could now see that there was a deep porch. All the windows were closed which didn't surprise him. It might help if he knew who was in the lounge. He crept past the recessed front door, noticed the spy hole, and continued on to the lounge windows. If they hadn't changed position both men were facing this way.

Galvin crouched and pushed himself up slowly to peer through the lower corner of the window. He withdrew just as slowly. Purcell and Michael Daley. He squatted against the wall and gazed across the water. No sign of the Morris yet but time was now critical. He rolled away and straightened against the wall.

There was only one effective way of getting in that he could see. Crouching again he crawled past the angle of the house towards the exit drive, rose, and then walked heavily and quickly towards the front door whistling loudly. He kept his head averted as he went past the drawing room windows, swung into the porch, rang the bell and turned his back to the door still whistling and outrageously off-key.

Galvin had one hand in his pocket and the other, at chest level, held the Browning, safety catch off. He could feel himself being scrutinized through the spy hole. He broke into song so that if someone called out through the door to ask his business he could pretend not to hear. It was a gamble; it always was.

The door opened but Galvin didn't wait to see any more; he swung round swiftly and smashed the door back as soon as it was ajar. He had a brief glimpse of a startled, wild-eyed Daley whose reflex action brought a gun into view from behind his back but Galvin crashed his Browning round the side of Daley's head before he could do anything about it.

17

Joe Aspel was summoned to James Powell's office and he knew immediately that it spelt trouble. Powell appeared quite calm as he told Aspel to take a seat. "You heard what's happened?" asked Powell taking out a cigar.

"The bomber blew himself up while our men were watching."

"Crap," said Powell.

"Oh?"

"This guy could handle nitro in his sleep according to all the reports I have. You got something different?"

"No. No matter how well a man knows his stuff he can still make mistakes."

"Not that kind, Joe. Not that man. Do you know he never had a conviction?"

Aspel didn't reply. Of course he knew. He was sitting there to be the butt for Powell's bad mood, so he decided to say as little as possible.

"Never had a conviction," repeated Powell. "Clever. A slob by all accounts but clever just the same. Blew himself up? In his own bomb factory? I don't go for it. He was hit and by somebody cleverer than himself and by someone who knew as much about his own game as he did. Now that makes a rare bird, doesn't it?"

"According to the New York reports he was setting up another job. It's possible that he was getting ready for it when it went sour."

Powell nodded wisely. He felt a little better now the cigar was going. "That's what they want us to believe, isn't it? Well, it's difficult to blame the New York team for what happened; they lost a few eyebrows themselves. They intended to pull him in as soon as he had set his bomb; they had to wait for that to pin something real on him. What have you got on Ross's target?"

Aspel hadn't been looking forward to this question. "Nothing. A junior manager in a computer business. No record, no linkage with the mob or anyone like that. Mr Average." He could feel the steeliness of Powell's stare from across the room.

"And you tell me that Ross took himself out? There never was a target. It was a set-up. Someone's ahead of you all along the line and I'm choking on it; that and the inability of the FBI to cope with it."

Aspel sat with crossed legs and folded arms, staring at the plush carpet.

"So where do we go from here?" continued Powell. "I'm asking because our new President would like to know. Not unreasonably. I mean he could be next."

There was no obvious sarcasm in Powell's tone but Aspel was under no illusion. "There was some stuff in Ross's apartment that could link him to the IRA. And there's that strange business of the banker George Farrell being kidnapped in Ireland."

"That it? We've been reduced to those two items, the first of which you can throw in the trash can? That's part of the set-up. And Joe, I know you think so to. Don't try to placate me. After a reasonably good start we're running out of options."

"It's a round-the-clock job. Something will come out of it."

"Maybe. What worries me is that even if it does is it going to disappear in front of our eyes like the rest has done? Have you any leads on Milton Purcell yet? We must trace that son-of-a-bitch."

"He's simply disappeared. We've also checked in Ireland on both sides of the border. Nobody's heard a word about him. Maybe he's been hit too."

Powell shook his head slowly. "He's around. Find him."

Aspel said, "We figure that the bomb was in the form of an attaché case, both exterior and lining made of high explosive plastic. The detonators were probably fixed through the hinges."

"And how did it get on board?"

Aspel spoke carefully. "Squire could have asked Rossi to deliver goodies to a friend of his in London; probably showed him the contents. That would account for why the bomb was in the hold."

"There's one flaw with that idea. Maybe because the

218

Soviet Ambassador was on board, sniffer dogs and PD-4s were used." Powell laid his hands flat on his desk; Aspel could see the worst was coming. "Even if the dogs had a bad day a PD-4 is so sensitive that it can pick out one particle of explosive for every million parts of air."

Aspel was about to voice a retort when he thought better of it. Perhaps Powell was already aware of it but he did not think his chief was trying to goad him or score points. He nodded. "I did know. We'll just have to keep on working at it."

"Find Purcell," Powell instructed again.

Mandy Squire was drawn to the newspaper report as if it had been printed especially for her. At first she thought it was strange, how it so quickly caught her eye. And then she realised why. George Farrell. The moment she saw it she realised that it was the name she had heard Sam use on the telephone. She sat down at the kitchen table and read the article through.

Apart from the name, why should a news item about a New York banker who had been kidnapped in Ireland excite her so much? She read it again and sat back. There was a link between this news item and Sam. It was crazy but she knew it and she was pleased that she had been alone when it first caught her eye; she did not want to be talked out of her conviction. Anyway, there was an easy way to try to find out.

Mandy picked up the telephone and put it down immediately. She went upstairs and packed a case and went next door to ask her neighbour if she would look after the two girls for a couple of days. She called a cab and drove to Washington National Airport.

There were many good reasons why she should not have acted so impulsively: Mrs Farrell might be away; and she might be about to make an absolute fool of herself. It did not matter. The name of the bank had been mentioned in the news report and from that she could get their address and she could take it from there. Anyway, to get away from Georgetown for a day or two would be like escaping from a cage.

By now, Mandy was convinced that Sam had done a terrible thing and as a result had been unable to live with

219

it. She wanted to know exactly what and desperately hoped that this would be her first break. She felt a tremendous relief as she took her seat on the Eastern shuttle to New York, unaware that a tail was sitting two rows behind her. For the first time since Sam had died she was doing something positive. For the first time since his death she felt alive again.

The kidnapping of George Farrell had put a damper on his wife's liaison with Dave Santos. Farrell was in trouble and everything else would have to wait.

It did not take the media long to comment on the odd coincidence of Farrell's kidnapping taking place at a time when so much else was happening in Ireland. And from this, strange and unwonted rumours began to spread which worried many people; Santos and his partners were increasingly aware that it did not help their bank's reputation.

Santos had been in constant touch with the kidnap specialists in London, but the outlook seemed to be grim. There was little else he could do and he was preparing to leave earlier that day to visit Judy when the receptionist rang to say that a Mrs Squire wanted to contact Mrs Farrell.

"What does she want to see her about?"

"She says it's about Mr Farrell's kidnapping, sir."

"How does she strike you?"

"Quite serious."

"Send her up."

When Mandy Squire entered his office Santos at once noticed that she looked ill. Her eyes were haunted and it appeared that she might not have slept well for some time. There was a feverishness about her that disturbed him; "Sit down, please, Mrs Squire. I understand you have some news about George Farrell."

She sat on the edge of a chair, uneasy now that she was here, but determined. "I didn't say I have news of him, but that it's about him. You are his partner, I understand? It's Mrs Farrell I want to speak to."

"Let me hear you first. I promise you that I'll take you to see her at once if you have significant information. Where are you from?"

"Washington. My husband was in the Secret Service, a member of the President's detail. He died the same day as the President."

It was enough to rivet Santos to his chair. He sat back and listened with increasing concern. There was no proof of anything, no actual evidence. Santos realised that if he considered the whole business logically he would toss it out of the window. But it all came down to a matter of *feelings* and they dictated that he take Mandy Squire to see Judy Farrell. In his situation, any lead was worth following.

On hearing it all over again Santos could see how flimsy it all was but Judy was caught up in it straight away. When a calmer Mandy had finished relating events for the second time she felt a great weight lift from her mind. She did not know these people, but in their way they were just as anxious as she, and she trusted them instinctively.

The three of them sat in uneasy silence for some time before Santos said, "It's no use; we've got to tell the FBI. We can't stall on this. Let them sort out the detail. If we are reading too much into this then let them find out for us."

The call came as a relief to the FBI who by now knew that Mandy had made contact with Judy Farrell, and to them, that began to make sense. From that point they began to look into George Farrell's whole background: friends, college days, clubs and associations. And they asked Judy Farrell for any photographs, other than studio shots, that she might have of her husband. Old albums were dug out and some disturbing snaps were found.

Don Helary used a call box. When his number answered he spoke at once, "Where can I find Purcell?"

"Just what the hell do you think you're doing ringing me here? Or contacting me at all for that matter?"

"And just what the hell use are you if not for emergencies? I could have called you at the Embassy so calm down. I must find Purcell; where's he likely to be?"

"You must be mad if you think I can answer that. He could be anywhere."

"The most likely person to look after him this end is Hogan. So where would Hogan hide him?"

"You've lost touch. Even supposing Purcell is over here he's the type to make it alone."

"If he thinks he's a target he'll make contact some time. Hogan must have a list of places."

"And you think he'd give them to me? They'll use all kinds of safe houses scattered around the country. Look, there's one possibility. I can get a list of properties owned by one man who has occasional contact with Hogan. It's just a chance. And if that doesn't work, you're on your own. I'll leave it at your hotel."

Helary heard the phone click out and he swore savagely into the receiver before putting it down.

Daley reeled back, slipped and fell, and his gun slid through an open doorway. Galvin could see that he'd not hit Daley cleanly and followed up quickly, trying to keep one eye on the other gun. Daley, with blood running down one side of his face snarled at Galvin and tried to climb to his feet. He was quick but Galvin was desperate and racing against time.

Galvin kicked Daley's legs from under him as he was half way up and then bent to strike him behind the head with the heavy Browning. Daley fell flat on his face. Galvin swung round to find Purcell pointing Daley's gun at him. The last person he wanted to harm was Purcell.

"Move and I'll fire," said Purcell in a shaking voice.

Galvin noticed that the gun was wavering. He had to think quickly. "You'll never hit me. You're shaking like a leaf."

Purcell was out of his element. And he knew it. It was one thing raising money to buy arms for other people to use but quite another to squeeze the trigger himself. "It's me you want, isn't it?"

"I just want to talk to you. Put the gun down before it goes off."

"Talk to me? Kill me you mean." Sweat was bursting out on his forehead and the gun was now shaking hopelessly. In desperation he fired and the shot was too close for Galvin's comfort as it smashed a mirror behind his head. The roar unsettled Purcell more than the effect and he almost dropped the gun from shock. Galvin kicked at Purcell's gun hand and Purcell cried out but he got a better grip on the gun and clung to it desperately. Galvin moved in and side-swiped Purcell with one hand while

222

grasping the gun with the other. Even then he had a job removing the gun, and had to break Purcell's trigger finger in getting it free.

Purcell yelled with pain and sank to his knees holding his injured hand. Galvin turned to watch Daley. Putting Daley's gun in his waistband Galvin ripped Daley's jacket off and used the sleeves to tie his arms behind his back. He then removed the trousers and tied his legs with them. He rummaged for a handkerchief and roughly gagged the man. It was crude and he hoped it would last long enough.

As he finished with Daley Galvin saw Purcell trying to creep into the lounge. He almost screamed his threat. "Don't do that or I'll have to shoot you."

"You're going to shoot me anyway." Ironically Purcell's voice was steadier now he no longer had the gun.

"Come on," said Galvin. "We're leaving. Out the back way and make it quick."

Purcell was still nursing his hand. "No. You might as well kill me here."

"Okay." Galvin levelled the Browning, worried about the time factor and alert for the return of the car. "Let's get it over."

"Wait. Okay, we'll talk."

"Outside then and move fast."

They went out the back and to the rear of the terrace. The shallowest part of the retaining wall was opposite the far end of the lounge and directly in view of its windows. Galvin hustled Purcell along and said, "Okay, climb on to the bank."

Purcell swung round. "How the hell can I climb up there, look at my finger for Chrissake."

The finger was swollen and purple at the lower joint and was undoubtedly very painful. "Bite your lip. Now get going or I'll shoot the thing off." At this point the wall was about four feet off the ground.

Purcell managed to get up and was struggling on his hands and knees on top of the bank when Galvin quickly hoisted himself up some few feet from him.

"Let's move it," said Galvin and pushed Purcell up the steep incline towards the bushes where the binoculars had been left. It was a fair climb but Galvin was increasingly concerned about the Morris returning and kept glancing over his shoulder to the the opposite coast road.

They finally reached the position of comparative safety and Galvin retrieved his binoculars and slung them round his neck. They were facing the villa, and therefore the bridge and the far road. Without the binoculars the villa was not at all clear and the position was good. Galvin made Purcell crouch close to the bushes while he himself was on slightly higher ground but still out of sight of the villa. He told Purcell to turn his back to him so that the American could not see Galvin. It was a good psychological advantage for Galvin who said, "Now talk, Purcell."

"I can't understand why you were so anxious to find me. I'm no threat to you. Never have been and never will be. So why do you want to kill me? Who else will you find as good?"

In the villa Galvin had got the impression that Purcell thought he was somebody else, or at least represented somebody else. Now he was absolutely sure. But he had to maintain the pretence and he thought very carefully. One slip and the sharp-minded Purcell would see it. "Oh, you're good all right. None better. But if you're no threat why hole up with someone like Tierney? Why hole up at all?" Galvin knew that he couldn't be too tentative but he had to get it right; he waited anxiously for the American's reaction.

Purcell started to turn his head but Galvin stopped him with a quick, vicious threat and a jab with the Browning in his back. "I only came over to keep an eye on things, see how they would work out. I wasn't running. And then I read about Farrell and realised what was happening. You were cutting off any connection that might show your funding. I understand that. But I'm no George Farrell, and what did he really know? I'm the very core you work through. There are no written records. Nothing. You could not have it safer."

Galvin found his hand moist on the gun. He felt unsteady and in danger of giving himself away. He was on the verge of receiving the greatest information of all and the fact made him nervous. He was feeling his way with every question. He took a huge chance. "The records are

224

in your head, Purcell. And that's dangerous to us. That's why you ran and that's why we had to find you."

"What the hell do you think I'm gonna do? Tell the Feds? I'd be slitting my own throat."

"Maybe you've already done that. Maybe you think you can do a deal with the FBI and maybe that's why we will have to kill you." Galvin was finding the role easier to play but who did Purcell think he was operating for?

Purcell beat the air with his sound hand. "Shit, you're just not thinking it through, are you? If I'm unsafe now I was unsafe before it all happened. What's the difference?"

Galvin floundered momentarily. "Because it went wrong, that's the difference." He thought he had made a terrible mistake when he saw Purcell stiffen but quickly realised that Purcell was preparing himself for the worst.

With little hope in his voice Purcell said, "You'll never get anyone to trust you again. You'll lose far more than me. Nikov knows I'm totally safe. He knew I was the only one who could handle the finances. Nothing's changed."

Galvin's mind was screaming, desperately trying to make the connection. *Nikov* – that bastard second secretary who'd once worked in London? How the hell could he handle this? Somehow he said, "Nikov is missing."

"Missing? *Missing.* Oh, my God. There must be someone else who knows." And then a terrible thought occurred to him. "You've taken him out?" And then slowly, "If you've burned him why are you taking so long over me?" A slight quiver was back in his voice.

"I didn't say we'd killed him. I said he's missing, maybe running scared like you. Tell me the arrangement."

"Tell you? A hit man? You've got to be kidding. Get someone from Dublin."

In a voice he could no longer trust, Galvin said, "I'm all you're going to get between now and a bullet in the back of your head. Your life is in my hands. It's up to you. And me."

Purcell shuddered and Galvin encouraged the fear by letting the muzzle of the Browning just touch the American's neck.

"Nikov is one of you Russians who's not too keen on *glasnost* as you must know. Some of you would not trust *any* peace deal with America. I had to feel my way round it but the result was that he agreed to underwrite any financial losses to us as a result of new legislation. It was a delicate arrangement dependent, but not actually spelt out, on the President taking a dive, provided that in no way was Nikov involved. It was an understanding between us and one from which we would both benefit. You must know this; otherwise why would you be here? Damn it, there's no way I'd betray Nikov or you, we'll always need your money."

Galvin was dry-mouthed, his mind bursting, but he had to go on. "Of course I know. I thought there might be something else."

"What else could there be? You've been going around cutting off all the fingers that might point to Nikov. Squire's dead. Farrell, who didn't even know of Nikov's existence but knew someone who did, has gone. I don't know if Hank Ross is still around but I'd be surprised if he is."

"That still leaves you." Galvin didn't know how he got the words out.

"What the hell are you worried about? I'm in the shit up to my eyebrows. I have to keep my mouth shut."

Galvin felt he was losing his grip. The shock had been enormous. He was sitting on information that could start another world war. He felt sick and shaky and had Purcell not been facing away from him he was quite certain he would have betrayed himself. He recalled with horror that the Soviet Ambassador had been on the flight; he must have been brutally sacrificed.

Purcell stirred at Galvin's long silence. He felt the gun against the back of his head again and closed his eyes and prayed. He thought he had said enough to convince the man he believed had been sent to assassinate him; perhaps he had even said too much.

At the moment Purcell was too afraid to think clearly; with a gun at his back his usual ice-cold logic had deserted him. Yet he was puzzled that the man behind him had claimed he knew what had been said yet had insisted that Purcell relate it. Perhaps he and those who had sent him wanted to know if there was anything Purcell knew that they didn't. He couldn't bear the strain any longer and he burst out, "For Chrissake put me out of my misery one way or the other."

The frantic plea snapped Galvin from his trance. "I'm going to take a chance on you. You're right, we do need you. You can turn round."

Purcell swivelled to face Galvin. Relief was sweeping through him. "You've made the right decision," he said breathlessly.

"When you get back to the villa don't let them know what's happened between us. When Tierney and his mob get back just tell them I was bringing a message for your ears only and that the heat's now off you. With the whole country looking for them you'd better get away from there as fast as you can. And if they ever find out what you've just told me you're dead anyway. Good luck."

Galvin slipped away and made for his car. When he reached it he switched on and thought that he had done Purcell no favour. If Purcell left the villa he'd be back on the open road and sooner or later would be found. Galvin cruised down the steep incline, reached a secondary road and eased his way towards the bridge. Something began to niggle at him about what Purcell had told him. Something did not gel. Purcell was a money man; a manipulator of funds. It was his life, all he really knew or needed to know; was Purcell himself missing something? Was he so close to what he did best that he'd overlooked what others did best?

On reaching the other side of the bridge he noticed a stationary car tucked in a wider section of the narrow road leading straight ahead. It was a small, dark green Fiat and he had the vague sensation of having seen it before. It was parked near to the place he himself had used when he had hidden to watch the villa. He made a mental note of the registration number and then turned right, away from the car and on to the estuary road.

As he drew out a snub-nosed Morris 1000 came out of a concealed drive and swung across to block his way. Galvin braked frantically and skidded. He glanced behind him as he swung to a stop. Two men with levelled pistols had come out of the bushes to cut off his rear. He realised that he had lost concentration after the shock of what Purcell had told him. Tierney must have returned some time ago.

Tierney stepped from the Morris and ran towards Galvin, knowing he was taking a risk on the road. "Don't try anything or we'll cut you to pieces. Just get out and climb in my car." Tierney was holding a gun in his pocket and was enjoying himself but it was Connolly behind him whose bruised and battered face showed the most pleasure. Galvin glanced in his central mirror. The two armed men had closed in and were now directly behind his car. He knew that it would be hopeless to try to shoot it out.

18

Galvin lay trussed and bundled in a corner of the dining room. His lips were cut and bleeding and his ribs had been so badly pummelled that he had difficulty in breathing. Tierney had only stopped Connolly and Daley going even further because he had to know what had happened between him and Purcell. When Daley had accused Purcell of going off with Galvin he hadn't denied it but had pointed out that he'd had a gun at his head.

Tierney no longer trusted Purcell. He had not wanted him there in the first place; he had distrusted the American's sharper brain from the start, but Hogan, who had foreseen something of what might happen had warned Tierney to toe the line. Purcell was important to the whole movement; without him there would be no American money. But Purcell didn't fit in with those in the villa.

It was important to Tierney to establish his authority and that could only be done by getting at the truth. He was satisfied about Galvin who would get a large calibre slug through the back of his head once he had finished with him, but first he had to work out the Galvin–Purcell connection. Purcell himself was holding back and that irritated Tierney because he knew he'd be in trouble with Hogan if he tried to beat the truth from him. All he could do was to work on Galvin, and for that he needed to keep him coherent.

The dining table and chairs had been pushed back to make more room. In his corner, away from the window, Galvin noticed that Pat Sullivan was missing. Daley had a long bloody scar down the side of his face, and he was still screaming for revenge. Connolly too. Well, they'd get their chance, but not yet. Tierney said, "I want just Milton and myself in here, the rest of you push off for a while. I don't want distraction, okay?" The tone of his voice told them not to argue.

Tierney then hooked one of the chairs round and sat down to face Galvin who was staring at the floor. Tierney spoke to Purcell, who was standing behind him, "Take a pew, you need to listen to this."

"A pew?"

"A chair. Do you know who this feller is?" When Purcell shook his head Tierney added, "His name's Laurie Galvin. At least we think it is. He's either working for the Irish intelligence service or the British. He's been spying on us. He's also a member of Sinn Fein but that's his cover. Now tell me what happened between you."

Galvin briefly caught Purcell's eye as the American glanced down; he shook his head almost imperceptibly. Purcell's mind was logically tracking events. "I don't think he is," he answered blandly.

"Jesus. You don't think he's a spy? What do you need to be convinced? He was carrying a Browning and he's got laser bugging equipment in his car. What do you think he needed that for? To listen to the radio?"

Purcell hesitated but he had no intention of being panicked; even with a gun at his head he hadn't done that. Tierney was watching Purcell closely.

With a warning look at Purcell, Galvin managed to speak coldly, *"Hovezi maso na hribkach. Svestkove knedliky,* Purcell."

Tierney glanced at Galvin, confused and shaken by what he thought was Russian.

Galvin added, *"Zelne Zavitky. Kulajda . . . Tierney."* He shook his head again in warning. Galvin knew no Russian and he was banking on the other two knowing none either. He was quoting two Czechoslovakian dishes from *Svet,* a Czech magazine that was sent to him regularly as part of his cover to endorse his political leaning. He and Riley had enjoyed a lot of laughs over the pronunciation. Even now he didn't know whether he had got it right or not and he had forgotten the last part of the last recipe. Riley had even tried to make two of the dishes and they'd finished up disasters.

Purcell was bewildered. He too, thought that he had been listening to Russian and that Galvin was trying to warn him about enlightening Tierney.

"What did he say?" Tierney demanded.

But Purcell did not know and he didn't want Tierney to think that he hadn't understood. "He's not a spy. Not against you, anyway."

"So tell me what went on?"

The ruse had worked: Galvin had managed to confuse Purcell just at the moment Tierney was beginning to make him have doubts.

"I can't go into it. There are reasons."

"Reasons? With this treacherous bastard? They'd better be bloody good reasons or you'll land up with him."

"Don't be ridiculous. You want good reasons? How about not receiving another nickel from American funds? Is that a good enough reason?"

Tierney was really out of his depth. He *knew* that Galvin was a spy. But what was the tie-up with Purcell? He wished that Hogan was here. "Are you saying that this rat is involved with our funds in some way?"

Purcell was tired, in pain and exasperated. "It's not so simple. You must trust me."

But Tierney didn't trust him. He didn't understand him at all. Things were going on he didn't know about and he didn't care for that. He turned to Galvin. "Okay, so you tell me. Your lousy life hangs on your answer."

Galvin's words were slurred through lacerated lips. "If Milton won't tell you you can't expect me to. This is over your head, Tierney. And even if I told you you wouldn't understand. Just accept that you have your job and we have ours. Whatever it looks like to you, believe me it's in your best interests to drop it."

"Believe you? Where did you get your combat training? You practically destroyed Connolly in that pub."

Cagily, Galvin turned to Purcell. "You know I can't tell him. Ring Dublin and get this sorted out." It was sheer bluff hanging on the thread of the earlier illusion.

"Nobody's ringing anybody unless I say so," Tierney burst out. He had the strong feeling he was losing his grip and was searching for a way to restore it. He could deal with Galvin easily enough, but Purcell was an intrusion and was now supporting Galvin. It didn't make sense unless Purcell himself was in the deep end. If he called Hogan it would be an acknowledgement of his own failure to cope. He rose only to sit on the edge of the table, an

231

Ingram sub-machine gun still in his hands. The villa was well away from the others; a quick burst would solve all his problems but it might create others more serious.

After a few moments of indecision Tierney stood up again. He spoke to Purcell, "You come with me."

They left the room and Tierney closed the door behind him. Galvin tried to analyse his position. He couldn't maintain the bluff for ever. Purcell apparently still thought he was a Soviet-hired assassin and was hedging his bets but there would come a time, and it had almost happened just minutes ago, when Tierney would lay the lethal seeds of doubt. Unable to do anything other than sit and await their return, his mind had switched to Riley when Connolly walked in carrying a pistol in one hand and a phone in the other which he plugged into a socket by the door.

"I've been told not to touch you. Yet. My turn will come though, and Michael Daley owes you a few too. Something to look forward to, boyo."

Connolly was enjoying himself as he stood gloating over Galvin. He glanced towards the closed door and suddenly gave Galvin a vicious kick in the side. Galvin rolled and groaned.

"My foot slipped," said Connolly, still grinning. "But I know you're bored there so I thought you might like a little entertainment." He put the phone and the pistol down on the table and pulled a slip of paper from the back pocket of his jeans. He waved it at Galvin. "You'll enjoy this." He dialled the number on the slip.

As the number rang out he gazed down at Galvin, who suddenly felt sick at heart. "Riley? Riley Brown. Don't hang up now for Laurie would like a word with you." Connolly listened then said, "Well now, I can't tell you where we are but I can tell you he's here, alive and well. Alive anyway. He's a bit tied up at the moment but I'll see if I can get him to say a few words. But first there's something you should know."

Connolly lowered the mouthpiece then openly laughed. Galvin had never felt so wretchedly low and tried to blot out the sound of Connolly's voice. Connolly continued. "Your darling lover boy turned out to be a British agent. A spy. Can you imagine that? Spying on us all the time he

232

was. Using you as his cover. Were you really stupid enough to think he loved you?"

Galvin wished he could die then. It would have been better had Connolly kicked him to death rather than force Riley to suffer in this terrible way.

"Would you like him to confirm it now? Just a quick word." Connolly came forward to hold the phone in front of Galvin's lips. Galvin turned his head away. He could hear Riley's distress over the phone and simply couldn't face it. "You bastard," he spat at Connolly, "You stinking bastard." And the words travelled down the phone. If he tried to say what he wanted to say to Riley, Connolly would cut him off. Anyway, he couldn't deny the accusation; it would only prolong her agony and sooner or later she would find out the truth. He was tempted to shout out his location but that would put her in danger. Instead, in an agonised voice, he called out, "I love you, Riley, what-ever . . ." Connolly crashed the phone down on the cradle and began to kick Galvin into oblivion.

Some time later, as he came to, he heard a terrible commotion from nearby and someone yelled out, "For Chrissake don't kill him yet." He was too far gone to make sense of it, but someone was suffering in another room.

Riley recognised Connolly's voice instantly and almost slammed the receiver down but he caught her attention just in time. At first she listened to what she thought were lies but in her heart, for some time now, she had known that wherever Galvin was it had nothing to do with his probably mythological sick sister.

With increasing nausea she listened to Connolly, and her depression deepened until she barely knew what was happening. What made it worse was that Connolly's vitriol served merely as confirmation of what she had already begun to suspect. Even so, nothing as bad as this had entered her mind. As much as she detested Connolly, and after this she would loathe him the more, she slowly accepted that she was hearing the truth.

And then had come the awful moment when she had heard her beloved Galvin calling Connolly a bastard, but with no denial of what Connolly had said. And the worst moment of all was when she had heard Galvin say he loved

233

her. It was too much. She had lowered the phone not knowing that Connolly had slammed down the receiver his end, and finally it had dropped from her hand.

It seemed to her a million years before she realised what had happened and she stared blankly at the floor to see Hercules playing with the instrument. She bent down in a state of shock to retrieve the phone and slowly put it to her ear. The dialling tone had returned. She put the phone back on the cradle and sat down. Hercules jumped on to her lap and started to lick her face. She clung to the dog, her last link with sanity.

Tyson, who had managed to retain a degree of panache even in oilskins, had taken his sea-going launch *Emerald* beyond Dublin Bay. There was a stiff swell but he took her away from the busy sea lanes between Britain and Ireland. He much preferred to be out of sight of land during these rare meetings and had not enjoyed being moored at the time he had met Hogan. But in the cockpit with him now was someone much more important.

Radavitch didn't show himself until they were well out to sea and then he came up from the cabin to join Tyson at the wheel. Unlike Hogan he didn't mind the sea or its motion and found it bracing: an escape from the Embassy routine. He clung on with stubby, powerful hands, as the boat yawed. His features were Slavic. Quite tall, he appeared awkward beside Tyson. His brown eyes were reflective and gave nothing away.

The *Emerald* was an escape in more ways than one. It meant that Radavitch, by arrangement with Tyson, could go on board at his leisure once he had satisfied himself that the Irish Special Branch weren't watching him. It was a good, secluded place to wait, the perfect rendezvous.

Radavitch had a heavy, broken accent but knew just enough English to cope. He stood next to Tyson who was peering through the spattered windscreen with hands on the wheel. "Have you no idea at all where Purcell has gone?" He almost shouted to make himself heard above the sound of wind and engine.

Tyson seemed not to hear until he answered some time later. "It's not easy to find someone who's hiding in Ireland. Most people don't realise just how much space there is. If the Garda can't find Tierney and his crew what chance have you of finding Purcell? How many people can you possibly mobilise over here?"

Radavitch steadied himself as the bows bit deep and two huge streamers of spray arched up. "More than you have provided, but perhaps not enough. It is essential to find him. You must help."

"Purcell will surface some time, old boy. He has to. If you search too hard you'll draw attention to yourselves. People notice strangers over here, particularly in the rural areas where he's most likely to be."

Radavitch said firmly, "You seem to think that Hogan knows where Purcell is. We must get it out of him."

"That would be a big mistake. Down here he's the King of the Provos. He might well know, but threatening or persuading him could do you far more harm than having Purcell on the loose." Tyson turned the wheel and said, "Are you sure Purcell is so important?"

"What he knows is not the sort of information we want others to discover. It could be disastrous."

Tyson looked worried, "Wait a while. Wherever Purcell is there's no way he's going to jump into the arms of the FBI. He's trying to show you that there's no need to worry. He'll surface; he'll have to. And he'll probably try to change identity. That's when you'll get him. He's no danger meanwhile. Don't interfere with the Provos. It will backfire; there's no knowing how they would react."

"You forget the FBI will be looking for Purcell too."

"No I don't. But if he's over here then I would think they stand far less chance than we do, wouldn't you? Look, I'll go through all the properties I've obtained over the years. Some are rubbish tips but they have been useful on occasion. Some I bought for a song and others at market value. The Provos have been known to use one or two although they prefer their own boltholes. You never know. I'll look into it." Tyson glanced over at the Russian and hoped he had done enough to placate him.

Joe Aspel reported to James Powell with mixed feelings. He handed over a file and said somewhat unevenly, "This is a report on George Farrell, investment banker; the guy who was kidnapped in Ireland."

235

Powell noticed Aspel's unusual grimness. He took the folder and opened the cover. "Anything you want to say before I wade through it?"

"There's not a lot but it's dynamite, nevertheless. Mandy Squire saw a link between her husband's death and Farrell's kidnap. It wasn't the kind of evidence that any court would accept but it was convincing enough to her to contact Mrs Farrell. They got together and decided to call us in with what they had. That file is the result. You want me to stay while you read it?"

"No. I'll take my time."

Aspel for once seemed reluctant to leave. He was willing Powell to get on with it. "Okay. There are some interesting photographs there. I'll be outside if you want me."

Powell stared across the desk. "Go back to your own office, Joe. I do know how to get in touch with you."

When Aspel had gone Powell took out the photographs; most of them were snapshots but there were some professionally taken group shots among them. Afterwards he read the report; his hand was shaking as he held the notes which showed surprising links between certain people. Aspel was right, there was not a great deal of information but it was potential dynamite. He was quite pale by the time he had finished and he sat back in something of a daze. He glanced at the file. He needed more information than he had. He rang Sir Gerald Fowler in London and when he had finished talking with him buzzed his secretary to make an immediate appointment with the President.

The policeman walked up the farm tracks and saw the dilapidated building and the pyre of car wrecks looking like some surrealistic modelling.

Finbar O'Leary knew all the outposts in the general area. Smallholdings, outlying houses, isolated pubs always miraculously busy, there was little he didn't know about the people and the properties on his patch. And he had a good idea where some of the illicit poteen stills were. There had been one on this deserted farm until it had been broken up. The remains of the stills were in what was left of the barn at the rear of the property.

O'Leary remembered the place when it had farmed well

and had brought Dan Driscoll, its owner, a reasonable return for his hard work. But Dan's wife had died and his daughters had married and had moved out, and his two sons had no interest in farming. One had gone to England and the other to America. When Dan himself had died the place had already become run down as he'd lost heart and age had overtaken him. The place was worth just what the land was worth which was too little to bring now-successful sons back to Ireland, but it still belonged to the family.

O'Leary had left his small car at the broken-down gates at the foot of the drive. It had been some time since he had called here. It was reasonably safe and there was little to steal and the location was too remote for vandals. His memories stirred as he approached the house and as he recalled the near-perfect brew that Dan had made at the back. Dan had added aniseed to some of the poteen to make a kind of liqueur which was more palatable to the women. O'Leary had pleasant memories of the place and it saddened him to see what it had become.

He was sweating a little by the time he reached the door. His short, chunky frame was encased in a heavy winter uniform topcoat and it was really too soon for it. Since the Farrell kidnapping he had called on many outlying farms whether occupied or not. It was plodding, hard work and it had been taking place all over the Republic. It was a slow, painstaking system which had, over the years, produced good results.

O'Leary could see at a glance that the place had been visited fairly recently. There were tell-tale signs all around and once inside it was even more apparent; there were wide areas like the table and chairs which had suddenly become dust free. And when he went round the down-stairs rooms he noticed that one chair was missing. O'Leary could write an inventory of the contents from memory.

In the kitchen he could see that the old carpet under the table had been disturbed and he knew a cellar trapdoor was underneath; Dan had stored some of his bottles down there and sometimes the smell of aniseed had escaped into this room. O'Leary pulled the table back, kicked aside the carpet and opened the trap. He didn't much care for the smell that greeted him; there was more than stale air down there. Half way down the stairs he saw the rough, untidy bundle that had been George Farrell and as he ventured further, even in the bad light, he could see the mess that had been made of him.

Detective Chief Superintendent Keane rubbed his lined face and tried to rejuvenate his circulation. His thick grey hair was hanging forward in uncharacteristically untidy strands. He was tired to a point of being unable to sleep and that could be a dangerous condition. He had just come from the mortuary to see the pathetic remains of George Farrell and was reflecting that Farrell's money hadn't done him any good at all.

Keane was now finally satisfied that the Provos were not guilty of Farrell's cold-blooded murder even though it had been carried out using methods they had made their own. But whoever had executed Farrell had not done sufficient homework on the organisation they had blamed. The request for money had not been followed up – something the Provos always took care to do, and Keane was satisfied that Farrell had been kidnapped solely in order to be executed. The rest was rubbish.

He sat at his desk, the office in semi-gloom with a desk light on and the door open to the long corridor beyond. He felt he didn't want to be cut off just then and the building at this time of night was lonely and creaky. He had been wondering just how many police forces were now operating in his country. The CIA were out there somewhere, as were MI5 and perhaps MI6. None of them should be on his soil but he was realistic about something as big as this, something that Farrell had known about. Anyway, he had a good working relationship with London's Special Branch. On IRA matters they would be mad not to co-operate.

Keane was glad of the company when Chief Inspector Matt O'Riordon came in. Keane nodded to a chair. He groped in his desk drawer and produced two glasses and a bottle of Paddy. He poured out large shots and didn't ask O'Riordon whether or not he needed water or white lemonade. They silently raised their glasses and drank it neat. "Any luck yet with Sean Hogan?" Keane asked.

The younger O'Riordon shook his head. A slim,

nervous man, he admired Keane who gave the impression of being a plodding senior officer put out to grass in an office where he wouldn't get in anyone's way. This, he knew, was far from true and he also knew that Keane was very highly regarded at London's Scotland Yard. "He's moved out from his usual place. We have a list of alternatives; he's bound to pitch up. You still don't think PIRA did Farrell?"

Keane smiled wryly, "I'm bloody sure they didn't, though I wouldn't tell Hogan so easily. I want to do a deal with him." He rubbed his nose. "He could be in trouble himself if we don't find him. There're some bloody queer things going on but I'm gradually forming a picture and believe me it scares me to death."

Heavy footsteps hurried along the corridor towards the office. A young fair-haired man dressed in a neat suit knocked on the open door. "We've picked up Hogan, sir. We have him downstairs. Shall we take him to an interview room now?"

Keane thought quickly and shook his head. "Bring him up here. He's not under arrest so you needn't hang around."

A few minutes later three sets of footsteps approached and the burly Hogan stood in the doorway, two men behind him. "I hate this place," said Hogan.

"Of course you do," Keane rejoined. "It smacks of justice and law. You should spruce yourself up before coming here."

"At eleven thirty at night? Jesus. What is it you want?"

Keane wearily pushed his chair back. "Take the weight off your feet." He turned to O'Riordon. "Close the door, Matt, but stay. I don't want any misunderstanding about this meeting." To Hogan he said, "Tell me where Tierney and his boys are and I'll issue a statement to the press to say we don't think PIRA kidnapped George Farrell, now deceased."

"So they killed him." Hogan had been expecting it yet he still felt surprised; it must have been too late for the news bulletins unless the police were suppressing it until Farrell's wife was told.

"You should know better than anyone."

"Don't try that." Hogan was worried about the way things

239

were going. Nothing was straightforward any more. "I can't tell you where Tierney is. I don't know. I haven't seen him around for some days."

Keane glanced at O'Riordon who was leaning against the door. "Then there's no deal."

"It's your duty to tell the public that we didn't do the Farrell job if that's what you think."

"I didn't say I thought it. I said I'd do it but you have nothing to exchange. If you didn't do it I believe you know who did and that's why you're so anxious. So tell me that instead."

"If I knew who did it I'd know what to do about it."

"Let's stop messing around, Hogan. I'm tired and I want to get home to save my marriage. If you don't know who precisely did it, and I'm not convinced, then who was behind it?"

Hogan shrugged his heavy shoulders. He really wanted more time to think, but he could see that Keane wasn't going to give it to him. "I don't know."

"Did Tyson throw out any ideas when you met him the other day?"

Hogan's gaze was suddenly too steady. He should have expected that Keane knew about Tyson for it had to happen one day. He wondered how long Keane had known, or was he merely flying a kite? He had to test the strength of it. "And who the hell is Tyson?"

Keane yawned and shook his head. "I offered you a fair deal. What's more important to you, your so-called movement or loyalty to a thug who will eventually bring you down anyway? What the hell does Tierney matter? He's an embarrassment to you. You must be pretty scared."

So Keane had been bluffing about the meeting with Tyson but Hogan didn't like the way things were going at all. There was too much muddle, too many people involved and too many shadows. The intangibles were swimming all around him. His only consolation was that Keane, in spite of his resources, was groping too. "Scared? Of you?"

"I'm not likely to kill you, am I? But there's killing going on right now and there are much bigger leagues than yours involved. I'm sorry you won't co-operate, Hogan. If

240

I were you I'd watch my back. And if you come to your senses give me a ring."

When Hogan had been escorted off the premises and O'Riordon had returned to the office, Keane said, "He's between the devil and the deep blue sea. I didn't expect him to betray Tierney because he would be signing his own death warrant if it got out, but I thought he might give a pointer to the bigger issue which could even be more dangerous to him."

"Do you need a pointer?"

"Oh, yes. I'm not sure I've done the right thing letting him know that we know about Tyson. I was trying to drive a wedge but he called my bluff; still, it might work on him like a time fuse. There's manipulation going on, Matt. And there's a nasty, deadly feel about it. Hogan's not sure of himself at the moment and that's not like our intelligent, aggressive and fearless Hogan at all. At all. He's worried and it's not about me." Keane moved this way and that in his swivel chair, the spring squeaking. "I know we're stretched but get some extra men on him. And tighten up on Tyson; check on his properties, he's got a few, some he probably can't even remember."

Keane paused for a few moments, the quietness of the building creeping into the office with the increasing night chill. "And dig up some extra men to watch the Soviets." He noticed O'Riordon's expression. "I know it's difficult but I reckon it's important right now. Borrow some from the Garda, anywhere. And, particularly, I want Radavitch screwed down; that bastard slipped us yesterday and there had to be a good reason."

As O'Riordon saw the trend of Keane's thoughts, he too felt uneasy; the possibilities were terrifying.

19

Riley Brown had suffered the worst night of her life. Happiness had been squeezed out of her with brutal savagery. But as much as she loathed Connolly she did not doubt the essence of what he had told her. Her world had turned upside down: her spirit crushed, her mind clouded by acute depression, she no longer wanted to live. Galvin had come to mean everything to her. And Galvin had been secretively operating against beliefs she had held from childhood and which he had claimed to share. She felt bloodless, the only warmth from the small furry bundle in her arms who, aware of her mood, intruded into it in the only way he knew. It was Hercules's liveliness that probably made her hang on.

She had taken him out for a walk, barely aware of the frequent stops the puppy imposed on her. She walked for miles until Hercules kept looking up, silently pleading that even his energy was drained. The long night ahead was something she could not face and when she arrived back at the flat she wanted to run out again. The problem of sleep was partially solved by taking two sleeping pills she had obtained from her mother at an earlier time for another problem, and she somehow resisted taking more. They got her through the night.

But dawn solved nothing, though the effects of the pills mercifully dulled her mind. As the morning wore on she found herself holding Hercules and sitting in front of the oven. Two things finally got through to her. If she gassed herself she could not bear the thought of taking Hercules with her; the dog was innocent and wanted to live. And then, more reluctantly, the danger Galvin was obviously in came slowly through her depression and grew stronger. It was one thing wishing him dead in a state of shock and anger, but quite another to realise that he was actually going to die – and knowing Connolly, most brutally. She might hate Galvin now but to let him die at Connolly's hands was a prospect becoming too unbearable to contemplate.

She wanted to die but she could not bear the thought of Galvin dying, not at the hands of the Provos anyway, whatever he had done, however much he had hurt her. She was in a phychological maze. She could not run to her rebellious friends, who she now realised with horror would welcome Galvin's execution. Nor could she run to the police who had often harassed them and represented an authority any self-respecting member of Sinn Fein would despise. She didn't know what to do. But the urgency of the dilemma forced her from depression in an effort to cope with an increasing dread. She felt sick at what Galvin had done, at how he had betrayed her, but was terrified of what would be done to him.

She rose slowly but close to panic at the amount of time she had already lost. She slipped on a light coat, put Hercules on a lead and left the flat to look for a taxi.

Keane rose when Riley was ushered in. Perhaps he spotted her quiet despair as she came through the door. He thought she was a pretty girl, very feminine, unlike some of her banner-carrying screaming friends, but perhaps he was seeing her out of context. "Sit down, Miss Brown. What can I do for you?"

She didn't know where to start. Now that she was in the office she was lost and suddenly wanted to flee. Hercules was still with her and she fidgeted with his lead.

Keane said gently, "You insisted on seeing me, quite vehemently by all accounts. You are here, so am I, so start at the beginning." When he saw her fumbling for words he added, "I know it might be difficult talking to a policeman, but let me tell you your father had no trouble doing it."

"You knew my father?"

"Pat Brown? Who didn't? Now there was a firebrand for you." Keane smiled. "I often thought he was trying to live down his English name. But he was of the old school, Riley. He didn't really belong to the modern version of the IRA. I always had the impression that he joined because he felt he should." He was tired but the lies came easily.

"That's not true," Riley flared. "He always wanted one Ireland."

"Don't we all? Even the Brits. We're all caught up in history; it won't go away with bullets and bombs."

"The Brits don't want it. They'll never want it."

Keane chuckled. "Ever been over there to ask them? Most of them would pull the plug tomorrow if they could manage to do it without the inevitable bloodbath. Is this what you called about? To convert me?" Without being patronising Keane had spoken like a long-lost uncle.

She shook her head, aware that she was now more comfortable talking to this grey-haired man with the roughed-up features. Her mouth suddenly dried but at last she blurted out, "My boyfriend," and then fiercely, "My ex-boyfriend is a British spy. They're going to kill him."

Suddenly, Keane was all attention and gradually extracted the story but even now Riley could not give names apart from Galvin's own. When she had blurted it all out piecemeal and he tried to put it together he found he had very little. It was time to be tougher. "What you've given me is not enough to help him. I assume that's what you want me to do?"

As if to protect her image Riley burst out, "He deserves to die; he's a traitor." She was close to tears. "He pretended he was helping the cause."

"Maybe he was. He saw it a different way. He was doing what you've been doing but he was probably trying to avoid bloodshed."

Riley stiffened. "I should have known you would have supported someone like that. He lied to me. Again and again."

"Would it have helped your relationship if he hadn't? Tell me, Riley, who knocked you about so much? Galvin?"

"No, he . . ."

"Sorted out who did? Wouldn't that be an expression of love?"

Riley rose. She was muddled and could take no more; she felt she had achieved nothing.

"Sit down," said Keane, "if you really want Galvin to stand any chance at all. Now stop beating about the bush. Is the feller who knocked you about the one who phoned? Was it a revenge thing? And if you don't give me his name perhaps you had better leave and let Galvin take a bullet in the back of the head. After they've finished with him, of course."

She almost gagged. "Connolly." Even now it was difficult to get out.

"Gerrard Connolly?"

Riley nodded feeling as if she had committed some dreadful sin.

"Don't let it worry you. The file we have on him would revolt you. Is Tierney with him?"

"I don't know who's with him."

Keane stared across the desk. "And you don't know where the call came from?"

"No."

Keane waved his hands helplessly. "What do you think we can do? Where do we start looking?"

"He went down to Cork some days ago. He said he had to arrange some car-servicing deal but I suppose that was all lies too."

"You're talking about Galvin?"

"Of course." Riley hesitated. "I do believe he actually went whatever the reason."

Keane sat in despair. "Well that narrows it down to an area of a lousy few hundred miles. Riley, I understand you are trying to save Galvin but you've given me nothing. Can't you dig up anything else, something to pinpoint the place. *Anything?*"

Riley clasped her hands together. She was pale, and without make-up her fading bruises were more noticeable. She said, "I've wasted your time, haven't I?"

"You've done your best. And you did the right thing coming here." Keane felt a strong and sudden surge of compassion: he felt sorry for the girl; she didn't really fit into her own background. He could think of some of her friends who would let Galvin burn in this situation and feel no remorse. She was obviously crazy about Galvin and the whole business had knocked the stuffing out of her. "Did Connolly say Galvin is a British spy?"

"Yes. But Laurie didn't refute it when he had the chance."

"What did he say?"

She broke down as she told him and he came round the desk to sit on its edge.

"Galvin obviously said what was most important to him. And anyway, Connolly would say that, wouldn't he? He wanted to hurt both you and Galvin; you spurned him and Galvin probably knocked the hell out of him. Has it occurred to you that Galvin might be with Irish Security?" Keane was fairly sure that Galvin wasn't but he hoped the little deception might ease her feelings; she was in a bad way. "We'll take a chance and concentrate on the Cork area," he added. "We're already looking for Tierney; that's an open secret. And where Tierney is, Connolly will be. In view of what you've told me that also means Galvin will be there."

Keane helped Riley to her feet. He said, "I'm pretty sure who does know where Tierney is. Sean Hogan. Is it possible that you can get something out of him? I've already tried. That would help Galvin, wouldn't it? We have to move fast, Riley." But he was thinking that they were already too late.

Hogan had been shrewd in directing Tierney to the villa at Kinsale. It was on open view but in a way that attracted little attention. It formed part of a general scene and the others around it were too far away to be a danger; most were screened from each other and there was considerable space between them. It was some distance from the centre of Kinsale, yet it was sufficiently near to obtain supplies. With a clear view of the approach road across the estuary and to the bridge, Tierney and his men were safeguarded from surprise. They were hidden from sight of the lesser-used road coming down from behind them.

While the police searched everywhere, their concentration was usually on isolated country dwellings similar to the one in which Farrell had been found. There were many places to hide and town searches invariably took in certain streets and terraced houses which had sometimes been used for kidnap purposes; needles in haystacks.

Tierney did not know that the villa was one of several properties owned by Tyson. He had never met Tyson nor knew much about him; that was a privilege reserved for Hogan. It was highly restricted information, as it needed to be. Hogan was still in Dublin and phone calls which Tierney had made to Hogan's home remained unanswered. Tierney had seized on a call which had come through last night but it had been a wrong number. He was lost without the decision-making abilities of Sean Hogan and he realised how much he relied on his burly leader. He needed to raise him because he wanted to deal with Galvin and Purcell and Sullivan, who was already almost dead.

Tierney did not understand that Hogan was himself under pressure, a pressure which included close surveillance from Special Branch; and that restricted his movements considerably. Hogan could have evaded the police but there were not usually this many and he knew they were being extra vigilant.

In fact, Hogan wanted to get down to the villa at Kinsale just as much as Tierney needed him to, but he had no intention of leading the police there and he had to be absolutely certain that he would not. He knew that Tierney would be sweating but as yet he knew nothing of Galvin's presence. He compromised and dropped into one of Dublin's green pillar boxes an envelope addressed to John Hopkins at the villa. He knew the postman was used to occasional guests staying there and equally he knew that at this time of year it was always empty.

Tierney received the envelope the morning after he had caught Galvin. The name on it did not stop him opening it. There was a torn off piece of paper inside with a Dublin phone number and a list of times, nothing else. Tierney recognised Hogan's scrawl and guessed that his chief was in some difficulty. But at least he could now contact him; the times were those when he would be available and the soonest of those was at midday. He was relieved; he did not want two bound men about the place and he was fed up with Purcell. What he really wanted to do was to get rid of the two traitors, tell Purcell to go to hell and then choose his time to flee the country for one of the overseas havens. He checked the time; there was an hour and a half to go.

Galvin was in a bad way but could see that Sullivan was in a far worse state than himself. Until they had dragged Galvin into the utility room he hadn't known it was Sullivan he had heard being beaten up.

The trussed figure was propped against a washing

machine but he knew little if anything of what was going on. His narrow features were battered and swollen. His eyes had almost disappeared into puffed slits and his mouth was a blood-red gash.

No explanation had been given to Galvin as to why Sullivan was like this, but he didn't need one. He was the man who had been laying the trail for Galvin to follow. Galvin was shocked by the sight of Sullivan, the real hero, the man who had taken the real risks to finish up like a pulped cabbage. He felt sick and humbled.

Galvin assumed that Sullivan belonged to the Irish Security Service and that Dublin and London had co-operated; which was something they did more often than people realised. He had tried talking to Sullivan in an effort to bring him round but had failed. He wondered bitterly why Tierney hadn't finished the job.

The utility room had clearly become a no-go area. It stank and it was obvious that Sullivan had not been removed for even the most basic needs. Galvin had been treated a little better – which showed that Tierney was still confused and undecided – but it could not last. When Galvin thought like that it was best to turn away from Sullivan; he hoped it would end with a single bullet. It was later that morning, when in a sudden spasm Sullivan moved and rolled over, his body twitching, that Galvin saw from the blood stains at the back of Sullivan's trousers and the awkward position of the legs, that he had been knee-capped. Galvin was suddenly sick. Afterwards he closed his eyes and had to turn his back.

He was still facing the door well after midday when Tierney and Connolly came in. Tierney appeared as if he had made up his mind and seemed to be more settled. Connolly was openly grinning so that Galvin knew the worst was about to happen. Both men were armed, but they did not come too far beyond the door and stood gazing down at Galvin and Sullivan who were both at the far end of the narrow room. Behind them Galvin could see Daley bobbing up as if trying to get a better view. And behind Daley lurked Purcell.

"You say you're working for us," said Tierney. "And Purcell seems to think you are but he's not as sure as he was. In fact he's weakening quite a lot."

248

"Of course he is," replied Galvin. "You've been working on him. But he knows what will happen to him if he gets it wrong."

For once Tierney wasn't angered or confused. He pulled Galvin's own Browning from his hip pocket and laid it on the tumble dryer next to the washing machine. "We're going to let you prove it," Tierney said with a grin. Connolly by now was laughing openly and Galvin didn't like the feel of it.

"We like to be fair," continued Tierney. "I mean we haven't killed you. You see him." He indicated the pitiful Sullivan. "We proved he's a spy. The bloody place is full of spies. Caught him writing out a little message while we were in Kinsale so that he could leave it somewhere for you to find. It gave our location and identities. Wasn't that good of him, now? I mean that's how you found us here, isn't it? One of Pat's little directions left for you at the farm? But we'll give you a chance to show that you're one of us. We couldn't be fairer now, could we? All you have to do is to shoot Sullivan through the back of the head. Execute the bastard. Then we'll know for sure whose side you're on."

Galvin managed to keep his voice steady, "I'm a political, not a field man. You know that damned well."

"Will you listen to him?" Tierney turned to Connolly; both men were grinning widely. "Not a field man, so. Then what were you doing with that Browning and the bugging gear in your car? Were you on your way to a Sinn Fein rally, now?"

"A shot will be heard all over the place."

"Nobody heard Purcell's when he smashed the only decent mirror in the place. Besides we can arrange a cushion for you. Untie him. And, Laurie me boy, don't try anything or you'll get a gut full of slugs."

Daley came through to untie Galvin and he enjoyed doing it as roughly as he could, giving the odd punch in the kidneys. When the job was done Daley rejoined the others who had now crowded into the room. Two Ingrams and a Colt pointed at Galvin, who had remained on the floor.

"Get up," said Tierney.

Galvin climbed up shakily. His legs were weak and he had to steady himself against the tumble dryer very aware that the Browning was close to his hand and that the others had only to squeeze their triggers. He felt dreadful, his mind sluggish when it had never needed to be so sharp.

"Pick up the gun and watch how you do it."

"He should be hooded." Galvin reached for the gun as he tried desperately to find a solution.

"We're fresh out of hoods. You'll just have to manage without one."

Galvin was holding the gun and wondering whether Tierney was bluffing. He was balancing the gun in his hand and could judge that the magazine wasn't full. But was it empty? Would Tierney trust him even with one round? If there *was* only one round, particularly if it was already in the breech? It was impossible to gauge by the weight or balance of the gun. If he took a chance and turned to fire at Tierney that was as far as he would get before being shot to pieces. And if that happened the knowledge he carried would die with him. When he looked at the gun his hand was shaking. Galvin glanced over to Tierney and Connolly; all he could see on their faces was evil. "Wait till Hogan hears of this little lot." It was his last chance.

"Hogan has not only heard of it but instructed it. He was on to you a long time ago. Just put the gun at the back of Pat's head and squeeze the trigger. Then we'll all have a drink."

"No. *NO*. You're mad, all of you." Purcell bustled forward. "You're crazy to shoot anyone here. You'll have problems getting rid of the body, there'll be a mess to clear up. If you have to do it then do it away from here, at night." Purcell could not stomach it. This scene was not for him. He did not want to know this part of it.

"Piss off," said Tierney. "I've had enough of you. Now get on with it, Laurie or we do both of you at the same time."

Purcell yelled, "Right, that's it, you jerk. I'll tell Hogan about this. You're brainless. I'll take my chances without you." He stormed out, his arm now in a rough sling.

Tierney didn't turn a hair, relieved that Purcell had

gone and that he could get back to the business at hand. He spoke softly, his voice full of menace. "Laurie, this is your last chance."

His stomach churning, Galvin moved towards Sullivan who gave no sign that he knew what was going on. Then Sullivan's eyes flickered and he seemed to be trying to turn his head. Galvin heaved and placed his free hand against the wall. He managed to push himself away and step forward. He bent down slightly and lowered the gun so that it pointed at Sullivan's head. Someone said, "All you have to do is release the safety catch." It could have been anyone's voice.

Galvin placed the gun at the back of Sullivan's head still not sure whether the whole ghastly business wasn't set to try his nerve. The room was suddenly completely silent. Gradually, a slight wheezing from Sullivan intruded but it merely increased the tension. Galvin took one last look round at Tierney, Connolly and Daley to see that they were no longer grinning. He turned back to Sullivan who had moved his head slightly, almost as if he wanted to make it easier for Galvin. Sullivan's lids flickered as he tried to open them, then he nodded almost imperceptibly in an attempt to offer Galvin his understanding.

Don Helary and his wife Una had motored through the night to reach Kinsale before dawn. Una had parked the car and had rejoined him. Having received a list from his telephone contact, Helary had rung round Tyson's various properties the previous evening, and when someone had guardedly answered the phone at the villa near Kinsale he believed he'd found them: Tierney didn't know enough for him to worry about, but Purcell was another matter: his death would prove useful in many ways.

Quick to size up a situation Helary and Una had found an area from where they could safely watch the villa. The place was on the high ground across the estuary and almost opposite the villa, the exact location which had been explained to him. They had mounted a powerful telescope on a sturdy tripod with its extending legs drawn in so that the profile was low. By early morning Helary had satisfied himself on the frontal approaches and windows.

By mid-morning Helary had seen enough through the windows to know that several men were inside and he thought he had detected Purcell as one of them. He removed the telescope from its mounting, fixed a clamp to the top of the specially made tripod and inserted a high-powered rifle with a telescopic sight and a silencer. Some time later the Morris 1000 left the villa; as far as he could make out Purcell had not been in the car and he continued to wait. Later, he saw Galvin's car cross the bridge, having come from a point well behind the villa but at that time it had meant little to him. The car disappeared from sight below him and then he heard it skid. There were voices but he could not distinguish the words.

Helary could not see what was happening below him but it was over very quickly. A car door slammed, then another, and two cars started up. The car that had just crossed the bridge was now returning with the Morris 1000 close behind. When the cars reached the villa he held the unmounted telescope to his eye and saw a struggling man hustled inside.

Helary did not know Galvin but he was puzzled by what seemed to be a kidnap. He did not know why his hunch should grow, but now, more than ever, he was convinced that Purcell was there and that the IRA were holing him up. During this time neither he nor Una had uttered a word. Now they glanced at each other and Helary nodded. They continued to wait.

Detective Chief Superintendent Keane had worked in a different way. The files on Tyson had thrown up some useful information on some of his property deals. He had a villa in Kerry near Glenbeigh, a large maisonette in Cork City, a villa near Kinsale, and several rural smallholdings, three near the Ulster border.

As far as Tyson was concerned, Keane was working from a gut feeling. He had known for a long time of Tyson's communist connections and his occasional association with the Provos – Hogan in particular. Tyson was by no means the first millionaire to be tied up in such murky dealings but there could be no complaint about the cover wealth could provide in such a situation. Tyson's weakness was that he had been at it too long.

252

Keane worked on what Riley Brown had told him and took a chance on concentrating on the Cork area which narrowed the checking of Tyson's holdings considerably. The Cork property was quickly dismissed by discreet enquiries made by the Garda at Union Quay; they were willing to vouch that Tierney was not there. Glenbeigh was an outside possibility but really too far.

Keane did not use a telephone ruse to find out if anyone was at the villa near Kinsale. He worked through the local post office to discover that a letter had been delivered to the villa that morning; the postman confirmed that the villa was occupied. Keane immediately contacted the Superintendent at Union Quay police station in Cork City and made certain arrangements. He himself organised a helicopter down to Cork airport and a light plane for some of his men.

By early afternoon the villa was surrounded, but at a distance. All surveillance was the villa side of the estuary which made it much more difficult for Tierney's men to detect. Most of it was at the rear on the higher ground. As Galvin had already found, there was plenty of cover. Too many IRA men in the past had effectively escaped in open country. The road both sides of the villa had been cut off by armed policemen hidden in the shrubs, and the entrance to the bridge was covered in the same way.

When Keane and O'Riordon were rushed from Cork airport with their own men the approach had been made in a baker's van over the bridge but then up the road leading to the high ground well beyond the villa. They had not disembarked until they were over the crest which they had then approached on their bellies. They had lain with binoculars focused on the villa area but, due to the surrounding growth, only those policeman nearer to the building actually had any view of it.

Unaware that Helary and his wife were well hidden across the estuary, Keane resigned himself to a long wait. Listening devices were on stand-by and a back-up helicopter was waiting behind him over the crest. So far he was satisfied with the arrangements. Lying beside him, O'Riordon was not at all happy. Something was wrong and he wondered if his chief felt it too?

*   *   *

253

As yet, Helary and Una had not picked up any sign of the police. For one thing, when dealing with someone like Tierney, the police were only too aware that they had to be ultra careful and had made the best use of the ample cover; at the moment, they were well back from the villa. And Helary and Una's concentration had been solely on the villa itself for they could not afford to miss the slightest opportunity.

Una suddenly stiffened. She held the binoculars steady. Someone was hurrying out of the villa with his hand in a sling. "My God, it's Purcell. Making for the larger car."

Immediately Helary traversed the rifle. He could see the shape of Purcell clearly now but identification was more difficult. "You sure it's him?"

"No doubt at all," Una confirmed, still gazing through the more powerful binoculars. "He's taking his hand from the sling. He's going to get in the car, you'd better be . . ."

But Helary didn't need prompting. He took careful aim, made sure the rifle was firm, then fired. The figure in his sights threw up his arms, the white sling flying, and collapsed on his back. Helary, now from a very narrow angle because the body was supine, nevertheless fired once more and knew that he had done the job. There was no roar of shots. Instead there were a couple of quiet, almost apologetic belches which barely reached the road below and were not heard at all across the estuary. Helary dismantled his equipment rapidly.

Galvin knew that he couldn't take the gamble. Whatever reason entered his mind, that the gun was empty, that Sullivan was virtually dead anyway, that he had to get his information back, none of it worked. He resigned himself to dying with Sullivan and was about to swing round and hope that he might just take Tierney with him when there was a tremendous shouting and Mooney, the least important of the group, burst in wild-eyed and panicking. "They've shot Purcell, they've shot Purcell."

"Who, for God's sake?" Tierney grabbed Mooney by the jacket and shook him. "Who?"

For the moment Galvin was ignored and in that moment he knew there was no round in the gun; they would never have turned their backs on him.

254

"He's dead by the car. It must be the police," yelled Mooney. "Don't go out for Christ's sake."

But Tierney was thinking that the police wouldn't pick one man off like that and leave the rest to barricade. He snapped to Daley, "Lock these two in."

Nobody troubled to take the Browning from Galvin but he heard the door key being turned. If only he could lay his hands on some ammunition. He pulled the breech back to make sure he was right about the empty chamber. In their panic Tierney's mob had forgotten to bind him again and the small opaque window was an open invitation. Galvin looked down at Sullivan again. But he couldn't risk moving him. Poor sod. Barely able to breathe Galvin climbed on to the washing machine and opened the window and squeezed through, dropping blindly down to the other side.

He heard the panic at the side of the villa where Purcell had kept his car and it was far too near to where he was crouching. Racked with pain he managed to reach the far end and somehow climb up the bank as fast as his injuries would take him. He was on the point of collapse when an uncompromising voice with a Cork accent said, "Move another foot and I'll shoot the arse off you."

20

Galvin found himself looking into the short muzzle of a Uzi sub-machine gun and was relieved to see the blue uniform behind it. "Laurie Galvin," he gasped. "I've just escaped from the villa below."

"You'd better not try to escape from me. Take that gun out of your waistband and be bloody careful how you do it. And then turn on your face and put your hands behind your back."

Through split lips, Galvin said, "The gun's not loaded. For God's sake call somebody up. A killer is escaping and one of your intelligence men is dying. He's in the utility room. For Christ's sake get an ambulance."

"Just do as I say, now. The gun first."

"Look at me, you silly bugger. Look at the state of me. You can see the rope marks on my wrists. For God's sake get cracking."

The garda wasn't convinced. He still had his gun levelled and was pulling out handcuffs with his other hand. Galvin, seeing he would get nowhere, carefully pulled out the Browning with finger and thumb and dropped it to one side. He started to roll over and then swung his legs round viciously to hook the garda behind the knees. As the garda collapsed Galvin called on his reserves to reach for the Browning and to crash it down on the back of the man's head.

He lay crouched and panting and in deep pain. Every area where he'd been kicked and punched throbbed, but he had to rally. He shakily climbed to his feet and groped for the garda's two-way radio. He switched to send and spoke breathlessy, "To whoever's listening. There's a man called Sullivan in the utility room. He's an Irish agent. He's dying. Get to him fast. And be good to him; he's a bloody hero."

Galvin bent to grab the Uzi and collapsed. As he tried to get up he heard movement through the shrubs, and, peering up saw an armed figure go past him down the hill. And then he saw another. He kept face down in the undergrowth, praying that neither he nor the unconscious garda would be seen. When satisfied that he was beyond the cordon he managed to climb to his feet. He glanced down and hoped that he hadn't hit the garda too hard. He turned away from the villa and started to climb the incline. Somehow he had to find transport.

Tierney gazed round confused and worried. He looked down at Purcell who had two wide blood stains on his chest and who was not quite dead. Mooney, scared at what had happened, had run back indoors. Tierney, Connolly and Daley weren't so feeble but they were confused. Tierney correctly believed that whoever had fired had done so from across the estuary and had been after Purcell himself. The police would not use a silencer; this was the work of a professional hit man. But, in spite of his reasoning, he still felt trapped.

He decided to put Purcell out of sight in his own car and had told the other two to help him when an amplified voice called out, "This is the police, Tierney. You are completely surrounded. Drop your weapons and lie flat on your faces."

Tierney froze, holding his Ingram rigidly. He had just convinced himself that the police weren't involved and now they were here and he couldn't bloody well see them. He turned towards the villa. Connolly and Daley, the other side of Purcell, jumped over the body with the same thing in mind when a fusillade of shots spattered between them and the villa door.

The Police Superintendent in close control of his armed men knew that if Tierney and his gang got back inside there would be a bloody siege that could last days and probably result in the loss of life of some of his men. Tierney spun round and started firing at random and the others joined him. They blasted into the shrubbery where they knew the police must be hiding and they killed one man outright. The Superintendent didn't hesitate. He gave the order to fire and Tierney and his friends found themselves in a cross fire that had them spinning and

257

gyrating and finally collapsing and twitching on the terrace in a variety of grotesque positions.

There was a lull when nothing happened at all and the sound of gunfire seemed to creep around the hills like a fading whisper with the smell of cordite strong in the air. And then slowly, cautiously, the police began to show themselves and came forward on to the front terrace to observe the damage. Inside the villa they found a cringing Mooney with his hands over his head, begging not to be shot, and the pitiful Sullivan lying where Galvin had said he would be.

Galvin heard the firing just as he reached the crest of the shallow hill. There was no point in waiting whichever way the battle went. He started to ease himself down the rough incline on the other side of the hill. He suddenly stopped. Below him a police helicopter was waiting on an even patch of grassland. He continued on and when he thought the pilot could see him he waved his Uzi in greeting; some of the Garda were bound to be in plainclothes.

As he got nearer he tried to keep the gun up to hide his battered face. The pilot, who heard the firing, came part way towards him, eager for news. Galvin brought the gun down and levelled it at him. "Sorry, mate. As bad as it looks, you'll just have to accept that we're on the same side. Take me up and make for Dublin but fly above the back roads."

The pilot was taken by surprise and was on the point of refusing when he saw something of what Galvin had been through. Then he saw the eyes and the pain and the weariness and realised that Galvin would do what was necessary to get airborne.

Galvin added, "I've no time to explain. We're after killers. Look out for a dark green Fiat. I don't think they'll use the main roads, these people are cockroaches. If you don't move I'll open the fuel cocks and empty the gun into the chopper. It's up to you." It was a gamble. The Fiat might have no connection, but it was an odd place to park and someone had shot from that area. What's more, the car had been there about that time.

"Killers, you say?" The pilot moved towards his machine.

258

"As bad as those bastards who I hope are being shot up right now. Someone shot Purcell and I reckon I know where the shots came from."

The pilot had never heard of Purcell. It didn't matter. What did was the way Galvin held the gun and his battle hardiness. Determination was about all that was holding him together but it seemed to be enough; the pilot began to hurry.

They took off and headed inland passing over the villa at low altitude. As Galvin looked down he saw a sea of faces raised towards them and he had a good view of the scattered dead on the terrace. The place was crawling with police so the bloody battle must have satisfactorily ended their way. He thought of Sullivan and hoped that Tierney and his mob were suffering a similar fate. He was almost all in but forced himself to keep going for a while longer. They crossed the estuary, gaining height as they left the small flotilla of boats behind, and, on the coast road, police cars racing for the bridge.

Galvin was not sure just how much ground the Fiat had covered. Whoever was driving would have been away as soon as he had done the job. He knew that he could be wrong but did not believe it for a moment, and there was an easy way to find out.

The pilot was the first to sight the Fiat. It was travelling below them between high hedgerows on an empty secondary road.

"Carry straight on," bawled Galvin. "Don't give the impression that we're following."

They left the Fiat behind them and then Galvin yelled, "Drop me off about three miles further on. Make sure there are no turn-offs they can take."

The pilot glanced over uneasily, because he now had an inkling of what Galvin might do. Well, there was a gun pointing at him, it was sufficient reason to obey and he had begun to believe in Galvin despite the fact that he hadn't even volunteered his name.

The road was empty for as far as they could see. The pilot had brought the chopper down on a straight stretch and hovered as near to the ground as he dared without fouling his rotors. Galvin eased himself to the edge.

"Can you manage?"

Galvin nodded. "When I'm down go and fetch the cavalry." He jumped the remaining few feet. He hit the ground as if he'd jumped from a roof top. He lay there breathless for a while and then painfully dragged himself to the side of the road. He pushed himself into the hedgerow, crouched, and waited.

His timing was good. The Fiat came into view in no obvious hurry. It was doing about forty-five miles an hour as Galvin stepped into the road some distance in front of it. He checked the registration number as it came towards him. At first he kept the gun barrel down but the Fiat gathered speed and someone leaned out of the passenger window and fired at him. It almost took him by surprise but he had time to move before the shot was fired and it was all he needed to know. He sent a burst into the front tyres and the Fiat careered across the road in a wild skid and finished nose first in the thick hedgerow.

A door burst open and a woman jumped out firing wildly at him with a pistol as she ran. Had she kept still she might have hit him. Galvin took no chances, he gave her a low, short burst and she fell face down crying out in agony. He ran towards her and wrenched the gun from her hand. She glared and cursed him and tried to grab his ankles but he stepped away and spun round to see what was happening to her male companion.

A dazed Helary was trying to take up position behind the car and had produced another pistol. Galvin sent a short burst into the bonnet just in front of Helary's face. Two rounds ricocheted too near and a sliver of metal cut into Helary's cheek. The shock made him reel back and Galvin called out, "Drop the gun or I'll shoot your bloody head off."

Helary dropped the gun and looked over to where his wife was lying in the road whimpering.

"I've smashed her legs up a bit," said Galvin easily. "She won't walk for a while but where she's going it won't matter too much. Come round this side of the car."

When Helary came round Galvin told him to back up against the car and to put his hands on his head. When Helary had done this Galvin said, "Now tell me all about yourself and who sent you." By now he was surviving on

260

sheer willpower but he loathed the treachery of Helary; it acted to spur him on.

"You dumb bastard. There's no way we'll talk."

"You're not working for the Russians that's for sure. They'd use their own." Galvin took the Uzi in his left hand and the pistol in his right. He fired the pistol and a huge spurt of blood flooded from Helary's left ear. The impact made Helary spin round and scream out in pain. He bent forward over the car with a hand to his ear and blood streaming through his fingers.

"Straighten up."

Helary came round slowly, his lips curled back, venom glaring from his eyes. "You've taken my goddamn ear off."

"The left ear. Next I'll take off your right. Then your knee-caps. Get it through your thick head. I've just seen what's happened to a colleague of mine because of shits like you. You're going to talk, whoever you are, and you're going to do it before the police get here." Galvin fired again and Helary's scream was terrifying.

The shoot-out at the villa hit the headlines worldwide because the press were informed that the dead IRA men had been responsible for blowing up the parts of Air Force One including the "black boxes" that might have proved a bomb was used on her; they had been covering for Provo comrades in America. The Provos had the worst press they had ever had and world opinion, especially that which had been delicately poised, turned swiftly, and in the majority of cases, permanently against them.

What the IRA had been seeking to achieve – the safeguarding of American funds which a hostile American President had been poised to eliminate – had blown back in their faces. It was inevitable public outrage would now cause the funds to dry up more dramatically and effectively than any legislation could have done.

It was against this background of frenetic media coverage, and the going to ground of the IRA to avoid the fury of local people who had hitherto tacitly supported them, that Sir Gerald Fowler met the CIA Deputy Director Paul Sutter in London. In a quiet mood, Fowler took Sutter to lunch at his club in Pall Mall. They had a table in

261

the far corner of the restaurant and were partly screened by a huge marble pillar.

"I'm going to take you for a ride on this lunch," Sutter stated bluntly. "Let's face it you've been taking me for one for several days now."

Fowler smiled thinly. "Have what you like."

"You're a smooth bastard," Sutter retorted, not unpleasantly. "It suits you to blame the IRA, doesn't it? And it suits the Irish too. You two have been ganging up on Uncle Sam. You've been doing it from the start. Neither of you wanted anyone else to take the blame. You both wanted to kill off the IRA – well, as much as you could anyway."

"We put good men at considerable risk to prove this for you. What more do you want of us?"

"The truth, old buddy. You think PIRA really did it all on their own? Bullshit. That crap will cost you more than a fillet steak. You owe us."

"On the contrary."

"What does that mean? Explain why Purcell was shot. Not by the police but by an assassin. And who burned Farrell? PIRA go down for that too but you know they didn't do it. The Irish had that villa surrounded yet, someone still got to Purcell right under their noses. And whoever it was got clean away. Now that's really something. Couldn't be that the Irish wanted to get him out? That the hit man might have thrown up too many problems?"

Fowler looked pained as he tasted his wine. "Yes, it does suit us to blame the IRA. It suits us very well. Better than suggesting that the Russians were behind the whole thing, thus accelerating the onset of World War III."

"The Russians? You don't really surprise me. It would be like them to sacrifice their own Ambassador."

When Fowler did not reply Sutter sat back and said, "You have evidence?"

"The death of Purcell *could* look like a Russian killing. After all they have poured considerable funds into the IRA and are therefore involved, if only indirectly. I'm not saying that there are not a good many Russians who are glad it happened. Just as there are many Americans and for the same reasons: their governments were giving too

262

much away. The armoury was being gutted and military men and hard-line industrialists wouldn't care for that at all. But I don't think it was the Russians."

"Because they had their man on board? Who're you kidding?"

Fowler sipped his wine, but with no sign of enjoying it. "I simply believe that they would prefer to protect Purcell. If they were looking for him it was probably effectively to hide him, to make sure nobody else could reach him. They failed."

"I find that a strange attitude. You know more than you're saying."

"Indeed. So I'd better say that you – not too subtly – pushed us towards the belief that the IRA did the job, and then led us to the suggestion that someone was behind them. By using the Helarys it could look as if Ivan was covering up the contacts leading back to them and that they might have killed Farrell and Purcell. I suppose you anticipated that Farrell would run scared if anything went wrong. He was strongly against the President – and the poor fool was willing: the perfect patsy. Irish background, secret funds to Noraid making it appear that he was linked to the IRA. Did you organise that for him? Not a nice way to treat an old friend."

Sutter had gone very still. Coldly he said, "I don't like your kind of humour."

Fowler ignored the remark. "Poor Purcell added to his own downfall. He knew how to raise funds like nobody else but he knew nothing of people. The Russians had supplied him with masses of money and he thought that was where the danger to him came from. That was a bonus for you but you really did not need it. You knew we would arrive at the Russians and we did. But our man in Ireland went beyond that."

Sutter gazed round the dining room before replying, "I don't intend to listen to any more of this crap." He laid down his napkin and stood up.

"You'd better listen to my insanities first, Paul. We got Don and Una Helary. Not the types to talk. Our man had to shoot considerable parts of Helary's ears off before he did. Cabals are nothing new. Arrogantly, you considered your President was taking far too many chances. It's my

263

belief that Air Force One was *not* blown up too late. I would guess that the timing was exactly how you wanted it. I would also guess that the fuse was changed at some point in order to make sure that it was delayed. I know that you acquired some of the stuff the Czechs researched to cover the scent of explosives so as to confuse dogs. And I suppose you had an acolyte similar to Squire to fix the PD–4s . You manoeuvred your Irish-American connections, people like Farrell. Everybody knew that the IRA couldn't do it alone but with the right backing they had plenty of motive. So you made it possible and manoeuvred events so that everyone had to keep quiet unless they wanted another world war. You wanted the IRA to be blamed but more importantly, you wanted the Red Hand to be seen behind them. That would certainly scotch any possibility of an American-Russian arms deal. In your lifetime, anyway."

Sutter's face was ashen. "You'd better substantiate this, or by God, I'll screw your whole service. You won't find a bigger patriot than me."

"That's what they all say: all those who step outside their country's constitution in order to protect it from itself. You know what's best, of course, but you have to stab your own country in the back in order to achieve it. You're just another bloody traitor, Paul. If you want a patriot then you'll find one in the Irish agent whose life hangs by a thread, or in our man languishing in an Irish jail.

"The FBI have most of what they want. They have the background to your association with Farrell. And they've seen through his IRA affiliations, at least, his pretended loyalty to the cause. You must have known that the poor devil would panic. But his Irish background was useful to you. It all fitted so nicely. The FBI know all about two members of your Joint Chiefs and the chairman of Anacosta Aerospace and a distinguished list of other patriots. They've collected all your carefully planted clues. Oh, and I was asked to inform you that they have John Smith. Another proven acquaintance of yours, and Farrell's too, I believe." Fowler gazed across the table at Sutter's grim face. "Squire did you a favour by being unable to take the burden of guilt; another weak link in your cabal. But you should have given more thought to his gutsy wife."

Sutter, shaken to his core, sat silent, his mind working furiously. He barely heard Fowler saying, "I don't suppose I've really shocked you. Yes, we do spy on our American allies. You pushed a little too hard and too soon towards the IRA theory at the start. You had better make some alterations to your plans. I understand from my masters that your President has made several decisions. As you said so long ago when we first started down this particular rabbit hole, none of us want a Kennedy sort of mystery. A courtroom speech is out. I believe an extra-judicial solution has been found. Check your insurance, Paul. You're about to have an accident. Soon. Run, Paul. Run now. Try to find somewhere to hide."

The news of Farrell's death had been devastating to both Judy Farrell and Dave Santos. They met in Santos's office on a wet, cold day that was a foretaste of November now almost here. The nature of the shock was not so much the death itself, which had rocked them, but the brutal way it had happened and the mystery which still surrounded it. They had to accept that for reasons they did not understand, the IRA had killed George Farrell. The FBI had been very helpful to them but had no further information to offer.

The death, at first, drove an inexplicable wedge between the couple as if they separately believed that in some way they were responsible. The guilt of their affair, blossoming as it had while Farrell had been under tremendous pain and duress, hung over them until logic slowly returned. And when it did, their love for each other and the way it had come from such a tragic background bound them even more. Farrell, in the end, had served some useful purpose though it was doubtful if he would ever have appreciated it.

Mandy Squire collapsed on to a chair and stared at the letter in her hand. Her lips trembled and then she broke into uncontrollable sobbing, the tears flowing down her face and running off the end of her chin to fall on the letter in great blotches. It slipped from her fingers and she covered her face with her hands. Her shoulders heaved as the pain, bewilderment, and the huge strain of simply trying to cope with life, gradually eased away with the tears.

When she could cry no more she stared into space before eventually wiping her face dry. She bent down to pick up the letter with an effort. She read it once more. Gradually her back straightened and her shoulders squared and her head lifted as if she had found new strength. She placed the letter on the table and tried to wipe the tear stains from it. But it did not matter, it was still perfectly legible.

After a while she decided to start packing. When the girls came home they could help her finish. They would all leave this place and go far away to start life all over again. Mandy had driven herself to the verge of insanity trying to find the answers about that part of himself that Sam must always have kept hidden from her. In Judy Farrell she had found one friend who shared her problem.

She picked the letter up again and read it once more. It was from a bank in Vienna, Austria. It appeared that she was now two million dollars richer.

Galvin made no effort to rise when Reg Palmer entered the room and placed his lanky frame on a wooden chair across the plain table from him. He was surprised that the Irish police authorities had allowed a British MI5 man into one of their prisons, even as a visitor. But Galvin was already aware of some of the privileges he had been granted and he had been treated very well. For his own safety, after medical treatment, he had been placed in an isolation cell; IRA prisoners would not be slow to kill a British spy being detained if the news spread round the prison.

Palmer came straight to the point. "You'll be out soon. We've done a deal. And we were all on the same side. But you are now known as a foreign spy. You won't be able to live here any more. We'll fix you up in the UK, provided you act sensibly."

"Sensibly?" Galvin's body was still a mass of pain. He'd had far too much time to think about Riley since he had been in jail; he was extremely depressed and did not much care what happened to him.

266

"There are problems. You've read the papers. You know the IRA's taken the rap. That's the way it's got to stay, Laurie; it's the way we all want it. You know far too much for the peace of mind of too many interested parties. There's a report that the Russians are already on full alert, an exercise they call it, but it's for real. They know someone tried to set them up; they're just waiting to see how it turns out but leaving nobody in any doubt what will happen if it swings against them."

"I understand the reasons. You think I'm going to tell anyone?"

"No. Not at all. You might be offered a good many inducements, though. Ivan would like to know what you know. And you're an open target for any frustrated IRA man who feels he'd be doing the cause a service by casting your bits to the four winds."

"I *have* given it thought. You'll get no more reassurance from me than that already given on oath under the Official Secrets Act."

"Good man. We'll get you back under escort just to play it safe. We'll have to set you up with a new identity, maybe a little surgery here and there. Your nose has always needed straightening since someone flattened it."

Galvin shrugged. He didn't much care what happened. "How's Sullivan getting on?"

"He might well recover but it could take months. He's in good hands."

"He should get a fistful of medals and a massive pension."

"I agree. Don't try to see Riley Brown. We couldn't cope with the security angle. It's such an obvious place for you to go."

"There's no way she would want to see me. She'll never forgive me for that and I can't blame her."

Palmer stood up. There was no police escort in the room, another sign of the privileges Galvin had been accorded. "Yes. Well, you can telephone her if you like. I've made arrangements for the use of a secure line. One call. Well, maybe two. Entirely up to you. They've been extremely co-operative over here."

*   *   *

267

"Riley?" Galvin was almost afraid to say her name. The small office wasn't ideal for such a call and a garda was nearby pretending not to listen.

"Yes." The reply was tearful, the tone of resentment clear.

"It's Laurie." He already knew that she knew. "I couldn't phone you before, I've been having treatment. I'm in prison."

"That's the best place for you. I hope they keep you there."

But she hadn't hung up. "I'm sorry for it all. Perhaps one day I can try to explain."

"You won't get a chance. There's nothing you can explain."

Galvin glanced at the garda. "When Connolly phoned you I'd been bashed about and was tied hand and foot. I still managed to say I love you. Believe me, it was no time for lies." He thought he could hear her quietly crying.

"It's too late. You've destroyed everything I believed in." She was having difficulty in speaking at all but still she didn't hang up.

"Look, I won't be allowed to come and see you before they take me across the water. Would you be able to call here? Just to say goodbye? Just the once?"

There was a long pause. "There wouldn't be any point. I would hate you all the more if I saw you again." She was now crying openly.

"I understand. Don't cry, Riley. One more thing and I'll hang up. If you won't come to see me yourself could you just bring Hercules along? I'd like to say cheerio to the little scamp. I think I can swing it so that they let him in. You'll have to have him on a lead, of course."

The wait was so long that Galvin thought she had put the phone down. When she finally spoke he could barely hear her through the sobs. "What do I have to do?"

He spoke quickly. "Just pitch up this afternoon at say, three. If I can't fix it just like that I'll give you another ring and sort something out. Give him my regards."

"It's just so that you can see him, you understand."

"Of course."

"I'll bring him then. At three."